DRAGONFLY

Frederic S. Durbin

ACE BOOKS, NEW YORK

THE BERKLEY PUBLISHING GROUP
Published by the Penguin Group
Penguin Group (USA) Inc.
375 Hudson Street, New York, New York 10014, USA
Penguin Group (Canada), 90 Eglinton Avenue East, Suite 700, Toronto, Ontario M4P 2Y3, Canada
(a division of Pearson Penguin Canada Inc.)
Penguin Books Ltd., 80 Strand, London WC2R 0RL, England
Penguin Group Ireland, 25 St. Stephen's Green, Dublin 2, Ireland (a division of Penguin Books Ltd.)
Penguin Group (Australia), 250 Camberwell Road, Camberwell, Victoria 3124, Australia
(a division of Pearson Australia Group Pty. Ltd.)
Penguin Books India Pvt. Ltd., 11 Community Centre, Panchsheel Park, New Delhi—110 017, India
Penguin Group (NZ), Cnr. Airborne and Rosedale Roads, Albany, Auckland 1310, New Zealand
(a division of Pearson New Zealand Ltd.)
Penguin Books (South Africa) (Pty.) Ltd., 24 Sturdee Avenue, Rosebank, Johannesburg 2196,
South Africa

Penguin Books Ltd., Registered Offices: 80 Strand, London WC2R 0RL, England

This is a work of fiction. Names, characters, places, and incidents either are the product of the author's imagination or are used fictitiously, and any resemblance to actual persons, living or dead, business establishments, events, or locales is entirely coincidental.

DRAGONFLY

An Ace Book / published by arrangement with Arkham House Publishers, Inc.

PRINTING HISTORY
Arkham House hardcover edition / June 1999
Ace mass market edition / October 2005

Copyright © 1999 by Frederic S. Durbin.
Cover art by Merritt Dekle.
Cover design by Judith Lagerman.
Interior text design by Stacy Irwin.

ISBN: 0-441-01338-4

ACE
Ace Books are published by The Berkley Publishing Group,
a division of Penguin Group (USA) Inc.,
375 Hudson Street, New York, New York 10014.
ACE and the "A" design are trademarks belonging to Penguin Group (USA) Inc.

PRINTED IN THE UNITED STATES OF AMERICA

10   9   8   7   6   5   4   3   2   1

For my grandmothers,
Emma Wilhelmina Adams
and
Julia Craggs

1

OF SMOKE AND SHADOWS

BAD things were starting to happen again in Uncle Henry's basement. These were things that had happened before, when the wind swung round, when the trees all felt the blood rush to their leaves after the exertion of August and the idling of September; when the chuckle-dark harvest moon shaped pumpkins in its own image, brought its secret wine flush to the scarecrows' cheeks; when the rich bounties of the land lay plump for the taking and the light left them alone for longer and longer at a time. But when the trouble started before, I was too young to remember.

That October I was ten, going on eleven, and Uncle Henry was fifty-eight, but he looked at least a hundred when the things started happening again in the basement.

People were moving around down there. And that wasn't half of it.

THE best place to begin telling the story, I guess, is with a memory of the beginning of all that. The first event was late on a Friday evening, and I was walking home after a school Open House, where my job had been to show a filmstrip about tobacco in the Old South—it was a class project that some of us had made; even now I can see those luminous crayon frames of big green leaves and a plantationer I'd designed after Colonel Sanders. I had to show it over and over as parents milled in and out of the room, admiring our artwork, terrarium, and pausing to watch exactly three and a half frames of the filmstrip. I can remember thinking to myself, "If fifth-graders' attention spans were as limited as parents', we'd be in big trouble."

My Uncle Henry couldn't be at the Open House because he had a visitation to do. I accused him of scheduling it on purpose to coincide with the Open House, but he denied it. He was probably telling the truth—especially since visitations pretty much *have* to be in that narrow time window between when a person dies and his funeral.

So I was walking home about 8:30 or so. It was dark and windy. I remember that wind, tearing around corners, gusting up dry leaves against the school fence like surf. As I walked away from the lighted building, cars were drifting past me, cars full of my classmates and their parents, some laughing, some wordless, some picking at each other already—taking each other for granted, like people do. Some would stop for hamburgers on the way home. I was thinking of my mom and dad and feeling lonely.

I passed stores, most of them dark, and houses, most of them light. The wind picked up two empty paper cups and twirled them, playing the sidewalk like a xylophone, *tap tap tock tap*. Zipping my jacket, I hurried after them, kicking them back into play when the wind fumbled them. The moon wobbled free of scudding clouds and drew the wind up breathless. Watching like me, the wind let the cups, the leaves, everything fall, dropped hair over my eyes—and pivoted slowly, gaining speed again, sweeping up the debris on Park Street (where, ironically, no parking is allowed), sucking it all up to the moon.

My spirits were rising as I hurried through the night, as I realized that Hallowe'en was not far away. I spread my arms and took a running leap at the moon myself, letting the wind catch me from behind, imagining just for an instant that the pavement was dropping farther and farther away beneath my feet. I careened up over the fence, swished between the electrical wires, changed my trajectory by snagging the flagpole and slinging myself around it as I soared, free as a flying saucer, into the black October sky.

Then I was on the sidewalk again, dancing with my shadow, playing my old game. My lifelong struggle had been to twist and caper in such a way as to outwit that black outline of myself—its feet never failed to anticipate where mine were coming down, always slipped sideways at the last second to meet them just as they touched ground. Along two blocks I sparred with it, trying every maneuver I knew as it circled beneath me. I whirled around street lights, hoping to use the angle of the rays to throw my shadow off balance just enough to beat its pistoning feet by a fraction—one day, I vowed, I would plant my foot on a perfectly clean, lighted patch of concrete, and my all-knowing nimble partner would be left with an unlit face considerably covered with egg. But I didn't do it that night. Even when I seized a tree limb to suspend myself for what I hoped might be a disorienting split-second, my shadow wasn't fooled.

Sometimes I got a little scared of my shadow. Usually it was perfectly ordinary, but once in a while, I thought I'd glimpse it making a subtle mistake; just from the corner of my eye, I'd be conscious of the swinging of my backpack mirrored on the sidewalk, the motion of my arms, the bouncing of the pony tail I sometimes wore. And then, the skillful imitation at some point would lag an inch behind—I'd shoot my gaze around, and that dragging shadow hand or foot would whip back into synch—*whoops! heh, heh, you almost caught me there!* Then I'd run home without stopping to check again.

Giving up my game, I cut through the park and into the alley behind the bank. The leaves of the elms hissed their dark melody, and a loose fence board shrieked when I pulled it—this was October, and I was thinking of making a jack-o'-lantern. I skipped from shadow to shadow of the pillars in the rear portico of the bank, enjoying both my invisibility when buried in darkness and the spray of silver when I soared through open spaces.

I was just gearing up for the final sprint home when I saw the two figures.

At first, I thought the willow-branches blowing over the sodium light in the parking lot were just making a bizarre optical illusion. In the alley, out behind Kohn's Furniture, it looked like two men were standing. One was hunching forward over something on a tripod—taking a picture?—and one was standing at a distance in front of the other, holding up something in his hand. Although there was nothing at all threatening in their posture, I was startled—and deeply unsettled, as I realized when I felt my heart racing and skin crawling—by two things: one, their overall color seemed somehow wrong—their billowing jackets and trousers were black, but it was a *luminous* black, as if the two were images from one strip of film spliced into another; that's the only way I can explain a dissimilarity in the flow of their clothing and that of the darkness and bricks around them. The other thing that disturbed me was the way they vanished when a pair of headlights appeared at the far end of the alley—it wasn't like two men simply getting out of the way of a car, but more like soldiers or spies, professionals of some kind with a desire to remain undetected. They moved simultaneously, stepping quickly into the shadows between buildings.

I was just thinking I'd backtrack and go home by a different route when the pair of headlights cruised up alongside me and I recognized the gleaming outlines of the hearse. Uncle Henry leaned over and swung open the passenger door. I'd never been so happy to see him.

"Is your visitation over?" I asked.

"No, but it's winding down. I thought I'd take a coffee break. Thought you'd be right along." He grinned his warm, leathery grin. "Why don't we stop for a hamburger?"

I told him about the two men, asked him if he thought they might be robbing the bank. He backed the hearse up the alley, but if the two were still lurking by the furniture store, we didn't see them. What we *did* see was the tripod, still standing where they had left it. A small tube was affixed to its top. With a shrug, Uncle Henry drove on.

"What was that?" I asked.

Henry's eyes behind his round lenses showed that the situation was as baffling to him as it was to me.

"Surveying equipment."

* * *

I knew Uncle Henry had some weird ideas, and that kids at school thought he was plain crazy. Sure, it was pretty bizarre that he whistled the Death March when he walked around town, and that he chatted with the people in his mortuary as if they could chat back; but then, no one blamed barbers or grocers for being cheerful at their work, and no one raised eyebrows at a dentist who might take note of the dinosaurs' teeth in a museum. I wholeheartedly enjoyed picnics in the cemetery where the flowers were so vibrant and the grass so lush, where I'd make garlands and chains and bouquets as Henry talked on and on, pushing up his wire glasses and helping me to memorize "Thanatopsis," word by word, line by line. He knew lots of poems about the brevity of life, from Housman to Dickinson to the Bard of Avon himself; he actually *celebrated* what they had to say. "Death," he often told me, "is not something to be afraid of." No, he wasn't so odd when you got to know him. And he had always been kind to me. I spent a lot of my childhood with him, because my mother was away on one coast making movies and my father on the other doing business. Sometimes I caught my teachers gazing at me with sad eyes when they thought I was working on division or social studies; they thought I was neglected. But they didn't know Uncle Henry. Come to think of it, handy as they are with bulletin boards and graphs—I have to hand them graphs—and long division—there's a lot teachers don't know.

Sorry—I'm a girl. Not that I apologize for being a girl, but maybe you were thinking I was a boy; being an only child in a house full of books like Henry's, I read a lot, and I always hated it when the author would sort of forget to mention until chapter nine that the main character wore glasses, or had a beard or something. So let's get it all out on the table: I was about average height for my age when I started fifth grade; I had dark, shoulder-length hair parted on the left side (my left, your right) and very dark brown eyes. Boys called me skinny, but Uncle Henry said that was only because they couldn't find anything else about me to pick on, and that it was natural for girls my age to be slender and ready to sprout up like a nightshade mushroom.

As I was saying, I knew that Henry had his idiosyncrasies, but I also knew what I saw and heard—and there were definitely some things happening in the basement.

In the wee hours of October 15th, I was jerked wide awake by a noise—

RRR-RAARNNGG-RAAAANN!

—the grinding of metal sawteeth through wood. Impossibly, it came from directly beneath my closet. I knew it couldn't be Henry; he was long turned in—my clock said 12:30—and anyway, he didn't own a power saw. I sat there with my knees against my chest for I don't know how long, the bedposts vibrating, the closet door rattling. Even the frosty moonlight rippled along the baseboards, like water does when you thump the side of a tub.

Then, as abruptly as it had begun, the shrieking stopped.

Mustering my courage, I called out in a voice that was really pretty tremulous: "Who's there?"

There was only silence at first. I almost wondered if it hadn't been the most realistic nightmare of my life; but then a cracked, door-hinge voice whispered from the closet—

"Dra-gon-flyyy . . ."

My heart turned a somersault, pounded so painfully I thought I'd faint. I peeked over the teddybear-printed mountains of my knees. Simulated knothole eyes in the wood grain paper of the door stared back at me. "Wh-who are you?"

"Don't mind us," hissed a different voice, this one like sandpaper. *"We're building a stairway."*

A *stairway?*

"It's almost finished," said the other and gave a dry chuckle.

"Sooooon," wheezed the rough voice. *"Soooo-ooo-oonn!"*

That was enough for me—pausing only to scoop up my sleeping bag, I skimmed across the moon-surf, bolted for Henry's room, the railings of the sunken den going *whick-whick-whick* beside my ear. My view through them of the room's lower level was as in the light of one of those strobes at the mall, a thousand pictures separated by fractions of a second, now this, now this, now this, threatening something new with each shutter-guillotine-chop: what will be next/ what will be next/ maybe this time maybe THIS time, some horrid inter-posing thing an inch away, oh what/ oh what/ oh—

"YAAAAHHHH!"

I crashed into Uncle Henry at the door of his room, Uncle Henry in his cotton pajamas, his face so brittle in the moonlight—suddenly so old. Tears of relief ran down my nose.

"Voices—" I began, "under my closet—"

"I know."

I blinked, dragged my sleeve across my face. "You do?"

"They were talking to me, too. 'May I have this dance, Henry?' 'We're almost finished building, Henry.' I heard them hammering under my night table." He pulled me into the room, fastened the door.

"They called me Dragonfly—" (Oh, yes, I forgot to tell you that—Uncle Henry always called me Dragonfly, although my name is Bridget Anne.) "How do they know our names? Who are they?"

Henry quieted me, tucked me into my sleeping bag right up against the headboard of his bed, crossways. "They're not good people. I don't know much more than that. It seems they're invading the basement again." His eyes clouded, turned toward his own closet. Getting up, he wedged a chair under his doorknob.

Kissing my forehead, he smiled reassuringly. "Don't worry, Dragonfly. We'll just have to get Mothkin to help us again."

I calmed down as I lay there, blinking up at the crucifix over his bed. It was a night of scratching branches and rattling acorns, but I felt safe with Henry sitting beside me, stroking my hair. Comforting it was to be believed; how many children are left to face darkness alone, their parents scoffing at the bumps in the night? Henry not only heard them himself, but he knew enough to call in a qualified person.

THE next day was a holiday, and we spent it carving jack-o'-lanterns. I had never heard of having more than two or three, but Henry drove us out through the chill smoky-scented morning to get at least a dozen from Samson's Market. Two bag boys helped us line them up on the floorboards and in the back seat like smooth, bright basketballs.

"Don't break an axle, Mister!" grinned one of the boys as he hefted a huge, oblong pumpkin into place between the two front seats. "What you going to do with all these, anyway?"

"Lot of pumpkins, isn't it?" answered Henry. "I could open my own market, couldn't I? Or make enough pies to feed the neighborhood."

I admired Henry that way; he did such a good job of giving people normal-sounding answers without ever telling a lie that he could usually come across ordinary even when doing something moderately strange. For example, he didn't come right out and say, "I'm going home to make thirteen jack-o'-lanterns." That was an art. It helped, too, when he went shopping in his old blue Plymouth rather than in the hearse—although I guess we could have fit an awful lot of pumpkins in the hearse.

Driving home we rolled the windows down and let the clean, purple-smoke smell wash over us, let the sparkles of the stubble-fields dazzle our eyes. I always marvel at October, how it can be so full of opposites. It's as if, since the leaves are doing something so dramatic and carefree in changing all those colors, the Earth thinks it can get away with anything, and runs around irresponsible and mad for a month or two before it goes to bed. It's positively primal—full of wild rituals and cunning, changes and smoky figures dancing around fires, faces peering around the trunks of trees. October is the owl season—the long shadow season. Take that smoky smell: you don't see all that many people actually burning things, but that smell is everywhere, drifting behind the rarity of the air like hidden darkness pooling behind the light, like Earth makes it somewhere in secret and slips it into the scheme of things, thinking no one will notice. The leaves come twirling down, and the wind waltzes them round and round, blowing from every direction at once. Black cats come east, come south, who knows from where, just for this season, just to see it. The days are warm yet cold, clear yet hazy; the world lives but dies. And the sun, pretending that it's not losing its grip, that none of this is happening, pours down more and more light that's all the while thinner and thinner. By All Hallow's Eve there's just nothing left of reason or fatness or gold—there's nothing but dark music—and the trees gasp naked and frail into November. Who wouldn't be worn out after a month like October?

This jack-o'-lantern business was all part of dealing with the people in the basement, of letting Mothkin know about our problem. We gave them scary faces, happy, sad, laughing, scowling, crescent-eyed, zigzag, mouths fanged, toothless, froggish. Then, with the falling of the dark, we set them aglow in as many windows as we could, some on each side of the house. It must have been quite a spectacle seen from the millet field, or from out on the road lost in darkness where frost covered the mailbox. We were just lucky no one called the fire department.

We made a lot of pies that month—a *lot* of pies. Henry made good use of them, taking them to bereaved families as a specially nice extra service of the funeral home. We roasted mountains of seeds, which Henry kept in giant candy dishes in the parlor and in his office. Those first jack-o'-lanterns were looking pretty shriveled and powerless by around the twenty-fifth; we were obliged to replace them with a dozen more, so of course we were busy again making pies and roasting seeds. It seemed that this Mothkin had told Henry long ago that if he ever had trouble with his basement again, to set these jack-o'-lanterns in his windows, and Mothkin would see them from afar.

We definitely had a problem. There were unearthly noises almost every night, increasing in volume and frenzy as the lightless bottom of the month drew nearer—poundings and wailings, the grinding of metal and the murmur of dozens of voices, the hauling of great loads that slid beneath the kitchen, beneath the dining room, sending the carpet up in runnels like mole-ridges in the garden. *"We're going to finish!"* croaked someone under the den. *"More nails!"* Once there was terrible laughter and the galloping of hooves all night long. The upper deck and stairway of the two-level den twisted and throbbed. Whoever it was seemed to be building a *city* down there, raising a pyramid, having symphonies and circuses. On the night of the twenty-eighth beginning at 2:00 A.M. they had an event like the chariot race in *Ben Hur,* round and round and round the water heater full tilt while crowds cheered in chain-saw thunder voices. Henry shook his head and said it was just like before, that he hoped Mothkin would come soon. Of course we didn't dare to set foot in the basement or open the door the slightest crack even by day.

I was awfully curious as to what was happening down there—honestly, wouldn't *you* be squirming to know what it was if your floors thumped by night as if an inverted giant were dancing on their undersides?—and as to who Mothkin was and what he intended to do about it, and as to what had happened before, Henry wasn't sure himself.

Our lives went on as normally as one could expect. I went to school days, and Henry worked, and nights I camped in my sleeping bag in his room, under the crucifix. Sometimes I would rest my chin on the warm lid of a jack-o'-lantern and gaze out over the waving millet, searching the blue crystal stars, searching the streak of the gravel road that led away into a paradox of shadows so remote, so interwoven by witch-hands, so unfathomable that no one, I figured, could walk out there at night in the month of October and come through alive—no one except an owl, who could fly so didn't count, or a black cat, who didn't count either, since it could pass along through cracks like a breath of ground mist.

My curiosity almost got me in trouble one night, when I just couldn't sleep through the racket and slipped out to the living room, where I saw a tall, shadowy figure moving near the basement door, and something—or some*one*—else perched in the top of a half-bare tree away through the window at the end of the hall. That was in the small hours of the twenty-ninth, after the chariot race. I was back like a paddle-ball on an elastic string to Henry's room, and I didn't venture out again. I always have been too curious; that's really what got me into it, after Mothkin came.

He came on Hallowe'en night.

It was about time, too, because Henry and I didn't know *what* might happen in our house on that wildest and darkest of all festivals at the very bottom of the moondrunk month. A cat was yowling somewhere out by the back fence as soon as the sun slipped down, and over the millet field in lethal circles a bird of the night swept low after the unwitting revelations of tiny pulsing things. I often imagined that the burls on the trunks of the oak trees were lumpish heads peering around, eyeing the moon as it rose red, hanging forever on the horizon, wreathed in vapors, the ponderous dread god of the pumpkins. Our jack-o'-lanterns worshiped him as he levitated, as he waxed monstrous, showered them and all of us with his now dusky orange effulgence.

I laid my chin on the translucent crown of our largest creation, his flickering heart charming shadows, beguiling and repulsing them, so that they fluttered and whispered primly just beyond the windowpane. My arms could barely reach around him to clasp hands beneath his molten grin. Together we watched the blue mists creeping and waited for Mothkin.

The old house was full of sighing, as if it, too, dreaded the night. Joinings cracked like tired knees, and the scufflings of Henry's feet on the carpet bounced away and got lost among walls weary with sound. Clocks ticked after the supper hour, after we washed and dried the dishes with frail feathers of hands, putting away the objects of our workaday lives to make way for the business of the dark. Henry puttered in his mortuary for awhile, then sat reading under a brittle eggshell lamp. Strangely, there was hardly a sound from the basement. I reasoned that the people down there had finished whatever preparations they had been making, and they were waiting, too. For Mothkin? For midnight? For the Prince of Cats? It was anybody's guess.

Then Mothkin came.

2

MOTHKIN

AT first, I thought it was just the dancing reflection of my
jack-o'-lantern's left eye in the window glass, a wavering,
bobbing flame. But it was moving, making a steady course for
the house. The mist parted before it and swirled grandly
closed behind. I called Henry, who smiled and nodded, bouncing on his toes and rubbing his palms together. "It's him," he
chuckled.

I held my breath, watching the light come. It was a jack-o'-
lantern, its candle a glimmer just sufficient to forge through
that bottomless, web-woven night. Mothkin was not the jack-
o'-lantern, you see, but carried it as he strode through the millet; that was the first we saw of him. He himself was
practically invisible behind the glowing shell, its grin the
widest I had ever seen on a pumpkin.

He had just stepped into the yard when a hideous shriek
erupted right over my head. Thinking my days on Earth were
ended, I screamed, dropped to my knees, burying my head in
my arms. There was the whirring of wings and a second cry
from the Angel of Death or whoever it was—farther away this
time. Henry lifted me to my feet and squeezed my shoulders,
his eyes fixed on the yard. I blinked at a winged shape tearing

along over the grass, homing like a missile on Mothkin. Tall, swinging the jack-o'-lantern, he never slowed his pace but stalked deliberately up the yard.

The Angel of Death gave voice a third time, closing the distance. Mothkin's bottom-lit face was calm as he turned to meet the charge. At the last second, the Angel veered in the flashing orange-dark, circled the black-hooded figure three times, and shot into the frosty sky. Crossing under the clothes-line, Mothkin's light set fire to the jewels of dew along its green length.

A feather twirled slowly down from the eaves outside the glass—a magnificent owl's feather. The Angel of Death was an owl, watching and waiting with me unseen in the chilly hours after sundown.

Uncle Henry pulled open the door, and there stood Mothkin, black cloak billowing, eyes twin pools of ink. *"Pax sit vo-biscum,"* he intoned, tracing two fingers together through the air in the sign of the cross.

"Et cum spiritu tuo!" cried Henry gleefully, catching our guest by the shoulders, pulling him into the hall. "Mothkin, Mothkin! We thought you'd never come! It's so good to see you! You saw our lanterns!" Henry was beside himself, practically dancing, bolting the door, rubbing his palms. "Can I take your cloak? Or—your pumpkin?"

Mothkin scanned the room, head cocked to one side, listening to the spaces between Henry's words. Flinging back his hood, he tucked his jack-o'-lantern into the crook of an arm, and paced slowly about, stepping carefully in the pools of orange light that shifted and spread before him. His hair was blue-black, curling over his ears and collar; he dressed in plain grey workman's clothes, like a plumber. I must have watched open-mouthed, as if following the movements of a fire-walker, while Mothkin *prowled* the front hall and parlor, his shadow a giant on the ceiling. Lifting his free hand at times before his face, he seemed to be fingering the shadows of the house, testing their fabric, examining their weight.

Henry's eyes shone. He was a child seeing Santa Claus in the secret depths of the night. Our visitor sidled up to the warm-air register in the foyer, just beside the table that holds the book that guests sign at a funeral visitation. For a moment

I thought he was looking for a book to sign, but then I noticed he wasn't peering *at* the tabletop but *over* it, keeping it between himself and the register on the floor. Gingerly he set his lantern on a corner of the table. He sighted along his nose, still as a technician about to defuse a bomb—then whirled, the space where he had stood filled only by the hem of his cape. Whisking a velvet pillow from an armchair, he came in low from the side, mashed it firmly over the grating, and snicked shut the vent control.

A muffled curse drifted up from under the floor—just a single, filthy word in a guttural voice, followed by silence. Henry and I exchanged amazed glances, our scalps crawling. Mothkin produced a short, hooked tool from a pouch on his belt and twisted something at one corner of the grate. I didn't know a person could *lock* a register, but I'm sure that's what he was doing. Finished, he sat back, feeling for vibrations in the floor.

"Would you like some coffee?" asked Henry at last.

"That would be nice," answered Mothkin, retying the lace of one work shoe.

THERE was actually something of a cozy atmosphere as we sat around the kitchen table, munching pumpkin seeds and drinking coffee from huge mugs that I liked to call "the caveman mugs" since they looked hewn from stone. Mothkin said little, and what he did say didn't make a lot of sense to me; I can't report much of our conversation—this was all quite some time ago, and the smalltalk we made in the kitchen really pales beside what happened after. Mothkin had left his pumpkin to watch over the locked register, and he sat with his big hands wrapped around his cup, his face swathed in rising steam. It really was hard to say just how old he was, for although he was wiry and athletic like a boy, there were crow's-feet above his swarthy cheeks and such deep lines at the corners of his mouth that his face resembled a mask—with its long nose, powerful chin, and thunder-harboring eyes, it had the capability of amplified expression.

Henry introduced me as his niece Dragonfly, and Mothkin accepted the unusual name without a sideward glance. "I'm charmed, I'm sure," he said with a lopsided grin, the wrinkles around his eyes deepening.

"Are you a priest?" I could not resist asking. You sure couldn't tell what he was by his clothes or anything else.

"Of sorts," he said, looking at me so hard without blinking that I squirmed in my chair. "But then, aren't we all?"

Mothkin asked for a full report of all that had been going on recently, which he got. Henry had me explain some parts which I knew better, and Mothkin listened as he closed and locked the kitchen registers, finishing each job with a deft twist of his mysterious tool. Apparently these registers weren't as dangerous as the one in the foyer, judging by the more casual way he approached them—maybe because they were smaller. A jack-o'-lantern by the refrigerator pressed its nose against the glass and grinned into the night. The clock above the cabinet said 7:32 P.M.

"Time to get started!" said Mothkin suddenly, draining his coffee cup and setting it down with a *bang!* Then he was fishing in his many pockets, checking the contents of a small backpack he shrugged from beneath his cloak.

Henry rose unsteadily, shuffled nearer. "Will you be—?"

"Yes. I'll be going down again. It's the only way."

Down! I know my eyes widened at that. Whatever the *Down!* was, he was going to descend into our basement to deal with it—from the moment I heard his intention, my mind was made up: if Mothkin was going down there, so was I—I *had* to see it for myself. I pressed my lips together and swallowed hard, squeezing one fist in the other. We were sitting on something big; I was old enough to realize that the things going on down there were not the typical problems other people had with their basements. Other kids *talked* of slimy wrists and knees that stirred below beds, of things in the basement that walked but did not breathe, of faces at the window. But what was under our house was real. I was scared, yes; I'd have been a fool *not* to be.

"They'll be guarding the basement door," said Mothkin. "I was expecting it last time, and it still almost got me killed. Are there any other ways down?"

Henry and I thought of it simultaneously. "The laundry chute!"

We hadn't been tossing any laundry down it for a month, since our machine in the basement had become enemy territory—we'd been washing our things laboriously in the bathtub, using an ancient washboard Henry found in his closet. But there was a square hatch in the wall of a nook off the kitchen. You could shove an armload of linens through, and they would tumble like ghosts in free-fall through musty darkness and land with a *whoomff* in a rolling bin beside the huge glass-fronted washing machine. Mothkin seemed pleased with the door when we showed it to him, though he wouldn't let Henry open it. He steered us all into the next room before we even talked about his descent.

"They're sitting down there listening to our footfalls," he said in the kitchen again, setting on the checkered tablecloth a glass cylinder with an ornate silver cap. This was a delicate lantern, the size of a soup can, into which he fitted a blue candlestick. "And they can hear the murmur of our voices. They know I'm here, and they know I'll be coming down. What I want you to do is this: when I get into position, walk as quietly as you can to the basement door and talk in whispers. Just stand and shuffle about secretively there. With any luck, they'll concentrate their reception plans on you—don't worry; you're perfectly safe as long as you don't open the door."

Henry nodded, wetting his lips. "What about you? I know you're an expert, but . . . is there anything we can do to help?"

Mothkin struck a match, touched the flame to his candle, and closed the tiny door. "Just *stay up here*. No rescue attempts under any circumstances, *please,* no matter what you hear. You have no idea what you're up against. I'll be back as soon as I can." He was uncoiling a metallic cord. "Of course, you can *pray*—that would help."

"Right," said Uncle Henry, pumping Mothkin's hand. "Take care, and good luck."

"Thanks, but luck's got nothing to do with it." Mothkin covered his head with the cowl.

I had a hundred questions as they stood there shaking hands in the lantern light, an aging mortician and a midnight monk. How had they met? What sort of person was Mothkin—where did he come from—what was he planning to do? But I had a bigger question, the one I'd been asking myself throughout the Black Cat Month, in waking hours and in haunted dreams, scooping out handfuls of pumpkin pulp, doing homework, watching Henry as he greeted the people who came to visitations, the uneasiness flickering behind his spectacles. (He worried that the other folks, the folks below the patterned carpet, might start up early tonight, might wallop on the floor and dump the rows of potted lilies—but it never happened; the house was always quiet when there were visitors about. It was as if the basement people wanted to keep their presence a private matter just between us and them. That gave us a lonely feeling, as you can imagine.) That big question was, who *were* the basement people? What on Earth were they doing down there?

I meant to find out—and I couldn't tell Henry what I was planning; he would never have allowed it, not with Mothkin's warnings about our basement situation. I watched quietly as Mothkin tied the end of his cable to a column, a narrow partition between the foyer and the entrance hall. The line was anchored around his waist. Paying out cable, he backed into the kitchen, shouldered his pack, and picked up the lantern. "All right," he nodded. "Do your thing."

"It's about an eight-foot drop," offered Henry, "from the hatchway to the laundry bin. There should still be a pile of sheets and towels—"

Mothkin shook his head. "Nothing will be the same, I assure you. Your basement has been rebuilt. If they've blocked off this laundry chute, we'll have to rethink."

Henry pursed his lips, nodding. He folded his arms, palms rubbing the leather patches on the elbows of his sweater, glanced from the clock to Mothkin. "One more cup of coffee?"

"No." The dark man took a last look around the kitchen. "It's time to do some trick-or-treating. Goodbye, Dragonfly." I couldn't see his eyes, but only his weathered cheeks, his jutting chin. "When I'm through the door, I'd better get to the bottom fast. Hanging on a line, I'm a sitting duck. So someone should plan on closing the door as soon as I'm through."

"I move quickly," I said in a hurry. "I'll do it."

Mothkin gave a single nod. "Walk lightly, girl."

He stepped softly to the edge of the kitchen. Henry and I

hurried toward the hallway. Mothkin became a long, floating shadow, then vanished into the gloom.

We padded toward the basement door, its chipped white paint luminescent in the dark hall. The deadbolt lock in its gaskets glinted coldly, like part of a gun. The cast-iron knob hung loose on its mooring, dislocated, as if it had been trying its utmost to pull away from whatever terrors lay beyond the door. Our feet on the moonslick carpet scuffed wakes in the knap. The door towered higher and higher.

I tried to imagine the people—*were* they people?—that waited for us just beyond it, crouching on the top stair, perhaps hanging sloth-like from the ceiling—bulldog-faced stranglers in slouch hats, all red-rimmed eyes and gnawing on darkness and drumming unclean nails in the dust.

The hall light on its brass chain snickered slowly to and fro as we passed beneath it, Henry's legs wobbling like poorly-managed chopsticks. He clutched my shoulder with a ghost's hand. We drew up under the shadow of the door—a shadow not made of the eclipsing of light, but by an obstruction of the life and warmth that flowed elsewhere in the world. It was a mighty rectangle of nothing, slabbing the entrance to nothing, a sheet of white ice.

Yet people—? Things—? lurked in the absence, terrible enigmas calculating sums that ended in death.

"There is a side to the moon that we never see—" echoed the voice of my science teacher in my head. *"As it revolves, it rotates in such a way that it keeps its back forever to space and that one single face toward Earth."* The face it wants us to see, my mind always finished. What was the moon hiding? And what about our basement door?

I remembered that we were supposed to be whispering, so I looked up at Henry and asked, "Have you got everything?"

His eyes jerked away from the door, blinked, and then he answered, "Yes, I think so. Do we really need all these potatoes?"

"You know it's best to be prepared. *I* think we should bring a few *more*, actually, but you're right about them slowing us down if we have to make a run for it."

We came to a stop, close enough to stretch out a hand and touch the frostily-glowing wood. With trembling fingers,

Henry turned the jittery knob a quarter-turn and released it, letting it panic back into place.

"The door's still locked," I hissed, rising to my tiptoes and coming down hard on my heels for good measure.

The silence behind the door inflated.

"I know, I know." Henry dabbled two knuckles on the frame, two lost pinball bones looking for a hole to vanish in. "Just making sure the knob still works. Wouldn't want it up and quitting on us at a time like this. Did you go to the bathroom?"

"Yes, I did. Did you?"

"Mm-hmm . . ."

Seconds ticked away. We shuffled our feet and babbled on, the skin on our stomachs shifting with that feeling you have when your head's safe beneath the pillow, but the whole length of your back is exposed to the monster straightening slowly up, easing the kinks out of his appendages that have been cramped for hours and hours under your bed—you're not safe, not at all—if he doesn't rip into you at 1:15, he can still do it at 1:45, at 2:01, or maybe he's saving you for that death-sweat hour of 3:14. Henry and I were playing Russian roulette with that door, tapping on its frame, jiggling the knob. That dime-store deadbolt was nothing, nothing at all; if they'd wanted us, they could have had us. We weren't fooling anybody but ourselves.

I'm ashamed of the way I handled the stunt—it embarrasses me to relate it. Hearing the whispering open of the laundry chute, I decided to have a coughing and sneezing spasm. I knew Mothkin would be through and down, so after a good wheeze, I burbled, "I've got to get a Kleenex!" and was off like a spit watermelon seed for the kitchen nook.

Goodbye, Uncle Henry! That last glimpse of his stooped figure, his balding head shining in the lamplight, the thought of how worried he'd be was almost enough to trip up my feet. I'm a traitor, I heard myself think; if Henry pulled this on me, I'd never forgive him. But he was safe up here, I reasoned, and I'd be back before he knew it.

Ha. Ha. Ha. We tell ourselves exactly what we want to hear, don't we? Reason is a slave to desire—it always was, and always will be.

I dashed through the dining room, spotted Mothkin's cable stretching away through the kitchen, and banked like a Cessna, gathering speed. Tables and chairs rolled away—the chute loomed into view, lighted from below by Mothkin's lantern. The cable jerked slightly, flakes of paint spiralling floorward. My right hand came up, fingers curled, tracing along the cord.

Suddenly, there was a whistling of the cable through space, and it was whipping out of my fingers, rocketing down the chute. Mothkin had some way of retrieving the line when he was finished with it; it was gone, and the lamplight seemed impossibly far away.

I wanted to shriek, but decided to save my breath—I wasn't going to be cheated out of a chance to see the basement. Thinking of the linens I remembered in the clothes hamper below, a great soft pile only a few feet down, I completely forgot Mothkin's assurance that the basement would not be as we had left it. Hands fanning like a diver's I launched myself, but caught the sill in my stomach, discharged all my breath. Streamers of cobweb swirled as I yanked the door to close it and slid face-first into the shaft.

If the metal bin had been in place directly beneath the chute, I'm quite sure I would have broken my neck. I can only credit my guardian angels with the fact that my ribs were spared in my belly-flop against the sill. The door struck my flailing legs and rebounded, my mouth widened in what would have been a scream had there been any air to power it, and I was plummeting head-down into darkness. I'd have to say that that's just about the most foolish thing I've ever done— maybe. You can judge better later, after I've told you about someone named Sylva.

Mothkin was there in a rapidly-growing circle of lamplight, much farther away than he should have been, the lantern at his feet as he stepped into position, arms spread. He caught me deftly, swinging me low and around to break my momentum, but I still saw a river of stars. He staggered sideways, depositing me on a wooden platform, the worst of his goblin-grimaces on his face. His breath hissed through clenched teeth. I lay there retching and gasping, and he dragged a hand across his mouth.

Above us, there was the sound of footsteps.

Slowly, the sunbursts behind my eyelids receded, doing a burn-down from yellow to orange to green. Getting to my knees, I began to take stock of my situation; there were several incongruities hitting on my mind. First, there shouldn't have been a wooden platform for us to be on—there had been nothing of the sort in the basement. And I had fallen a whole lot more than eight feet. On top of *that,* nothing around me was in any way familiar—the washing machine was gone, as were the laundry bin and the water heater, the shelves of Mason jars, and the furnace. The place we were in was *huge,* a shadowy warehouse of lumber and platforms, stairways and crumbling, dank-smelling earth. There were parts of the house's underside visible over our heads, pipes and timbers and floorboards; but in places, these were obscured by strange pillars and leaning bulwarks, stacks of things that might have been shingles. The door leading down from the hall was nowhere in sight.

Mothkin was right: the people in our basement had remodeled. I would never have recognized it as a place in my uncle's house. It was no longer ours. Accustomed as I had necessarily become to the idea of mysterious people inhabiting the basement, I was not in the least prepared to comprehend the sheer *size* of this place they had built.

3

The Basement Stairs

THE wooden platform was a landing on a haphazard stairway, the steps of varying sizes and angles of inclination, as if it had been built with either no blueprints at all, or with out-and-out malice toward pedestrians. Turning, it vanished around a dust-shrouded column above us and descended to darkness below. We seemed to be alone—at least for the moment. Mothkin said nothing as he wound up his cable.

The footsteps belonged to Henry; his frantic face appeared in the chute, pale in that distant aperture of houselight. Guilt twisted my insides as I watched his mouth working, head jerking from side to side in consternation. "Dragonfly!" he kept repeating. He extended a thin arm toward me, fingers quivering—it was way too short to do him any good. He was at least twenty feet above us.

Mothkin shook his head.

"Rope!" cried Henry, snapping his fingers, floundering to pull himself out of the chute. "I have some in the—" He froze, then deflated. "—In the basement."

"I'm sorry, Uncle Henry!" I called, my eyes stinging. I regretted my legerdemain. "I had to come see what's down here. I'm all right, and I won't stay long!"

Mothkin turned in a circle, studying our surroundings. Then he lifted his face again. "Henry—"

That was as far as he got, because we both saw something terrible. To the right of the laundry chute, a furnace pipe protruded from some shapeless wooden cornices like an exposed dinosaur bone. Following this line, our eyes picked out a junction of the house's floorboards and a shattered edge of the old basement wall, a place where cobwebs fluttered in a draft from an impenetrable gulf. It was a cave, plunging deep back into the crazy construction work. Across its jagged lip, a black shadow was advancing.

For a moment we stood squinting, trying to separate imagination from legitimate perception. Whatever the shadow was, it moved independently from the other shadows, a dozen feet across. Gliding through the masonry, barely visible in the feeble light of Mothkin's lamp, it held a smooth course, forward and a little to the side. In a most disturbing way, it traveled along a concave surface, skittered up a wall, and increased its speed.

It was going for Henry.

If I could have seen the thing more clearly, I would have been a step closer to unlocking a mystery that would vex me for some time. All I knew for the moment was that its apparent purposefulness filled me with horror. "UNCLE HENRY!" I screamed. "LOOK OUT!"

Mothkin took charge.

"Henry," he said gently, but with a deadly serious tone. "Listen to me. Close the door *now*." He was gauging distance, figuring out how much he had time to say. The shape moved unswerving toward the open hatch.

"Henry, I'm sorry to be abrupt, but your *life* depends on this. You've got to get inside that door *now* and close it. I'll look after Dragonfly and bring her up as soon as I can."

The shadow cruised over the furnace pipe, ten feet from Henry, closing fast.

Mothkin's voice rose. "Enemy coming your way on the ceiling! Close the door, man! Get inside!"

I was wailing, choking, my hands trying to cover my eyes, my eyes refusing to be covered. "Uncle Henry, *get inside!*"

"NO TIME!" roared Mothkin. *"NOW!"*

Henry blinked, wavered, confused at first by our instructions and then wrestling with his need to ask questions, to offer advice in return, as if he sensed that, by closing the door, he might lose us forever. At the last second, realizing his peril—perhaps responding more to some innate warning system than our words—he pulled back. He didn't see the thing; it was behind him. Jerking backward in the confined space, he caught his shoulder on the frame and hung there stunned. He shook his head, which dislodged the glasses from his nose. Reflexively closing his dangling hand, by some miracle he snagged the wire frames as they fell. Slipping back like a sack of potatoes, he fell into the kitchen nook, heaving shut the hatch no more than an arm's-length ahead of the shape.

Mothkin and I wilted in relief, watching as the black thing settled over the mouth of the chute, changed positions, and drifted in a few lazy circles. He raised the light, tried to get a better view, but the object was moving soundlessly back the way it had come. Finally it disappeared into the hole behind the wall.

The light from the kitchen was gone. Henry and his reassuring world were gone. The little indentation that marked the laundry aperture was one tiny shadow on a vast and passionless ceiling. I glanced down at my white, trembling hands. With every passing second, I was becoming sorrier for my impulsive decision to come down here. What had I expected to find?—Something like a carnival, perhaps, with pennants and eerie popcorn vendors lounging among our piles of garden hose and retired kitchen cabinets—maybe with rides, too, flame-colored cars suspended from the clothesline, controlled by a one-armed ticket man—a funhouse in the old coal room, and a grand circular midway with the furnace in the center, the heat of its blue flame filling calliope pipes as chariots pounded round. Truth be told, I hadn't thought much at all. I had been scared of the people and noises in the basement up until the time I heard that Mothkin was going down; I've never been able to stand being left out of anything.

This dim world that had been our basement was *gigantic*, smelling of dampness and an evil presence as penetrating as the mist which slid through the air in layers, clung to the edges of pillars and braces, beaded on the lid of the lantern.

I looked at Mothkin, a stranger about whom I knew nothing, except that Henry trusted him. I really couldn't read his emotions at all. He had come out of the night with a jack-o'-lantern, and now I was alone with him in enemy territory. I wished I had brought along a sweater. Mothkin had taken a second lantern from his pack, and now he handed it to me. His apple-mummy cheeks bunched slightly—a smile? But his eyes echoed the dark.

"Are you mad at me?" I had to know.

"No. It's obvious to me you're supposed to be here."

I brushed hair from my eyes, clamped it behind my ear. "How do you know?"

"Because you're here. But listen to me, Dragonfly: we're in danger. Believe me, you cannot even *begin* to guess what a dangerous place this is. I know you've got a child's mind, a mighty imagination, and those will do us some good—but they can work against us, too. I can't take you back until we're finished here. With all this shouting, I'm quite sure we've lost any surprise advantage I might have had, but we're not where they expected us to be. To try to get out now would be death— I'm not exaggerating. They'll kill us if they can. That much is at stake—and a whole lot more."

"Mothkin—"

He hushed me with his eyes. "Little girl, you're a doll hanging by a thread over a well, and there are clacking scissors and flaring matches every way you swing. We've got to blow out those matches and get past those scissors a pair at a time. You're going to get cut and burned, but remember, it's the thread that gets you out—got it?"

I didn't get it. Why do teachers always speak in parables?

"Do what I say. Don't do what I don't say. Don't believe everything you hear. Don't believe everything you read. *Do* believe everything you believe. And, as you value your life— *don't* take candy from strangers."

My head was spinning.

"Keep your eyes open. We're going down." His voice softened. "I'll try to find you something warmer to wear as soon as I can."

Whirling away, he bowed his head, his back to me. He stood still for a long time, and I switched my lantern nervously from my right hand to my left. The darkness pulsed around us with every movement of the candles' flames. There was a scurrying as of tiny feet atop a bank of loose earth. Peering in that direction I could see nothing.

"Mothkin," I whispered at last, "what are you doing?"

"Praying." He picked up his lantern, stepped to the edge of the landing. "You'd do well to do the same. Watch your step."

He started down, and I hurried to follow, the fingers of my right hand pressing against the wall of rough timbers. The stairs creaked beneath my tennis shoes. How did Mothkin walk so quietly? The footing was uneven, in places slippery with condensation. Soon the platform was far behind, and we crossed several more, the stair winding, encased in chill vapors, lightless. Already far below the street, we still descended between wooden troughs, low walls, pillars, mounds of shattered concrete—the old floor of the basement?—fractured pipes, past the skeleton of a rusted motorcycle. Ominous caves loomed up in broken distances, mildewed soil and rubble like dried vomit on their chins—I wondered if there might be hundreds more of the things like that which had gone after Henry. At times, rounding a bulwark like the slipshod gable of a house, we would catch a glimpse up a chimney at the distant floor of the funeral home, the merest glimmer of electric light filtering down through a register or a crack in the wainscotting. I thought of Henry pacing from room to room, unaware of the abyss just beneath the squeaking boards, his footsteps dislodging dust to sift down, down, feeding the darkness.

In the library at our school, there was a plastic model which had always fascinated me. It covered a whole wall, a three-dimensional map of the ocean floor, the features molded in brown plastic, the water represented by a transparent blue film. I loved one name I read there: Challenger Deep, a trench of unthinkable depth. Now Mothkin and I were walking in just such a place, the secret floor of a lightless ocean. Henry's floors were the thin veil, less substantial than the blue film— beneath the kitchen, Brick Shelf, twenty-five feet down. Along under the veranda, Gable Range, seventy feet below the Earth's surface. And under the funeral parlor's soft, wine-colored carpet, down below the flower stands and the rows of folding chairs—Lost Echo Deep, a thousand feet straight down!

Icy drafts wafted suddenly around crumbling structures towering purposeless in the unsteady light—impossible heights and depths unnerved me, more suggested than actually seen—full of whispers, scrabblings of creatures with no bodies, visible sometimes as glittering pairs of eyes. What finally intimidated me, though, were the shadows. I was gradually forced to redefine that word, "shadow." It had always communicated to me the blocking of light, a dark patch cast by something interfering with a light source; but the shadows down here were altogether different—unrelated to light, having *substance,* almost their own *smell,* like the blackest leaves on the floor of a forest. They rustled, dragged hems over piles of stone, lined themselves along the gables of slanting rooftops (—rooftops of *what?* I wondered—) and followed us. I was sure they were going before and behind us, conspiring, preparing to swarm together and drown us beneath their accumulated midnight.

I thrust my lantern at them, and they danced backward. They shifted, rolled and billowed in ways that no living creature could move, reminding me of laundry on a clothesline. Yet this clothesline that held their corners in place was itself moving, slithering through the waste, tightening itself around us. I whirled twice, convinced that something like a black sheet was spreading open behind me, the hood of a cobra. Both times Mothkin glanced back at me. Clutching the small warmth of the light to my chest, I tried to control my breathing, tried not to betray my terror with whimpers and gasps as I moved in as close behind his fluttering cloak as I dared.

But as we reached the biggest landing yet, a rough platform of timbers set with chairs, a table, and arched over with a gargantuan slab of leaning stone, it became too much to bear. Looking up at the monolithic piece of granite, my peripheral vision swimming with the shadows—the undulating shadows—I found my legs unwilling to move. This was a trap if I had ever seen one; the slab was going to slam down on us while they all watched and shifted, and they would go on watching and shifting even when the lights were gone, when we were entombed. I folded my arms around the lantern, unable to go further.

I must have looked something like a paralyzed deer in the headlights. Mothkin laid a hand on my shoulder.

"Don't let them get to you, Dragonfly. You are doing exactly what they want. Yes, they're there. Yes, they want us dead. But they are only shadows." He glanced from the darkness to my face and brushed a hand across his mouth. Obviously, I wasn't convinced. He peered up at the overleaning stone.

"I think it's time to call Quillum," he said.

"What?"

"Quillum is the Great Shadow Lord, the master of every shadow that ever danced by chamber or pit beneath the earth. It's time to put some fear into these."

There was nothing I could say as I watched him step gingerly off the platform behind the large wooden table. For the first time, I noticed that there was a human skull on the table, dry and ancient, its empty sockets by chance fixed directly on me. But a skull is a skull; it didn't frighten me like the shadows did. I found the strength to back up onto the stairs, retreating into a narrow place between walls of tumbled rock. Here, if the granite fell, I might not be flattened—I might only be buried alive. Smothered by the shadows, I sagged to a crouch.

Mothkin had disappeared around a pile of loose stones. The platform and skull faded into dimness and a hollow beyond it was lighted by his lamp, which also threw a field of illumination across the smooth slab above us. In the downwash of reflected light, the shadows hovered back a little, and I could have sworn I heard a collective inrush of breath. Then there was even deeper silence. An eternal and diffuse body of tiny ice crystals spiraled before my eyes, the ubiquitous spirit of this place. Its touch upon my face, my hair, I clamped my lips tightly shut, lest it lunge down my throat and fill me with its frigidity, make me forever its own.

I wished Mothkin were back within my sight.

"Dragonfly." His voice seemed impossibly distant, a whisper across space. "This terror you feel—you must overcome it if you hope to be of any use down here—if you hope to stay alive. Do you see why?"

I opened my mouth, closed it again. Granules of ice swam in the dark. Fear possessed me, became my universe, taking every ounce of my power to move or think. "Yes," I whispered, closing my eyes against it.

"Good. Now I will tell you how you are going to overcome it. You are going to extinguish your lantern and sit with fear in the dark."

My eyes flew open.

" 'Unthinkable,' you want to scream. It is unthinkable. But there are limits to the usefulness of thinking. There are dangers, and there are fears; what assails us now is *only* a fear. Do not let it breathe, Dragonfly. Enter its domain and let it be finished."

My heart pounded—it was crazy, the idea of blowing out my lantern, crazier even than coming down here. It was plunging into the sea in pursuit of the sea serpent. "No!" My voice was a squeak.

"*You* live, Dragonfly, not they. Show them you know that. Defy them with a puff of air!"

I gazed into the mist around me, its billion crystals shimmering, blue and lifeless. Years before, I had formulated what I called the Act of Ultimate Courage, had considered it often, but never carried it out, never expected to think of it as anything but a hypothetical situation. The Act of Ultimate Courage would be to walk alone into the cold back bedroom at night, where no one slept and Henry kept the Christmas tree in a box in the closet—to walk in there *without turning on the light,* right out to the center of the floor, shut your eyes, and *trust,* as only an adult could trust, that nothing would touch you. Another Act of Ultimate Courage was to stand in that bedroom in the dark with your back to the mirror, to be immune as only an adult could be to the fear that faces emerged there, faces of people with pale, pale skin and teeth of iron, people with red hair and red lips and mouths torn open back to the ears . . .

Mothkin had spoken of my child's mind, my imagination, of how they could do us some good, but that they could work against us. I suddenly understood him—or at least the part about how they could work against us. The shadows thought they could defeat me by reminding me of a cold back room and a mirror that frightened me. Commanding my fingers to stop trembling, I opened the lantern, lifting the delicate latch. The flame wavered, vulnerable and alone. "I'll light you again; don't worry," I told the candle in my mind. "And as for *you*—" I glared at the shadows, "it's time for you to wither and die. I am coming into your house. I am sitting on your steps. And, Shadows, I come to you *in the dark.*"

With that, I blew out the light.

There was one terrible instant as the darkness closed in when I was seized by doubt—the ice vapors were touching me, the shadows creeping near, and what else? What else was sitting above me on the stairs, what bloated face with ragged lips was looming up out of the cracks, all red hair and filthy nails reaching . . . ? I felt the circulations of the life within me—made a fist of real flesh, of true bone, and set the lantern calmly down beside me on a step I could not see. Folding my hands in my lap, I raised my chin, even smiled into the warmthless nebula.

"Good," said the voice of Mothkin, seeming not nearly so far away this time. His light still flickered across the slab, but I was alone at the bottom of a deep well of darkness.

The fear was gone. I was conscious of the stairs stretching above me to where the shape on the ceiling had tried to swallow Henry, conscious of the caves we had passed at every turn—yet the quiet voice of my mind spoke with confidence: *There is no one on the steps behind me. I know that without turning around.* I was just going to call out to Mothkin, demonstrate the steadiness of my voice, ask him why he, too, did not put out his lantern; but then a flash of motion drew my gaze upward.

A lone black shadow stole across the edge of the lighted slab. It was not amorphous like the ones that hung over the stairs, but a bold, vast one with edges sharp as the hole a stone cuts through ice. I watched in fascination as it grew and grew, the shadow of a long-fingered hand, an arm, a monstrous body.

"Quillum," hissed Mothkin. "Quillum is awake."

It rose like a bat, sweeping across the ceiling, stretching arms and legs like black rivers. Back and forth it moved, round and round the flickering granite stage. It was more or less human in shape, but enormous, swooping and pouncing. Its face was beaked, birdlike.

I was sure it was Mothkin's shadow; he was stepping back and forth over his lantern in the hollow. What he achieved—or what we achieved together—was a rout. The spaces around us lightened by several degrees even before my lantern was rekindled, and only natural shadows quavered on the stairway. Something like an invisible wall retreated as "Quillum" vanished, returning to his infinite tunnels, his minions quieted. The feeling was like in a summer storm, the air oppressive and cloying one minute, and the next, after the cloudburst, there is a wave of relief and your body and spirit stretch out.

The light shifted as Mothkin reappeared around the rock pile, his face unquestionably grinning this time. There was something in his eyes that gratified me almost more than our victory: respect. "I knew I was right," he murmured, relighting my candle. "You're here for a reason." His eyes narrowed. "Round One is ours, but Round Two is coming, Dragonfly. You have courage, but that, too, is a two-edged sword."

"What do you mean?" I was a little put out at his glossing over my Act of Ultimate Courage. After all, *I* was the one who had blown my lantern out. "I thought we just proved shadows have no teeth or claws."

"*These* don't."

He was already turning to continue the descent.

The farther we went, the more orderly the construction became, as if the builders had spent more effort on their labors in the deep, and had merely scooped holes and slapped boards together in the pits just beneath the funeral home. We met no one on our stair, which I had begun to think unusual considering all the noise that arose from down here—but then, in wider places lower down, we had glimpses of other stairways, dozens of others, many much broader than ours, and I realized we had only been tripping down a cobwebby back alley of sorts. "That one," said Mothkin at a shadowy bend, pointing across a gulf of jumbled bricks at a flight of steps ten feet wide. "I suppose that's the one that leads right up to your basement door."

He shrugged off his backpack and reached inside. Producing two velvet cloths, he fitted them over our lanterns, completely blocking the light. By lifting a cunning aperture sewn into the material, we could aim a slender beam of light directly at the stairs before our feet.

The passage became defined by walls of stone blocks, each fully two feet across. Training my beam upward, I found that the ceiling had soared high out of sight. Here at last we saw a living thing that was more than a pair of eyes: Mothkin's beam picked out a shiny, almost luminescent blue lizard, its skin color like none I had ever seen. Its tongue darted out and in, its gemlike eyes marking our passage. The temperature was dropping. I shivered, wishing *now* that I had brought a *jacket.*

A light was growing somewhere ahead, first a smudge of grey against the black, then a dull red, then bright enough to show us the sweeping arch of the passage down which the stairs twisted.

"Do you know that color?" asked Mothkin.

It was firelight, but darker somehow, redder. Drunker. *Lustier.* "The light of jack-o'-lanterns?"

"Fire at the heart," he whispered, "leaking through the tight orange skin of the Harvest Moon. That's the name of this whole infernal operation, scooped out of the dark souls of basements. Welcome to Harvest Moon."

Our stairway joined another, became twice as wide. Mothkin listened carefully to the stillness before proceeding. As the light increased, we could see patches of trailing moss clinging to the high walls and growing, miraculously, in a near-total absence of light. Our breath swirled before our faces, mixing with the dank mist.

The red light was spilling from a square window in the right-hand wall. Motioning for silence, Mothkin beckoned me to follow him for a look inside.

4

HARVEST MOON

I T was only when I peered through that glassless window into the radiance of a hundred hanging lamps that I began to grasp the evil of this place. Mothkin kept me back away from the sill, so that our faces were wreathed in shadows. The lamps, shaded with dull orange oiled paper, sputtered shifting light over long tables on a floor of stones and littered straw. At the tables sat about forty children, thin, dressed in rags, their hair tangled. They hunched over their plates, ate ravenously a dark green substance like particularly limp, oily spinach.

"They're prisoners," muttered Mothkin. "Eating sparsely."

"What are they eating?"

"Sparsely. It's the bitterest of bitter herbs, a specialty of this place."

Gazing at the sparsely with glassy eyes, they ate and sat stiffly in high-backed chairs. The meal had obviously just begun, but it was over even as we watched—there was so little food, and no conversation.

"Don't look now," said Mothkin, knowing full well that I would, "but *that,* coming out of the corner, is one of the foulest things on any world."

A tall figure circled the farthest table, passed beneath a

lamp, its face shaded by a wide-brimmed hat of black felt. It strode down the center of the hall, hands buried in the pockets of a loose coat that hung to its knees. As it turned, I got my first look—which I'll never forget—of the devastation under the hat. That face was little more than a skull—at first, I thought it *was* a skull, until glowing eyes emerged from the caverns under its brow, and I saw the deeply-etched wrinkles in its sallow skin. The thinness, the down-turned mouth gave the wasted countenance an appearance of insatiable hunger.

I jerked back as if slapped, feeling somehow *dirty*—the eyes, sweeping left and right, made smudges on the essence of all they touched.

"Eagerly Meagerly," breathed Mothkin. "That's its name."

It—he—walked up and down the chamber, never uttering a word, pausing now and again. Under his gaze a child would wither, slide down in his chair, and clench the edge of the table. The nearest children would glance about close to panic until Eagerly Meagerly passed on, the nails of his boots going *click, click, click.*

Mothkin had slipped past the window and was beckoning me. Horrible as the scene was, it was hard for me to leave the window; the children were pathetic, breaking the silence only to sneeze or cough—and when they did, Eagerly Meagerly would turn in their direction, narrowing his eyes. Many of the prisoners were my age, and some were much younger, their clothing, hair, and skin color indicating that they came from various countries. My heart went out to them—how long had they been here? How had they come? Their sadness became my own, and I vowed to help them.

Mothkin was urging me onward, hurrying with his bull's-eye lantern trained on the steps. There were iron chains fixed to the walls now, rings and collars for holding prisoners. The stair ended in a slope of loose, broken stones and mud. A wrecked wagon lay on its side, a row of bats dangling in restless sleep from its sideboard. The mist brought smells of rotting cloth and garbage, of animals, the Hallowe'en odor of burning, and—and of onions, the smell of chopped onions that makes the eyes water. Picking our way over the boulders, we reached the bottom, vapors of unreality swirled away, and there lay the haunted kingdom of Harvest Moon.

There was no sky—only far, far above, the winking of mineral highlights in a cavern ceiling. We saw a town—perhaps a series of towns—walls, peaked roofs, and towers, jutting in a crazy jumble over the knees of a black mountain. Firelight danced in the windows, behind the shutters, sputtered here and there on lampposts in the narrow streets. Figures shifted in the shadows; carts passed with a clatter; cats yowled on fences. A wagon thundered along an avenue, thick smoke rising from a flaming pot on its high seat, its driver a silhouette with flying cape and peaked hat. Higher up, the steep slopes bristled with forests—yes, trees that existed without sunlight, sucking their life from deep waters. Over all shone a flushed and indiscreet moon; how it was engineered I did not know at the time, but its bloated, ruddy disc hovered over the peak of the mountain, where the image of a black horse towered in the glare, a colossus of iron. Smoke poured out of the moon—that fact alone convinced me it was a clever facsimile, not the real moon. It smoldered like a bonfire in the sky, sending up a haze that rolled and brooded over the landscape, stirred not by wind but by the drafts of the deep Earth.

"Hallowe'en Town," I whispered. I had not forgotten the children; I could *feel* the evil of this place, suggested in every winking spark, every baleful shadow, in the false moon that choked the sky. But I was, at the same time, enchanted by Harvest Moon. It was all I had found to love in the wine-dark festival being celebrated with masks and costumes in the world above our heads—a place of frost-white mists, of disembodied chuckles, of the whirring of owls' wings and the glow of their eyes. Magic spread out from the tree roots here, a deceptively alluring pestilence, drawing all in, leaving no survivors. It called me in a liquid chant, its rhythm thrilling a depth of my heart that had slept since earliest childhood. Part of me wanted to clap hands and dance over the rocks like a gazelle, to let the smoke fill and carry me, whisper to me the things of mystery and delight long forgotten in the schoolrooms and under the unfeeling sun. For I sensed that there *were* secrets here, wrapped by the roots of time, framed in the sorcery of burning wicks. The liquid sounds called me more insistently, using my name, confiding that only a sensitive heart, a heart that came in joy and willingness, could share these secrets, this fluttering rapture.

Mothkin's voice seemed harsh, intrusive when he spoke. "Do you hear the water, Dragonfly?"

Water? I forced my mind to consider its perceptions one by one, not to be swept into their dream. Yes, it was water that I heard as a plaintive call—running water.

"That is the River Abandon, which lies across our path ahead. The bridge into Harvest Moon will be guarded." He poked his face up over the rocks, slithered higher for better vantage. "Two of them."

"Two of *what*?"

"Guards. You are about to meet the inhabitants." He slid back to join me. "There are ways past guards. You were right; this *is* Hallowe'en Town. And it's time to go trick-or-treating."

"Won't they recognize us?"

Crawling on hands and knees, he motioned me to follow. "The guards on this bridge have neither eyes nor ears—down here, appearance is icing on the cake. They look *inside,* at how people *feel*." Blowing out our lanterns, he stowed them in his pack; the moon gave us more than enough light—and the less light on us, the better.

"Now, Dragonfly, I'm hoping we can pass ourselves off as citizens, so think melancholy. Dredge up all the sad thoughts you've got—dog hit by a car, a loved one's passing, anything. Don't let one happy thought intrude until we're over the bridge."

I frowned. "Thinking sad thoughts will fool them?"

"No one here is really happy, so projecting sad thoughts is the way to blend in. Subject matter is irrelevant; it's the emotion that counts. Wail out loud if it will help. Can you do it?"

I nodded, thinking of my parents. There were things I could be sad about.

"Just *don't* get curious—if you let your sadness evaporate, you'll have more attention than you want, I guarantee. Only sad thoughts, no matter what you see or hear. Okay?"

"Okay."

"And if it doesn't work, be ready to run."

Affecting a wooden, strengthless gait, we rounded the last rocks and came within sight of the river channel, a cleft gouged deep in the stone. The river charged foaming and grand in the moon's twilight between walls glittering like ancient ice, riddled by mossy caves. The voice of the current was loud, the voice of an eternal and indomitable will.

Spanning the gorge was a strange bridge—it seemed constructed more of shadow than of wood or stone, for grey smoke swirled along its arch, obscuring the footing, and trails of moss groped down toward the water, twisted on its piers. At the far end, where the path rose toward the town, two guardsmen waited—they wore black, hooded robes that covered them head to foot, leaned on heavy scythes, each the very picture of Medieval Death, the Grim Reaper. They must have perceived us as we lurched into view, but they did not stir.

Mothkin stepped onto the bridge, and I followed, sighing as pathetically as I could. Closing my eyes, I summoned up my own ghosts. The faces of my family hovered there, materializing from the frosty mists. My grandfather had seemed to love me like no one else—I saw him suddenly in a beam of purest sunlight, swinging along his garden path, tapping his cane as he always did on the raised bricks beside the rose bushes. Reaching out to him, I shoved into his hands my crayon sketch of the Mountains Beyond the Distant Stars— always done in purple and blue, for those were the only colors that existed there—he took the paper and smiled. He listened to my stories of Hal, the boy who climbed the Thousand Stairs to rescue the Princess Miriel from the Tower of the Hag— Grandpa always asked the right questions, nodded and sighed, laughed and rubbed his eyes all in the right places. I had seldom spoken of those Mountains since that last day he and I sat in the gazebo in summer sunlight. His kind, wrinkled face dissolved in roses and sun. How quickly he'd vanished!— listening to my story one day, gone the next. None of us had known it would be the last day. If we had, I would not have been so quick to skip off to the movies. "Stay for supper," he had implored; I'd hesitated a little, and that made the memory worse—I almost stayed with him. But I chose the matinee, left him standing in the gazebo with my crayon drawing.

The tears were coming hot and fast. I clutched at my loneliness, my mother's rigid back as she stood before the mirror, brushing her hair. *"Decide, Bridget."* That was her battlecry. Did I want to be dropped off at the movies or the mall? Did I want money to eat out with, or did I want Mrs. Cain to fix supper for me? So many decisions, but Mom wasn't part of the package, even when she was in town. She had to keep her appointments; her script didn't call for a daughter. Then there was Dad. I swiped at my eyes, barely able to see the guards, now much nearer. Dad's battlecry was, *"Ah—I just don't think that's going to be workable."* It wasn't *workable* that he come and see my play at school, that he make Christmas or Thanksgiving or my birthday, either, although I'm sure we could have bought a pretty good cake with the money Mom left for me. Having an accidental daughter must have been *really* unworkable for him—or so it seemed to me, in the long climb through grade school. I loved them, and they loved me, though none of us knew how to show it very well. I sometimes call those our "In-the-Dark Years"—there was the awareness that something was lacking that need *not* be lacking; it was like putting your arms around smoke, like picking up mercury.

We crossed right between the two unmoving guards, their weapons glinting. It was only when Mothkin gripped my arm that I was again aware of the groaning passion of the River Abandon, its voice even stronger than before. Within the boundaries of Harvest Moon, it became a Siren's dangerous song; I whirled to face the water, stumbled forward to peer down into the channel. Its breath rose, lifting my hair, freezing the tears on my face. The water tumbled, echoing in the dark. Foam burst over rocks, hurled flaming pearls at the moon, gathered smooth and secret in the hushes of coves. Tottering at the brink, I was only dimly aware of loose pebbles stealing away beneath my feet.

Mothkin pulled me suddenly backward, and the guards swiveled dark-filled skulls to face us, winelight red on their scythes. Across the river a commotion arose; there was torchlight, the clattering of hooves, and harsh yelling.

I found my feet and ran with Mothkin through ditches overgrown with clotted brambles, under arbors thick with alien vines. The smoke swirled densely in places, fed by burning piles of garbage and vegetation that sputtered and coughed up the smell of wildness, lit the arches and brickworks with a pagan murk. A thought came crazily: *The October burning smell—is it all manufactured here?* Night birds exploded from black shrubs as we passed, owls watched from the limbs of witch-trees, and shapes of things like dogs bounded over haphazard fences, sped together in packs glimpsed only as bristling backs through vapor and wan light. There were hedges, shriveled brakes, trunks burdened with knotted burls. Spectral scarecrows loomed functionlessly in groves of bracken. With the leaning trees and overhead trel-lises, it seemed we were half outdoors and half in, neither in brightness nor dark; it was a world of opposites, like October. We dashed on through a diffusion of orange moonlight, pur-sued or unpursued, we knew not, and the mist swallowed us whole.

That was how we came to Pink Eye Street.

That's what a signboard said at a corner where we broke from the trees: the ominous junction of Pink Eye Street and Too Quiet Street. The latter ran straight before us into the town's heart, deep as a canyon between high buildings that leaned together. It *was* quiet, absolutely avoided by the carts, a gallery where shadows pooled and a solitary black cat sidled over the cobbles.

"No change down that way," murmured Mothkin, "but they've rerouted Pink Eye."

"So you don't really know where we're going?"

"Sure I do; we're going over there." He pointed toward a low fence that paralleled the busier avenue.

"Shouldn't we go where there aren't as many people?"

He glanced sideways at me from beneath lowered lids. "Feel free to offer suggestions, Dragonfly."

I shrugged, missing his point. "Okay."

"Come on." Crouching, he flitted toward the fence. "I want to have a look around. It's easier since they put up a moon."

We relied now on stealth, dodging from shadow to shadow, lying low as carts racketed past. Some carried passengers, some garbage in reeking mounds, and many were tilt-carts, their cargo draped with canvas shrouds. These were pulled by a variety of beasts—black horses, goats, sway-backed mules, a camel, and one species I had never seen before—a powerful creature with the size of a horse but the horns of a goat, drawing carts in pairs, surging and writhing like teams of living springs. The drivers and passengers were usually dressed in black, often concealed beneath hoods, slouch hats, or opera capes. The faces we *did* see were pretty disturbing, pale skin stretched nearly to ripping, enormous, staring eyes under high-arching brows. For the most part, we stayed out of sight and they took no notice of us, although at times a face would turn sharply in our direction, eyes fixed on our hiding place, and the driver's head would pivot fully around like an owl's.

"The people aren't all skeletons like the guards," I observed.

"No." Mothkin steered me around a puddle. "These can see and hear—*and* sense your feelings."

It became painfully obvious that my clothes marked me as one from the outside, so Mothkin darted across the street to go rooting in a trash pile and found a tattered black hooded cloak. Its almost *visible* smell made me choke when I held it, the essence of smoke, onion, and fishbones. Taking pity on me, Mothkin handed me his own cloak and donned the filthy one; I protested, but he wouldn't exchange again—at last I was forced to put his on and hurry after him as he moved up the street. I felt a little safer now from the burning eyes—but none of the drivers were wearing tennis shoes.

At about this time, as we crept along what seemed a line of shops, each ground floor window covered by iron grating, a clamor erupted in the direction of the bridge, the same stamping and shouting we had heard at the river. Diving into an alleyway, pressing ourselves against the bricks, we waited—and the noise grew with a grinding of wheels, vibrations ringing deep in the stone. Mothkin drew from his bag a weapon, a dagger with an ornate hilt, which he buckled around his waist.

Then with a flapping of cloaks, a wave of mounted figures swept by in the street. They swirled and eddied like foul scrub-water, some pausing to wheel and look backward—tall, gaunt men and women, some riding the horse-goat animals and some running on foot. A black coach crashed along at the center of the confused column, twin lanterns dangling above its seat, a noxious smokepot fuming on its roof. The driver was both fat beneath his velvet vest and extremely long of limb, a combination which made him resemble an insect. At his side, jingling against his striped trousers, was a gigantic pair of silver scissors. A tall stovepipe hat crowned his head, and he held a smoldering cigar between his teeth, precisely in the center of his mouth.

"That's his toady," whispered Mothkin, "and the big boss is in the coach. This must be the party that was staked out under the funeral home. Look—you can see how mad they are they didn't find us."

I wasn't sure if I could see anger in the cadaverous faces or not, but there *was* a kind of infernal glow leaking out from the draped windows of the coach. The vehicle's wheels were not rimmed with smooth circles of iron, but were cut in the pattern of a star like four large-toothed gears. "For the stairs!" I gasped. "It's made to go up and down stairs!" It couldn't have been the most comfortable ride, either on stairways or on the level.

The procession rumbled up Pink Eye Street like a scudding storm and turned at a corner somewhere ahead, into a street that ran up toward the mountain. A few carts swerved frantically to get out of their way, the lead riders cursing them, the complaints echoing back through the cavalcade.

With a clattering rush they were gone, and Mothkin nodded with satisfaction. "The riders aren't fanning out to search the streets; they've probably left a detail to guard the bridge, and doubtless they're scouring the upper brickworks for us—but they don't seem to suspect we've gotten this far. Round Two, complete. Round Three is on the way."

"Where do we go from here?"

His answer was interrupted by a voice from the alleyway behind us, a dismal lane leading back toward Too Quiet Street. The voice was of a quality I heard then for the first time—less a human voice and more some wondrous symphony *mistaken* for human speech—that's the only way I can describe what sounded like a singing of wind, a tinkling of bells, the growling of distant beasts.

> "See, Procrustes, the jackals are walking around
> Tightening the knots of their circles . . ."

A curious light was in Mothkin's eyes as we searched the murk, but saw only the alley stretching away, sagging stoops and shuttered windows.

"This way," whispered Mothkin, laying a hand on my shoulder, "quietly." We crept back from the street front, close under the wall of a building. The grey stones radiated chill.

Water glittered on the pavement, and the vapors flowed along Too Quiet Street in a white river.

Another phrase of the poem followed, echoing, indefinable. It was farther away now, and I could not make out the words exactly—something about a *"blind giant eating up the ground"* and a *"three-fingered scissor man."* As the sound faded, a candle was lighted in a low doorway ahead, spilling a pool of warm light into the alley. Mothkin slipped forward, skirting garbage piles. I glanced up at the dark windows, at the rooftops, at the burnished shield of the moon.

Peering around the door frame, Mothkin entered, and I hurried up behind him. In a space enclosed by plank walls, with only room for a table and a twisting iron ladder, the candle burned. Beneath its brass holder was a note, neatly scripted on an unusual beige slip of paper. He glanced over it and handed it to me. I did not read it in its entirety just then, but I certainly did later, by the light of the candle, and this is what it said:

> Up and down the land of leaning stones
> The night breeds ghosts, and I have seen a few;
> Gibber and clack they go, the moving bones.
>
> On Pink Eye Street they are the empty ones;
> They grin with hollow skulls the evening through
> Up and down the land of leaning stones.
>
> As the Lean Man his sickle hones
> They pass the grates of Number Fifty-two;
> Gibber and clack they go, the moving bones.
>
> The moon turns over with a sickly groan;
> They know the darkness better than we do
> Up and down the land of leaning stones.
>
> You lean toward night and think you lean alone.
> Just when they died it seems they never knew.
> Gibber and clack they go, the moving bones.
>
> The Emperors of Air, the ice-cream clones
> Cold the wind blows through, the wind blows through;

Up and down the land of leaning stones
Gibber and clack they go, the moving bones.

Puzzled, I watched Mothkin climb the spiral ladder without a sound, thrust his head through a trap door. There was a peal of quiet laughter in the outlandish voice of the alley singer, and a single, sharp chuckle from Mothkin, who waved for me to follow him.

"Close the door, and bring the candle," he instructed.

Wondering, I did as I was told and found myself in a loft so cramped that the peaks of our hoods almost brushed the ceiling, our feet met at the trapdoor as we sat around the walls, our knees under our chins. Mothkin helped me up, and I saw in the single candle's light that another person was here, but couldn't get a good look at him until Mothkin had finished shutting the square door and, as an afterthought, opening it a crack to drop his odorous disguise into the room below. Then he settled back, running his fingers through his hair with a sigh.

For the briefest of instants, I thought I was looking into the face of an owl. That's how the man's smile was, bent down in the middle like a beak, eyes huge and suggestive of a nocturnal animal. He wore a green tunic, his trousers and boots of supple leather.

His eyes glowed at me, then flicked to Mothkin. "You've brought someone." That voice was *surpassingly* strange.

"Yes," answered Mothkin. "It seems so appointed. *Eirene eie soi.*"

"*Kai to pneumati sou.*"

I thought my hearing had gone suddenly dysfunctional.

The stranger said, "Mothkin, is it?"

Mothkin answered, "Yes. And this is Dragonfly."

The stranger inclined his head. His hair was the color of chestnuts, his cloak like fathomless smoke.

"And you?" asked Mothkin. "What shall we call you this time around?"

Still in awe of his voice, I blurted out, "You're—*you're* the alley singer."

He held up a finger. "Good idea! My name is Alley Singer."

Mothkin laughed. "Well, Alley Singer, are we reasonably safe here?"

Alley Singer smiled his owl smile. "My dear Mothkin, this is Harvest Moon. Safe? But I'll say yes, if it will make you feel better." He moved the candle for a better view of our faces. "This was a ticket office or something. And now it's a hoooole in the wall. Best place, if you want to hide." On that "hooole" his mouth was very round.

"Been here long?" asked Mothkin.

"Long enough. Something's doing, as I suspected, at Number Fifty-two."

"All right, we'll have to check it out." Mothkin sighed again. "Any leads on what he's up to now?"

"It is biiiig, my friend. Same old thing, only ever-so-much-moreso. Going to taste like dishwater."

"Great." Mothkin nodded to me. "Dragonfly, you must be getting curious. What do you want to know?"

I stared at him.

"First," said Alley Singer, "I must know. Do you like my poetry?"

No sooner had I opened my mouth than Singer's hand shot out and clamped over it.

Mothkin's dagger was out, and I thought for a horrible second I was about to be run through—but then I noticed that their attention was on a square portal I had not seen in the roof.

There was the slightest scraping sound, as of a foot on the shingles outside, the clink of a latch, and the hatchway was thrown open. This was behind Mothkin—he scrambled across the floor, dragging me with him.

In the square a face appeared.

I could not hold back a cry at the sight—a sharp face, widest at the forehead, tapering to a receding chin, the whole framed by wisps of backswept hair, fine and cornsilk blond. The fire-green eyes of a cat burned down at us.

"Green Man," mewled the stranger. "Knew I'd find you here." His grin spread sideways over a face pasty-pale with smudges of green. "Mind if I drop in?"

"Noyes." Alley Singer's eyes blazed. "Enter at your peril."

The sickly one's lips peeled back in a laugh, exposing long, long canine teeth.

Even I could see that he was a vampire.

5

THE GLASSWORKS

"JUST a word or two." He held up a long-nailed hand, as if to show he was unarmed. "A little chat, and we all go on our ways. Fair? Anyway," he said with a gesture toward the blade in Mothkin's hand, "you have the advantage, do you not?"

"*If* you're alone," snorted Mothkin.

I would not have thought it possible, but the vampire was wriggling in through the hatchway, which seemed barely wide enough to admit his head. It was as if his bones became liquid, letting him ooze in and land with a *plop* where Mothkin had been sitting. His black clothes smelled much like the disguise we'd found in the garbage, and when he sat with drawn-up knees, the chamber was cramped indeed. His sideways smirk allowed one lethal fang to glint in the firelight.

"Make one move," murmured Singer, "and, believe me, you're ashes to ashes."

"Oooooo!" The vampire opened his mouth, waggled his greenish tongue. Settling back against the wall, he picked his teeth with a fingernail.

"State your business," said Singer.

The vampire, whose name was Noyes, crossed his bony legs. One mold-dusted wingtip shoe twirling in the air before us, he spoke in his pathetic, half-strangled voice. "You weren't hard to find. You don't move with the stealth you once did."

"Nor does Project Nowhere," interjected Mothkin. "Since when have you had people running around *measuring* things up there?"

"Survey teams," chuckled Noyes. "The time is close."

Survey teams?—the men in luminous black I had seen skulking in the alley. Measuring things? "What's Project Nowhere?" I asked.

Two pairs of eyes communicated that I ought to seriously consider shutting up; the third gleamed with a hungry light.

"Ah," sighed Noyes. "Yes, I suppose stealth is not so easy when one is leading a lamb to the slaughter." He laced his fingers behind his head, half-lowered his eyelids. "You've brought me a present, have you, Green Man?"

Singer leaned a little closer. "You want a present from me, bloodsucker?"

"Consider it. I found you first, because I'm dazzlingly clever, and this is my neighborhood. *He'll* find you before long, and then your party really *will* be over. As I see it, you have one chance to cut a deal that will make us all happier."

"I do not cut deals with undead, gorger."

"You might start." The vampire's red lips were draining of color, starting to match his face. The laxity left his expression, and it turned to ice. "Give me the child," he ordered, aiming a long finger at me, closing one eye to sight along it. "And then we all walk away. I never saw you." The hand became a colorless fist. "Refuse, and you die first, *then* I take the child. And, no"—he flicked his thumb in Mothkin's direction—"I'm *not* alone, Grey Man. Touch me, and you won't leave this house." If his face were less pale and blotchy, his teeth tucked away, Noyes would have looked almost cherubic then. "Do we have an agreement?"

Mothkin's face was, as always, unreadable.

Singer grinned. "Good work, boy! You're a smart little lid-kisser. But you think like a vampire; you just haven't been at this long enough."

Noyes raised his eyebrows a fraction, looked amused. "No?"

"You're really after the promotion, aren't you? You no longer have a grandmother to sell, but you can find plenty else—you intend to relieve us of this child and *then* hand us over to the boss, right? Win his favor, and you're a shoo-in for Operation Groundmist."

Now the smile was looking forced. "You know about Groundmist."

Mothkin turned his dagger over in the candlelight, studying the blade. "Tell me about Groundmist," he said quietly.

At the time I wondered angrily why I couldn't ask questions like that. It all boiled down, I decided, to whether or not you were an adult—but under the eyes of the vampire, I didn't feel like doing much but lying low behind Mothkin.

"Oh, it's a new one," answered Singer. "The spearhead of Project Nowhere, that they're all chewing on right now at Number Fifty-two Pink Eye Street behind locked grates. Hain's brainchild—place three Harvest Moon vampires outside by the bottom of the year, to speed along the work up there. Our moldy friend here would give his pinkies to be one of them."

"Sucking blood in the land of opportunity," mused Mothkin. "Ambitious fellow, aren't you? Love to get yourself an advance on the boss man's vision for the future."

"Oh, he's got visions, all right." Singer glared at the vampire. "Bloodsuckers by Christmas, with expansion to lycanthropes in the new year."

"Big time," growled Mothkin. "Hallowe'en all year long."

"Well," said Singer, "it looks like we're at a stand-off."

The vampire cleared his throat. "You're refusing my offer?"

"Wake up, mulch lips," snarled Singer. "We do our homework. I've got the facts sheets on you, and lots of friends have copies. Assuming you hand us over to the boss, we tell him how you run your business, Mr. Chairman of Project Changeling! Snatch thirteen children, turn ten over to Meagerly; snatch nine, turn in five. You're gorging yourself on fresh young blood while others of your unholy kind are starving. I wonder what Mr. Hain does with those who abuse their positions?"

"Well, then," said Noyes, nodding slowly, lips mashed together. "It is obvious that I cannot hand you over to Hain. The alternative—"

"—Is that you gut us right here and now," finished Singer. "Only that doesn't look so good either, because we're number one on the 'wanted' list—if Mr. Hain learns that you held out on him, that you took upon yourself the honor of doing with us . . ."

"You won't have an ear to land on." Mothkin rose to a crouch. "So I suggest you slither on out that window, call off your dogs, and go back to your faithful stewardship."

The candle was burning lower. Shadows flickered about the chamber as Noyes, too, got his feet beneath him. Once more his unwholesome eyes passed over us each in turn, and his lip curled.

"Is that what you suggest?" His single exposed fang glistened, a string of saliva from its tip trailing down his chin. He rested a hand on the ledge of the hatch. "You've kept your ears open—that is obvious. Little escapes you. Before I go, I will answer your question, little lamb, that you may know, when you die, what your blood has been used to feed. Project Nowhere is the future, the glorious destiny of the human race, beginning with the extension of Harvest Moon into the golden feeding grounds of the world above. Yours, young one, is a land flowing with milk and honey. We are 'Nowhere,' the hidden kingdom; soon we will be 'Now Here,' the Realm of Harmonious Night!"

My two companions gave him the benefit of no reaction whatsoever, and the vampire hated it. "When you've finished, Mr. Noyes," said Mothkin, "the window is right there."

"I oversaw the rebuilding of Pink Eye Street after you finished with it—is it nine years ago already?" Flexing his fingers in the air, Noyes appeared to relish the jaggedness of his nails. "We've made some improvements; I won't be needing the window." With that, he hurled himself against the boards beside me. I had not even time to scream as he swooped past and vanished *through the wall*—which was, in reality, a concealed door. As Mothkin once more dragged me to safety, I caught sight of Noyes landing in a spin, teeth bared.

Other shapes loomed up from their hiding places. The wall of our tiny room swung open to annex the adjoining building, what looked to be a vast, shady warehouse; I could discern boxes and ladders, balconies and dubious alcoves. Our chamber gave onto a balcony at the second-floor level; there were two more above it, festooned with cobwebs. I saw three vampires besides Noyes—one perched beside him at the wooden railing, one leaning casually against a brace on a balcony above, fluttering his clawed fingers playfully in our direction, and one making a dizzying leap from a ledge to the top of a tower of crates, skipping over the precarious heights toward us as a child crosses a brook from stone to stone. Black capes spread winglike behind them, formal tails on their coats giving them the appearance of twiggy insects. The bloodish moon peered in at the high glass windows, mixed with the lights of the town to cast the vault into an eerie twilight.

"The gang's all here," muttered Singer.

The vampire out on the peak of boxes pistoned his feet, throwing up an apron of dust about his knees. "Shall we dance?" he screeched, tossing back his balding head to shake with laughter.

"And now," said the creature that leaned with Noyes on the railing, "you die." He stepped forward, a thick-necked brute with blond hair shaved so close that at first glance he seemed to have none, his eyes blue as gas-jets. Fangs bared, he lunged at Singer.

My hands covered my eyes, but I heard a sound like a whistle, like the thump of an axe into wood, and then an animal roaring. Looking again, I saw the blue-eyed one spin ballet-style. Six inches of a wooden rod were sticking out of the left side of his chest, and the vampire clawed at it as he went down, rebounding from a stack of boxes, smearing the wall with his blood. I remember thinking that vampires bleed a lot more than human beings.

Singer had shot him with a small crossbow. I saw it now, about the length of his forearm, as he drew it from under his cloak and laid another bolt on its deck.

Mothkin had sheathed his knife and armed himself with a wooden club, sharpened at its tip.

Still against the railing, his mouth agape, Noyes decided, for the moment, on flight. He leaped over the rail, caught a pulley rope, and swung to another section of balcony. Mothkin took the advantage of a few seconds to remove something else from his pack.

Using a metal key to wind his crossbow, Singer observed the wounded vampire as its blood—and the stolen blood of its victims—fountained from around the bolt and from the twisting mouth. The arms and legs flailed as if the vampire were making a snow angel. I stood transfixed, watching the dark pool spread beneath the body, reach the railing, and begin to flow like a midnight waterfall over the edge. Slowly, the creature's thrashing stopped.

The dancer from the stack of boxes came in like wind, soundless at first, his fury rising as he cleared the rail. Mothkin avoided the charge by inches, diving backward into the gap between two cases of cans and dusty implements. The vampire connected heavily with one of the cases, hurled it aside, cans of oil and paint crashing from its shelves. Lunging into the space after Mothkin, the creature vanished, but his pitted, pimpled face lingered behind my eyelids like a nightmare sun. His tall silk hat, dislodged by his collision, rolled to a stop at my feet.

"Rip out his wheedling throat, Sparks!" hissed a voice from above, and I saw the vampire on the upper balcony, his face as puckered and obese as a toadstool. His piggy eyes behind rolls of fat glowed yellow as he dropped like a missile down an open stairwell to the balcony beneath.

"Dragonfly," said Singer, his unearthly voice close beside my ear, "hide yourself."

I could not muster the strength to move as Mothkin reappeared on the top of another case, this one lined with glass beakers, his pursuer a mere step behind. Dislodged by their feet, the beakers flew and shattered.

Cackling, the piggy-eyed one blossomed from the shadows, landed ahead of Mothkin to cut him off.

Mothkin hesitated, slashed backward with his weapon suddenly, catching the balding one off guard. His pike emerged from the back of the creature's cloak, and I expected the vampire to fall. Instead he wrenched free, twisting his body, and laughed—although the weapon had pierced his stomach, there was no blood. Seizing the shaft in both hands, he pulled it out, eyes throwing sparks, tossed it away. It fell end over end, clattering on the floor far below.

"Too bad," said the vampire, straightening his tie. "Doesn't count if it's not through the heart."

Mothkin glanced right and left, midway between them on the ledge.

The fat vampire, he of the yellow eyes, giggled like a child and spread his round hands. "Mothkin, Mothkin," he crooned.

"Pye," said Mothkin. "How long has it been?"

"Twenty-one years." The vampire pulled back his cowl, exposing fully his misshapen head. He looked to have been horribly burned in a time past; lank hair grew on only half his crown, his left ear barely recognizable as such. "Look on your handiwork, Grey Man. I have counted the time, awaiting our next meeting." He rocked from toes to heels, his fat undulating. "This is the night of repayment!"

"Who will have the pleasure?" asked the other vampire. "Mr. Pye, or I?"

Pye waggled a stubby finger. "Mr. Sparks, Mr. Sparks—"

What he would have said must forever remain a mystery—for Mothkin, making good use of the split-second that Pye's admonishing eyes flicked beyond him, reached to the small of his back and drew out a slender wooden knife he had placed in his belt when Noyes fled. While Pye was still forming the next syllable, he flung it underhand, his arm curling.

This time, he did not miss the heart.

As Pye fell, sounding and *looking* like a murdered pig, his weight splintered the railing of the lower balcony. Upending when he struck its edge, he rolled lazily, cartwheeled to the floor below. Floorboards cracked, and he settled at last with one leg dangling down through the ceiling of the basement.

Then Sparks tackled Mothkin from behind and locked mold-splayed fingers around his throat.

But you must be pretty anxious to hear what was going on about then with Singer and Noyes.

As Mothkin was leaping into the cover of the standing cases, as Sparks was making a mess by pitching over shelves, Singer dashed in pursuit of Noyes, following our balcony around to its right end.

There Noyes—almost but not completely a coward—reared up in his face and made something like a stand, swinging a globe of glass. Singer collapsed his knees just in time, glass spraying in all directions. Turning again, Noyes launched himself across a gulf to another section, his formal shoes skidding when he landed, pinwheeling his arms.

The two balconies on which they stood were separated by a gap of a dozen feet. They faced each other, the vampire's green cat eyes smoldering with hatred. He dragged the back of a cadaverous hand over his moldy face. I wondered how old he was. And I had discovered an important difference between Hollywood vampires and the real things—there was nothing suave or even remotely handsome about these guys; nor were they from Transylvania.

"It's too far for me to jump," said Singer.

"Yes," agreed Noyes.

Or to shoot with any accuracy, I noted. Now that the cross-bow was no secret, Noyes could probably dodge a bolt at this range.

"But not too far for a vampire. Why don't you come over here, and let's finish it?"

"I don't think so," said Noyes.

Spotting a catwalk higher up, Singer turned to a ladder.

I didn't like the vampire's smile. Noyes watched him climb, aiming beakers and bottles at his head, his knuckles. Pulling his hood over his face, Singer climbed, the missiles catching the moonlight, reflecting dark rainbows.

The abundance of breakage brought a fact home to me which would probably have been obvious to a better-trained eye: we were in a glassworks. On the ground floor, where Pye was about to alight, there were worktables, carts, racks, and crates of glass products. Long tubes for blowing glass in bubbles leaned against a brick wall, near a row of ovens. So Noyes had plenty of ammunition. He must have gone through hundreds of dollars' worth by the time Singer reached the cat-walk and shook himself like a dog that has been swimming, glitter flying from his clothing, catching the ruby light.

Then he started across a simple board suspended from brackets, only feet from a broad, many-paned window near the ceiling. As he edged forward, using the cables that served as its handrails, the plank swayed a little to and fro.

Noyes was screaming with mirth, lobbing pop fly bottles, not even aiming, through the glass behind Singer. I wondered if he had lost whatever sort of mind vampires have. Panes folded, flew apart. Shards as big as I was fell in amber spirals, in emerald cascades.

Singer was crossing the moon now, his silhouette black and impossibly far away—but suddenly I thought I was seeing double.

Rubbing my eyes, I looked again. A tiny shadow, a smudge, seemed to have detached itself from the lunar surface, beginning to grow, dancing and diving in the smoky nimbus, far away beyond the glass.

It grew larger, a falling leaf, a—

I screamed the air from my lungs as the glass behind Singer erupted, knocking him to his knees, setting the catwalk into a jerky, uncoordinated swing. One end yawed and crashed out through another pane of the window, and its passenger gripped the plank for his life.

It was another vampire. This one came in transforming; outside the glass, he was a great black bat. He got big and heavy enough to force an entrance, and when his feet hit the catwalk, he was an old man with floating white hair and a goat's beard—that's all the longer it took to change.

Noyes stopped throwing things, raised his fist in a wild cheer. "Adrian!" He clicked his heels. "You're beautiful! Join the party!"

The old man, hardly more than a mummy of bones and leather skin, showed Singer his sizeable fangs, closing the distance with a wiry bound. He lashed out with both hands, one armed with claws, one with a jagged piece of the window.

Singer evaded the thrust, forced the vampire back with a kick, and fired his crossbow point blank.

There was only a *plunk!*—and the vampire crackled like a bonfire. He was laughing. Dust rose from his waistcoat as he rapped horny knuckles on his chest. *Clank, clank!* "Iron plate. Don't bother reloading." He came forward with the glass shard again, gashing Singer's face. I couldn't see how bad it was at that distance, but the man staggered and the vampire was on him, all stick arms and scissor legs. I watched the piece of glass come floating down, down, streaked with Singer's blood.

"Now, boy," spat Adrian, the old one, "now."

Pressing Singer's neck against the wire, he wormed his ancient body, rocking the catwalk into dizzy motion. Harder, faster, he splayed his frame, forced the man sideways, kicking his legs off into space, pointing his head at the window. A vampire, you see, has uncanny strength, even if he looks old and dried up. It's part of the curse they exist with, like the magic of being able to change shapes and come through wearing clothes when they're done, not like poor werewolves that have to run around naked until they find the pile of clothes they wriggled out of under the moon.

It was clear what this Adrian planned to do: put Singer's head through the window, then use the fractured hole as a guillotine. The catwalk was shuddering, bouncing, threatening to come loose from its moorings, getting nearer the window with each swing. Singer's feet scrabbled helplessly in the air.

Sorry; I'm going back to Mothkin and Sparks now.

Mothkin and the pimpled, snarling vampire were rolling along the top of the display case, Sparks attempting to throttle Mothkin, their struggles knocking ornamental bottles to the floor. The case had a glass front, and their knees and heels left sprawling spiderweb cracks along its length, the blossoms of ghost flowers. Glass tumbled in deadly rivulets, highlighted by the swollen moon.

Mothkin broke bottle after bottle over the vampire's head, ground the jagged ends into his face and neck. I was glad I couldn't see any better from my vantage point.

"Gouge away, Michelangelo!" hooted Sparks. "This face can't get any worse!"

Mothkin could only wheeze, his throat compressed in the cold hands, his struggles getting weaker.

"Grey Man," hissed the vampire, "you have failed. That which is not becomes that which is. The Kingdom must open." I think he would have had Mothkin then if Sparks had been a man and not a vampire; Mothkin's arms were going limp. A man would have crushed his opponent's throat until all struggles ceased—but Sparks was a vampire, and he wanted to drink. And it's no kick at all, I'm told, for them to drink from a dead man. His heart has to be beating, or the blood is something like cold coffee, I suppose, or curdled milk. Sparks wanted Mothkin alive, and to bite his throat, he had to let go of it.

As the fangs descended, Mothkin heaved upward with his knees—either he found a last ounce of strength, or he'd been playing possum—I never did ask him. He got Sparks off-balance and thrust him back with both legs.

As if the motion were slowed to replay a sports event, their two bodies parted like those of trapeze artists. Sparks, stretched at full length, arched over—and came down. Inverted, he was back-diving, arms over his head, crimson eyes locked on my face—my blood just sat dead in the tubes.

Was it chance—accident?—luck?—that lined him up perfectly? Mothkin often said he didn't believe in luck, that nothing happens by accident. But, well, remember how Pye's plummeting body splintered the railing of the balcony? It couldn't have been choreographed better: yes, there was a stave of the broken rail sticking up, very wooden, very sharp—and yes, Sparks landed on it.

No, this isn't a fairy tale—it didn't pierce his heart. But he lay there cursing, trying to get free by working his way up the spike that protruded from his waist.

Mothkin rolled down from the case, gripped its edge. Gasping, he sagged to his knees, pressed his face to the wood. The cabinet stood in ruins—I don't think one available surface remained intact.

Unsettled by the rocking of the structure, a tower of crates, each full of several dozen bottles, toppled slowly into the wall, slats flying apart, pulverized glass spuming like water. Pieces of the boxes rained down; granules flowed over the balcony in a river of stars.

At the end of the swath of wreckage, Mothkin climbed to his feet. Opening his pack, he got out another wooden spike.

Sparks slavered, hissed, broke boards.

Mothkin didn't make any speeches; he just stepped up quickly and finished the job.

You may be wondering why vampires bleed so much—I

know *I* was at the time. They bleed anywhere from three to ten times more than the average human being with the same injury, although I don't know just how much laboratory data there is on the subject. It's because they drink so much blood. You know that old sickly cartoon belief that you can put blood into your veins by drinking it? Well, for vampires, it really works that way; I guess they have special stomachs, or maybe none at all. They gorge themselves, and if that heart is pierced, you get *jets*.

So there was Pye lying on the main floor, and Sparks directly above him, leaking profusely, head and arms hanging from the edge of the balcony; and there was Mothkin like a tired gunslinger, wondering how he could help Singer.

Ah, yes—Singer. He was getting strangled, too, and about to have his head delivered through a sheet of glass. Adrian's disheveled hair flopped like a pompon with his exertion. Grappling at the vampire's throat, Singer ripped loose the cloak, and it floated down, a black parachute. Singer's hair brushed the glass at the extremity of the yaw. On the next swing, his head would go through.

"Mortals," leered Adrian. "So short-lived."

Wriggling onto his side, Singer pulled a surprise of his own; he, too, had had a moment of leisure to stick something into his belt. I saw it glint, an iron spike about eighteen inches long.

The vampire snorted, enjoying the moment. "Pitiful! It has to be wood to work!"

Singer's head cracked the glass. The pane burst outward, a hole opening dead center, broken pieces sprinkling down outside. Again the catwalk swung away, jerked, and one mooring bracket popped free, flinging its bolt high across the room. A metal clamp crashed onto a balcony, and the plank tilted sharply.

Adrian wasn't distracted; he was the oldest and wisest of that particular graveyard quintet—wise enough to wear an iron plate under his shirt.

"Iron," coughed Singer, aiming the spike, "for iron." He ran it into the vampire's throat, just at the knot of the rumpled string tie.

The point shouldn't have been anywhere near the old one's heart, but he *howled,* clung to a cable by one wizened hand, his crickety legs pedaling the air; his head rolled as if it were about to come off, and his black, hateful eyes glowered from the floor of the glassworks far below to the face of the man on the catwalk. Suddenly, *smoke* was belching from the vampire's mouth, his nose. His wordless screams, more full of fury than any I had heard, choked abruptly to a stop.

Singer drove the spike deeper with his heel, his cut face a mask of blood. "Has to be wood?" he croaked.

Adrian vomited smoke, lashed with his free hand, but Singer was already climbing off the swiftly-unmooring plank into a stairwell. The vampire's skin puckered, as if what little substance he had between bones and flesh were disappearing.

"What about holy water?" said Singer. "Doesn't seem to agree with you."

The spike, you see, was a hollow tube, a syringe. Singer had injected the ancient one with holy water, which can kill a vampire as surely as sunlight or a stake through the heart.

The plank let go, and so did Adrian. Together they fell— the long board, the brackets, the cables, and the vampire— from the very highest point in the room to the very lowest. I think he tried to assume the shape of a bat as he fell, but I guess he was too far gone—what slammed into the floor and lay still amid the debris was a smoking carcass with staring, glazed eyes, neither bat nor man.

It had all happened in a few minutes, but it seemed as if I'd been gripping the rail for an eternity as I let out my breath. The damage to the glassworks was awesome—smoke rose, boards were fractured, and the underground breeze blew through the newly-made ventilation, swirling the dust from balconies. The Glitter Fairy had been everywhere, it appeared, generously distributing wheelbarrow-loads of ground glass in every color of the rainbow.

Just as the last of the air sighed out of me and I crumpled, tears stinging my eyes, a terrible grip seized my arm, whirled me around.

It was Noyes.

6

TOO QUIET STREET

"IT'S over," he grated, eyes about to pop out of his head. I won't say his breath was fetid on my face, because I don't think vampires breathe. But his body and clothing reeked overall, exuding waves of damp and unspeakable decay. It's more than the odor of tombs and their own undead flesh—I think what assails the nostrils when confronted with a vampire is the putrefaction of what lies *inside* them, the dead thing that is *alive* in mortals—the soul. Vampires have to walk around with rotting souls until Judgment Day, or until they meet a stake—which is six of one, half a dozen of the other. They really are wretched beings.

"We're out of here, little lamb," he said, wrapping cold arms about me, dragging me toward the anteroom where we'd talked. The hand he cupped over my mouth was an instant ahead of my scream. "Hey," he added, almost apologetically, "don't look at me that way. Everyone has to eat."

He started through the swinging door, the one he had used to surprise us earlier, but then thought better of it. "Not that way—that's no good." Hefting me to his hip, he opened a square hatch in the floor, stepped into space as a fireman does when sliding down a pole—except there wasn't a pole. We dropped a level to the ground floor, and he landed easily, bending his knees.

I struggled, but he was obviously experienced at stealing children; with one arm, he held my mouth shut and pinned my arms, leaving himself a hand free to open doors. His fangs were very close—or one was, anyway, because he was doing his lopsided grin from nose to ear.

"Yes, everyone's got to eat," he repeated, sidling cautiously out of the building and into an alley. "Little lambs have their clover, lions have their meat, and some people, I've heard, even like chicken tetrazini."

He found a dark alcove, where rats as big as squirrels picked over garbage and scurried for cover as he kicked them away. "Begone, friends," he said gently. "I don't need you today—got something sweeter. Much, much sweeter." He pressed me into the bricks, his hand still covering my mouth.

His eyes were huge, loathsome, hypnotic. "Got to drain you now, lambie. You're a little too much trouble to take along, things being what they are." He flicked back greasy hair, his lips full and red. It's sickening how a vampire's lips change color with his mood.

I tried what heroines have been doing in movies for years—I kneed him as hard as I could in the groin. Let me tell you, it doesn't work with vampires.

He ran that green tongue over his fangs. "You're afraid, little one. I can *taste* your fear."

Can you?—that gave me an idea.

The picture of the guards at the River Abandon came to me—they had "seen" only my negative feelings. The shadows on the stairway, too, had relished my fear.

(*"—The golden feeding grounds,"* Noyes had said, *"of the world above—"*)

(*—feeding grounds—*)

(*—think melancholy—*)

I had one chance, and I gave it all I had, filling my mind with a picture, something far from this alley, a picture of summer light—an empty gazebo—Grandpa's cane rolling in slow motion, down one step, down two, *tock, tock,* settling at the bottom where they had found it—

I sucked breath, suddenly able, because Noyes's hand was gone from my lips. "Little *lamb!*" I heard the vampire say from a thousand miles away.

Sunlight, roses. I skipped along the path, singing "I Saw Three Ships," a Christmas song, although it was summer—

mom mom i'm home mom

Sunlight, open windows, curtains floating, smell of the new tar on the road—

what do you mean where is she mrs. cain why

Silence, silence; the tears were coming now.

grandpa grandpa can't be can't be

Crayon sketch fluttering in his brown hand—

(—"Now *this*," said the vampire from the backside of the night, "is *delicious!*")

what do you mean how can a heart just stop not his

Cane in the soft dirt, by the bricks—

mom i don't like this mom don't go mom why

(—"Better than blood," said the vampire, "better—sweeter—")

Tears were pouring down my face, and I felt fingers brushing them, playing with them, saw Noyes licking his fingers.

"More—!" he hissed. "Remember more! Give me more!"

And I did it. Boy, did I do it. I sent him pain, searing images, every dark and bitter heartwound of a childhood. I faxed him dead cats, lonely evenings, and Mrs. Cain's mascara; dredged up treasures of darkness; tossed griefs out of my storehouse with both hands.

He was feeding off my pain, off the milk and honey he so desperately sought through Operation Groundmist, and was oblivious until Singer hauled him off his feet and Mothkin drove the stake weapon through his heart. He fountained all over the alley, but he didn't scream, because Singer jammed a wad of cloth down his throat.

Mothkin was astonished to find my neck intact, but then his eyes began to glow again with that same respect and joy they had shown me on the stairs. He squeezed my shoulders. "Another round complete!"

Singer, too, understood. "If the bloodsuckers can pull warriors out of the air," he murmured, wiping blood and dirt from his face, "so can we. Well done, Dragonfly."

* * *

WE moved quickly. I learned we couldn't leave the vampires in their present state; if someone pulled the stakes from their hearts, they would be up and around again, carrying bigger grudges than ever. Singer and Mothkin rounded up the bodies, cut the heads off, and stuffed the mouths with garlic, of which the men carried an ample supply. Then heads and bodies were stacked on a bed of whatever flammable items we could find and ignited, right out in the middle of the floor; when reduced to ashes, the vampires would be irrevocably destroyed. We might have gathered the ashes and dumped them into running water for good measure, but Singer assured me this was enough, that we'd be wise to get off the premises before the fire brought company.

I regarded him blankly, my senses dulled with exhaustion. "The fire will bring company, but nothing else we've done here has?"

His smile was still there, although a long slash lay from his nose to his left ear, oozing blood and looking extremely painful. "The neighbors will come to put out a fire, because it threatens their houses. They'll usually lie low for a fight, especially one with vampires."

"Not everyone around here is a vampire, then?"

"Everyone in Harvest Moon sucks pain. Most *don't* suck blood. The vampires feed off these townsmen, even if their blood's not very good—that's why the vampires all want in on Groundmist." Mothkin stowed the last of his gear and we scampered out of there, driven by a surge of blistering heat. The alley was already lit with the fire's flickering, voices crying out in the gloom.

I looked back at the windows, the eyes of the inferno. "Who's going to pay for all this?"

"Adrian," grinned Singer. "It's his glassworks."

Mothkin shot him the goblin-glower. "You picked us a good hiding place, Alley Singer. Really good."

IT was warmer in the town than it had been on the stairways, the result, I gathered, of all the smoldering that went on.

Things were burning whichever way you turned, including the moon itself, which spread a layer of fog to be stirred by updrafts. There were cookfires, bonfires in huddling gardens overleaned by rotting stone walls, and the smudge-pots smoking on wagon seats. Although the frigid white mist pooled in alleys, eddied in dooryards, its chill was perceptibly lessened here.

We followed an alley that cut back from Pink Eye Street, bordered by a prodigious leafy arbor. Moving quickly, we looked back and could see the glare our adventure had left over that district. Flame stood in a tower, reflected on the underside of the smoke. My poetic thoughts at the time were of apocalypse—my unpoetic thought was that we were arsonists. There were obviously different rules in effect here—did that include lighting fires in people's glassworks?

My hands shaking, I relied on Mothkin's arm for support; I was ten years old, and I'd just spent the most traumatic hours of my life. Mothkin and Singer were here to fight. It was clear to me that, from the moment I saw the captive children, I'd joined the war—maybe it's true that in all members of my gender there is something of the mother instinct. In one evening, I knew I'd taken a step down a road from which there is never a returning.

Mothkin and Singer always moved with a purpose; that's one of the things about them I remember most clearly. They discussed very little, as if able to read each other's minds.

A wall of piled stones ran through an orchard where the soil lay deep and spongy. Some men in high-collared cloaks were whispering among the trunks, the moon casting their shadows long over the bracken. They turned pallid faces in our direction, their knitted brows suggesting that they were searching for something—or someone. The tallest, an angular man with eyes and hair the color of frost, put his gloved hands on his hips and took a step toward us. As his short cape rose with his elbows, his silhouette resembled the hood of a cobra.

"Down!" hissed Singer.

We collapsed against the base of a wall.

The breeze ruffled Mothkin's hair as he peered over the edge. Long moments passed while overhead, autumn leaves spiraled toward earth. How did they keep it up? I wondered—

it was incredible that leaves could grow without the sun; how they kept falling forever in an autumn that never ended was a strange, dark miracle.

"Did they see us?" I asked when Mothkin gave us the all-clear signal.

"Not quite."

"But they're looking," said Singer. "Stay low."

We moved at a crouch, our shoes making sucking noises until we crossed a fence and scrambled back into the shadows of an alley.

It's often said about children—and animals—that they know intuitively whom to trust. I had hardly a clue who Mothkin and Singer were, but I liked them. Think about it; they were made to order from the mind of a child: adults who saw the phantoms I saw, moved with me through the same dark, and fought with grown-up strength and experience.

The moon lit our way, kindled flashes of moisture like sequins on the rats. It never changed position in the "sky"— there was no day, only a night of hoots and howls, of hinges, tenebrous vines, and the swelling of enigmatic fruit.

Cutting across a garden thick with nettles, where a gang of thorny creepers were frozen in the act of strangling a scarecrow, we borrowed an outhouse. It was a ramshackle hutch with a sagging roof and an odor that led us to it. Mothkin went in first, and when he declared it safe I braved its reeking blackness while my comrades stood guard outside. This is an episode that gets quietly left out of stories, but I'm including it in mine—not only because I remember the relief it brought me, but since that mundane act removed the last thread of doubt; this was no dream. Harvest Moon, in all its hideous splendor, was a part of my waking life, and its people were real enough to need outhouses.

What a place this was!

First of all, I was lost after three turns; no street pursued a straight line for more than a hundred yards. At sudden forks, plank walls shot up like ships' prows to cut the path in two, black ships blown in from the gulfs between stars, all harbored here and half-sunk in stone to form a town. Rats glistened through the gutters. Candles burned behind windows shuttered and barred.

Everyone who passed was the villain of another tale, flitting out of a doorway, gliding with a sweeping cloak, watching us from beneath a lowered brim. Some traveled in groups, funereal women, sunken-cheeked men, most silent, some screeching with inebriated laughter, supporting drunken fellows, some glancing fearfully over their shoulders. It was a haunted place, and its people were haunted. One black-bearded giant dragged the corpse of a thin man by the hair. As we passed, he looked murderously in our direction but made no effort to be discreet. Yet another specter was a being so ancient his bald head was a shriveled walnut, the two bones in each forearm clearly pronounced as he gripped the leash of a slavering woolly thing that must have been a dog.

We kept a lookout, but the frost-eyed man did not reappear. The others who passed mistook us, I suppose, for a bedraggled gang of their own; Singer and I were masked by our cloaks, and Mothkin, with his raven hair and jutting cheekbones, looked perfectly at home.

There were children, too, nothing like the prisoners we had seen. These children had pale cheeks, shuffled along in the wakes of adults or stalked each other like panthers. I thought a group of them were fighting, but I saw it was a game; it involved pouncing out of hedges, slapping, scratching, and penalties for the losers. Some were made to walk along fence-tops carrying heavy stones while the winners flogged them with sticks, and others were dragged along the pavement by the heels. The losers took the abuse quietly, hardly lifting a hand to protect themselves as they were bruised, even bloodied. Different groups played it in gardens all across the town—it was the only game they knew.

The more I watched, the more terrible I realized their activity to be: the children moved ceremonially, as if following the steps of a ritual, and I was reminded of chess; dozens of rules seemed to be in use, rules of movement in proximity to one's opponents. Those who hid were not well-hidden—rather, their positions beneath trees and against warped fences *represented* hiding, the stiff, hopping courses of others bringing them close enough to be attacked—with acts of simulated vampirism, suggested gorings, *actual* tramplings—in one instance, an "attacker" bit her victim's hand until it bled.

I watched from the corner of my eye as Singer hurried us past that particular garden, where the children circled under the willow trees. The bitten child, a skinny boy perhaps six years old with hair so blond it appeared white, sagged to the ground, his face contorted as he clutched his hand. I was about to rush to his side when Mothkin snatched my arm, pulled me onward.

"It's not easy, but try not to feel anything," he advised. "Compassion stands out here like a beacon."

"There's nothing innocent about these children," added Singer, "or their Game."

As we hurried away, I noticed dark fruit among the leaves—the trees were not willows at all; they drooped, but the raindrop-shaped leaves were a pale blue. Independent of the air currents, the leaves were *moving*.

Until I saw the phenomenon on several other trees, I was sure my eyes deceived me—for under the leaves, oily in the moonlight, were thousands of *moths*. Their blue-black wings pulsed, patterned with silver crescent moons.

They're not *growing* there," said Mothkin with a smile at my incredulous face. "They're feeding on the fruit. Those are bittermite trees, an atrocity of nature unique, as far as I know, to Harvest Moon. The berries are so small you can hardly see them from here, and taste so bad that those Lammas moths are the only things alive that can stomach them."

Then I noticed that the fruit of the bittermite trees, too, was used in the children's Game. The losers were made to shinny up the trunks, shoo away moths, and pick a handful of berries to chew under the scrutiny of the victors. It was hard to watch the Game as the hours and neighborhoods slipped by, but impossible *not* to watch. Cornered children went down while others pressed around them, reaching hands that fluttered like the feeding moths.

" '*The jackals are walking around,*' " quoted Singer under his breath as we skirted a large playground, " '*Tightening the knots of their circles.*' "

That was the way it worked in Harvest Moon. There was no curfew, no law that I could perceive, and thus no crime. Night went on, and games went on until exhaustion imposed a temporary halt. Children didn't go to any school but the

School of the Night, and their parents drove carts at full tilt and slaughtered each other. Vampires drained blood.

I learned a lot on my first night there.

Worry nagged at me; finally I asked when we rested in a moss-grown stairwell. How long would it be before the townsmen we passed stopped glaring and started snatching? By now, this "boss" must have known we were no longer on the stairs.

"Word's not quite around yet," said Mothkin. "When people know who to look for, things won't be so easy for us."

"So let's go," muttered Singer. "Not much farther."

MY feet were beginning to drag when we came across a cobbled way overleaned by brooding houses, where not a single figure stirred beneath the lamps. The brawlings that went on behind the shutters elsewhere were nonexistent. Glancing at a signpost, I realized we had come out on a farther stretch of Too Quiet Street, although we had been crisscrossing toward the moon for several hours. The town was much larger than it appeared, with neighborhoods tucked away in folds and cracks of the cavern floor, dark sectors walled with limestone, other dusky quarters rising on slag hills beyond. Piles of stone interrupted the layout at times; often shacks had been built with ridiculous lack of foresight directly on the uneven slopes, and had then settled with the stones, shuffling off their foundations, winding up on their sides or completely inverted, sometimes in pieces. Everything—this slipshod construction, the smoky carousing, the children's games, suggested a people utterly heedless of value, responsibility, or respect—they had but one purpose. As they played, they expanded their borders. Even I could tell that the buildings here, nearer the heart of the great cavern, were older, much older than the ones near Pink Eye Street. Harvest Moon was a cancer of witches, spreading and spreading below the ground.

"Why is it so quiet here?" I whispered, as Singer led us through the swirling mist. The street was aptly named. It seemed to be waiting.

"The people are afraid of this street," said Mothkin. "No

one lives or does business here. The houses and shops are just a front."

"Why?" Even the footfalls of my tennis shoes were loud.

"They say it's haunted by demons."

"It is," said Singer quietly over his shoulder. "No one wants to wake them up."

The mouths of alleys yawned; eaves hung like teeth.

"You're not afraid to come here?"

"No." Singer directed us to a pathway between brick buildings on the far side. "I come here when I want a little peace."

Mothkin and Singer were like that: just when I thought I had something figured out, they surprised me again.

SINGER had another surprise for us.

In the crumbling shed behind an empty tavern in Too Quiet Street, Singer kept a wagon. I'll never forget my first glimpse, the murky moonlight almost warm upon it when Singer flung open a door. It sat on iron-rimmed wheels, a blackwood contraption of warping sides, scratches, and splinters, oil-smoked and battered. It had an enclosed cab for passengers and a platform at the rear for a guardsman. Lanterns, tarnished and dented, hung from four hooks above the corners of the cab, and two brass lions' heads flanked the driver's seat.

"Cinderella's coach," grinned Singer, checking the harness. "Right where I left her. I knew she'd come in handy."

"Have a look, Cinderella," said Mothkin, helping me step up into the passengers' compartment. The door squeaked on hinges as weary as I felt.

"I don't feel like Cinderella," I said.

"Well," smirked Mothkin, squinting up at the moon, "it's a long time after midnight. At least you've got a coach, not a pumpkin."

"And we're not turning into mice," added Singer. He stepped out into the night. "If you'll excuse me, I have to find my team." So saying, he vanished around the corner.

For the first time since coming into the basement, I experienced a sort of peace. The lunar radiance was gently reflecting from the brass lions, their mouths open, manes streaming. I climbed to the high seat and ran a hand over one, enjoying the coolness of the metal, the smell of the leather reins, the bouncing of the springs as I ascended.

I smiled down at Mothkin, who paced about, running his fingers through his hair. "How is it, Dragonfly?" he asked softly.

"The coach?"

"Everything. This place. Can you finish it?"

I nodded, stroking the lion's mane of golden flame. "Henry's always shown me that you have to finish what you start." Which was true—if you took apart the clock, for example, you had to fix it and put it back together. If you didn't, you were left forever with a mess of springs and gears and oil on your hands.

"Yes," said Mothkin. "That's right."

As we waited for Singer, Mothkin and I strolled across to observe our surroundings from the side windows of the shed. We were on fairly high ground, and had come up through a jumble of buildings on the downhill side. The windows afforded us our first look at where we'd been heading since leaving the glassworks—the edge of the forest, where the town ended and the mountainside began.

The vista was breathtaking—twisted trees draping black foliage over vast slopes of jutting, broken rock, all soaring up through misty air to where the mighty image of the Horse towered in amber light. Its flat eyes glinted as it stood astride the highest ridge, ruling the town, expressionless as that other gigantic equine conqueror that brought doom through the gates of Troy. As I think now, it seems that the image of a black horse was the perfect manifestation for the soul of Harvest Moon—for, like its predecessor at Troy, this colossus loomed out of the starless gulfs with disaster in its belly—this vile country, this place that moved and *grew*. Once through the gates of the world above, it would burst upon mankind with dreadful finality—Pandora's box, wolves loose among sheep, the most ghastly jack-in-the-box ever built.

Also, though I would not realize it until much later, my Uncle Henry was a tiny, unseen part of that view beyond the windows. And I was a tiny and unseen element in the landscape over which he peered.

My thoughts were like vines and whirlpools in my head. Climbing back into the cab, I drew the cloak around me and pulled my feet up onto the seat, settled into a corner. Mothkin stalked in slow circles, his head cocked as it had been in the funeral home, listening to the silence of Too Quiet Street. His shadow swept back and forth past the open door of the coach, and I remembered with a smile Quillum, the Great Shadow Lord. What a long night it had been!

Images of the night's journey took shape behind my eyes—coaches racing around corners, tilting on two wheels as the drivers whipped black horses; oceans of mist; children with staring eyes and blood-smeared fingernails; houses on houses, houses on rock piles, houses crowding each other and climbing, climbing—they rose in mountains, shoving up their gambrels, and in the windows white faces with fangs laughed and laughed—dark things hooted in gardens, and darker things skittered behind walls, bounded over the bordering fields. The moon boiled the whole pot of midnight stew.

I could feel myself slipping into an old, old dream.

Music came to me from a time as far away as a lost roller skate, a time buried and rusted in a garden deeply overgrown.

(bridget anne what on earth is the matter with you)

The Trovers, creeping through the autumn night!

(silly thing you were laughing in your sleep)

Moonlight—

(must have been a good dream but your father and I would like to get some sleep)

I *did* dream in the wagon—dreams of dark distance, of the shimmering gemstones of the Trovers, down where the ceilings ran with roots and the furniture was roots.

(trovers? honestly bridget you should be writing scripts if only you spent as much energy on picking up your toys)

[the trovers pick up her toys for her dear didn't you know only sometimes they don't give them back and that's why we needed another new teddy bear]

The Trovers lived under the back garden and had a passage up through the hollow oak (only no one *knew* it was hollow)— from there they looked out through a hole and saw every softball that went over the fence or into the weeds, and then, quick as scissors, they were up through a trap door and gone again, sporting a new trophy—and I never saw the ball again. Over the years they collected from me a whole quiver of arrows, one by one, half a dozen balls, and uncountable small objects—marbles, dollhouse furniture, bits of colored glass I saved on a ledge behind the garage. They stole up in the dead of night to spy from rooftops, to snatch the plastic glo-clickers from the spokes of my bicycle. When a dog barked suddenly at three A.M., I knew he had caught wind of a Trover, or glimpsed one's green eyes glittering in the hedge. I drew floorplans in my head of their huge storehouse, that dripping, echoing place that ran all beneath the neighborhood, deep down, stacked and strung with railroad spikes, hubcaps, bottles and beads, racks of comic books, sheaves of handkerchiefs and mismatched mittens, fleets of matchbox cars.

In my dream—a dream I'd had over and over again since I was small enough to take baths in the sink—the King of Rabbits had come to a meeting with the King of the Trovers, whose name was Trover Cleveland. (How beautifully flexible is the reasoning of childhood dreams!) They were eating blue eggs—I marveled again at the sky-hued shells littering the floor. Over their heads, up on soft moss-mats, the Moon Dancers spun through the trees, braiding the three threads of music, laughter, and wilderness.

It seemed to last for hours and hours, but such is the illusion of dreams, unbound by time—dreams, the great telescopes of the imagination. I was vaguely aware that Singer was back, that he and Mothkin were conversing, then resting and standing guard in turns—but I kept one foot in my dream, lay warm and serene in the shallows beneath consciousness—

—UNTIL a sound struck like a stone. The awake-world intruded with lantern light, acrid smoke, angry voices—and all music was ended. Darkness snicked shut like a deadbolt, flecked with flame.

We were being attacked.

7

FIRE AND ICE

MOTHKIN swept out of the flickering gloom as my eyes fought against sleep and the smoke. He snatched me from the coach, whirled me like a doll, dropped me behind his back as a snarling shadow sprang around the wagon's front. I glimpsed only red, feral eyes as Mothkin's dagger sliced air, made contact, and the thing in the darkness howled.

He thrust again, his free hand shoving me toward the back of the room. The walls shook beneath a fierce pounding and the thunder of inhuman cries. The thing fighting Mothkin retreated with the speed of wind up and over the driver's seat. I saw it more clearly then, in a flood of torchlight from the doorway—it was like a man, yet its knees bent horribly backward, the wiry body covered with grey hair—then it was gone, and Mothkin backed a step in my direction.

Its blood trickled over one of the lions on the coach, dripped onto the floor. Mothkin's blade, too, was stained with it as he glanced at me, then at the doorway, where shadows leapt and danced.

Suddenly, a splay-fingered hand shot from beneath the coach, swiped at Mothkin's leg. He stumbled with a cry, threw himself away from the carriage. The enemy's snapping head emerged, jaws flecking the floor with spittle—the long-eared head of a wolf.

A second monster loomed in the door, silver fur glistening. One edge of its muzzle peeled back as it rumbled like a chainsaw.

Behind us, the window shattered, and Singer's face appeared there. "Down!" he cried, swinging his crossbow into play. Light flashed on the silver tip of the bolt as it streaked past my ear, struck home in the creature's chest.

I saw it stagger backward into two dark-cloaked figures, the torch-bearers. Then Mothkin was nearly throwing me through the broken window, and Singer was guiding me toward a descending stairway between dank, slime-covered walls of earth.

"After you. *Go!*" ordered Singer, sliding another bolt into his weapon. There was the muffled shriek of a beast; Mothkin dove through the window, whirled in a patch of nettles at the corner of the building—facing the alley, he flicked his wooden knife into the shadows. Someone groaned, and a body slumped into the weeds.

The torchlight shifted and grew. Feet were running in our direction.

Beneath me the ramshackle stairs protested, sagged to one side. I caught the rail as the entire wooden structure impacted with the wall of the chimneylike defile, shrieked, and pulled apart. Singer caught me under the arms; we vaulted through space as timbers collapsed like a ruined scaffold, steps splintering, nails freeing themselves from worm-eaten prisons. Black air whistled past us, and we landed in a patch of yielding grass rooted in mud. He covered me as junk hailed around us.

In a few seconds all was still. Cautiously, I raised my head.

"KNEEDEEP!" said a clotted voice an inch from my face.

It was a bloated black frog, his back misshapen, as if he wore the drippings of a wax candle.

We were at the edge of a sluggish canal only inches deep, its sole function the removal of waste—it smelled of things best left undiscovered. The shed and the end of Too Quiet Street were on the clifftop above, and all that magnificent view Mothkin and I had admired earlier rose before us: the sloping wood, the rocks, the High Horse. This stream had been concealed from us earlier by the crumbling lip of the cliff.

My belly was soaked with the liquid oozing beneath the grass, reeking of gutters long uncleaned, of yellow gone black.

"Okay?" whispered Singer, turning me over, lifting me out of the coarse grass.

I took stock of my arms and legs, caught the breath that had been forced out of me. "Okay."

Mothkin had not joined us on the stairs; he was up behind the shed, dodging in and out of shadows. Swords clashed against his knife, bodies dropping at his feet.

Like those who'd hunted us in the orchard, some of our attackers were wrapped in scarves and long coats—the others were werewolves. Beneath a full moon that could not wane or set, the hunger of these beasts never abated. They were true in-betweens, not wolf, not human—a Harvest Moon lycanthrope could never be represented in movies either by a trained animal or a person in a suit. Skinny legs, a long face, eyes and ears constantly probing the night for the next kill—if you can't imagine it, I'm relieved in a way. I hope you never can, and you never meet one.

They had Mothkin surrounded. I could see them streaming around both sides of the building, werewolves lolling their tongues, stretching humanlike hands with three-inch claws, men with torches and swords. Mothkin killed them, maimed them; Singer fired his crossbow again and again, as fast as he could wind it up, but Mothkin was pinned between enemies. A massive brute pounced on his back.

As their bodies collided, the sagging lip of earth gave way, and they plummeted into a stand of high, scraggly weeds at the canal's edge; they must have struck in only inches of water, judging by the sound.

I screamed Mothkin's name, lunging forward, but Singer pushed me into the shadows at the foot of the cliff, where vines and fungoid growths seemed born only for the purpose of rotting. "Go that way quietly," he commanded, pointing away from where Mothkin had fallen. "Stay hidden."

"I'm going with you to—"

"No!" There was no trace of his smile. "They're coming down. I'll be with you as soon as I can."

I looked deep into his eyes, trembling uncontrollably, terrified that I had already lost Mothkin, and that I would lose Singer, too. "Are you going—?"

"To find him." He shoved me away. "Run!"

Then the vines waved, and he was gone.

I had no intention of leaving them; I supposed that if I stayed put a minute or two, Singer would shuffle out of the mist with an injured Mothkin, perhaps carrying him. I didn't want to think about the possibility that he might return alone, ashen-faced, and tell me there was nothing we could do. I prayed then, as Mothkin had suggested to me on the stairs—I had never been a great one for prayer, but I tried it then since there was little else I could do. Pressing trembling hands together, I shrank back into the vines and asked God to save us, and to be with Uncle Henry, to keep him from worrying. I opened my eyes, and Singer wasn't back yet, so I prayed for the children Eagerly Meagerly had in that filthy hole in the wall; I asked God to show me a way to get them out of there.

The next time I opened my eyes, worms were falling on me. With a gasp I jerked away from the wall, flicked the pink-black mottled things off my cloak. I edged along the wall, the vines brushing at my hood, the river in its odorous bed seeming to gurgle with discomfort.

Looking for Singer, squinting through the tendrils of decaying plants, I scarcely heard the ghost of a footstep ahead. When I nearly walked into a shadowy figure, I don't know what kept me from jumping straight back to the clifftop.

—Well, I do know. It was his face, particularly his eyes, which were the blue of ice that blazes in starlight—not the ice of winter, which ends, or even of the Earth's poles, on which sunlight whispers at least. These eyes held the glittering essence of the frozen fire at the end of galaxies, where the lost rocks drift that were once worlds—drifting eyes, so far removed from light that they produced their own. Yes, they were eyes of fire. My gaze was sucked into them like boats to a vortex—I could almost hear the rushing of the seas.

The eyes belonged to a boy, who seemed perhaps a year or two older than I was, though he was taller, his thick, back-swept hair that powdery brown which is almost grey. His gaze ignited something in me, and suddenly the conflagration that inhales autumn leaves with a roar had left me without air.

My knees gave way, and his lean hands were on me, drawing me up, electricity quivering in his fingertips. I truly could not breathe, could only hang in his grip, swim in his eyes. His hands grasped my arms, but it was my soul he held trembling before him.

His face was very close, a face of wildness and angles, bushy brows joining over a long nose. His tongue slid once over pointed teeth. I have seen faces since that remind me of his—the faces girls cannot resist in their earliest teenage years, the faces they hang on their walls, and at which their mothers shudder. There was an animal smell about him which clung to my borrowed cloak long after he released me. Yes, I used to seek for it, weeping when it had faded utterly—but I'm running away with myself.

"I am a werewolf," he said. He had nothing to hide, and nothing in my eyes was hidden from him, I'm sure. "Who are you?"

"Dragonfly," I gasped. For that was my real name, more real than the one recorded on my birth certificate. Uncle Henry knew what was real, and I had never felt how real I was until that moment. The world would never be the same for me again.

"Dragonfly," he whispered, smiling. "I am Sylva."

Sylva! The name spoke of the soughing of wind in pines spiced with night. He was a Moon Dancer, all I had ever dreamed them to be.

"Come with me," he commanded.

"Where?" The coursing of the stream was the rushing of blood through my veins, and all the world was silver and amber.

"To dance into the arms of the night."

My breath was gone, but somehow he breathed for me, the torches of his hands sustained my heart's beating. Nothing in the hypnotic eyes of the vampire had approached the power in Sylva's gaze, the strength of his spell lying not in its overriding of my will, but in its unlocking. Swept from my mind were all thoughts of Mothkin and Singer, gone like shooting stars that burn as they fall and never touch earth. I felt no doubt, no remorse; I was his because I wanted to be.

"Your hand trembles so!" he laughed, with the subtle humming of an aeolian lyre. "Does my touch burn you? Then here!" He plucked a strand of cobweb from the crumbling wall, placed one end in my hand and tripped away. "Come, come! Do not let it break!" It drifted and swung in the air between us, never quite stretched to the full. Rose petals hold the dawn less gently than he held that thread, fleeing backwards, fleeing sideways, and I scrambled after.

At a bend in the wall we reached a cave tunnel, where the sewer stream was joined by a fresher current. Ahead, a stone dam blocked the river bed, the fouled stream emerging from a culvert in its base. The black forest crept down to the stream here and across the top of the dam, thick stems and knotted vines drooping over the flood. From the opening in the cliff at our right, a breeze lifted our hair with the clammy kiss of deep channels and pure water.

"This cave," he murmured over the music of the converging streams, "runs beneath the length of Too Quiet Street." He leapt across the current by three step-stones, and I followed, guarding with all the passion of my life the filament that connected us.

"Look!" Sylva balanced on a flat place below the stone dam, the creepers of the thicket hanging close above him.

The moonlight penetrated only a short way into the cave mouth, but there was another light deep within, shimmering on the walls, stringing diamonds across the water. The river flowed along a crack in the floor, and the light filled the tunnel, shifted in patterns that almost suggested figures, bodies that floated and merged in the air, beautiful and ethereal.

"Those," he whispered close to my ear, "are the demons of Too Quiet Street, so greatly feared in the village."

I turned back to him, and again felt the rest of the world disappear. "You are not afraid."

He laughed easily. "A werewolf fears nothing." Playfully, impossibly, he began to twirl the cobweb around his finger like a kite string. How could it not break? His hands were long and narrow, the hands of an artist, their backs covered with a fine brown fluff.

"Do you know how I found you?" he asked.

I held my end of the magical filament, waiting for him to reel me in. "How?"

"The same way the others did. I smelled you."

"What do I smell like?"

His eyes twinkled. "Like purple, and silk, and moonlight on wisteria."

I laughed. "Really?"

"Like stars, and the motions of stars. Like a deep, still lake, and the rippling of grass." He closed his eyes, inhaled. "Willows, and the thoughts of willows. Roots, and glimmerings, and the sparkle of stones. Wonderful aromas, Dragonfly. And so very rare here."

Something unpleasant stirred within me, something that would have manifested itself in a shiver or a frown had I been any more in control. A hint of chill in his tone, his hungry nearness, some fleeting suggestion of his words—whatever disturbed me, I remembered the leering face of the vampire Noyes, his green-flecked cheeks and swollen lips. Certain of the vampire's phrases, too, echoed in my ears: "feeding grounds" and "everyone's got to eat." I recalled Noyes's drunken ecstasy as he sucked leechlike at my memories of pain.

"Can you smell me now?" Still I did not doubt Sylva, at least not with my heart; I knew only confusion.

"Of course," he breathed. "Though not like I could, Dragonfly, when you were dreaming."

"Dreaming?"

"Your dreams," he whispered, "are as lovely as they come. Beacons—brilliant beacons in a world of darkness. Sometimes I am cold, Dragonfly. But wrapped in the cloak of your dreaming, I would never be cold again."

My eyelids fluttered. He was near again, only a foot of thread remaining between us. The ground tilted, and I doubted the power of my legs to hold me up. I could feel his breath, warm and sweet, whereas the vampire had had none. Sylva was alive; he was the night.

"Dream for me," he intoned, as softly as if the words, too, were cobweb. "And I will teach you what it is to be free."

My lips parted, but I could not speak, could only nod

weakly as my eyes overflowed; I knew that what he offered was all I had ever dreamed. He did not want my blood or my pain—all he asked were dreams.

I stepped forward, but something struck between us like a silver bolt of lightning, cutting the night with a steely hiss.

Sssssssshhiinkk!

It was a giant pair of scissors, two feet long, thrust down from the overhanging branches. It snipped the cobweb in two.

Sylva's yelp of surprise became a snarl—the scissors twisted suddenly, flipped up and to the side; their point drew a terrible scratch across his face from his left jaw to his hairline on the right. Howling, he lurched backward, fell into the stream.

The scissors withdrew, and a pair of hands took their place. Locking on my arms, they jerked me up into the whip of branches.

Lanterns flared as cloaking velvet was whisked away, the stream gone, and I was in the heart of a tangled thicket, a dozen bulbous faces scowling at me like a ring of poison mushrooms.

Directly above me, his face shadowed by his stovepipe hat, was the driver of the coach we'd seen on Pink Eye Street, the coach with stars for wheels. The cigar in his teeth winked fire. Across his striped knees, the scissors threw the light back in a hundred dancing sparks.

Holding me aloft in one hand, he pulled a gold watch from the pocket of the vest that stretched over his bloated belly.

"Nearly midnight," he croaked, lips writhing around the cigar. The corner of his batrachian mouth opened to issue a stream of smoke. "Time to go."

Then he stood, his spindly legs unfolding. Carrying me through the crowd, he hooked his warted chin toward the stream, gave an order that chilled me as if ice water had been injected into my blood.

"See that it doesn't follow us."

Several black-cloaked figures left our group, and I heard the sliding of swords from sheaths.

As loud as I could, I called to him. "SYLVA! RUN AWAY!"

The scissor-man slapped my face so hard that I woke up only to feel a carriage seat beneath me, and was aware of the bouncing of its wheels as they raced over cobblestones.

8

Number Fifty-two

I awoke only halfway, to the flaring of a match. We sat in a velvet-lined coach, the windows draped to shut out any view of the passing town. The cigar-man was folded up beside me, his head hunched forward as he arranged a variety of gleaming objects on a shelf in front of him. The compartment was full of his smoke. Only one eye was visible to me as he half-turned, spewed fumes from the corner of his mouth, and touched the match to a spoonful of yellow powder. As the powder ignited, the carriage swung sharply to the side, and his leathery hand snaked out to steady the apparatus.

The powder burned quickly, its gases passing up a metallic tube and through the liquid in a bubbling decanter. He lifted a larger tube connected to the vessel's top, popped it into my mouth, and clasped my jaws and nose shut with his hand.

"Breathe deeply," he grated. "And sleep without dreams."

A horrible sweetness invaded my senses, oiling my nose and throat like honey. Clawing at his hand, I tried to smash away the equipment with my knees, but none of my limbs seemed inclined to obey. My fingers did little more than brush his wrist as the jangling scissors on his knee drifted slowly out of focus.

Then there was a long and bottomless darkness.

* * *

THERE are times when you wake up and feel you have scarcely closed your eyes, and you are surprised to note the leap in the clock's hands, the sun's height. And there are times when you're aware you've been dreaming all night, your mind exhausted from the roller coasters it has ridden, the thousand images and interwoven plots. It was with neither of those impressions that I lifted first one lid and then the other, that I lay blinking away the heaviness.

It had been a deep, deep sleep, the sleep of the hibernating bear. I would not have been surprised to learn, like Rip Van Winkle, that twenty years had passed since the ride in the carriage. A thick, syrupy taste lingered in my mouth, and with a bitter sinking in my chest, I remembered Mothkin, Alley Singer, and the blue-eyed boy who said he was a werewolf. I searched frantically for his smell in my cloak, and it was there. Falling back with the cloth bunched on my face, I looked around.

At first I thought it was a trick of my awakening eyes, but the ceiling actually slanted, much higher toward the foot of my bed and almost within reach over my head. The slats composing the walls were painted a lifeless grey. There was no furniture but the brass bed, scarcely larger than a cot, and a row of empty hooks affixed to the far wall suggested that my bedroom had been made in a kind of attic or passage where tools were normally kept. A faint, unsteady light shone through a transom above the door.

There was a *click,* and the door dragged open on pained hinges. I pulled up my knees beneath the unpatterned grey quilt, steeling my nerves for whatever might appear. I gasped in spite of myself as a cheerless face thrust toward me.

It was a man of middle-age, his face as puffy and without color as that of the vampire Pye. Appraising me with eyes practically closed by excess flesh, he dragged a serving cart into the room. As he shambled backwards, wheeling in an array of covered dishes, his black clothing *shone* softly, like that of the figures behind the bank.

Placing a polished rosewood lap tray before me, the man set out a breakfast on fine china, the plates patterned with fili-

grees of vines. He was silent, save for the cavernous hissing of
breath through his nose, his eyes shifting within the folds of
his face as he laid out ornate spoons and forks of various sizes.
The small, thick quantity of his hair was parted impeccably,
glistening with oil.

He lifted the lid of a silver egg cup. I stared at the egg, its
shell perfectly blue. Other dishes held fried sausages, sliced
bread, cheese, fruit jelly, and wedged apples. My hunger was
fierce—the server had hardly gotten out the door before I
yielded, unable to remember having enjoyed this much the
simple pleasure of eating. The food was gone in minutes, and
I was just pouring myself a cup of a steaming, ruby tea when
there came a knock at the door.

For a moment I sat still, feeling the courage drain from me.
I think I had a premonition that I stood on a fragile surface of
ice, an airless deep waiting inches beneath my feet. It was the
terror of facing the basement door, of standing with my back
to the cold bedroom mirror—only this time, someone *was*
there, waiting to step through. I could hear him, *feel* him waiting. "Come in," I whispered.

"Dragonfly."

He was tall. As he swept toward me, the chamber rushed
away around him, giving him space. Broad-shouldered, he
towered over me, and it seemed he was chiseled of a substance
other than flesh and blood—light reflected from his silver
hair, his red coat, so that he was a mirror in human form.

"Dragonfly." He leaned close, extended a hand, and I
shrank against the brass railing. His skin was dull and grey,
the only part of him that did not glitter, his smile a winter
smile.

"You are welcome in Harvest Moon. We have waited a
long time for your visit."

I would not take his hand, and at last he dropped it, cluck-
ing his tongue.

He finished pouring my cup of tea. "I trust that you enjoyed your breakfast." Raising his eyebrows, he waited for me
to speak. Deep crows' feet at the corners of his eyes contrasted
with the agility, the intensity of his movements. His bearing
reminded me of a cunning cat, a midnight hunter—perhaps it
was the slope of his forehead, the sleekness of his hair. I could

easily imagine him perched on a moonlit fence, his coattails floating on the breeze as he licked his wrist and slicked the hair, his angular green eyes gathering the light.

"I am Samuel Hain."

He folded his fingers on the lap tray.

"How do you know my name?"

The smile widened, showing his teeth. "I know a great deal more about you than your name. I've known you since you were—" he held up his hands twelve inches apart "—about this big. Dragonfly, you dreamed lovely dreams even then."

"How do you *know?*"

"I drank every one of them, of course." He shook his head, as if what he said were indeed a matter of course, as if I were foolish to ask. "Not that I was surprised; your Uncle Henry is quite a dreamer, too, and like yourself, quite a gnawer on pain. A good man is your Uncle Henry."

"Have you always been in our basement?"

"Not far away, child. Oh, how we all looked forward to your visits!"

I had been too young to remember it, as I said, but I knew that the trouble with the basement had begun long ago, when my mother first brought me to visit Uncle Henry. It had been an extended visit, and I'd figured out later that it had been a convenient one for my mother; she'd had to be in Europe, and that was before she'd discovered Mrs. Cain.

"You think I am your enemy, Dragonfly. That is what your 'friends' have told you." He put in the quotation marks around "friends" by waving his fingers in the air. "Nothing could be farther from the truth."

I narrowed my eyes. "What are you doing in our basement, then?"

"We're building. That's not hurting anyone. It's the two you were with that hurt and destroy. You saw what the A.P.K.s did to Adrian and his Glassworks."

"The vampires tried to kill us," I said evenly. "What's an A.P.K.?"

"They didn't tell you what they were, did they? No, they wouldn't. Your two fine friends, who change their names *far* more often than their shirts, call themselves Agents of the Peaceable Kingdom. They are members of a fanatical religious cult that seeks to crush self-expression and make slaves of us all. Do you want to be a slave?"

"No. But how do you explain the children?"

"Children?"

"The children that Eagerly Meagerly keeps."

"Friends!" he cried, clapping his hands. "We are all friends in Harvest Moon! You saw children tired and hungry from their journey—they have only just joined us. In time, they will relax and start to have fun—fun is what we're all about, Dragonfly. In the end, no one regrets coming."

I shook my head in disbelief. I had seen children *having fun* on my trip through the village. Were those colorless ghoul-children what Meagerly's slaves in time became, when all memory of joy and light had been wrung out of them? Did they grow up to become the scarf-shrouded drivers, the builders?

"They're stolen, aren't they? Stolen from their homes."

Hain rolled his eyes. "They are—*encouraged* to come. Invited. Is this not an intriguing place? You are here, Dragonfly. Were you 'stolen'?"

I met his gaze and felt the penetrating chill of the end of space, the bottom of the sea.

"What has happened to my friends?"

He shrugged. "I'm waiting for news of them myself. As soon as I hear anything, I'll pass it on to you." As he reached out and pinched my toe, I could feel the ice of his touch right through the quilt. I was glad I hadn't shaken his hand.

"The fact remains, little Dragonfly: you are here because you wanted to be; all that we are, you love; and what you do not yet love, you will love in time."

My teeth set, I shook my head.

He reared back like a wolf about to howl at the moon, and he laughed, the sound harsh in the wooden chamber. Then he crossed to the door, beckoned by curling all his fingers.

"Come, if you will not drink your tea. Come and see what a good time we're having here!" He held the door, his hair like silver fire.

Reasoning that I was doing no good drinking tea in bed, I swung my legs over the side, found my tennis shoes waiting for me, and brushed past him into the hall.

The ceiling was higher here, but it still slanted, and a row of windows cast moonlight in from the right. Lanterns hung from pegs on the left wall. Hain strode ahead of me, the gold buttons on the back of his coat flashing like a pair of eyes. The air was chilly after the closeness of my bedroom, and I drew Mothkin's cloak tighter, catching again that musky essence of the wild boy. Feet scraped floorboards somewhere beneath us, voices buzzed, a hammer pounded steadily.

I peered out a smudged pane at a margin of stunted trees beyond the street, a curve of road, and a rise of jumbled boulders where the mist hung like midnight laundry. With a start, I realized I was looking back at the gorge of the River Abandon with its guarded bridge, and somewhere, away through the mists, the stairway.

"You know where we are, don't you?" Hain paused at the top of a flight of steps. "This is Number Fifty-two Pink Eye Street, also known as Reception."

I was just turning away from the window when a movement caught my eye; I noticed a wagon rolling up the street at a good clip, its driver whipping the two flame-eyed beasts that pulled it. The heavy wagon careened between porches and posts, its wheels and the iron-shod hooves rattling the glass even at this distance. A feeling I didn't like nibbled at my stomach as the rig drew nearer, its firepot drawing a greasy black line through the air. The driver passed through a moonbeam, his broad brim shooting squid-ink shade over his face, his dun coat flapping after him.

"Just on time," chuckled Hain, ushering me toward the stairs. "Receptionist Meagerly and his Welcome Wagon! You, Dragonfly, can help us out. In fact, it's really the least you can do; you see, Receptionist Noyes used to handle things very well, but he will not be able to join us tonight."

The stairs squeaked under our feet, our shadows huge on the rich red wallpaper. At a landing, a chimney lamp burned on a round table. Above it hung an oil painting, gilt-framed, rendered in magnificent shades. It might have hung in any museum but for the subject matter: a narrow-faced man in a graveyard, his eyes bulging with horror as he climbed a sepulchre and kicked desperately at a sea of corpses' hands clawing up through the soil, perhaps a hundred of them, waving like a ghastly crop.

"That was painted by Mr. Noyes," said Hain with what looked like a rueful smile. "This used to be his house. Alas, you'll never know what a gentleman he was."

He'd been a gentleman in the alley, all right. I hurried past, and then we were on the ground floor, stepping out of an alcove into a salon from a nightmare.

It was an old-fashioned parlor, like the ornate lobbies of century-old hotels where my mother chatted with stage actors and movie producers in overstuffed chairs, glasses of firelit wine on the tables, the men with leather patches on their elbows. (She'd taken me to a few such gatherings one year when families were in vogue.) Yet in these wing-backed chairs crouched scarecrows with sunken eyes; in the smoking-jackets were grey-skinned ghouls, and on the settee stretched a werewolf, yawning contentedly. A fire blazed in a walk-around fireplace in the center of the room, the flames echoed in a thousand crystal facets on the chandelier. At a grand piano, a vampire with a cascade of raven hair reclined but did not play, his lips flushing a deep crimson as I entered.

Opposite the fire were a desk and a high-backed wooden chair. The scissor-man sat there, his cigar aglow, his face lit from beneath by the reflection off his scissors.

"Ladies and gentlemen, good evening!" Hain swaggered among them as they rose in greeting, the ice-faced ladies curtsying. It turned the stomach, really, the way they fawned. "I present Dragonfly, our honored guest!" He was resplendent in his coat, not one strand of his hair out of place. The audience applauded. The werewolf gave an expectant whine, shook his ears, and sat up on his haunches.

"Mr. Anselm, some music!"

The vampire turned to the keyboard, began to draw from it a pensive melody that captured all the subdued yearning of the river I had crossed, his mime-white hands bouncing as if on the current's crest.

"Mr. Snicker, are we ready?"

The scissor-man nodded once, his head wreathed in smoke, and offered Hain a cigar.

"Thank you," said Hain, twirling it elaborately through his fingers and lighting it by sticking it into his teeth and his face almost into the fire—I assume this was to impress the werewolf, who sat as far from the flames as he could get, and at whom Hain winked, issuing a puff of smoke.

"And now," he said, glancing at a clock, "it is time."

I did a double-take at the clock's age-darkened face. The right side was divided into three hours, with the number twelve at the top and three at the bottom—midnight to 3:00 A.M.—and after three, the left side measured from seven to eleven o'clock P.M.! Those were the only hours that existed in Harvest Moon—evening and the deadly small hours, when closet doors opened and terrors walked. The clock said it was now three A.M., the single hand pointing straight at the floor. An all-too-authentic skull on the top of the instrument opened its jaw somehow—if by means of a wire, it was invisible to my eyes—and clacked it shut, sharply, three times.

Hain pranced in a circle, puffing his cigar, rubbing his hands expectantly on his vest.

Mr. Snicker brought out a coil of silver cable, measured a length, and snipped it off.

"Bring out the mirror," ordered Hain. Then he bent down with his hands on his knees and grinned into my face.

"Dragonfly, *you're on deck!*"

The mirror was taller than I was, with three panes, hinged so that it stood by itself. Two figures in black hooded robes set it before the fire, removed its velvet cover. I watched the reflection it showed me of Mr. Snicker rising from the desk, the cable in his hands.

I whirled on Hain, indignant questions in my eyes.

"Watch the mirror," he commanded.

I saw the reversed image of the street door open, the back-lighted shape of Eagerly Meagerly lurking there. His gaze directly upon me for the first time, I felt again a sense of uncleanness.

The vampire's music swelled, pervasive as the mist outside. All moisture was gone from my mouth—I could feel the pulse in my temples. The chamber was spinning, the mirror seeming to advance on me, to loom wider. Anselm's skeletal hands plunged dramatically over the keys, his black mane flying.

Then Hain's talons locked on my shoulder, shoved me toward the glass. Within the mirror, which swallowed all the room, my image was effaced by vapors that were not in the chamber—the quality of light within was different from that around me. I struggled to turn away, to deny what my mind told me could not be, but Hain held me fast. In the mercury-backed glass, an alternate reality took shape.

Low chuckles sounded behind me. In the triple panes, I saw eyes of glass—faces of toys—teddy bears, stuffed horses with pompon manes and rag tails, a bumblebee with jingle bell wings; they leaned among the platforms of board games, straddled the roof of a doll-house. A door stood open just a crack straight ahead, and a string dangled, remarkably three-dimensional, right before my eyes.

I was inside a closet. A blue-and-yellow summer dress hung to my left, an upturned ice skate lay just inside the bottom edge of the mirror on my right.

Hain stepped up carrying a bellows from the fireplace. Kneeling, he fitted its nozzle to a hole in the base of the mirror's frame. As he squeezed a puff of air, the closet door swung slowly open.

Beyond was a bedroom with pink walls. Bare branches tapped at its window, and a single, pastel green horse with denim ears stood guard atop a bookcase, his button eyes rolled fearfully toward the closet. A clock in the shape of a sunflower beside him agreed with Hain's: three o'clock.

A mound stirred beneath the silky comforter on the bed. I knew by the way my scalp prickled that Hain—and everybody else—was grinning behind me. Though no one stirred, it was as if their *attention* shuffled up and crowded in, like frigid breath on my neck.

A tiny hand slipped out and hung over the edge of the bed.

Hain snickered softly. "Alycia," he whispered.

I opened my mouth, studied the dainty fingers.

"She'd *never* do that if she were awake, Dragonfly." His voice was laced with enjoyment. "As every child knows, one must never—*never*—wiggle an appendage over the edge of a bed!"

Faintly, I saw the image of Eagerly Meagerly, far away, reflected from the mirror on *her* nightstand. He was licking his lips.

"What is this?" I demanded, anger welling up over my dread.

"It's Alycia's bedroom," said Hain. "We're going to invite her here. More precisely, *you* are."

I stared. There was nothing to consider on this one—I simply *would not* do anything to help them kidnap a child.

"Dragonfly—Alycia will be very happy here."

"Don't lie to me, Mr. Hain. I know where she'll go, and what she'll eat."

Hain smiled patiently. "Not just anyone can go through the mirror. Mr. Noyes had a talent for that, but he had no charm whatsoever—he was a grabber and a runner. You, on the other hand." He brushed my hair, and I pulled away. "Alycia is six years old, a lonely child, like yourself. She has an imaginary friend Sheila; they do everything together. Just think how happy she'd be if you stepped out of her closet! You could be like a big sister to her. 'Come with me, Alycia,' you'll say. 'I want to show you a wonderful place behind the closet, where children play all night long!' "

I think if his hand had been close enough, I would have bitten it. "I won't!"

"No? You're not eager to please me? Then you must not care so much if we go up and get your Uncle Henry, do you?"

"You can't."

"Can't we?"

"You can't touch him, or you would have done it before Mothkin came."

"Dragonfly, I have strolled through the funeral home quite recently; I was especially amused by all the locked registers. Do you want me to recite for you the titles on Henry's bedroom bookshelf?"

I remembered the shadowy shape I had seen by the basement door—and the half-glimpsed thing in the garden tree. He might or might not have been bluffing.

"All right, then if you can, why don't *you* go in and kidnap Alycia?"

"A job like this seems made to order for *you*—don't you think so?"

Furious, I made balls of my fists.

"I could put a hook in Henry's foot," murmured Hain as if to himself. "Yes, that would be fun. Then I could drag him hand over hand, like landing a fish, into his closet." He giggled, gnawed his fingertip. "The only thing that could spoil it is if his old heart gave out too soon."

Tears spilled hot and stinging down my cheeks. As they did, I heard a sound like a rustling wind in October branches. Turning away from Alycia, I faced the parlor of Fifty-two Pink Eye Street. All around the chamber, the shrouded people were waving their hands toward their faces as if collecting an aroma, blue-black tongues slithering over withered lips; the noise was their inrush of breath. Even the vampire, who needed none, sucked air and trembled.

They were feeding on my distress.

"Thank you, thank you!" cried Hain, crushing my arms, lifting me off the floor. Mr. Snicker looped the cable around my ankle, drew it tight, tied a knot. It radiated cold, like every other implement in Harvest Moon. "Now go make a friend, Dragonfly! Ask her to drop in." He pushed me forward. Snicker held the cord, wrapped it around his wrist. "Don't try to escape," added Hain, "or anything else foolish."

I wiped my eyes, noted Alycia was tossing again. "Why doesn't she wake up?"

"She can't hear us, just as we can't hear her, although she is whimpering now in her sleep."

He gave me a final shove, and I stumbled into the glass—and through it. The surface slipped around me like ice-cold water the merest fraction of an inch deep. Then I was really in the closet—the light, the air pressure different. The pull-string of the closet's bulb bounced off my nose, and a toy car rolled away from my foot.

I caught the doorframe, regained my balance.

Alycia writhed beneath the covers, her breathing short, tearful, punctuated by mewling cries. It must have been a horrible nightmare—but nothing like the nightmare I was bringing her. I almost gasped with the pain I felt for her. What could I do? How could I—?

The plastic sports car glided across the beige carpet, glanced off a sneaker startlingly like one of mine, and clicked to a stop against the edge of Alycia's bed.

Behind me, the mirror was a flat black square, as if a giant sheet of ice rested against her hanging clothes. Eagerly Meagerly's ravaged face still glowered from her bedside mirror.

I stepped forward, dragging the silver cord. Letting my hood fall away from my face, I straightened my hair, wondered what I would say. Her voice was so pitiful, so young—

Like a cresting wave, the comforter came up. Alycia's face rose over its edge, her tear-stained eyes wide as violet pools, her mouth a perfect O.

She looked straight into my eyes, took in her breath to scream. But at the last second, she checked it, her surprise turning to fascination.

"Sheila?" she whispered.

God, I prayed, *help me!*

"No, my name is Dragonfly." My voice was shaky.

She appraised me, the last tears shining on her face. "Did you come out of my closet?"

"Yes."

"You've been crying." Her hair was an unruly nimbus of gold. "Did you have bad dreams, too?"

"Yes."

I felt the cord tighten, a warning tug.

"Alycia, I'm a girl like you. I—I've been watching you. I'm sorry you had bad dreams."

She hugged her knees, tilted her face. I knew she was trying to decide about me; curiosity played in her eyes. "Are there other people in my closet?"

"Yes, Alycia. I—"

The cable jerked, a little too hard. I winced as it cut into my skin, and my foot slid an inch backward.

Alycia saw it. "Why are you tied up, Dragonfly?"

"I—it's—" The pain reminded me of hooks, of a red-vested fisherman in Uncle Henry's closet. "It's so I won't fall and hurt myself, or get lost out here."

"It looks like it's hurting you."

"Alycia." I looked at her books, her rocking chair, the soil-stained overalls thrown over a hamper. If I led her to Hain, my heart would break like glass beneath a brick. I had her attention, and I gazed deep into her eyes. "There's a whole world behind the closet, and so many people—" How could I say it in a few words? How could I warn her in the time I had before I was yanked back? I blinked. What happened to me when I got there didn't matter. Uncle Henry would support me in this, I was sure.

"Don't go near them, Alycia! Don't ever let them get you!" I did not waste breath on screaming as my feet were pulled from under me. I was prepared to catch myself, so my wind was not knocked from me as I hit the carpet. "No matter what your parents say, sleep with *them*, Alycia! Stay away from basements, closets, and mirrors!"

The carpet sizzled past under my belly, one of her discarded shoes bouncing across my back. White-hot pain skewered my ankle, but I clung to the closet door frame just long enough.

"Don't trust strangers at night! Trust God—be ready!" My fingers slipped from the frame; I snapped my head back in time to save my chin.

Alycia had leapt to the foot of her bed and knelt gaping over it as if she were on a boat in a shark-infested sea.

As the mirror's tingling splashed up my legs, as a hand like a vise snatched my foot, I screamed with all I had. "GET OUT OF THIS ROOM, ALYCIA!"

I confronted meteoric eyes.

Perhaps I was dead, I told myself, but I took some comfort in a glimpse of Alycia bounding into the arms of a bewildered woman in the doorway—and even more in what was happening on this side of the mirror.

As Hain's fury practically discolored the air, his followers forgot their loyalty in the face of pure tantalization—they gathered his anger and basked in it, drank it in; it was far more potent and delicious than mine had been.

My confidence dissolved, however, when I looked again into his eyes.

9

SYLVA

As it turned out, I did not die then and there, nor was I flung to Eagerly Meagerly to be carted off. Hain marched me down a cobwebbed stair to the cellars, sat me in a bare stone room, and said he hoped I would seriously consider my situation and how my attitude and behavior affected it. Curiously, he left a lamp burning on the dank soil beside me. A key turned in the lock as if at a great distance, and his footfalls faded.

I was alone in a chamber that smelled of dampness, the whole weight of the village seeming to press against a ceiling supported by groinworks of brick. Dried grasses lay in shapeless decomposition, and a whitish cricket wiggled long feelers, probably puzzling at the light that had invaded his quarters.

Leaning against the driest corner I could find, I put my head on my knees and thought. Hain wanted to keep me—that much I was sure of. The fact that I had defied him, although it surprised him, seemed to make me even more interesting. I wasn't especially afraid for myself; obviously he only wanted to show me who was in charge while he considered how to deal with me.

Actually, anger was stronger in me than fear. The thought of the hunting they were doing over my head revolted me— they relished the role of boogeymen, played their wicked game by rules children could not but accept, for they were rules every child knew: there *are* monsters in the closet, you *can* be snatched by goblins in the mirror. How many times, I wondered, had this company chuckled unseen behind the mirror in our back bedroom?

I ached to see Mothkin appear from a secret passage, his arrow nose thrusting out of the hollow behind an arch—or to hear Singer's feline "Hssst!" at the door. Hain called them "Agents of the Peaceable Kingdom"—those words had a ring of familiarity; though I hadn't had time to mull them over before, it didn't take me long now to arrive at the reference: *The Peaceable Kingdom* had been a painting on the wall at my grandfather's house. I could remember him reading words from the Bible about the Rest-giver, about a coming Kingdom in which lions were supposed to coexist with oxen, and no one would be anyone's prey. No place could be more opposite than that, I thought, to Harvest Moon.

Settling back, I watched the oil burn down in the glass belly of the lamp. Again, I was thinking of Sylva. Now I could find no trace of his smell in my cloak. It was that immaterial loss, among the dozens of problems confronting me, that brought tears to my eyes, his face floating before me. How odd, it occurred to me, that I should grieve the most over a loss that was no loss at all—why wasn't I crying for Henry, or those who had journeyed with me—or even for my parents or grandfather? Why such tears for a lawless boy who danced on the river's stones? For all my abhorrence of the evil of Harvest Moon, I could not abhor him—for him, I knew only a hurt in my chest.

I cried long and hard into my knees, the oil gone, the darkness whispering around me. My anger and tears were only feeding the denizens of the village; surely they sat behind their barred windows, tongues sliding over bleached lips. Resolving to be as calm as possible, I counted griffins, floating by on cloud barges—I'd always liked griffins better than sheep. Sleep did not come, since I had awakened recently; resting, I listened to the scrabbling of rats in the walls. And I said a few more prayers.

* * *

THE time that passed in the dungeon was hard to reckon, but it was much longer than I had expected. The portly butler brought me meals on the serving cart; I had to laugh each time at the incongruity of being served on a rosewood board in a dungeon, but he never so much as smiled in return. On each visit, he escorted me to a nearby toilet, little better than the outhouse I had used above, and refilled the lamp, which would burn until about an hour before he came again. Since he was always accompanied by three hollow-cheeked swordsmen, I did not attempt escape.

Several days must have passed in this way. I worried about Uncle Henry, and what he must be thinking. Would he trust Mothkin and stay put? My greatest fear was that he would enter the basement himself, alone and totally unprepared for this place. If only I could have sent him a letter!—but I would have sent it to the wrong place.

With the dying of the flame each time, with the receding of the cart's wheels, my hope for rescue ebbed a little more—if Mothkin and Singer were alive and free, I reasoned, they would have found me by some means, by some arcane augury or sleuthing. Yet if they were dead, Hain would certainly inform me and increase my anguish. Why had they not come?

Always my thoughts returned to the werewolf boy. Had my warning saved him, or was his lifeless body tangled in the weeds of the foul river?

So the cycles passed, the dawnless nights of Harvest Moon, and in spite of myself, my anger mounted.

WHAT happened then seemed nothing less than an answer to my prayers. The lamp had burned out, and the meal was taking a long time in coming. Then there were footsteps, the ratchet of the key in the lock, and the door scraped open. Carrying a lamp, the butler entered and stood to one side, his face expressionless as ever. Blinking, I fought to adjust my eyes.

As my vision cleared, my heart leapt nearly out of my

chest. In the doorway stood a slender shadow with eyes of blue fire.

I gasped, covered my mouth with both hands.

He knelt beside me, the light fringing his tousled hair with gold. "Hello, Dragonfly."

Sylva! A silver scar ran diagonally across his face—the wound inflicted by Mr. Snicker. Smiling, he extended a hand. "Do you want to come with me?"

I could scarcely breathe, let alone speak. Having been alone with my thoughts for so long, and suddenly to be faced with him who had so much occupied them—mutely, I nodded.

Laughing, he caught my hands, and I cried out with the electric thrill as he pulled me to my feet, looked deep into my eyes. Such a versatile, passionate face he had! Emotion set it aglow. Bending close to my ear, he brushed back my hair. His breath was warm as he whispered, "You are free!"

Then we were laughing, dashing out of the dripping chamber and up flights of stairs. Hand in hand we fled, leaving the butler and his unmoving guards far behind. Doors with iron rings stood open before us, lamps lighting our way; the great empty house of the vampire Noyes echoed with our footfalls as we darted through curtained archways, skated over ruby pools of moonlight, danced in galleries of weird and faded splendor. Sylva seized me in his arms and slid down a marble banister—I squealed into the rush of wind as we parted shadows, darkness cresting over us and filling in behind.

He launched us expertly off at the end, and we whirled beneath a chandelier on which a thousand candles burned. To the left was an open doorway spilling firelight, where I recognized the furnishings of the horrible parlor; just as Sylva whisked me by it and out a side door, I glimpsed a figure standing there watching us, a long cape in silhouette.

The smoking orange moon had never looked so glorious. I giggled with sheer intoxication as Sylva lifted me beneath the arms and spun me in amber shadows, my cloak winging behind. Again, you see, the power of the place, and particularly of the werewolf boy swept me away; for as much as I knew of the evil of Harvest Moon, when I danced with Sylva, I was a part of it all, and wanted nothing more.

We glided around the corner, from the alley to the main street—there, I froze. Immediately before us, the iron-wheeled Welcome Wagon waited with its team. It faced away, toward the bridge, but the ominous shape of Eagerly Meagerly towered in the driver's seat, the shadows of the firepot garish on his upturned collar, his wide brim. He did not turn.

"Come along!" laughed Sylva. "I told you, you are free! Let's ride a ways!"

Aghast, I watched him skip up to the rear platform of the wagon, catch hold of a ring, and stand there reaching his fingers toward me. The goat-beasts snorted and stamped, long ears twitching, hides writhing with impatience.

"Come on!" called Sylva.

Sick with my loathing of the wagon and its driver, but overwhelmed at last by the pull of Sylva's eyes, I hurried to leap up beside him. I gripped the iciness of the ring—at once, a whip cracked, and the wagon trundled forward.

As it had when I watched it come, the craft bucked and veered unpredictably, now right, now left, now rising on two wheels. The beasts pulled in conflicting directions, their giant cloven hooves pummeling the road; a trip across town for them was one prolonged argument of the harness. "They are called 'Untowards,'" said Sylva. "The team that pulls this wagon are both named Louder."

I grinned, choking back my unease. "Louder and Louder?"

Sylva tipped his head and laughed up into the moon. We held tight as the wagon yawed, its iron running boards and undercarriage clashing with the cobbles, sending up plumes of sparks. Rounding a corner, we angled away from Pink Eye Street, away from the River Abandon. The grade rose, the buildings crowding in around us, as life-drained faces appeared on balconies to watch us pass, hovered in windows and behind the grillworks of smoky shops. On a deep-set porch, just as we clattered past, one wraithlike child held another's hand to his mouth and bit with all his might. I shrieked and flinched away, turned helplessly to Sylva. But he was looking in another direction.

A massive padlock bounced against the doors between our faces. From time to time, over the din of the wheels and the Untowards, I thought I could hear subdued whimpering from inside. Considering this, that we were coming from a Reception at Number Fifty-two, I thought about letting go of the ring, of taking my chances with a fall to the street rather than accompany this terrible conveyance any farther. Sylva, as if reading my thoughts, spoke into my ear. "Hold tight! You wouldn't want to fall here. We're in Cannibal Town!"

I stared at him. He pointed with his chin, and I looked to where a thin man shuffled out of a doorway. He leaned on a crutch, and I saw that he was missing an arm and a leg.

Disbelieving, I shook my head at Sylva.

"Don't fall off!" he said.

WE crashed over a bridge, then up a zigzag street where people had oily fires in rusted barrels, and children scattered out of our way. They watched us with glazed eyes, and one boy, his clothes in ribbons, chased us on spindly legs. He reached up with long-nailed hands, his mouth opening and closing like a baby bird's. When the wagon began to outdistance him, he dove through the air and belly-flopped on the pavement, skidded along with his hands on his nearly-bald head. Cackling, his playmates descended on him, and we veered up another street.

"Did he want to eat us?" I asked in anguish.

"No—we're out of Cannibal Town now. This looks like a Hallowe'en festival."

Tears stung my eyes as I held the ring with both hands, my knees trembling. But Sylva touched my shoulder, and I saw a sea of shiny leaves and glistening flowers.

"The Gardens!" he announced.

Rows of hedges flanked the road. There were straight trees wearing garlands of rubbery vine like Maypoles swallowed by the bizarre, verdant growth. Flowers in tended gardens raised heads of pink petals, sea blue, violet, deep jungle green. The blossoms were heavy, unwholesome despite their beauty; a phalanx of them actually wriggled around on their stems as we passed, the blue pods of their heads tracking us.

I gave a cry at that, and again Sylva laughed. "Moth-feeders. They sense our movement." Some of the pods opened, like football-sized mouths with Venus'-flytrap teeth, and snapped shut.

As I had noted earlier, the burning was everywhere—gaunt gardeners leaned on their rakes beside bonfires of turf and castoff vegetation. A few raised bony hands in greeting, and Sylva waved happily back at them. We thundered into a tunnel in the hedge, where the flowering vines swarmed over a trellis, moonlight falling in spears on the deeply-rutted track.

The wagon stopped so abruptly I nearly struck my face against the doors as the brakes screeched, sparked, and the Untowards strove to pull apart their yoke. The fragrance of the flowers drifted down to us, settling with the dust of our arrival—a haunting essence that whispered of things forgotten, of half-disclosed secrets. My impulse was to climb the trellis, to press my nose against the blossoms, to commune with the night and my deepest memories—I felt that if I were to gaze out any one of the tiny open squares above us, where the vines parted, I could peer back to my earliest childhood, to the life and truth behind the events—that I might actually see Moon Dancers.

In the sudden silence, a tremulous voice called from inside the wagon: "Help me!"

I stood still, laid my hand on the wood.

"Help me!" The one voice rose above a chorus of others, voices of children who sensed that their journey was over, dreaded what might be coming next.

I knew this voice, but I wanted to deny hearing it. Sylva caught me and helped me off the step.

"Alycia!" I whispered.

"Dragonfly?"

Just my name, a question, an agony of despair that sank like a dagger into my heart—it remained, burning inside me, as the Welcome Wagon shuddered and pulled away.

Then we were alone, the werewolf and I, in the dim and aromatic cavern of the hedge. He draped an arm around my shoulders. "Look," he said gently, indicating a door of iron-banded wood set in the leafy wall of the tunnel. "We're home."

The enchantment of Sylva's presence was everywhere—in the hedges, in the darkly luminescent gardens of the district, in the trembling lunar reflections of secret pools. The fingers that brushed away my tears brushed away with them the ache over Alycia—I have called it intoxication, this effect Sylva had on me as he led me from one end of the tunnel to the other, showing me the gardens and the moonscape. My thoughts were disorganized, drifting on soothing waves of honeysuckle, which twined round his house in abundance, heedless of the season and the lack of real light—there were also somnolent poppies, orchids, and most wonderful of all, roses of a deep red—yet these he did not show me at first.

He lived alone, taking care of the extensive gardens and the marvelous apartment by himself. For a long time at the beginning, I was overwhelmed by the beauty and wildness of the place; it was a child's dream, sculpted of living hedges, wood, stones laid in the earth, and spreading trees. I could not say where the house left off and the gardens began, for the whole affair was lighted by the moon through open trellis ceilings, and at least two walls of every room were growing hedges or vine-draped screens. It seemed to have the resolution of a house near the road, with chambers squared off and floored with planks; then, in arboreal corridors and unceilinged fern-beds, it *melted* as one went deeper, house consumed by gardens, until all that remained of structure was a path of flat stones sunk in moss. Having no rain to contend with, he indulged his love of the moon by making it always visible; he had arranged the house artfully to frame the orb in archways of trumpet vines, in crumbling brickworks, had given it pools on which to dance. "Languor House," I named it in the corners of my mind over which I still had some control.

There was little cleaning to be done in such a house, and no cooking at all. "I always dine out," he grinned, guiding me as one steers a sleepwalker to a table of melted and faceted glass in an open courtyard, where the mazes of his gardens began. I sat in a high-backed wooden chair, the moonlight shimmering up from the table, dazzling me until I changed my position.

"Do you like my table?" he asked, shooing a moth that had settled on the frozen lake of its flawless top.

"It's beautiful."

"It was made at Adrian's Glassworks"—I was sure his

voice shook a little as he vanished into another room—"where
there was a *fire*."

He returned with a soft cloak of blue velvet, just the color
of a clear night, wrapped it around me; it was lined with rich
grey fur, warm as a quilt in the crisp air. "You should keep this
about you, since I have no stove." It was true; I had seen no
fireplace, nothing like a kitchen.

"This cloak," he went on, pouring liquor into mugs of fired
clay, "is lined with the skin of my grandfather."

I had been stroking it, but recoiled at once, stared at him.

"Dear Dragonfly, you are priceless! Don't be morbid. He
was put to death for what Mr. Hain regarded as bad behavior,
and one doesn't let the pelt of a werewolf go to waste. My kind
isn't squeamish—will you still wear it? Good! A warm coat is a
warm coat." He handed me the cup, which smelled of sweet
wild berries. "It is a cloak of great honor, and I've always
wished for someone to present it to." His eyes trapped me
tighter than the walls of Hain's dungeon. "If you wear the skin
of my ancestor, Dragonfly, we can be closer than ever." Then he
lapped the drink, splashing it over his teeth and licking it off.

"What did he do?" I asked, tasting the liquor. Its warmth
stole over me almost at once.

"My grandfather?" He chuckled, waved a hand. "He was a
rogue—devoured all the wrong people. Mr. Hain was most
generous and patient, but even his magnanimity has limits.
My grandfather and a couple of his friends tired of eating
what they called 'the same old dust,' and one midnight they
went too far. They hijacked the Welcome Wagon, slashed up
old Meagerly—that's how he lost his scalp, and still wears
that hat—and had themselves a feast."

"I'm sorry I asked." My hands clenched the cup, and I bit
my lip, fighting to think clearly.

Sylva bounded into the gardens, plucked two handfuls of
flowers, his voice drifting back over the seeping mist. "All the
water comes up from below, probably from the same source
that feeds Abandon—it's magic, of course. Supplies the gardens, even the forests, with all they need. It's wine," he giggled, returning. "The wine of the Earth!"

"Sylva." I focused on my hands, deliberately avoided his
eyes.

"Dragonfly?"

"Why did Hain let me go?"

Busy with the flowers, twisting their stems together, he did not answer at once.

"Sylva," I pressed. "I want to know."

"Why do you worry?" He lifted my chin, forced me to look at his eyes. They only searched mine; he did not do with his gaze what he could have. "But since you do worry, I will tell you. I have no secrets from you, Dragonfly. He gave you up because I went to him and asked for you."

"Asked for me?"

"I asked him to let me care for you. He knows of the world—he knows I will gladly teach you the ways of Harvest Moon, and you will learn willingly. For him to teach you would amount only to his grief, for he knows you are already turned against him. But you will stay with me, you will learn—and you will dream dreams."

I only watched him.

"He had much to gain from such an arrangement, nothing to lose. He knows where you are, and that you will not leave us." He poured more wine. "Am I right?" This time he turned away, for he wanted my answer to be my own. With narrow eyes, he watched the moon.

I was ten years old, and the world was a place of more power and life and mystery than I had ever imagined. "Yes, Sylva," I whispered. "If—if what you say is true, then—then I will stay with you."

He smiled, twisting flowers, moths playing about the garden. "There is so much we can do, Dragonfly. I've been lonely—and so have you."

I reached across and squeezed his arm.

He looked at me earnestly, his voice low. "Can you accept what I am?"

I shivered, clinging to him. "What is that to me? You are a boy. You breathe; your heart beats."

"Yes," he sighed, stroking my hair. "Remember that, please, Dragonfly." He placed the crown of woven flowers on my head. "Then wear the skin of my kindred, and be one with me!"

Scampering to the pool on hands and knees, he lowered his face and drank, then howled at the moon. I listened with a racing heart to the deep-throated cry of exaltation, rose to meet him as he sprang back and swung me round and round. We shrieked with laughter, vaulted over the chairs, skipped in and out of the dark avenues of the bushes. I cannot express how I felt—how can one describe a first love? There was excitement, a nervousness as if a whole flock of birds beat their wings within me; there was a weeping joy at the touch of his hand, an all-consuming delight as his eyes looked into mine.

And yet, as he sat me down again, gasping, into my chair, there was a shadow under my heart. As he waved and cried out that he would return soon, as his flying hair vanished among the arbors, I was aware of the chill in the garden, suddenly empty and quiet; I felt as if I were older than I had been a few hours ago, older than any child of ten should be.

Laying my head on my arms, I wept.

IT was unnerving the way time passed without passing in Harvest Moon. Though hours slipped by, the cycles of nature never changed in any typical, perceptible way. Always, no matter how the clocks lied, it was the frozen moment of Now, a time of moonlight, and eternal autumn, the world arrested in the process of dying.

That first time Sylva left me, he was not away long. I had fallen into an exhausted sleep at the table, awakening only when he set a wooden box before me and softly called my name. I was stiff and sore from dozing in the chair. Feeling ill, I shuddered and tightened the cloaks around me. Perhaps the wine was to blame, perhaps the drafty house, or perhaps the stress of the last days; at any rate, I was feverish, the very thought of eating the food Sylva had brought for me in the box making my stomach churn. Scarcely able to hold my head up, I allowed him to lead me to a bed—a real bed, in one of the rooms that had two wooden walls.

He was deeply sorry for having left me in the open garden. Tenderly, he tucked me in, brought water, and washed my face. Giving me water to drink, he stayed beside me as I drifted in and out of sleep.

Ironic as it sounds, some of my fondest memories of Sylva

are of his gentle nursing, his nearness, his face etched in lines of concern. I don't know whether or not he enjoyed those first dreams I dreamed in his house, wild, distorted dreams of pursuit and delirium. I tossed, I burned, and he mopped my forehead. When at last my fever had abated, he told me in a voice hoarse with weariness and relief that two nights had passed since I had fallen ill.

WE passed an immeasurable time in his house—I don't know precisely how many days, for we chased each other through the gardens and flopped down to sleep whenever we exhausted ourselves, eating when we were hungry, washing in the sparkling pools. In that time after the fever, I felt a newness, a blissful ignorance, as if my life had begun again; I was indulging in the carefree childhood I had almost forgotten, abandoned when my grandfather died. Now his death, and school, and all the hurts and cares of my life were fading like the scar on Sylva's face. The wolf-cloak warmed me, but at odd moments, when I chanced to glance at Mothkin's black cloak, laundered and hung behind the front door, a cold wave rolled up inside me. At those times I remembered the faces of Mothkin and Singer, of Uncle Henry and Alycia, and I was nagged by a sensation of unfinished business, a suppressed urgency which I could have defined if I'd wanted to—but always, there was Sylva, there was moonlight on the roses.

Yes, the roses! They were a loveliness at the center of a lovely dream. One evening he led me to them, down a tunnel of the hedge, through a secret gate. The color of the sky just after sunset, sweet as deep summer's breath, they surrounded us in his private garden, pale ornaments, stars in the darkness of the bushes. There he brought out a harp and played it for me, sang in a starlight voice:

> Black raven of the night,
> Shining roses in the heart of the night,
> Show your beauty to my true love;
> Raven-hair, she is a rose,
> And beauty mirrors beauty mirrors beauty.

He took me in his arms and kissed me. Never since have I experienced anything more pure or fulfilling. Often, let me tell you, I scoff when I hear far wiser people talk of love, of making love; I understood more then in his touch than I have learned in all the interlying years. We were children, with the bodies and hearts of children. There was no sex, no greed, no comparison or agenda—there was only closeness, unsullied fondness, the scent of jasmine in his hair. I had saved his life at the river, and he had set me free—from the dungeon, from my veil of isolation.

Our evenings were full of activity; we worked side by side, tending the flowers, pruning the trees, gathering the apples which fell in a constant rain. A forever-autumn world is an eternal harvest. We sold apples and their juice to a lumpish peddler with a tilt-cart. (Pain, you see, was not the only sustenance in Harvest Moon; the people ate food to fuel their decaying bodies.) Dark bouquets we sold to thin-browed ladies in formal dresses—Sylva told me these were members of mourners' circles, clubs of ladies who whiled away their hours in reaping the sheaves of each night's mishaps—strangulations, cannibalizations, drainings, brainings, wagon wrecks—thriving on the pain, following after the bereaved like shrouded sheep. To hear such news, to meet the folk we dealt with disturbed me vaguely—yet these things were distant, only half-real now that I had a place to which I could retreat.

Harvest Moon money came in only one denomination: a copper coin larger than a fifty-cent piece, usually green and crusted, which bore Hain's profile and the words "Render unto Caesar." With some of his money, Sylva bought pretty clothes for me, baubles and trappings to make Languor House a home. And with some, he paid the old woman who cooked my meals—she had strings of white hair and a single yellow tooth, and she never spoke to me. Usually Sylva carried the steaming stews and breads across the field for me, but at times I would go myself. I even helped her with her cleaning when Sylva was away, or when he slept after a long foray. She would watch me with a milky eye and chuckle soundlessly when I arrived or departed.

Of course I knew where Sylva went when he was away. It was important to him that I watch him change into a wolf at least once—that I remained with him even then lifted a burden from him. It's one thing to hear someone is a werewolf, but to see his nose become a snout in the moonlight—to see his wrists lengthen, grow impossibly thin, his legs scissor backward, his ears become black twitching scoops—that is another thing entirely. It did not shake me; he never killed for sport, nor did he play with his victims like a vampire. He hunted only every fourth or fifth night, and I would have his clothes neatly folded and waiting for him on the glass table. Naturally I preferred to see him in the form that I could love.

Once when he was away, I took some paper and a pen and ink he had brought for me, sat in the rose garden and wrote down an idea that had always lain in my head—an idea about the people under the Distant Stars—more of that later. I suppose my subconscious was trying to tell me, "Get up! Wake up!" But at the time, I read over it as one does a letter one has written years before; this writer was a stranger to me. For a reason I cannot explain even now, I folded the paper and tucked it away in a pocket of Mothkin's cloak. Perhaps that somber garment had become for me the sole reminder of unrest, of things undecided, and so it was the repository for my stray idea.

I dreamed in Languor House, certainly I dreamed. He would play the harp, sending me to sleep with lullabies, and stay just beside me until I opened my eyes again to his angular face. He drank my dreams; they made him stronger, so that his need to hunt lessened—for me, that knowledge brought fulfillment. My nearness brightened his eyes, physically *sustained* him—does any lover dream of more? Also, by providing a werewolf with a nonviolent dietary supplement, I was saving lives, however wretched they may have been. In fact, our relationship was a contradiction to the entire activity of Harvest Moon—despite our surroundings, despite the very nature of what my darling Sylva was, we generated peace, we dwelt in the security of a hidden island. Sylva quickly hushed me when I voiced this idea, warning me not to boast before jealous shadows, and told me that I must not anger Samuel Hain.

The stealth that must surround our existence became clearer to me when I asked Sylva why I remembered so little of my dreams in his house—a fragment here, an echo there, a fading memory of pleasure when I awoke that filled me with longing. He answered in fewer words than were characteristic, even for him, explaining his nearness when I slept: he must drink the dreams quickly, for if they were allowed to linger, surely Hain would smell them across the slanting moonbeams—and they were so vibrant, so rich, that Hain would want them for himself. Sylva trembled so fiercely that I took him in my arms and wept.

My time in Languor House was growing short. My memories are the exhilaration of running with Sylva through the gardens, the simple warmth of hours spent with a spirit that mirrored my own. There was a sting of parting whenever my companion left me for the hunt—I could never remove his uncontrollable change, his need to kill. Always there was the vagueness, the disturbing sensation of unrecollected dreams, and of waking thoughts that never quite became clear. Always, when I looked at the dark cloak hanging behind the door, I remembered my love's trembling, the clouding of his eyes, and a black foreboding filled my heart.

I was a fool to think we could go on forever, to assume that Hain would really leave us alone, no matter how quiet we kept ourselves. Why did I not question? Why did I let myself fall so far, drift so deeply, so passively into his web? The answer: Languor House. It no more belonged to the werewolf than did the bogus moon, the trees, or anything else in Harvest Moon; all proceeded from the master of the dance, the Father of Generosity. Hain's game employed the ancient principle of the battering ram, the timeless rhythm of waves on the beach—islands and towers are seldom broken down by constant pressure. Rather, the game is always waves, force alternating with vacuum, defenses shattered by renewed assault.

His house of false security took the edge off my fear, gave me comfort and something to hold on to . . . all for the sake of what I would feel when Hain ripped it away.

LAUGHING, Sylva tossed me a dark emerald blossom, and laughing, I wove it into the chain I was making. We sat in the branches of a tree he called the lurkwick, which spread low limbs across the garden and bent its trunk as if frozen in the middle of a dance. Sap glowing with a cold light oozed from the tips of long-stemmed leaves, creating the illusion that thousands of candles were fixed to the branches. Of all Sylva's trees, I loved the lurkwick best.

Sidling down a limb, he dropped to the thistled grass beyond the hedge, waved, and sprang away into the darkness. Clutching the flowers, I waved back.

The darkness swallowed him.

He did not come back, not even when I had dusted the glass table and washed and mended some of his clothes. As I tried to stitch a patch over the tattered knee of his trousers, I smiled, thinking that a werewolf's clothes, even new, are as ragged as a vampire's are immaculate.

I gathered some flowers, arranged them in bouquets for selling—even sold some to ladies who tapped at the door or stood wailing on the road. Ignoring the hunger that gnawed at my stomach, I waited and waited, yearning for the swish of his feet in the garden, his howl on the far hills. But there was only silence.

When the neighborhood clock, an ivy-covered bulk at the end of the lane, struck midnight, then one o'clock, I began to worry. By the time the small hours gave way to the next evening, I was numb with dread, pacing from room to room and along the avenues of the garden. Every sculpted arch, every mossy stone unfurled memories for me, cherished times and experiences with Sylva. Night birds called softly in the thickets, and the odor of roses drifted in the still air.

At last I decided I must go look for him, though how I expected to find him in all of Harvest Moon I cannot guess. I passed through the house and was just approaching the front door, which gave onto the tunnel in the hedge, when there came a loud knock.

The blood drained from my face.

The knock sounded again.

I lay hold of the knob, tried to breathe, but it felt as if my lungs were full of cotton. The third series of knocks sent tremors up my arm. Swallowing on a dry mouth, I pulled it open.

Mr. Snicker was a giant in bulging velvet and stripes. His

dangling scissors flashed with the light of torches as he tipped his hat, blew a cloud of acrid smoke, and dropped a bundle on the doorstep.

Into my hand he stuck a creaseless square of paper, on which words were lettered flawlessly in a bold hand:

My Dear Dragonfly,

I hope you are well and have enjoyed your little vacation. A house is ever so much more pleasant than a dungeon!

Since you are entirely free to do as you please, I invite you once more to come and stay with me. I understand that Reception is not to your liking; not to worry! Come, if you please, to the High Horse—I am remodeling my Tenebrificium, and dearly wish to show it to you!

I am waiting for you—come at your convenience.

Most Sincerely,
Samuel Hain

P.S.—I notice your cloak is getting a bit threadbare—please accept this new one. It is just your size, and I know you'll like the color.

Mr. Snicker snipped the twine that bound his parcel, unfolded it, and laid it across my arms. Then he stepped back, carefully shaking ashes away from the splendid garment.

The sight and smell of it knifed through me, all strength leaving my body. There was no mistaking the dusky odor, the luxuriant fur, the grey-brown shade of the pelt.

I dropped to my knees. Every muscle in me went slack, and my last thought before darkness swept up to engulf me was the desperate wish that my heart, too, would give up its beating, which was now utterly meaningless.

10

TOOTHLESS BITES, MOUTHLESS MUTTERS

I recall awakening to a body stiff with ache, blinking leaden eyes, raising my head slowly from the threshold, where I had lain with my face on the skin of my beloved Sylva. Mr. Snicker had gone, and the door rocked in a draft from the shadowed road.

There was no reason to rise—not ever again. Letting my head fall, I surrendered consciousness once more. Uncounted hours slipped by.

Again I awoke, so empty that it seemed the darkness of the house would crush me as I rolled onto my back, shuddering with the pain of each breath. Wrapping my arms around my knees, I huddled in a ball. There were no tears. I touched the soft pelt on the floor, my fingers wooden, as if they belonged to somebody else.

Sylva!

How different, how ridiculous was this empty hide on the floor! As much as I wanted to refuse the idea, mine was the child's solemnity of acceptance; Sylva was gone, and my heart was broken. For the first time since entering Languor House, I saw Uncle Henry clearly in my mind, recalled his early lessons about the death that trafficked in and out of his funeral home. "People cling to these empty shells," he explained, answering my question about why the caskets were never closed until after the families had driven away. "They don't want to see their loved ones shut in boxes or buried in the earth. But, Dragonfly, this is nothing but a husk. The person who wore it in life was long gone before it was brought to me."

Nor was this skin on the floor my Sylva; he had gone, and the curse of his lycanthropy was lifted. I knew it had hurt him, having to kill. That was why Hain kept werewolves: they were efficient generators of pain, and they felt every slash of their claws in their own hearts; thus they were double-producers—perfect fodder, perfect slaves.

A movement caught my eye. Lifted by the chilly air, the black cloak was moving on its peg. I watched it rise, rippling along its hem as if mourning for my werewolf, for all the injustice of Harvest Moon. A ray of moonlight fell through an open screen behind me. Either its wan illumination played a trick, or a greater power was at work, showing me visions; I have heard and read many times since of people who, in moments of extreme emotion, are able to see beyond the scope of ordinary perception. What I saw, or thought I saw, was a swelling of the cloak, as if a body filled it (though no legs were visible below), and the profile of Mothkin's gargoyle face in the hood. The apparition lasted no more than a second, and then it was an empty cloak again, in a foyer of filtered light.

Yes, I thought, *it's time to put you on again, black cloak.*

With unhurried movements, I rose and walked to the room where my clothes were kept in a chest. Turning its brass key, I lifted the lid, found my flannel shirt and jeans, my tennis shoes. When I had changed into them, I took the black cloak from the wall, fastened it at my neck. Gently folding both werewolf skins, that of Sylva and that of his grandfather, I carried them into the gardens.

First, I went to the secret place of roses, where Sylva's harp rested beneath a velvet cloth. Tenderly, I gathered as many of the blossoms as I could carry, then locked the little iron-bound door forever behind me and made my way to the lurkwick tree.

At the tree's foot was the right place, all the gardens spreading away, the open fields a short hop over the hedge, and the myriad candles of the tree glimmering like the true night sky of the world above. Using Sylva's garden spade, I dug a shallow grave and laid them to rest there, the werewolf and his grandfather. Some of the roses I wrapped with them, and some I scattered on the soft earth. When my task was accomplished, I lay on the grave and wept at last.

THEN came a time of wandering.

The spell of Languor House was broken. I took nothing but the clothes I wore, climbed over the hedge by the lurkwick tree, where Sylva had gone out the last time, and never once looked back. I had no plans, no thoughts that I can remember, my heart and mind empty as the house, and as steeped in frost as the lands above must have been by now. In truth, winter had already come to Henry's millet field, blanketing it with snow.

Dark-eyed gardeners scratched at the soil, piled leaves and twigs on fires, and hissed at the skeletal dogs that tried to warm themselves. I greeted none of them, nor did they speak to me. By experience I had become what I had imitated on the bridge—yet another passing ghost of Harvest Moon, a tattered shadow gliding along the hedges. Sere grass crackled beneath my feet; wraiths of ground mist drifted among nettles and thistles.

The old accustomed crashes, rumbles, and laughter arose from the town, of which the largest part lay now over my right shoulder. The High Horse stood ahead and to the right, where the forested mountain climbed toward the moon. I stumbled on into a district of mist and silence, which suited my inner desolation; I had nothing to say, no urge to meet a soul, living or dead. Traversing a wide meadow, I wound in and out of a fringe of leaning lurkwick trees. Riding the darkness, a lone bat circled and was gone. There were wolf tracks in the mud beside a stream; feeling my insides twist, I went on, done with tears. The frail fire of leaves over my head cast shadows like webs of silver across the path.

Away to my left, a ring of firelight grew. I approached only near enough to see a circle of wagons in a clearing, to hear the murmur of voices and smell the aroma of roasting meat. Hungry, but not ready to eat, I pushed on into the wood.

It was darker now, the glowing trees growing only here and there, surrounded by dense brakes of lightless ones, their trunks worm-scarred and malodorous. Stumbling through nets of vines that clung to my ankles, made ripping sounds at each step, I imagined the plants moving in the shadows, crawling toward me. A conclave of black cats scurried in procession over the roots, crossing from left to right, toward the town. To this day I cannot guess where they had all been, or their purpose; there are intricacies of the worlds adjoining Earth that I suppose no one has ever fathomed.

The forest thinned, and I emerged atop a slope tangled with shrubs, boulders, and dying trees. At the base, a sluggish expanse of water lapped at a bank collapsed in places, choked with flotsam. It was a canal, but it reeked of an oily uncleanness beyond pollution. Perhaps a hundred yards across, it joined with others in the distance, a sprawling network of ditches and greasy waters, cutting the lowlands across to the foot of the mountain.

I scanned the system, trying to understand its function; at every intersection of canals stood a square, narrow building two stories high, with a peaked roof and three vents or windows high on the walls. Constructed of a steely metal, each was ringed with a fence, skirted by clumps of dark weeds gone to seed.

Moving down the bank, I observed a punt on the surface of a far waterway, its pilot slicing the water with a pole. He was dressed in the unnatural black hue I had come to associate with Hain's closest servants, his inner circle. The water, where it parted around the square prow and widened in a wake behind, looked as heavy as glue. Paths of moonlight oozed across the surface like spilled blood.

It was as if the kiss of the canal poisoned the shore, for all the bank was littered with dead things—rotting trees, some standing in dry skeletons which clawed at the sky—stinking weeds, and the bones of animals. I picked my way through a soggy deadland, something like an echo of my old curiosity drawing me toward the nearest fence-guarded building.

As I drew near, I could hear a gurgling, thrumming noise

from inside the building. Its walls were flat, non-reflective, seeming almost to produce their own inner light. The high windows flickered with a yellow glare. I stepped over a log, waded through slime puddles that sucked at my feet. The fence, which had looked imposing at a distance, was actually only as high as my chest. Peering into the overgrown yard, I laid a hand on the planks and could feel the deep vibrations through the wood.

I suppose I felt I had nothing to lose. I'd experienced Hain's generosity; what more could he do to me, even if he captured me? And what did I care? What was my liberty worth here, or my life? All these thoughts I would doubtless have amended in time, but then I was alone in the mists of grief.

Determining to have a look inside, I was just lifting one leg over the fence when a wagon rattled around a bend, its driver hauling back on the reins. Puffing black horses stamped, the steel brakes screeched, and the driver, a silk-hatted man chinless as a chicken, swung down from the seat, flicked his opera cape over his shoulders to free his arms.

I crouched in the weeds behind the fence. A fat black spider jiggled its way up my arm, and I sent it flying.

Another man with emaciated cheeks stood up in the bed of the wagon. Together, the two lifted down an oblong box and carried it to the door.

Following the fence, I adjusted my position and watched them vanish inside. A corroded padlock swung from the half-ring on the latch. The man had not had time to unlock it, so I reasoned it was in disuse; furthermore, the lock on the outside suggested I would meet no one within. I waited, the horses watching me with dubious eyes. After what seemed a long time, the rumbling grew louder, a grinding of enormous gears. When it had peaked and then receded, I heard the approaching footsteps of the men and hurried back around to the rear. They carried the box, obviously much lighter now, and loaded it into the wagon. Pausing long enough to blow up the flame of his firepot, the driver cracked his whip, and the rig clattered up the steep road.

What could this be, I wondered—had they carted in a corpse? For what? Was this a crematory? A processing plant for the cannibals? Or, in the tradition of Harvest Moon, something worse? I circled to the front, opened the gate, and slogged through knee-high grass to the door, a rectangle of the same shimmering metal. No one seemed to be about; the road disappeared around a wooded rise, the forest leaning over the bank down which I had come. To the rear of the building, the land fell in a low cliff to the canal.

A single doubt nagged me as I pushed open the door and peered into blackness: if no one was inside, why were the upper windows aglow?

Sourness and heat assaulted me from the open door. The darkness churned as with the winching of chains and sprockets, the wheezing of a cavernous bellows. Directly before me was an inner door—this one *was* fastened by a padlock—but an iron stairway wound upward to the right, following the wall. It was like stepping into the boiler room of a plague ship.

I suppose the anger was rising in me again—powerless and ignorant in so many ways, alone in Hain's evil world, the least I could do was try to keep surprising him. *Maybe* that thought compelled me to enter, or maybe it was curiosity; I don't know. It won't do to analyze my actions then with an adult's mind—it was a child that climbed those stairs.

The building sweated and *breathed* around me as if I were inside a living thing, the air stifling, condensation dripping from the rusted steps. Behind the walls of the inner housing, there was a ringing as of dangling weights hitting each other. Climbing, the stairs turned away from the light. In near-total darkness at the second-floor level, I faced a door edged with firelight. As I reached for it, the noise beyond it suddenly stopped. Fear crept up behind me. Had the building merely reached the end of a mechanical cycle, something triggered, perhaps, by the coming of the men with their delivery? Or did someone *know I was here?*

Perspiration trickled down my back, my heart pounding; rationality ordered me to bolt. I certainly could not remain on this stairway. Putting out a quavering hand, I shoved the door, and it opened with a shriek of hinges long deprived of oil. Before me lay a room dripping with moisture, cloying with stench, lit by lanterns on hooks.

The jumble of pulleys, gears, and pipes left little extra

room, exposed machinery crowding the chamber from floor to ceiling. Stepping gingerly over an oxidized pipe at knee level, I examined banks of levers sticking from the walls. Fitted with handgrips, they rested along a row of benches with iron foot rests. I edged nearer, fanning away a puff of steam that issued slowly from a mineral-coated pressure valve. There were four rows of ten levers, one along each wall. Something crunched under my feet—a fine dusting of what looked like pulverized clay.

Holding my breath, I crossed flickering patches of light and shadow, trying to understand what this place was. Heavy-linked chains snaked into holes in the walls and floor; as I circled, I saw a round opening in the floor's center and a pit within it like a gaping pipe, smaller in circumference than the hole; both the iron shaft and the first-floor housing around it were impenetrably dark, but the gurgling of water and a stench wafted up—I shrank from the hole, turned back to the levers.

Cautiously I sat on a bench, put my feet on the rest like that on a barber's chair; I could swivel it up and down by angling my feet. The benches had clearly been made for people to sit on and work the levers—but where were these people? Who lit the lanterns?

Taking hold, I pulled tentatively. At first the lever would not move—I pulled harder, feeling resistance, and slowly, pushing against the foot rest, was able to bring it up to my chest.

Something skittered up the wall, a dark shape. I gasped, letting go of the lever, which swung back to its original position with a crash—now I saw what had moved: a lead weight, half-enclosed in a wall shaft in front of me. When I pulled the handle, the weight crawled up through an opening; when I let the lever return, the weight came down, and a metal shaft rotated. This building was a machine, or series of machines, that operated by manual labor. What was it for, I wondered? Where were—?

A prickling sensation stole up my back, over my scalp. Pulsating, the shadows seemed nearer, denser. My heartbeat was audible in my ears. In my fancy, booms and pulleys subtly twisted, steadily moving in.

The lanterns flashed, then nearly went out as a puff of air

escaped some quirk of the architecture. Quivering, the tiny flames righted themselves—except for two, which guttered and sent wisps of grey smoke from their ornamental lids.

Scritch-hhh!

I spun around with a gasp, certain I had heard a footstep somewhere back in the corner—only silent benches.

Whick-kk!

Behind me again, near the door—

A face!

I screamed, sure of what I had seen among the ranks of chains. Whirling, I tensed to dash for the stairs, but my way was blocked. Eyes glinted in the darkness. My hands tore at my hair, tried in vain to cover my face as my mouth shaped meaningless words.

They came forward from the shadows, from their hiding places, shambled on twisted legs, misshapen hands groping toward me. In a circle they advanced, and I saw that they were children—children with brown, grainy skin that crumbled and flaked as they moved. Some had only one eye, some were missing a nose or a mouth, only smooth brown skin where there should have been features. On some, one ear was grotesquely oversized; some had none at all, or a single arm, and stubby, impossible combinations of fingers. The very worst were those whose faces had been pulled in opposite directions, the mouth far to the left, the eyes on the right, the nose stretched between. Walking was an agony for them, seeing and reaching gave them pain; shaped of clay, they were not built for such activity.

They were built to suffer.

Torn between terror and sympathy, I staggered backward—and found myself standing on air.

The open shaft!

I lashed out with my arms, shrieked with pain as I caught the pipe's rim. The edge was too narrow—it was like trying to hang from a knife-blade. My elbows were jarred numb, my fingers unresponsive; I dangled outside the pipe in the hollowness that housed it, but the rough-cut edge of the floor was beyond my reach—I had no strength even to try.

I thought once of God.

"HELP ME!"

And then I dropped into darkness.

11

THE NUMINOUS WOOD

THERE was a far-off explosion in my ears as I hit black water and shot into its depths, my only awareness the heart-freezing chill.

I sank forever, my flesh afire, arms and legs flailing in a void without light, without resistance. Then I felt a rhythm in the water, the steady pounding of something huge, something close beside me: the engines in the building had started again. Hurtling like a bubble on a wave of pressure, I swallowed water, which rushed over my face, dragged back my cheeks in what must have been the parody of a grin. Light flared behind my eyes; the hand of the canal sought to crush me.

I was moving in horizontal free-fall at a speed I could not reckon, ripples of orange light now above me, now below. Somehow I had avoided the machinery; by some unseen floodgate, I had been vomited into the outside current. Farther away now, the booming of the machine sent impulses past and through me.

As my head broke surface, as I coughed water from my lungs, the moon swam out of focus, seemed to melt in the sky.

Along the whole length of the canal, nightmare visions began.

Trees flexed limbs, knotholes winked, and mounds of dead leaves rose and fell as with labored breathing.

I knew these things could not be real, not even in Harvest Moon, yet that knowledge did little to lessen my terror as the canal blazed into flames that roared in my face without heat, as the water became transparent, showing me a mass of serpents writhing beneath my kicking feet. Some were the size of whales, with fins of bone and elephantine tusks—some were eyeless and livid, gyring in figure eights—and millions on millions were tiny shoestrings of death, venom trailing from their fangs.

I could see no water—it was as if I floated in air above them—yet I could feel the water's loathsome, icy touch. And I could see the debris that rode on the surface, the detritus of the poisoned wood. Striking with my hands, I felt the water part and shower around them, the suction of undertow dragging me toward the boiling monsters. Fighting for air, I seized a bobbing log, clung to its oily solidity.

The melting moon turned white, elongating slightly, sprouting hair at the top. Two of its shadowy patches opened and became eyes—eyes glazed with horror. A nose thrust up, a mouth split open—and it wore the face of Uncle Henry.

I had no breath for a cry, could only make a noise like choking as the Henry-Moon's eyes flicked left and right, surveying the landscape. Then he screamed, mouth engulfing his face, the features destroyed like the faces of the machine house children.

Losing shape entirely, the moon sagged and fell in a molten teardrop, coated the High Horse, and the land was lit only by the burning of the canal. The Horse reared up, suddenly animate, kicked its colossal forelegs, and charged down the mountainside, trees flattening beneath its iron hooves.

I shut my eyes, shook my head.

Even Harvest Moon had rules—it was a nightmare, to be sure, but it didn't flow and reshape itself. Vivid as these changes were, they could not be real. Perhaps, I thought, I had gone mad during my encounter with the children. Perhaps I had struck my head in the fall. Or—

The canal itself.

That was the answer. It was the influence of the midnight

canal I had ingested that caused me to see the Horse descending toward me, to see animated skeletons dancing on the riverbanks, to feel a hand—

—a hand on my shoulder—

I went stiff.

—eyes on my back—

There was no doubt what sat behind me. I had felt their presences before, and they were indelibly burned into the part of me where shapeless things still, no matter how old I get, breathe at night.

I heard their chuckles when they knew that I knew. Slowly, slowly my head came around.

They sat on a floating tree, their red hair bouncing in frizzles like uncoiling springs. White eyes with pea-sized pupils gathered the light, shined it on me. The ripped messes of their mouths flapped with their laughter.

"Dragonfly!" gurgled one, raising clawed fingers, the nails caked with filth.

"Missed you at the mirror!" grated the other.

In the cold back bedroom, I had never seen them; on the stairs, I thought I had conquered my fear of them once and for all—but now we were face-to-face. There was no denying the reality of the hand that encircled my throat.

I did what I had to do: I fainted.

THE hands, the hands! They clutched my shoulders, pulled at my collar. There was pain everywhere, the stench, the clinging wetness—with a cry, I struck the hands away. A voice reached me then, gentle words drifting down through my panic.

I opened my eyes.

I thought I had somehow escaped Harvest Moon, for the face hovering over me belonged to a weary, kindly person that might have been my grandmother. It was the humanity of her expression more than her faded green sweater and heavy glasses that told me she was an outsider like myself.

Brushing bedraggled hair from my face, she said, "Can you hear me, Sweet Pea?"

"Yes," I answered weakly. I was still in the canal, at its edge, where it meandered beneath a wooded bank. Hanging around us were limbs draped with moss like yaks' hides. My cloak had caught on the log; it was the chafing of the wood that made my back throb.

"Let's get you out of the water." Heedless of the mud that sucked at her tennis shoes, splattered her dress, the woman supported me, disentangled my cloak.

Leaning forward to help, I gasped with the pain of movement, slumped against her.

"There, Sweet Pea, we've got you loose."

Through fluttering eyelids, I checked the moon—it was back in the sky now, and the iron Horse stood in its accustomed place. The water, too, was as blackly opaque as a river of oil; if monsters truly seethed in its depths, they were hidden.

My arms and hands trembled with the strain of the past hours. Even the resiliency of childhood was almost spent. No bones were broken, but my legs were so chilled, so tired that I could scarcely move them up the lizard-haunted bank. The woman half carried me, and somehow, amid all the tainting of the canal, her sweater still managed to smell of herbs and wood smoke.

When we stood dripping between the knotted knees of the wood, she turned toward a thicket and said, "Come on, Willie."

Peering from among thorny branches was a boy no more than six years old, his eyes round. He wore a baggy yellow shirt and blue pants that reached exactly to his knees. In his arms he cradled a white kitten.

"Don't be bashful," said the woman. "This poor child's half drowned. Lead us home, Sweet Pea."

Now Willie was Sweet Pea. Without a word, he headed quickly into the woods.

The woman walked with a hitch, her ragged shoes expelling mud at each step. She was little and square—not fat, just shaped like a box, with slightly bowed legs. She kept an arm around my shoulders, murmured encouragement.

The forest was a cavern, spangled in places by self-illuminating trees.

Smaller flowers, too, produced light. Just beside the path,

they resembled jack-in-the-pulpits, but a pale violet light reflected from their petals upon the tiny "men" on the stages.

Unseen animals scrabbled in the canopy overhead, the carpet beneath. The mist swirled through the trees, like yawning, stretching ghosts on ghost mattresses. There was the scent of loam and breathing moss.

I was relieved to see the cottage in a clearing. It was back under the limbs of a spreading tree, some murky, stately cousin of the oak. Grass fingered up through the stone path, and the house appeared to be sinking in the undergrowth, ferns lapping at the windowsills. Firelight danced in the windows, and a cloud of fragrant smoke rose from the chimney to dissipate among the branches.

Inside, I sat on a stool as the old woman heated water in an iron kettle, dumped it into a wooden tub. All the while she talked to me, patting my arm when she passed to search for towels and clothes. There was an abundance of both in massive wooden trunks. I must have resembled a shivering alley cat, my hair ratty. Hunching over a cup of tea, I absorbed the warmth.

The boy, Willie, had an entourage of cats. They sidled from every corner of the house when we returned—a thin black matriarch with a crooked tail; a sleek tom the color of rain on ravens' wings; two or three wispy tabbies somewhere in color between grey and orange; a tiger-tom who limped; and five kittens, of which the white one was the largest. Rattling a pan, Willie called them in his piping voice, led them outside to eat and play.

The woman helped me to take a bath, scrubbing my back, washing my hair with her strong, gnarled hands. The grime of the canal left me in clouds. She dressed me in a warm, clean nightgown which hung over me like a potato sack.

Only when she had turned back the covers of a springy little bed did the tears come. I was wracked with sobs, all my pent emotion bursting its gates. I clung to the old woman whose name I didn't know, and I howled as she rocked me and sat right there until I was worn out and sinking into exhaustion.

"Try to sleep now, Sweet Pea."

I dried my heavy eyes. The woman's kindness and the hot

bath had drawn out much of my hurt like venom from a wound. Still, something bothered me, a sense of incompleteness. The source occurred to me as she was tucking the blankets under my chin: she never smiled. She was warm and real, but her eyes were sad.

My consciousness remained for a few minutes, even after my eyelids had sagged nearly shut. Floating in the comfort of the bed, I watched her wash herself in the water, then drop our shoes and all our mud-stained clothing into the tub. She paused only to remove something from the pocket of a garment, examine it briefly, then spread it near the fire to dry.

The sizzling of meat awoke me, its aroma filling the cozy room.

I sat up to find the lame tiger cat curled at my side, his warmth like a patch of sunlight on the thin quilt. Sunlight!—I had almost forgotten the feel of it. He opened one eye to regard me, yawned grandly.

"Stover likes you," said Willie, who was dangling a piece of yarn for the kittens to bat.

The woman was frying salted pork and spinach in a black skillet. She worked at the fireplace in one wall, her hands busy with spoons and turners. Soup bubbled in a pot, and potato cakes browned on a fender. It could have been the morning scene in a country house a hundred years ago, except that darkness reigned beyond the windows, its constancy broken only by the glowing trees.

Strips of moonlight showed between the planks of the roof, through chinks in the walls; the cottage wasn't built to withstand wind or rain, of which there were none. It would do the job of holding heat and keeping out most prowling animals.

"Feel better, Sweet Pea?"

"Yes," I said. "Thank you."

"My name's Clara, and this is my grandson William."

"Hello." I drew up my legs and tried not to disturb Stover. "My name is Bridget Anne, but my friends call me Dragonfly."

"Well, Dragonfly, we'd like to be your friends. Come and eat." She set her pans and pots on the square table in the room's center. There were two chairs, and she pushed the stool from my bedside to the table.

Without being asked, Willie hopped onto the stool, giving up his chair for me. I thanked him and told him I'd be happy to sit on the stool, but he said, "No, no!" in such a serious voice that I gave in.

There were only two beds in the cottage as well—it was one room, the single door leading outside. The room was well-furnished for daily existence, but there was a conspicuous absence of ornament, and none of the toys one would expect a boy of six to require. I noticed one more thing: amid all the neatness and order of the house, Clara's sweater had a button missing. It was the third one down from the top, the second one up from the bottom.

I ate hungrily. Clara and Willie chewed slowly, studying me. The cats rubbed against our legs, but none jumped to the tabletop.

When I slowed down, Clara poured tea. "How did you come to be in the canal, Dragonfly?"

I knew we wanted to hear each other's stories, so I settled back and told them mine.

They listened to every word, shaking their heads at Hain's cruelty, Clara reaching across to squeeze my hand when I spoke of Sylva. I had lost my energy for tale-telling by the time I recounted my flight from Languor House, so I left out the harrowing encounter in the machinery house—I said nothing of the misshapen children, but only that I had stepped into the open shaft and fallen into the canal.

"Do you know anything about the canals?" I asked at last. "I saw terrible things in the water."

Willie nodded soberly. "We know all about the canals. You're brave, Dragonfly."

"Thank you."

Clara removed her glasses. "The canals, Sweet Pea, are Samuel Hain's big, dirty project. The Gypsies have told us. It's not just water, you see; Samuel Hain makes them foul. He drops in murdered bodies, bones, the magical garbage from his house, the potions of his witches, and some things even the Gypsies don't know about, probably. Those waters are one big stew-pot."

"But what are they for?"

"It's what they *are*," Willie said. "Nightmare in its liquid form. The pump houses swallow the stuff, shoot it off through pipes under the ground."

"Pump houses?" I leaned forward. So *that* was the purpose of the metal buildings. "Where does the water go?"

Clara stoked the hearth. "Up through the caves, through frost and boneyards, under the swamps. He can open culverts and shafts to any town on Earth, just like he can get through any mirror." The fire threw shadows across her bulbish nose, glinted in her lenses.

So the men in black clothes, measuring our town, had been there to hook up Hain's pipes.

"He pokes holes in rusty valves," Clara continued. "Deep down in places where rats drown, in corners too tight for workmen from up there to squeeze; if they don't know what to look for—and they don't—they never see his connections."

"His canals feed into city water, and—" I was making connections of my own, and they chilled my blood. No fluoride or chlorine could take out what Hain put in. People gulped down his tainted water every day, completely unaware. Naturally bad tempers got worse; babies cried more, unable to talk about what they saw. People dreamed bad dreams. Wives nagged, and husbands snapped back. "When children can't sleep," I thought aloud, "what do they ask their parents to bring them?—*glasses of water!*"

"That's throwing oil on the fire," said Willie, far more serious than even I had been at age six.

I clenched my fists, my old passion rising again. "And Hain feeds! People are poisoned into dreaming and—"

My anger.

"Clara," I whispered, "if he can feel my dreams and strong emotions, he must have felt me just now. That means he knows where—"

But Clara assured me we were safe in this forest, the Numinous Wood. It was woven with Gypsy spells, which masked it from Hain's casual perceptions.

"Now it's your turn," I said. "Will you tell me how you came to Harvest Moon?"

12

PEA MUMMIES

IT had begun for them, too, in a funeral home—not Henry's. Willie had been five then; this was last October, a year before the trouble in our basement. They had been attending the visitation of Clara's sister, Lily, who had died of heart failure. Late in the evening, when nearly everyone had left, Clara was talking with Bill Shaver, the funeral director, and Willie's parents were on the front steps. Willie and his cousins were playing around in the back room, where family members sit and drink coffee. Just as their mothers called and the cousins left, Willie heard a noise, a *click* from a dark corner, behind a staircase.

He saw a door swinging open under the stairs, like a closet, with a light shining inside. The light, flickering and orange, filled him with dread. He turned to run, but a tall, grey person sprang from the door, crossed the room with a whisper of striped trousers, and seized Willie in an icy grip. A giant pair of scissors jingled at the man's side—Mr. Snicker.

Clara, coming to find Willie, looked through the door and saw a stairway stretching into the dark, saw a grasshopper-legged man with her grandson over his shoulder. Shouting for help, she dashed after him.

The funeral director, Bill Shaver, arriving at the doorway, seemed to look right through them all, though Snicker's torch flared brightly. Bill only stood and cocked his head, as if he heard faint sounds far away. He started down and vanished before Clara's eyes.

Bill Shaver's basement had looked normal to him. It meant that either Hain had some control over who could come into his realm, or he shut down his doorways quickly after using them. The funeral home made sense, too: Hain devoured sadness. Funeral homes, where people mourned, would be his ports of entry in every town.

Gazing into the fire's coals, I pondered Hain's plan of attack. His people had to eat—they could only bleed each other for so much. It seemed their population should be steadily decreasing, which made Project Nowhere urgent. Vampires could drain a little blood and leave their victims alive, but werewolves had to devour flesh—they preyed upon birds and wild beasts, too, but they could not resist the challenge of hunting villagers. The natives themselves were hard on each other, often inflicting death in their quest to extract hurt.

I considered the canals: whereas Hain stole children as a delicacy from the outside nearly every night, consumed their nourishing pain, I thought the real staple would have to come from the nightmares, the ill will produced with the water. The canals were the lifeblood of Harvest Moon.

It was a blessed relief to be thinking clearly again, free of the influence of Languor House. "The pump stations," I said. "We have to destroy them."

Clara and Willie looked dispirited. They saw no hope in fighting.

"What happened then?" I asked. "How did you get away from Mr. Snicker?"

The Gypsies, who wandered in bands throughout the forest, had rescued them. When Snicker snatched Willie, the scissor-man had been alone. Hain's people must have just opened up shop underneath Bill Shaver's, and Snicker had been looking things over. Clara, struggling not to lose sight of him and Willie, had seen them reach the bottom of the stairs, on the far edge of the wood from here. As Snicker was loading

Willie on board the wagon he had parked there, the Gypsies jumped from the bushes.

Telling me the story now, Clara smacked her fist into her palm. "The Gypsies' leader, Lurkwick—that's his name, just like the tree—tumbled old Scissors into a mud bog. The others fetched me down, and they tried to take us back, but a whole caravan of builders came up the road to expand the digging under Bill's. So we all dashed off and camped here and there."

The Gypsies had decided that their singing, drinking, and perpetual wandering was no lifestyle for the old woman and her grandson, so they had built this cottage. "They visit us," Clara explained, "bring us food and everything we need, and they're always keeping an eye out for a way to get us home."

CLARA and Willie needed the exercise of a good walk to raise their spirits, so I cajoled them into following me in a loop through the groves opposite the canal. We hiked along a trail that followed an overgrown gully. Tapestries of branch and moss drooped on all sides, the ground damp and spongy; already I had muddied both knees from slipping on the hill above the cottage. The farther we got from Hain's waters, the more prodigious the plant and animal life became. It was often difficult to distinguish flora from fauna; certain roping vines slithered away at our approach, veined leaves blinked filmy, hooded eyes, and one shape I had been sure was a squirrel turned out to be *growing* on a tree, sprouting conical fruits. Darning needle insects with luminous abdomens droned past our ears. Upturning a log soft as sodden cardboard, Willie showed me a fleet of snails whose translucent shells burned with a pale green fire. Once the sharp grey face of a fox appeared in the bushes, the cats all standing in stiff arches until it withdrew.

I asked about the glowing trees, which looked as if they came with reading lamps. Rubbery vines coiled around the trunks, and from their trumpet-like flowers, a soft radiance shone over the blossoms of the trees themselves. Clara repeated the Gypsies' explanation that the vines and trees were partners in the dark domain; the light cast by chemicals in the vines' flowers aided the trees' growth, and the vines, in turn, flourished on the magical waters brought up by deep-questing tree roots from the Abandon River.

Clara filled the lap of her skirt with dark amber berries the Gypsies had shown her. They were sweet, with a hint of dusty astringency; popping the tight skins with our teeth, Willie and I spit the oblong seeds into the ravine. We tried to outdo each other, aiming for forks or rotted openings in the trees—one of Willie's direct hits brought a furious chattering from the depths of a woody cave.

Hope was awakening in me for the first time since before my imprisonment at Fifty-two Pink Eye Street. "The Gypsies," I asked, "why are they helping you? Don't they come from Harvest Moon?"

"No," Clara said. "They're from outside. In their wagon trains, they drive in and out of dreams. They were here in the forest before Hain built Harvest Moon and closed their doors."

Willie bit into a sour berry, made a face and spit at least ten times.

"Will the Gypsies come back soon?" I asked.

"Before long, I expect." Clara had all she could carry, so we steered toward home.

"Good. We'll have to talk to them." I watched the moon, visible between the leaves in its sea of smoke. I had an idea for how to spend our time while we waited for the Gypsies, a way to build up our courage for what lay ahead. Thinking back over my handful of years, I remembered Uncle Henry's remedy, used when I would come to him, my eyes clouded with glimpses of the long corridor of the future: "In the meantime, we're going to tell stories."

"Stories," Willie whispered, keeping a stone in motion with his feet. "It's been so long since we've thought about stories."

"But we need them now." I felt an old familiar thrill in the pit of my stomach—the excitement of the movie theater when the recorded music is still playing, just before the house lights dim.

* * *

BACK in the cottage, I followed my ears and found a tarnished pocket watch on a shelf beside the stove. It was a man's lidded watch on a long chain, and calibrated regularly, not according to Harvest Moon time.

"From the Gypsies?" I asked, bringing it to the table. "May we use it in our game?"

Clara nodded, and I handed it to Willie. He looped the chain around his neck and clipped it, so that the watch hung like a pendant on his chest.

"Good," I said. "We will play for only twenty minutes, twice a day—once after breakfast, and once before bed—until the Gypsies come. If we discipline ourselves that way, Hain won't have time to find us, even if we make dream energy. We'll tell happy stories, to help us remember how good life is outside Harvest Moon."

Willie nodded emphatically. Clara sighed and shrugged.

And so for twenty minutes each "morning" and "evening"—as we anticipated our game, we began to recapture the feeling of day and night—we unlocked our memories and let the stories carry us far beyond the walls of the little cottage.

Willie's tales were the best. They were not tales, exactly; telling us what we could see, he would lead us on journeys. In our minds, in the flickering firelight, we visited the deep-sea gardens of the mermaids, we rode the back of a whale among the mountains of ice in the North Sea. We saw the sun again, felt its rays on our faces, and Clara was unhindered by her limp. She swung easily onto her white horse, clung to his mane as he galloped. My favorite trips were to a secret island floating in space, forever hidden by the shadow of the moon. Willie found a bridge there from the moon's dark back, and we discovered it was the Kingdom of Cats. He could understand them, and they told him that his black tom, Egor, was the prince of their realm; Egor had been lost in Harvest Moon when he was too young to remember, but they knew his face—and the sight of the fish-gardens there jogged Egor's memory. He regained his kingdom and was crowned with a sapphire crown. We were so caught up in the celebration that we nearly went over our twenty minutes, and had to come sliding back down a moonbeam at the last second.

All the cats came with us in our travels. Even Stover, the

crippled tiger tom, was able to scramble and pounce and run as fast as the others wherever we went.

Clara's stories were always of animals; she remembered old tales of clever animals who banded together to outwit robbers and defeat monsters. I liked the humility of her characters and the way they used their differing talents for the common good.

The Gypsies were many nights away, longer than usual, according to Clara. We lived for our forays; we thought of them throughout our days as we cooked and ate the dwindling foodstuffs, as we cleaned the cottage or walked in the woods. When we were not engaged in storytelling, we tried to keep our minds as quiet as possible, so as not to alert Hain. Keeping a quiet mind was no easy task for me and Willie in a forest so full of whispery ravines and things to discover. We unearthed rusty lanterns dropped who knows when by who knows whom; we found and brought home three more stray cats; and always we listened and watched for the Gypsies.

We took the lid, you see, off a well that normally stayed covered in Harvest Moon, and we drank from it. We were resisting Hain in a way that mattered.

Under one corner of the house was a sunken space that could hardly have been called a basement. It was accessed by a ladder and barely large enough to turn around in. Clara kept an extra washtub down there, and jars of the strange pickles and preserves brought by the Gypsies. As we resorted to eating even these, which tasted like unadulterated salt, Clara happened upon a packet of seeds.

They were tucked away at the back of a shelf which she reached only by standing on the upside-down washtub. What she felt with her groping hand to be a long-lost letter turned out to be a blank paper, folded carefully around a dozen spherical seeds, somewhat smaller than dried peas. "Pea Mummies," Clara called them when none of us could identify them as anything else. There was no apparent end to the curious stock left by the Gypsies.

Clara didn't hold out much hope for anything's growing from the Pea Mummies, but she planted them in a window box that she'd never used. A little firelight could reach it through the glass, and the glow of a luminous vine fell across it from the gable. Maybe it was this uncertain blending of lights that sparked the long-hidden life of the seeds—or perhaps, as Willie suggested, it was the sunlight from our expeditions that brought the seeds to life, for we gathered to tell our stories just inside the window.

Day by day we watched little golden shoots peek out of the soil; their progress became almost as great a preoccupation as our travels. Willie and I had a way of sensing in our sleep that the other was stirring, and each morning we hit the floor simultaneously, dashing to the window, elbowing each other for the best vantage. Within two weeks, the shoots became seedlings, and the seedlings became stalks. Delicate, coppery leaves unfolded, and buds formed, one at the top of each stem.

We were eating supper one night—pickles, potatoes, and cakes of flour and fish-powder—when we all heard a loud *pop!*

Willie dropped his fork.

Clara set down her tea cup, and we all exchanged mystified glances.

Pop!

This time, we could tell the sound came from the window. Stover perked his ears.

Poppity pop!

We were on our feet, tripping over our chairs. By the time we reached the window, the buds were popping like popcorn. When each bud popped, a shimmering flower hovered in its place. Every one bloomed in less than a minute—twelve breathtaking blossoms, three golden, three silver, three green, three transparent as crystal—and the center of every flower glowed a brilliant sapphire blue.

From then on our stories, bathed in the light of the Pea Mummies, grew ever more hopeful.

I could tell, however, that Willie missed his mother.

He spent hours and hours with the cats, "helping" them do things. I'd find him lifting them one by one onto the limb of a tree, where they squirmed and clambered over each other to climb higher or jump down. Only old Efya would sit patiently where he placed her, whirring steadily in her charcoal voice, her tail flicking slowly at the tip.

"What are you doing, Willie?" I'd ask.

"Helping the cats climb this tree."

He'd hold them on his knees, stroking their heads, feeding them, whispering to them. They were his comfort in the sunless stretches between meals, tales, and other chores. They followed him in a train when we walked in the woods, clustered lazily around him when he sat on the doorstep, and slept in a purring pile on the bed he now shared with his grandmother.

One evening I found Willie standing by the canal, his fingers paying out a jittering twine which was fastened around a yard-square piece of paneling, criss-cross, like a Christmas ribbon. Out on this raft were Efya, Stover, the two yellow-whites Wonder and Marvel, Egor, and the kitten Snowball. The newer strays had apparently not developed sufficient loyalty to Willie to go aboard; they were visible only as incredulous green eyes among the roots. The board caught the current, spun out from the bank, and slipped downstream, Willie scrambling along beside it, the cats a pack of hackles and flattened ears precisely in the middle of the raft.

I'd never known a cat to put up with anything it didn't expressly want to do, not a brushing, not being lifted, hardly even an unsolicited glance. But here were six cats allowing a boy to fly them like a kite in a dark and very wet river. When he'd reeled the boat in, when the cats had shot like six furry arrows into the weeds, I wound up his soggy twine and commented on what good friends the cats were to him.

He smiled his faraway smile. "They're Gypsy cats. Gypsy cats are smart. They know who to trust."

We were turning back toward the cottage when an uneasiness washed over me, a bony finger needling my spine. At the borders of my hearing, voices whispered words too soft to recognize. Whirling, I searched for who was speaking, stepping protectively closer to Willie.

A winged shape fluttered through the trees. I was accustomed to seeing the will-o'-the-wisps, the balls of luminescence that hovered up from the margins of the wood, where the canal probed tenebrous fingers into a bottomland livid with decay. For the merest second, I thought I saw a shadow pass across one of these spheres, obscuring its light—but when I squinted, there was nothing to see.

"I'm sorry," said Willie, tugging my sleeve. "I should have warned you." He held out his handkerchief. "It's the canal water. You don't have to *drink* it. It gives you the creeps even when you *touch* it."

My voice shook a little as I laughed, drying my fingers. We'd done no more than pull Willie's string from the canal. As quickly as it had come, the shuddery feeling was gone. I returned the handkerchief, and we called the cats, who appeared at once, sensing that the water games were done. Pattering over the black carpet, they followed Willie toward higher ground.

Yet as I glanced over my shoulder, something was there, closer than the bobbing globe of light. I sucked breath—it was really no more than a shadow, half-in, half-out of the greater blackness beneath a tree. An actual figure? A trick of the light? I couldn't look away, couldn't use my voice. When I thought my heart would burst, I found the impetus to run.

"How do you stand it?" I asked Willie later, when he was giving bowls of broth to the cats. "Touching that water when you play down there. Doesn't it scare you too much?"

He considered, helping Snowball find a place to wriggle in among the others around the bowl. "It's like seeing a snake. If you see it at a distance first, and walk up to look, it's okay—not like if it springs out at you. I know the canal is there, and what it does."

Willie was four years younger than me, but a lot braver.

AS in the house of the werewolf, I quickly lost track of the days. The friendship we three grew into was less intoxicating than the one with Sylva, yet more stable, a well-laid fire as opposed to an uncontrolled blaze.

The evening came at last when Clara asked me about the bedraggled scrap of paper she'd taken from my cloak's pocket. It was the story idea I'd written in Languor House. The letters had been blurred by their soaking in the canal, but they were mostly still legible, and my memory served to fill in those that were not.

"Read it to us, Dragonfly," said Clara. We had just returned from a short trip to the Kingdom of Cats, where nothing was happening at the moment. We had about twelve minutes left on Willie's watch.

"All right," I said, smoothing out the paper. "This is an idea I've had ever since I was smaller than Willie. It's only an idea, not a story."

Clearing my throat, I began to read.

"WHAT do they look like?

"Yes, let's see. They are about three inches tall. From head to foot, they are the color of the deep sea.

"They are born on a night of falling stars from the Silver Fruit of a tree in the middle of a desert. Their birthday is marvelous! A warm south wind shakes the Silver Fruit, and far and wide across the desert floats a sound like the jingling of hundreds of bells.

"Their food is the moon's dew. Their tails are for dangling them from the tree when they sleep. Their three-fingered hands are for joining with those of others in friendship.

"Until the day they leave on their journey, they do nothing but play, leaping from branch to branch, and they watch the moon. Their large ears can hear the lullabies of many thousands of years ago.

"One evening, most suddenly, they stop their laughter, and the first one simply begins to walk. And they all follow, hands joined, one by one. A quiet line of walkers in the dark desert—yes, it is the beginning of their journey. Where they go, no one knows.

"As for that, I do not even know their name. Shall we perhaps call their people 'the Star Shard'? They each have one yellow eye, and one blue; I have always thought this strange. And I wonder, with which of their eyes do they see truth?"

I finished, folding the paper. The stove crackled steadily, its warmth suffusing us.

For the first time, Clara was smiling. "A beautiful story, Sweet Pea."

"But a little sad," said Willie. "Why do they have to go away? It's sad, not knowing where they go."

Clara rose to tend the fire. "Not sad. Just unknown."

Together we gazed out over the flowers in our window box, out at the dark desert we must face. What chance did we have against our enemy? And yet, as I pulled the blankets up to my chin that night, I knew in my heart that, like Clara, I was ready.

Before I drifted off to sleep, I watched Clara, still awake by the fire. In the glowing circle of light, she sat with needle and thread. Her steady hands were sewing the missing button back on to her sweater.

13

MOON-O'-WAR

"**WE'RE** out of food, aren't we?"

I was helping Clara wash the wild potatoes she'd dug in the woods. Each one was the size of a marble.

"Just about, Sweet Pea. One more jar of pickles, and then all we've got is tea. Then we'll have to go berrying and rooting."

"Why don't the Gypsies come?"

"I don't know." She poked at the fire. "They've never been away this long. I'll bet they're up to something important. Maybe we'll be home in a little while."

Clara had seemed to awaken in the last several days, as if from a long sleep. The optimism she showed now, I guessed, was her natural personality, which had only been dimmed for a time. She hummed softly as she dropped the potatoes into the boiling kettle, stirred in an assortment of herbs.

"I hope the Gypsies are all right," said Willie. Standing at the window, he wound his watch, setting it by the chime of a distant tower clock. He had worked out a theory as to which Harvest Moon hours were which hours in our time. None of us, including Willie, cared whether he was right, so long as our system was different from Hain's.

"Lurkwick knows what he's doing, Sweet Pea."

I wiped the table and fidgeted with the cloth.

They *had* to come soon. Without them, or Mothkin and Singer, we didn't stand a chance. And the longer nothing was done, the more children were snatched through their mirrors, the more nightmares got pumped up into the world where night held only partial dominion. And the bigger, and bigger, and *bigger* Harvest Moon became. Willie and I could see wagons away on a hillside across the valleys—wagons hauling wood, hauling ghouls, hauling pipe.

Were they alive, those two strange men with whom I'd begun my adventures? I hardly dared to hope that they were alive, that even now they might be less than a mile away, combing the forest for me . . . No—if they were alive, I told myself, then their business was with the dark lords of this place. Perhaps they believed me dead, or still imprisoned. After all, they hadn't asked me to jump down the laundry chute. Certainly I couldn't expect that keeping track of me would be their first priority.

I paced the floor, absently pushed a broom. In a sense, I had turned my back on my friends—had I gone looking for *them?* What had I done with my freedom? Biting my lip, I stared into the darkness beyond the window.

"Come and eat." Clara set bowls on the table.

I flung the edges of my cloak over my shoulders to free my arms. "We've got to *do* something."

"That's right," agreed Clara, gently stirring Willie's tea. "And the something we've got to do is carry more water after supper—the ewer's nearly empty again."

She said grace, thanking God for our food, our health, our companionship (she included each of the cats by name), for our stories, and for the flowers which had grown in our window box. I peeped at these from the corner of my eye as she went on, waxing far more eloquent than she usually did in her table prayers.

The cats purred and threaded in and out among our ankles. With the crackle and fragrance of knotted briar, the stove warmed us. Behind the glass, the Gypsy flowers sent their perfumes into the deep places. To my eyes, they were like twelve tiny candles left burning to warm all the world's night.

When the dishes were washed in the last of the water,

Willie and I made our ten trips to the spring a short way into the woods. The Gypsies had declared this water pure, for it came from outside Hain's territory. We carried the bucket sloshing between us, emptied it again and again into the cottage ewer. I liked the crystalline breath of the spring, so cold it made steam even in chilly air.

Willie smiled across the bucket at me, and my eyes misted with a pang of affection. His fingers on the bucket handle looked so thin the darkness might freeze and break them off. I had always been the smallest in the circles of my life, a child among the powerful. Here was someone who seemed comforted by my experience.

THAT was the night the moon moved.

We filled the ewer, told some stories, took our baths, and made ready for bed. Inspired by Clara, I spent longer than usual at my prayers. The cats were curled like round pillows all over Willie's bed, and the fire had burned low. Clara sat just beside it in her nightgown, her needle busily mending a rip in Willie's yellow shirt.

"I've got a rip, too, in the knee of my jeans," I said dreamily, crawling into bed. "But don't worry, I'll sew it tomorrow—I want the practice." Clara had taught me to sew properly at that table before the stove. My mother never sewed things—that was Mrs. Cain's job, and she did not encourage spectators. So the pleasure of teaching me fell to Clara, and it was my pleasure to learn.

Just before I fell asleep, I was thinking of Clara's suggestion that we work together and make a dress for me, if the Gypsies would be kind enough to bring us some cloth.

Into my warm sleeping mind, a nightmare dropped. Like a black icicle, it skewered me into shrieking wakefulness—the picture of the half-seen shape in the woods. At my outburst, the cats sprang spitting and stiff-legged in all directions, and Willie tumbled to the floor with a scream. Clara, tangled in bedclothes, was a mass of thrashing arms and legs.

The figure from my dream loomed up before me, cowled and wraithlike, waiting. Still howling, I struck out with my feet, snatched my pillow, hurled it at the elongated nightmare, the faceless *thing*.

Flooff! The pillow struck its sunken chest. It expelled a rustling hiss of crypt-scented breath and flattened itself, dropping to the floor, spreading like a manta of death.

The cats rebounded, their wire-brush hackles doubling their sizes.

"WHAT?" cried Willie, "WHAT?"

I seized a chair, spun to face the oil-pool demon.

Shuffling free of the nightmare, my mind began to clear. In another second, I recognized the apparition I'd struck down: it was Mothkin's black cloak, which always hung on a peg opposite my bed. It lay lifeless and empty at my feet.

Clara was free of covers, getting to her feet.

I stood trembling, bathed in sudden perspiration. A frigid draft from nowhere lifted the cloak's hem, flapped it against the pillow.

The cats turned this way and that, perfect Hallowe'en cats, their backs arched. Glaring into every corner, they sensed danger but could not locate it.

Suddenly, Willie gasped and pointed at the window.

Amber rays of moonlight fell on the flowers there. As we watched, their slender shadows pivoted, the light growing brighter. Clara's shadow, too, swung over the bed, across the floor.

My whole body was shaking. Slowly I stooped, grabbed my cloak, and threw it over my shoulders. Straightening, I took a step toward the window.

"What's happening?" asked Willie, moving with me.

As we neared the glass, a tremendous sound shook the house, a rushing, the *snort* of a monstrous hog. We froze, clutching each other for support.

Clara put on her glasses, drew her faded sweater over her nightgown. She, too, was shivering. In the silence after the airy noise, the forest, even the settling of the cottage was utterly still. Only the molten light poured in, increasing.

Willie and I reached the window a step ahead of Clara. The clearing was brighter than any place I'd seen since leaving sunlight behind. Trunks glistened damp and shocked, every subtle crack of their bark unveiled, the candles of the lurk-wick trees paling to nothing. Shadows flitted helter-skelter in the grass, mice and lizards running for their lives.

We tilted back our heads.

The moon filled all the sky. We fell back from the huge-ness, the orangeness descending on our cottage. As it dropped, its surface blushing brilliance, coughing smoke through its skin, it spun slowly, like a gigantic world globe. Seen this close, the surface was a translucent membrane, pit-ted, scratched. It rotated, and a vague gout of fire glowed from deep within—and with the flash, another titanic *snort* rattled the window.

We squinted as a black triangle moved into view, stark against the glare, a shape three stories high on the moon's skin. And something beneath the triangle, a jagged line . . .

A face. A jack-o'-lantern face.

The obscene moon grinned down at our window, the mouth as long as a canal. Fire belched constantly in its bowels, its acrid smell flooding the glade. Our cottage was a matchbox beneath the moon's nose. I thought I could see pulsations un-der the face, black, swollen veins—and wiggling movements, as if all the moon might be full of writhing larvae, half-formed insects, embryonic spiders. Did Samuel Hain send it down on us—*to burst it over our heads?* Imagining, *feeling* myself buried alive under tons of whatever jittered in the moon, I sank to my knees.

Something burst, indeed, but it wasn't the moon; it was the door.

Boards splintered, flying asunder. The knob rolled around me in a wobbly circle. There, in the moon's bloodlight, was Eagerly Meagerly, his face dry as a hardened peel, rabid with hunger.

"TRICK OR TREAT!" roared a voice outside. The voice was Hain's; his bellowing laughter filled the clearing.

Meagerly lunged forward, a knife glinting in his hand. As he crossed the floor, two shapes assailed him, one sizzling up each of his legs, faster than thought. Wonder and Marvel, the two haze-colored tabbies, climbed his flapping coat, went like meteors for his face. They were defending us—defending Willie—with their lives.

I caught Willie in my arms, tried to cover his eyes.

The knife flashed.

Marvel landed with a horrible *flop* at our feet. Wonder was flung over our heads, shattered the window, her maimed body vanishing into the yard. I felt Willie slide from my arms as Meagerly dragged his sleeve over his features. He bought his intrusion dearly—long ago, Sylva's grandfather had taken his scalp. Now two heroic cats had taken most of his face. With a gurgling hack, he spit from between his teeth Wonder's severed tail.

I glimpsed a flash of red, of silver in the doorway. Hain was strutting to and fro in the yard, swinging his arms with delight.

Willie cradled Marvel in his lap. Clara gripped the foot of the bed for support. Before I could stoop to touch him, Willie threw himself at Meagerly. He kicked and punched, a blur of pummeling fists, his voice an implicating siren.

I sprang after him, my gaze fixed on the knife.

But it only hovered in the air. With his free hand, Meagerly lifted Willie off the floor, dangled him harmlessly at arm's length.

"You put him down!" ordered Clara, advancing.

I looked up into the mangled face, wondering what Meagerly would do—certain that if I moved, he would use the knife on Willie.

There was a *thump* on the roof—then another. Footsteps scrabbled along the peak, down the boards. Hain's voice drifted in from the side yard. "Santa Claus is coming!"

Meagerly turned, still bearing Willie aloft, and strode out the ruined door. I followed, not daring to breathe, Clara fairly hopping with indignation. Around us the cats followed their boy to the last.

Hain's soldiers filled the clearing, swords in their hands. They clustered funerarily, wasted faces agrimace, doffing their silk hats. A small army of them had come—slavering werewolves barely in check, horsemen, and wagon teams; an elite gaggle of vampires, engaged in whispered conversation among themselves at one edge of the glade; and the indescribable citizenry of Harvest Moon, clad like grave-diggers, bearing their lanterns in fish-chill fingers. I recognized the frost-haired man I'd seen in the orchards after our flight from the glassworks. An owl screeched in the trees. Horses and Untowards stamped, smelling of labor and lamp-smudge.

Out in the center of it all pranced the ringmaster, Samuel Hain. Resplendent in his tailed coat, he soaked in the moonlight, flashed his teeth, relished the whole of his orchestration. At their first clear sight of him, the cats spat, showed their fangs. Hain lowered his eyes to regard them, and they prudently disappeared into the bushes. I could sense them still there, torn between loyalty and terror, but Hain and his minions took no further notice of them.

He examined Willie as one might a dangling chicken in the market. Raising his eyebrows, he poked a finger at Willie's stomach, clucked his tongue. "Frail Boy." Willie hung motionless now, exhausted, returning his stare.

Clara marched toward him, her hair floating, shoulders high. I hurried to keep pace, consumed with my own anger—I saw no reason to reserve my emotions now; he knew where we were. Clenching my hands to stop their trembling, I looked again into that age-scarred, grinning face.

He spread his arms in a fatherly greeting. "Madam!" he said to Clara. "I have come to extend a welcome, for we've not been intro—"

Her hand was flying.

As he caught it, held the wrist, her bony fingers flexing before his eyes, I was again impressed with his catlike dexterity.

Allowing his face to harden into a thing of barely-covered bone, he pinned her fingers, kissed the back of her hand, and murmured, "Gently, Madam. Old . . . bones . . . break."

"Beast," whispered Clara. "You know your end."

"My end?" He laughed harshly, seized her other wrist and held her as if to dance. With a hand at the base of her throat, he shoved her back into the arms of the frost-haired man.

Clara protested with threats paraphrased from the Book of Revelation. I heard the Frost Man mutter that he was an expert at removing tongues; perhaps she figured that she might use her tongue to greater advantage later, for she fell silent.

As if noticing me for the first time, Hain stooped and rested his palms on his knees. "Dragonfly! So this is where you have been! When you failed to answer my invitation, I wondered what could possibly be more interesting than my Tenebrificium."

I wanted to hit and kick him—all the while Clara had faced him, I pictured myself attacking with teeth, knees, and elbows—but he had a power that shone from him, a chill aurora that froze my nerves, left my arms hanging like wood. That Clara had been able to strike at him was an indication of the concealed strength of her will.

"Clara is right," I said as evenly as possible. "You will be stopped."

The smile gone from his face, he towered over me, fists on his hips, like a schoolmaster near the end of his patience. "Child, you are accustomed to the ways of kindly old men. I have given you every opportunity to accept me as such. Now playing is over."

At his command, two shrunken-faced servants leapt upon me and held my arms as he glowered down his nose. "Bring their clothes," he said, and three more of the soldiers vanished into the cottage.

Spun by my captors, I found myself staring upward into the wonder of the moon, the moon of the Harvest, which waited above the cottage. There of course was Mr. Snicker, crouched like a grasshopper on the peak of the roof. Around him were four assistants holding ropes that stretched down from iron rings on the moon's lowest meridian. The great sphere's glow lit every twig, every cobweb, every huddled nest in the treetops. I could see now that the globe's skin was sewn of stretched rectangles, rippling and nearly transparent, shiny as silk but porous as gauze. Still the tubes twisted within, dark arterial lines—and the repulsive spidery shapes that climbed and labored were men—hundreds of men in the moon!

A square flap hung open on the bottom, from which a circular iron stairway descended to the cottage roof. Two black-garbed men were coming down carrying barrels on their shoulders, and two more, higher on the stairs, were just passing into the flickering hatchway. Smoke poured out from the interior, with a hot wind that made my eyes water.

Steadying his top hat against the gale, Mr. Snicker slid a wooden ladder down along the side of the house, and Hain scrambled up. He stood on the peak, hair and coattails whipping.

I was dumped over a bony shoulder and carried up next. Meagerly followed just below me, the mask of his face rising like a leprous moon. Blood soaked his collar, spattered his sleeves, his bulbous eyes rolling right and left; he wore nightmare like an autumn fashion. Next came the Frost Man, negotiating the ladder under Clara's full weight. "If you squirm, Granny," I heard him growl, "my landing on top of you will be the *least* of your woes." Behind them, our clothes were hoisted in a sack. Several of the ground crew climbed up and passed us on the roof, ascended the stairway. "Cast off," said Hain, and the four men released their ropes. The crowd dispersed, wagons pulling away into the night, and with a prolonged groan, the moon twisted overhead; the stairway shifted several inches, its iron coasters gouging furrows into the roof. The wooden ladder was borne up through the flap. Leaves shivered in the smoky draft.

Crowding onto the lower tiers of the stairway, the men of Harvest Moon set us down, told us to hold on tight and watch. Meagerly loomed in the hatch above, and Hain held the banister cables at the bottom of the stairs, his cloak in wild array.

Only Snicker remained on the roof. He stood, slowly unfolding his spindly limbs. Like a conductor, he checked his watch, the down-rush of air fanning his cigar, driving sparks from its tip. He blew a long, blue cloud from a corner of his mouth.

Glancing past us, up into the mouth of the moon, Hain turned on the lowest step. He raised his arm, opened his fist as if throwing Snicker a handful of flowers.

Snicker squatted, taking the cigar from his teeth, and touched it to the end of a fuse. In the coil at his feet, it branched into four, ran to each of four barrels positioned at the corners of the roof. As Hain stepped aside, letting him mount the stairs, the spark ran in spirals and S-curves over the roof.

The moon lurched, tipped up and back, belched fumes, and yanked us into the sky. Hissing over the planks, the four mooring ropes were pulled in. We slipped sideways, over the lurkwick, over a fringe of the forest. My stomach rolled like the landscape, and I clung to a cable, hair streaming across my eyes. Pushing it behind my ear, I saw a clear hilltop, washed in our light as we passed. We were still near the ground, and with a gasp I made out the shapes of the cats who clustered there, tails lashing. They were ours, all of them, watching our progress with the green eyes that have traced the courses of harvest moons for uncounted thousands of years.

A teardrop fell sparkling away from me on the bellows wind as I gathered my cloak around my neck and tried to tell the cats with my eyes what I wished for them, the unhomed.

Willie saw them too, and the light in his face made me turn back, squint into the increasing distance. Then I saw that the tabby Wonder was with them—Wonder was alive! Her tail was gone, one ear mangled from her battle, but she was alive.

That thought filled my mind as we rode into the vaults of night, as the grinning moon lifted us away, as the House of Peace was forever consumed in a blossom of fire. Our Gypsy flowers, which had given us hope, were destroyed.

But Wonder was still alive.

14

THE JOLLY JACK

THE moon rose, buoyed up by its gouting internal flame. Oily smoke bled through the pores of its skin, fanned behind us in a filthy wake over the town. Hain stood for a long time on the lowest step, hands gripping the cables, like a diver on a high platform. The monstrous moon-craft (for it *was* a ship, a hot-air balloon on a grand scale) passed like a torch over his domain—a vast, roving eye, peering into every dark corner.

Hain called to us over the rush of air. "Welcome aboard my fine ship *Jolly Jack!* First, let's see the sights—then a tour of *Jack*'s insides!" Eagerly Meagerly vanished inside the craft.

The furnace bag creaked as it twisted, cables twanging behind the veil of orange skin. Whereas the air that whistled through our stairway was biting and clear, the bag itself looked like a tremendous organ for the production of smoke and firelight. I felt as if I were a passenger on a dying star. Ordering us to hang onto the central iron pole of the stairs, our chalk-faced guards kept hands on our shoulders, hands that numbed our flesh like ice.

We rode in widening circles over the wooded mountainside, the misty ravines. Bluish patches of fog drifted in block-long shreds over the forest, sometimes parting before the wandering moon, sometimes stealing soundlessly in from the side or behind; whoever piloted the craft took pains to avoid these seeping clouds. The rigidity of Hain's shoulders suggested an inner tension as he scanned the ground, as he eyed the vapors groping effervescent fingers toward the *Jolly Jack*.

Willie sat two steps above me, his knees against my back. Feeling with my hand, I found his ankle, squeezed and held it. All three of us were barefoot.

Signalling to someone at the top of the stairs, Hain brought the ship to hover over a bowl-shaped depression in the trees. He studied it intently as Snicker stepped around us to enter the hatchway.

The scissor-man emerged with two more of the explosives kegs, one under each arm. Setting one down on the step, he lit the other's fuse.

"What are you doing, Samuel Hain?" asked Clara.

"'Nother housewarming, Granny," answered the Frost Man.

Snicker aimed where Hain pointed. With a grunt, he tipped the keg, sending it tumbling down into the sea of branches. Beneath the canopy of leaves, the barrel went off like earthbound lightning. Trunks flew apart; branches hurricaned upward with a *boom* that echoed in a complete circle around the horizons.

"Whose house?" Clara's voice filtered down the breeze from her position behind the Frost Man and Willie, nearest the top.

"Gypsy camp," said Hain, trying to survey the damage.

Snicker, too, gripped his hat and squinted into the darkness. Grey smoke rose from a new clearing, and not far away, I could now see the bobbing firelight that had drawn Hain's attention.

"There they are!" Hain half-turned, rotating his wrist in a signal to his pilot. "Now we've got them."

Snicker backed up a step, turned to retrieve his second bomb. His hoarse, wordless cry snapped my head around.

Looking up sideways between his knees, I barely glimpsed what had happened. The fuse on the barrel was alight, sizzling like bacon in a pan. It had five inches to go before it reached the hole in the lid.

Hain whirled, eyes blazing.

Willie shrieked, scrambled to his knees.

"Fire in the hole!" said Clara, slipping her box of kitchen matches, Gypsy matches, back into the pocket of her sweater.

There was no time. Snicker lunged for the keg. The Frost Man's expression was murderous as he rose over Clara. "You," he breathed. He was moving in to help Mr. Snicker dispose of the bomb when Snicker turned.

Clearly, the scissor-man hadn't expected anyone to be standing immediately behind him in the aperture between two cables, in the quickest avenue for getting rid of his hot potato. I don't think he even saw the black-cloaked man until he'd slammed a thirty-pound barrel into his chest.

There was a wheeze of expelled breath, the snapping of bone—and the burning fuse disappeared inside the keg. Under its weight, the Frost Man sagged like a boxer into the cables, his arms wide, head back. His feet came up, and he somersaulted into space.

The barrel detonated so close beneath us that the stairs shook, our cloaks rose over our faces, a cable snapped loose from its grommet. The balloon rolled in a gaseous upswelling, twirling our stairway in sick circles through a sky instantaneously brighter than daylight. A stench of vile chemicals spread on the buffeting wind, so foul it made us cough.

The good news for the Frost Man was that he fell clear of the barrel, and was as far to one side of it when it exploded as we were above it; the bad news was that it was perhaps two hundred feet to the treetops below. I'd thought Mr. Snicker was pale before, but now, with shoulders heaving, he was whiter still.

Even Clara was aghast at what had become of her interference. Hands over her mouth, she hugged the pole. Willie pressed himself against her. In a daze, I watched the cables swing, one like a strand of hair out of place, as the moon-craft slowly righted itself. The guard beside me looked from face to face, his neck, his tendon-strung jaw quivering beneath a paucity of flesh. Advancing on Clara, Mr. Snicker reached for the scissors jangling at his side.

"No," said Hain. He had been peering down into the smoke, motionless save for the flapping of his clothing. Now he looked up with a blank face—not blank with shock, I thought, judging by the sparks in his eyes—but masterfully restrained.

Snicker hesitated.

"Just take her matches, and do nothing."

Hain leaned back on a cable, gave a signal, and the *Jolly Jack* began to rise in a lethargic spin. The lights below us had winked out after the first warning blast, the Gypsies doubtless scattering into impenetrable thickets; I don't think even Hain was sure where they'd been.

Clara's lips moved, her eyes glazed—all I heard was her repeated phrase, "I killed that man."

"*Snicker* did, Grandma," said Willie, but she kept shaking her head.

I tried to comfort her. "Clara—"

"Silence," growled Snicker.

THE canals, viscous and littered with deadfalls, reflected our image as we glided over random punts and the somber pump houses. A shudder passed through me as I recalled what lurked behind those featureless grey walls.

Hain's back was toward us, regal and aloof as he surveyed his waterways. There were miles and miles of them, far more than I had guessed; they branched out from beneath the High Horse and ran far afield in loops and side channels to exit Harvest Moon in all directions. From our altitude huge pipes were also visible, rising from the sluggish waters to the walls of the cavern.

Coming about, we were able to see to the very extremities of the place, the great slopes up into darkness, the mazes of stairs, the jumbled piles of rotting brick and detritus. So bright was the light we cast that I imagined I could nearly make out the stairs leading to the crack where Eagerly Meagerly kept his prisoners. Carts and wagons raced like toys in the shadowy streets.

We banked, moving toward the town proper. As we rounded a shoulder of the mountain, I located the deep-cut course of the River Abandon, the moon-mad waters charging away into a dim region *beyond* the mountain of the Horse. My impression was of the endlessness of the deep places, the receding and receding of stony vaults. I saw mystery written in that nether cavern, mystery of which Harvest Moon, with all its peculiarities, was only the porch, the first well-lighted train platform. Even at this distance, the Abandon called to me; I felt its strange, seductive voice beneath my skin.

Hain rode his cruiser over the town, and his subjects were duly awed. They turned out in the yards, the alleys, crowded on the widows' walks, gazed solemnly upward. Wagons pulled up in the shifting light, drivers and passengers poking faces from gauzed cabs, from beneath silk hat or glittering pince-nez. Stalking vampire and fleeing victim alike paused in the streets, werewolves rested red-mouthed over their feasts, ghouls hopping the fences stopped to mark their master's passage. Scarecrows hung at attention; pumpkins shone like buttons on the bulging velvet breast of the ground. Owls stood in round-eyed salute.

Hain took it all in, the frozen tableau of smoky revelry, of brawling, biting, and drunkenness. He stretched loving arms toward the gleaming Horse, as if to cup its muzzle across the miles. Then he raised his hands over the dark gardens, his voice coming gentle and contented to our ears:

> " ' "There is a noise of war in the camp."
> 'But he said: "It is not the voice of those
>   Who shout in victory, nor is it the voice
> Of those who cry out in defeat,
>   But the voice of those who sing that I hear." ' "

We swung over the garden district, alight with the lurk-wicks, the lampvines, the candle creepers. My eyes stung with the memory of my only love, buried at the foot of a tree.

Now the jets of flame above our heads were less frequent, and the balloon settled lower. We passed the bustle of Pink Eye Street, where the burned-out glassworks had been erased by new construction; I could not even tell where it had stood. Details of the planked and shingled rooftops became clear, children halting the Game to gawk from the curbs of leaf-strewn pools. Skimming over orchards, we crossed the river, where the skeletal guards seemed not to have stirred since last they turned their heads to watch me enter the city of nightmares. Moonlight flared across the cavern walls in front, illumined the arches. Our stairway was nearly dragging the ground, and although I could see the main corridor yawning dead ahead, the ascent that led to the funeral home, I knew that escape would be impossible; not only had my guard seized my arm again, but a platoon of Hain's men awaited us on a mound of crumbling masonry.

As the moon drifted to a stop just short of the stone wall, a detachment scrambled down the slope, their boots striking up dust. Four of them caught the lowering ropes, steadied the craft. Black armor flashed beneath their robes. Firepots blazed on the seats of wagons among the stones nearby.

Before we knew he had returned, Eagerly Meagerly plucked Willie from the steps and held him by the collar of his pajamas. In his other hand, he held a small bag; I recognized Willie's yellow shirt bulging from the bag's neck.

The color drained from our three faces simultaneously.

Snicker anticipated our movements; as Clara struggled to stand, he yanked her arms behind her. My own guard had his knife out, held it before my throat.

"I'd guess your supper will be especially bitter, young man," chuckled Hain, "because your kittycats made a nasty first impression on Mr. Meagerly."

I wish I could have shown Willie courage in my eyes as he passed me, anything but the look of devastation I know was there. The knife was between our faces, and all I could do was form his name with my lips.

"NOOOO!" he screamed, stretching his fingers toward us as he was carried down the steps.

Meagerly had bandaged his face in the body of the craft, and now he was a gruesome Hollywood mummy, all oozing blood, loose ribbons, and staring eyes. Willie punched at the slouch hat, grappled the stained lapels, and Meagerly wrenched one arm painfully behind his back.

"A piece of advice," purred Hain, thrusting a finger at Willie's nose. "Don't invite retribution upon yourself. Someday we'll be friends, my boy! Think of that!" He trotted along beside Meagerly, stroking Willie's forehead. "When I'm through with these 'friends' of yours, they won't even remember that you existed!"

"Don't listen, Willie!" yelled Clara, before Snicker's hand clamped her mouth shut.

I ignored the shining knife. To shut my mouth, my guard would have to put it down—or else cut me with it. His other arm was busy holding both of mine. "I LOVE YOU, WILLIE!"

"It's all your fault that you're here, Willie!" cried Hain into Willie's ear. "Your marvelous mind makes us strong! Your delightful child's mind called us to your little house in the woods! Your grandmother and your little friend would still be there if it weren't for you!"

"IT'S NOT TRUE, WILLIE! HE WANTS YOU TO SUFFER!"

The guard crushed the air out of me; I fell back, gagging.

"Learn to love *me,* Willie," breathed Hain, blowing Willie a kiss. "Be my dear child—this is your home, forever and ever!" Giggling, he strode back to the ladder, motioned for dust-off. The guard dropped me to the steps, where I curled up to nurse my bruised ribs. Snicker blew a cheery smoke ring, and the balloon roared.

Meagerly became a tiny speck, working his way up the rubble pile with a boy under his arm.

Hain licked Willie's tears from his fingers. He was feeding—the ground crew, the moon crew, every denizen of the dark dance—they were all feeding their inhuman hearts with the pain of three mortals. I understood why Hain had allowed no punishment of Clara for lighting the keg; he'd wanted her safe and whole for this moment. Snicker and the guard would not let me weep on her shoulder, would not let her weep on mine. But weep is what we both did.

The moon climbed again, and with a grinding of sprockets and chains, the circular stairway was hoisted into its belly.

I had seen pictures of hot-air balloons; I had even seen the real things. There was a balloon club in the next town. Henry and I had watched the members inflating their giant craft on a school ground—one had landed in the millet field on an autumn morning three or four years ago. The sight of that snorting monster, descending into the field like an enormous lightbulb ablaze with color, was something I would not soon forget; but the ship in which I now found myself made that other seem like a primitive toy.

First of all, ordinary balloons dangled a basket to which the crew and passengers were limited in their movements. The *Jolly Jack*'s retractable stairway was only the beginning; nine-tenths of the space for the crew was within the bag itself. The source of the ship's fiery power was an engine in the shape of a brass dragon about twenty feet long, which hung suspended from cables at the center of the cavity, the grotesque face behind that of the jack-o'-lantern painted on the outside. A myriad of hoses connecting at the dragon's belly and throat ran to openings in a transparent inner bag, supported by a skeleton of wooden beams. The hoses distributed the hot air from the engine to the various parts of the gas bag and to its outside, for steering. A lighter, spherical cage of reedlike slats lay just beneath the outer skin, and to this cage was anchored a second transparent "tent." Between the silky membranes was a space of cooler air traversed by hoses, decks, and cables; this interlying area was for the crew. By a series of ladders, one could climb from beneath the dragon, where we entered, up between swaying curtained walls, past platform after platform of winches, pulleys, and weapons racks, to the "North Pole" of the moon, where iron rings held the moon stationary over the town when it was not in flight. Three exhaust vents near the bottom expelled hot air to control the ascent and descent. In this way, the *Jolly Jack* was a globe within four more globes, counting all the skins and skeletons.

Our avenue of entry, through which the stairway was raised, was directly into the crew space; at the "South Pole," this layer penetrated the hotter shell to the outer skin, so that passengers went in and out through a heat-sealed tunnel; the hatch could be left standing open with no loss of the hot air needed to make the moon rise.

The gleaming brass figure overhead, a constant brilliance spewing from its jaws, was the chief source of light, the orange Hallowe'en-light which had shone through the windows of the glassworks, into the rose-garden, over the sprouting Pea Mummies. It hurt my eyes to look into the leaping fire. Holding my breath, I tipped my head to peer up at the hazy outlines of crewmen high in the sphere. Behind two layers of the insulating cloth, their voices and the sounds of their tasks were lost in the steady rush of the flames.

Our stairway jolted to a stop beside a wooden deck, and Hain ushered us into the hold. Crewmen clipped chains over the cylindrical cage of the stairway to stop its swing while others closed the flap in the outer covering. We stepped around more barrels—presumably explosives—and rolls of rope ladder, crates, tools, and wooden ladders. Steadying himself by gripping taut cables, hand after hand, Hain led us to a ladder. "Come and see the wheelhouse!"

Clara scowled, her eyes puffy and red. "I'm not climbing up there."

Hain appraised her and shrugged. "Very well. Sit here, then. Come along, Dragonfly."

I hurried to Clara's side. A guard had fairly shoved her to a sitting position atop a hawser. My anguish over Willie had hardened into anger. "I don't want to see your wheelhouse."

Hain sighed, hands on his hips, and looked at the floor. "Dragonfly, Dragonfly. Such choices are not yours to make. When will you learn that? You will come, because that is my will." His eyes began to blaze, widening slightly. I tried to look away, but was trapped—even as I hadn't been able to strike him, now I was unable to disobey. I retreated a step, and the eyes pursued me; my vision became a swimming fog that permitted nothing but the eyes. It was beyond hypnotism, beyond the rumored mesmerizing potency of a snake's stare—what paralyzed my knees, constricted my throat was a glimpse of something *behind* the bulging eyes, something *within*. The pupils narrowed to slits, the irises altered their shape. The eyes of predators—the big cats, wolves—are devoid of passion; but these were windows into a consciousness that seethed with hunger, fury—and an unquestionable torment—though all I felt as a ten-year-old girl was that I would faint with loathing and terror. I knew then that Samuel Hain was a Monster; not in the sense of a thoroughly evil *man,* but a true Monster, such as have lain in swamps, in echoing caves, in the dismal places of the Earth since the beginning of time. I heard his voice sigh—the desolate sound of wind in a desert of poisoned trees—and I had the horrible feeling that I would die if he didn't look away.

Perhaps sensing this, he blinked, turned, and I dropped against Clara. As his towering, red-cloaked back materialized from the dark mist of my sight, I understood the agony of that sigh: for children alone burned with a flame of life, a passion equal to his own—only children spun kingdoms and phantoms from the webs of their dreams. Children were the believers, the imaginers, who provided him with life in the elixirs of their fears and visions, and whom he sought after—year after year—with a devotion like that born of love. Yet children could never be more to him than food, for no child could regard him with anything but revulsion; none would willingly stay at his side and dream for him, weaving jewels of cold beauty into his empire. I guessed I was not the first dreamer he'd tried to win over. I covered my face.

"Come, Dragonfly," he called.

I followed, drawn by the same power he used to harness such elemental forces of evil as Meagerly. He had given me suggestions and invitations before; now that he commanded, I could only stumble along in his wake, my head ringing and numb. Without looking back at Clara, I climbed the ladders.

WHAT Hain called the "wheelhouse" wasn't a house at all; it was a chair of polished wood carved with glowering faces, its legs shaped to resemble four claws. Set on a broad deck high in the sphere opposite the painted face, above and behind the dragon, it commanded a view of most of the ship's interior. At this height, about a quarter of the way from the top of the moon, we could see the crew arrayed below us; there seemed little for them to do but await orders, as the ship virtually flew itself.

Before the chair was an old-fashioned ship's steering wheel, which a black-bearded pilot offered to Hain. Billowing on a hot draft from the permeable inner veil was a black flag patterned after the traditional pirates' Jolly Roger; this one had an orange jack-o'-lantern grinning maniacally over crossed orange bones. The pilot stood at attention to the rear of the platform as Hain seated himself in the chair, took the wheel.

As a child, I did not question the steering and propulsion of the *Jolly Jack;* I might well have wondered at the absence of external fins, a rudder, or the propellers necessary to drive a dirigible. In the relative windlessness of Harvest Moon, navigation was accomplished merely by expelling hot air in the direction opposite the desired course. Hain spun the wheel to the left, and somewhere in the hidden valving of the dragon, the proper hoses were opened in series, causing the ship to veer to the left.

"New bearing Gypsum one-five," called a crewman ahead and to the left. "Slag Dome nine-three-zero, Chief City one-three-five."

I saw about ten crew members positioned at our level around the entire curvature of the balloon. Each man perched on a high stool set in an alcove off the main deck; these extensions stretched the lining of the inhabitable layer of the ship through the outer hot bag to the surface. Thus, these crewmen could peer out through flaps to monitor the moon's progress. A duplicate set of such stations ringed the craft below the equator for use when the balloon was near the ground, when the swell would block vision from the upper vents.

"They call out landmarks," explained Hain, "and I know where we are." He smiled, and for that moment, as he sat calmly in profile, his hands resting on the wheel, it was almost possible to forget what he was; just then, he might have been a kindly old riverboat captain, showing his granddaughter the tricks of his trade. His sloping brow, his cheekbones looked brittle in the flickering light.

"Actually," he confided, "the pilot's seat is the most boring in the house. You can't see anything!" Half-turning, he stretched out a grey hand. "Would you . . . like to try it, Dragonfly?"

His impeccable hair gleamed like chrome, his face weary, shriveled. Still, there was the memory of what I had seen in his eyes. Swallowing hard, I shook my head.

Then came his old, sad smile. How old was he? I wondered. Henry's age? Clara's? What a different path he had followed from theirs, even considering that he came from another world, another plane of existence. Showing me this fragility, I reasoned, was the next in his bag of tricks—I dare not be deceived.

A guard called from a rear viewport, "Slag Dome three-nought-nought."

Easing the wheel to the right, Hain waited for a report from the fore: "New bearing, Tenebrificium dead on, up seven-four!"

"Boneyard crew!" ordered Hain, adjusting the angle of ascent.

The lower guiding team jogged to their positions around the decks, and others climbed past us to access hatches above.

"Horse one-one!" A member of the upper gallery crew turned toward us, waving a hand. "Starboard! Starboard!"

I imagined the stark colossus looming up in the darkness ahead, its iron eyes flaring in the light of the advancing moon. Unconsciously I gripped the back of the chair.

Cutting back to half speed, Hain stepped aside. "Captain, take us home."

The pilot bowed, sliding behind the wheel, giving orders and listening for bearings as he guided the globe up and around to its mooring place. Once anchored to the ceiling, face to the wall, the balloon would be again simply a bogus moon.

As Hain led me to a forward observation deck, my attention was drawn to the marvelous engine. Its brass casing was exquisitely worked, shining amid the smoke and flame as if it were often painstakingly polished. Hain saw my interest, admired the dragon over my shoulder. "Beautiful, isn't he, this Light of Harvest Moon? I call him Conflagron."

I gaped at the astounding intricacy, the dimensions of the beast that eternally breathed fire. "What does he burn?"

"A vapor which rises from the depths of the mountain. He holds it in tanks in his belly. Three hundred of my people do nothing but keep him provided with full tanks." He grinned, watching my face. "When you have seen my Tenebrificium, I hope you will realize, Dragonfly, that there is more wonder and beauty to Harvest Moon than terror."

"You live on terror," I said, avoiding his eyes.

He laughed, whirling to peer out a viewport. "My dear girl—what is more wonderful than terror? It is only what you've been taught to think of terror that you find repugnant. In truth, there is nothing more beautiful in all the universe!"

15

The Tenebrificium

THE moon hung in the sky over the mountain's crest. Turned low, the brass dragon breathed smoky light but a lesser heat. The excess, vented against the rocky summit, gave birth to an abundance of garish flowers, a type which grew nowhere else in Harvest Moon. I felt a twinge of revulsion for these moon-spawned jungle blooms as I climbed down the stairway into their midst. Stems twisting to receive the heat, they reminded me in their indiscreet poses of painted ladies, blushing too fiercely beneath a veritable *weight* of hue.

As we topped the ridge, which commanded a view of the entire valley, I saw a doorway leading directly into the body of the titanic iron Horse. A suspension bridge spanned a sheer drop, a hundred feet straight down to the feet of the statue; the peak of the mountain was level with the Horse's back, and the bridge crossed a stone-littered chasm to the door in the right rear hip. Just as the balloon's jack-o'-lantern face was kept turned away from Harvest Moon, so this bridge and doorway were concealed by the body of the Horse from observers in the town below. Hain's black chambers filled the statue's belly as Harvest Moon expanded and rankled in the belly of the ground, its unwholesome influence no farther away than the twist of a spigot, a glance in the mirror.

I stepped gingerly over the clammy soil in my bare feet, hiked up my nightgown's hem. Gasping at the touch of stones, the whickering sting of dry sticks, the threat of mandibled pinching bugs, I refused any assistance from my guard. Mr. Snicker escorted Clara, her face drawn, hair floating in the downdraft. Surveying the garden, she sniffed. "You don't know from flowers, that's for sure."

We paused at the railing to look over the town's leaning gambrels, its bonfires—and the Numinous Wood, pulsing with wisps and marsh-lights. The *Jolly Jack* cast our shadows immense over the Horse's side.

Uncle Henry's book about the Wonders of the Ancient World was one of my favorites; I thought of it as we crossed the bridge, frosty air empty around us, toward the cyclopean shell of iron. I was sure the ancient sailors had felt this same prickling on their salt-burned skins as they glided in or out of the harbor at Rhodes, between the legs of the bronze Colossus. Surely each man must have looked up from his work and shivered every single time that statue's shadow blocked the sun.

Harvest Moon would remind me, too, in later years, of the Tower of Babel. Hain harnessed agony, sired pain and devoured it like Cronus his children. His rule undisputed in the realm of phantoms, he built and *built,* and not even the heavens, it seemed, were beyond his reach.

"What are you thinking, Dragonfly, behind that knitted brow?" Hain strode beside me, never an arm's length away, as if he feared I might leap into space.

I peered down between the slats; far below, the velvety mists cloaked the boulders in softness. "Of the Colossus of Rhodes," I said.

He chuckled with obvious delight. "So already you are finding the Tenebrificium a place of Wonder!"

"In the end," muttered Clara behind us, "the Colossus of Rhodes was hauled away in chunks on the backs of nine hundred donkeys."

Hain grinned over his shoulder. "I know. A.D. 672. I was there in person to watch. Where, Madam, were you?"

"Off the streets."

Was he joking?

"Come in, come in!" he said. "This is my Factory of Darkness."

THE Tenebrificium was all it should have been. Lit with widely-spaced chimney lamps, it was a midnight maze of corridors and foot-bridges over tiled waterways, some only inches deep, some in sunken channels twenty, thirty feet down. I winced at the chill of the floor, unmarked by scratch or scuff. Gritting my teeth, I breathed deeply and would not ask for my shoes.

Someone somewhere was playing Schubert's music to Goethe's poem "Erlkonig." I did not know the piece at the time, but I never forgot those driving, spiraling phrases on an unseen piano, the notes like the frenzied hoofbeats they were intended to represent. Years later, when the same pounding cadences charged at me from the plastic shadows of a music store, I clutched the counter and broke into an icy sweat.

Samuel Hain loved surfaces that glittered. It was his way, I think, of accentuating the darkness at the heart of things, this polishing of the stones, the floors, the fixtures of his home. Just as his clothes were sewn of spangles, his hair brilliant as if it were washed in mercury, so the bricks and chandeliers in his fortress were slick, hard, catching the tiniest glimmers of light, hurling back anything that was not silence. It was a cave of black glass, in which the faintest sounds from far away came skittering along the passage, lingered behind the archways. Lamps were reflected in a thousand convex eyes; the bricks in the walls had a melted appearance, their corners rounded, their surfaces bulging like cobblestones.

From all around came the splash and gurgle of streams like the circulating blood of the great Horse. Here in his "Factory of Darkness" Hain's workers added to the water its most potent pollutions.

Six facsimiles of Medieval Death stood guard at the approach to a long gallery. Even in the uncertain light, I could see that they were skeletons, not merely the hollow-visaged men of Harvest Moon; only blackness filled their eye sockets, and the bones of their fingers—"phalanges," Uncle Henry called finger bones—were wrapped like coils of dry cable around the handles of their scythes. To all appearances, they were long dead remains leaned into alcoves as threatening decorations, incapable of guarding anything; I knew better. But this time, I didn't have to sneak past them, and I knew they weren't going to hurt me. After all, Death's signs—the bones, the oblong box, and the body in the box—these things have no power to terrify. What frightens me is that which has life: beasts like Samuel Hain, viruses which thrive and spread in the dark canals of the body; and even my own organic mind, pulled to and fro by the input of senses, lighted by its own terrible lightning.

Hain knew his weaponry, and he used it well. The vestiges of the grave were points of nostalgia for him—the Death guards, the peaked roofs (what actual need *was* there for shingled roofs in a place where rain never fell?), the silk hats, the scarecrows, the orange moon. He had found his image in an age of the world before the electric light, when the imagination was at its zenith. He was Gothic; he was lofty towers twined with ivy, a trembling candle behind a shuttered window, the scrabbling of rats in battlement walls.

The gallery's ceiling was a distant skylight which admitted the lunar glow, much brighter here than in the village; no lamps were necessary. Weird statues lined rafters, balconies, even pillars against the walls—images of goat-horned men, grinning imps, many-armed fiends. Lighted from above, these overleaning figures were mostly in silhouette, a host of demons pressing down on air, on spirit—beneath their "weight" I found it difficult to breathe. Water fell by rivulets and gutters, streams joining streams, to be channeled into six vats on the second-floor balcony, three on a side. Fires crackled beneath two of the vats, the light wavering over the ranks of unspeakable watchers, making them appear to breathe, to flex leathery wings. The six containers overflowed through six primary gargoyles, their chins resting in their palms, their open jaws spitting jets into the central canal in the floor.

At each of the six cauldrons, a witch was at work.

Of course, I thought, swallowing hard. What was Hallowe'en without witches? If they weren't out criss-crossing the moon on broomsticks, if they conducted no midnight sabbaths in forest glades nor danced with their familiars nor hexed their way through the diabolic picnic-ground of Harvest Moon, it was because Hain had plenty of work for them right here. They were his master mixers—shocks of hair like the crowns of willows, warts and wens, hairy chins, dresses of silk, wool, and calico. One's face was olive-green, one pigskin-brown, the others in shades of bloodlessness and mold. They ranged in age, the youngest looking about fifty, the oldest a toothless thing nearly bald, who spewled her breathy spells between black gums.

The most terrifying of all was the witch at the very back, on the right. She was the witch of a thousand nightmares, hers a face that must have stared from my mirror at night— somehow, without ever having seen her withered face in the glass, I had known the color of her eyes, the fiery fright of her hair. She smiled at me, her mouth half-hidden by the hook of her nose, her bone-thin arms stirring her cauldron. This terrible Red Witch wore no hat—for no hat could have been forced over that hair's wiry chaos. I could scarcely move when I saw her. The delight in her eyes spoke as clearly as words.

All the witches quivered and clucked, cockatrice hens warming eggs of death. Shuffling in flame-shadows they sifted and stirred, sprinkled grains, dripped oils, strained shapeless things, chopped with cleavers, boiled, and poured. Their product, six elements of disquiet, flowed down into the canals. Were there more witches, I wondered, in other rooms, dozens more, hundreds more, all brewing bad dreams? Or were six enough, six hags stewing tirelessly, to poison the nights of the world?

"Carry on, Ladies!" cried Samuel Hain, sweeping us through to a door at the far end. Had the guard not prodded me along, I don't know if I ever would have summoned the courage to cross just beneath the Red Witch, whose eyes followed me.

After that place of moonlight, we were once again in the inky bowels of the Horse, the passage branching, veering, up stairs and down stairs, water falling around us. Archways yawned, trapdoors stood open in the floor with ladders stretching down to dripping vaults. Dry skulls ornamented pedestals like the busts of a museum; I remember one alcove—what I took at first to be dangling cobwebs was a row of severed hands, varying in size, livid with decay, each neatly tied to a cord. Clara exclaimed with disgust, and Hain, smiling, stalked on.

We crossed a bridge in a high, narrow hall, where a mirror-thin sheet of water fell on both sides and drenched us with a fine spray. This water must have already been considerably affected by Hain's additives; whereas I did not hallucinate, I could feel myself growing jumpy, a dark cloud's-edge of panic stealing over my mindscape.

Hain stopped, gripped the brass handle of a door, and pulled—revealing another dark hallway, this one devoid of any lamps. Taking a light from a bracket, he stepped through the door. The glowing mantle illuminated a corridor with walls of a dull, coppery cast. At its far end, we came into an unfinished area—the walkway was of planks nailed end-to-end over bare crossbeams. Between these lay a gauzy substance which had a muting effect on the light; I had only a vague notion that the walls curved up like the roof of a barn, braces and pillars flanking us around.

"This place will be breathtaking when we are finished with it," said Hain. "One section is complete already—this way!" He turned left, ducked beneath a beam, and led us around a stack of dust-covered plates that reflected his light. Where a workman had dabbled his finger in the dust, I could see that the plates were mirrors, piled as high as my head. Holding aside a drapery, he ushered us into an enclosed corridor that exited the chamber.

We found ourselves on another bridge, this one with handrails. The footing gave slightly under our weight—feeling the floor sag, I seized a rail. When I stumbled back a step, the floor rose where my foot had been and settled an inch or two where it was now, as if I were walking on a waterbed.

The view was amazing: the bridge crossed the field of a giant kaleidoscope, black mirrors whirling on soundless pivots, gemstone flowers and snowflakes blooming, bursting with a sibilant sigh. By the illusory spells of the mirrors, the effect stretched up and up overhead, plunged down beneath our feet to the center of the Earth. Dancing stars fragmented, comets soared, blossoming deep-sea gardens folded in on themselves and flew apart into galaxies. *Snick!* A thousand crystal spheres arose from the hearts of a thousand green glaciers. *Wisshhh!* With a whisper, the heavens rained crimson meteors.

The panorama spread along the bridge as we advanced. Hain's lamplight joined the array, the echo of his hair, his coat glinting behind a sea of golden moons.

"Lovely, is it not?" Hain turned in a circle, swung the lamp.

Clara had both hands on the rail. Although she was a dim shadow, her glasses flared with the moving firmament. "This bridge . . ." she stammered.

"Jointed every six inches," he said. "Footsteps on triggers beneath the floor set weights in motion and turn the machine. See how the recently-tripped mirrors spin the fastest?" He rested a hand on his hip. The cosmos flashing around him lit his face, his chest with a helix of purple and red. "Reduced to science, my kaleidoscope becomes as dull as a pulley here, a spring there. But equations fall short in the end." He gestured, made us turn and survey the slowing infinity of his handiwork.

I saw his point; this chamber held more than rotating panes, was more than the sum of its parts. Unfortunately, wherever there was beauty in Harvest Moon, there was, as close as the reverse of a coin, a corruption of beauty. No sooner had he finished speaking than a door behind him opened, and a row of figures approached, their feet pumping the whirling planes.

Hain greeted them warmly, stepped aside so they could pass us on the bridge. Mr. Snicker and the guard pulled us against the right-hand railing. Shaking off the squamous hand, I looked into the face of the first passerby—and could not suppress a cry as I met eyes lifeless beneath a thatch of strawberry hair.

It was a child, a boy my age. I had seen him in Meagerly's hole in the wall. The summery freckles were a sharp contrast now with the shadows of his eye sockets, the bruised pallor of his skin as he stopped in front of me, studied my face, and smiled. His lips drew back, twin fangs glistening in the corners.

"No!" I shrieked again, cowering against the rail. "You were—you can't be—"

"I was a mortal," he said slowly, the smile never leaving his face. "Now I am immortal. Not all of them became vampires—only me. I had the most potential."

A girl with raven hair hovered over his shoulder, rested an ivory hand on his arm. She, too, looked about my age, except for her eyes, which burned with green light, deep crow's-feet lining the skin around them. "Jarrod may get to be the new Receptionist," she crooned.

Could these be the same children who were eating sparsely only days ago? Days? Months? How much time had slipped away? The entire line was made up of children in ragged clothes, children with bleached skin; crowding close, they lifted flickering lamps, tried to get a look at me. An unpleasant odor wafted from them, not the smell of unwashed bodies, but of something alien and dark.

A tiny girl pushed her way to the front and ducked between Jarrod's legs to gawk up at me. No more than five, she had pigtails that stuck straight out from liver-grey ears and a dress made from a tattered cloth sack. Holding out a chubby hand, she burbled "Come play!"

I turned away, unable to look at her for long. Typical of a girl her age, she was missing a few baby teeth; but in every gap, a pointed, Harvest-Moon tooth was emerging. Whoever's child she had been, now she was Hain's.

My tears brimmed over, tears of anguish and rage. With all the solemnity of my years, I turned toward the man in the red coat and lowered my brows. Our eyes locked, the eyes of Harvest Moon's lord and a barefoot girl in a nightgown. Reaching up, I pulled my hood into place, drew the cloak tighter, but did not look away. From that moment, I think he knew he could never win me over, could never bully or beguile me into being his Hallowe'en granddaughter. I let the tears flow, did not wipe them away.

Clara's hand knotted in the collar of her nightgown. Some of the children had brushed past me and were tugging at her sweater, groping for her arms. "Come with us!" they called. "Be our granny!" Her lips formed words without sound.

"Yes!" said Hain, breaking from me with a wink. "Yes,

children, you shall have a granny in time. But now is the time to go out into your kingdom. Soar on the wings of the dark! Discover the night!"

"Life begins!" cried Jarrod, the fanged boy.

"Abundant life is yours!" shrieked Hain, spreading his arms. I thought I could even see a glint of moisture in his eye. "Go forth; now is the Hour of Misrule!"

Waving, they hurried past us, sought to pass each other, their impatient footfalls gyring the kaleidoscope. Jarrod patted Clara's cheek and whirled away. "We'll be waiting, Granny!" They were gone in the vortex of swirling stars.

Hain sidestepped me, towered over Clara. The mirrors covered her face with moving tattoos. "Wh—what have you done to them?"

"Done *to* them? Nothing! All that I have done is *for* them, dear lady. I've taken the shackles from their existence! Unhappy marriages, the deaths of loved ones, responsibility, the pain of parting—I've taken away Monday Morning itself! Not one of them wants to go back to all that—*not one!* Oh, if only the world understood me!" He clapped a fist to his breast, rolled his eyes melodramatically.

Clara shook her head. "You didn't answer me. What have you done?"

He waggled his finger. "Madam, you fear for the safety of your grandson."

"Give him back," she said.

"Oh, I will free him, when he learns to be free—when he is ready."

"No. Give him back now."

"Such dread," he smirked. "You are delicious!" Stroking his upper lip with a finger, he appeared to consider her plight. Then he looped an arm around her shoulders, spoke confidentially, like a salesman of used cars. "But let it not be said that Samuel Hain lacks generosity. I will offer you a way to buy back your grandson—*before* he is much educated. Are you willing to try?"

"No, Clara!" I started forward, but my guard held me in place. "He doesn't keep promises."

"This is no promise," he said, drumming his fingers on his lips. "It's—it's an opportunity for *penance*."

"Penance?" asked Clara.

"Of course. For your little stunt aboard the ship. I lost a good man up there tonight. A just judge like myself usually designs a punishment to fit the crime, but in Harvest Moon, we strive always to be productive. There is no shortage of work to be done; and there is a good job waiting for you, too, Madam, if you are willing."

She watched him from beneath lowered lids.

"Mr. Snicker will tell you all about it." Hain marched to the end of the bridge, held open the door through which the children had come. Our guards forced us after him.

"Sweet Pea," said Clara hurriedly, "I think we are to be separated, too. Remember—remember everything. God is with us, and with Willie."

We gripped hands for a second, but Snicker shoved her through the door, dragged her up a branching corridor. *Boom, boom* went his boots, his gold coat buttons winking at each stride. My guard clenched my arms, ignored the stamping of my feet on his toes. "I'm not afraid, Clara." I squirmed, and now my hood was half blocking my vision.

She turned sideways to smile at me—to smile!—as she was pulled into the throat of darkness. Sitting now, she made Snicker haul her like a bundle, her feet sliding along the polished floor. I surged toward her, but fell back in the iron grip. Hain moved between us, shutting out our last glimpse of each other.

But he would never efface the image of Clara, who did not struggle against her captor—that picture would remain like a photograph of the heart.

I was shivering beneath the cloak and the flannel nightgown, my feet on the glacier of the floor looking positively blue. Only Hain and the grey-faced guard remained with me now. The Tenebrificium was silent, save for the distant passage of water through its echoing crypts. "Come," said Hain and crossed the intersection of the halls to a stairway of brass, each plane a mirror that gleamed in the lamplight.

Climbing, his figure rose, the cape brushing the walls and steps—light *sprayed* from him, sparked around him; he *was* a kaleidoscope. Reaching a door at the top of the stairs, he stepped into a nimbus of moonlight on a floor of black and orange tiles, punctuated with brass posts in the shapes of cornstalks—leaves and ears, even the splaying roots were engraved in minute detail. Where the tassels should have been, a gas flame burned at the top of each stalk. Bronze jack-o'-lanterns rested on the floor, a bonfire crackled in an urn, and two or three scarecrows leaned on poles.

Above us the enormous bulb of the moon shone through a broad skylight, which lay open to discharge the smoke from the urn. Hain paced slowly among the lights of the spacious chamber. I turned in circles, my eyes drawn to the sweeping windows, to the spectacle of the town, nestled in its woody dells and valleys. Our vantage was straight down the nose of the High Horse. We had come through the body to the crown of the head, where the graven forelocks served as curving dividers between expanses of plate glass. The massive ears soared up on either side. In spite of myself I ran to the windows, gazed in awe over the rooftops, hills, and gulfs of never-ending dusk. When a cloud of my breath obscured my view in one place I hurried to the next, cupping my hands against the glare from a cornstalk lamp.

Hain waited until I had made an entire circuit of the crescent of windows; then he beckoned me toward the rear of the hall, where a frieze spread over the dark wooden wall, obscured, from my position, by the blaze of the *Jolly Jack*. Starting toward him, I noticed that there were others in the room, men and women in somber, elegant dress, all of them seated in overstuffed chairs, on wooden stools, or on a sofa that stood to the right of the door. Some sat with hands folded, others stared as if in meditation out the windows; a few were reading hard-backed books bound in cloth or leather. I avoided their glances. My guard joined those to my left.

"This is my Hallowe'en Lounge," said Hain. "And these should interest you—some historical carvings."

I followed his gaze to the panel over the door—it became clearer viewed below the stream of moonlight. In a tableau of unquestionable skill, a series of figures took shape; it was a bas-relief rendition of a medieval village stricken with the Black Plague. Emaciated corpses lined the streets, mourners rent their clothes, and wagons bore away the dead. Skeletal Death prowled at noonday, his scythe in hand, his long finger aimed at a ragged man who clawed at his own throat. Rats glowered in doorways, in the foreground, or scurried along the alleys.

Grim as this much of the carving was, the lower part depicted Samuel Hain and a group of his people in what appeared to be a basement just under the street. Their clothing was different—older—but the features were unmistakable; there was Hain, his smile from ear to ear, his hands upraised toward a row of stacked bodies. Snicker stood on his right, his scissors poised like a sword. Instead of his top hat, he wore a pointed cap like a wizard. All the company was adorned in the flowing robes of the Middle Ages.

"Now *that*," said Hain, "was a very good century! The fourteenth—Europe and Asia."

I faced him, looked into those eyes-within-eyes, those windows to the collected nightmares of the ages. "You *are* that old, aren't you?"

His laughter rose like a rattle of autumn leaves.

"Older, dear girl. Much older! I first tasted the pain of your world in Persia, in Babylon—I was young then, only learning how to reap. I came again with the Black Death—that was the first venture of which I was wholly in charge—my coming of age. Ever since, you children of humankind have been . . . in my blood. You're addictive."

I remembered what Henry had told me of the Plague, one of the darkest chapters in world history—whole towns decimated, their populations cut in half, and the halves cut in half, hardly a family left untouched by bereavement. "You—you *caused* the Plague?"

"Not I. That pestilence was a gift from my father, he who was a friend of two Kings Herod. His arts were always greater than mine."

"Is he dead?"

"We do not die, Dragonfly. He hunts in other fields now."

Moving forward, he showed me a second panel, this one of a moonlit ceremony. A ring of cloaked figures held torches and branches of trees—in the center of the ring was a towering pyre. "The Celts—my dear old friends. Those were the days, Dragonfly, in which men and women dared to dream! Do you happen to know if you and your uncle are of Celtish stock?" He ran his fingers fondly over the wood. "I nearly established my Kingdom on Earth that time, little one. I had my very own cult among living, breathing men of the world of light!" He fell back, shaking his head, hands folded on his chest. "They *worshiped* me."

I leaned forward to study the strange symbols below the scene. "I can't read this. What does it say?"

" 'The Fear and Reverence,' " he intoned proudly, " 'of Samhain, Lord of the Dead.' "

"Samhain? Is that you?"

"Yes. I allowed them to choose for me a name. My father disliked 'Osiris,' which his first cult called him. But I loved the ring of mine. The Celts were so terrified of me—I was the master, and they were puppets on my strings!"

Fear made them weak. That was the first lesson Mothkin had taught me, and I vowed to remember it when it counted. Turning away, I perched on the edge of an easy chair, put one foot on top of the other for warmth. Hain's was an old, old face. I was not so surprised, really, to learn just how old it was—not after I had looked into those eyes. He claimed to be immortal; that was discouraging. But I also knew that he had been defeated before—even with a cult of worshipers on Earth. On my back I could feel the gazes from around the room. Trying to ignore them, I drew a deep breath.

"You are not human. What *are* you?"

Clasping his hands behind his back he studied the carvings. "I want you to think of what happens when you drop an ice cream cone on the sidewalk."

"It melts."

"Yes, it melts—and what else? Sometimes even before it melts?"

"Well, if dogs are around, one of them licks it up."

He held up a finger. "Precisely! The wandering dogs. Your loss is their gain. And if they leave anything behind—?"

"Ants."

The finger swung around. "Yes! Ants! Nature wastes nothing. Animals die in the woods and are consumed by others. Parasites feed on trees. Everything that lives must eat."

I knew *this* litany. " 'Little lambs have their clover,' " I offered, quoting Noyes, " 'lions have their meat.' "

He held up his palms. "It happens that my people come from a place where emotional energy is consumed as food. Is that bad? Is it bad, little one, for you to eat hot dogs?"

"Eating hot dogs doesn't hurt people."

"Do the ants hurt you when they eat your dropped ice cream? You dropped it, didn't you? Beings with minds experience emotional pain—it's a fact of life. We only enjoy it."

"You do more than enjoy it. You *cause* it! Stealing children—piping them nightmares—"

"Development," he said, shaking his head, "of natural resources. We take only what we need, no more."

Gnawing my lip, I watched the gaslight flutter shadows over his face. His charm was a dangerous thing; I could feel the fire of his eyes eroding my anger. The wideness of his grin, the shining of his hair filled my vision as he stepped closer.

"We are not unique—by no means! The energy we use is negative, but there are those who devour the positive. Oh, there are countless, countless harvesters of the Earth's bounties. Yes—we are gardeners; think of us in that way."

"There are—others? Other places like Harvest Moon?"

He tipped his head, down and up, the grin close, closer. "You want to wage a war against me, Dragonfly? Then where will you stop? You who would be a judge over the cosmos—if Samuel Hain must be stopped, will you attack next the Muses, who inspire men to create works of art and poetry that they may drink from the rivers of joy these works produce? Will you leave your world behind, and search for my father, Osiris the Great, out across the stars? Surely he—the eater of worlds, the elder lion—surely *he* must be destroyed! Take up the sword, little one, and you may wield it forever, unable to rest—and think of all those your anguish will feed!" His eyes glowed like his airship, his face inches from mine. "Is that the existence you wish, child—forever and ever?"

My will faltered. Unformed words jumbled, dissolved as caped children played ring-around inside my head. I shook, fell back into my chair—even the upholstery felt inflexible, frozen. I wanted Clara, and Willie. I wanted, suddenly and fiercely, to go home.

Hain whirled on his heel, clapped his hands. "So you are still a little girl, and not an eternal warrior! Well-chosen! Good!"

He paced through rays of moonlight, his form eclipsing, as he passed, the distant bonfires in the valley. Turning my head to watch him, I wiped my eyes, hugged my knees to my chest.

His voice rose softly through the pumpkin-light. "Mr. Angore will show you to your quarters—by the time you are rested, I'm sure I will have thought of something worthwhile for you to do. So I will bid you good night. Feel most free to dream!"

16

VINTAGE TEARS

I allowed a bearded steward with fiery eyes to lead me down the stairs of brass, through the tortuous mazes of the Horse to an apartment prepared, obviously, for my occupation. A four-poster bed was curtained with lavender, the knob of each post carved into a replica of the Horse's head. Walls of an airy, pinkish hue were decorated with framed pictures of flowers and large-eyed kittens such as a little girl might like. In the center of the room stood a roll-top desk and a chair with a red cushion. A gas chandelier cast a bright, yellowish light, and the deep nap of the carpet, midnight blue, was a blessed relief to my feet.

As Mr. Angore showed me a door which led to a bathroom and a control for shutting off the light, I wiggled my toes and basked in a stream of warm air from a vent. "There is hot water in the tub," he explained in a monotone. "Your clothing has been placed in the dresser. You may turn off the lights to sleep; when they are off, you must ring this bell and I will come and light them again. Do you have any questions?"

My thoughts were a muddle, my limbs suddenly heavy as bags of sand. Swaying, I clutched a bedpost and shook my head.

"If you require anything, ring the bell."

I was glad when he was gone with a dragging of his mold-scented cape. A bolt scraped through rings as he secured the door from outside. When his footsteps receded, the silence was broken only by the faint hiss of the chandelier.

Parting the curtains, I collapsed across the bed and thought I might sink forever in its cedar-scented depths. The smell reminded me of the trunk at the foot of Henry's bed, where he kept quilts his wife had made—Aunt Chessie had died before I was born. For me, this was *her* smell, this closety aroma of cold weather with long, cozy nights. What hands had made this comforter beneath me now? Some dour seamstress in a gable chamber of the village—or was it stolen along with a half-sleeping child, yanked into the frozen-pond undertow of a mirror?

An ache stabbed through me, the need to be held by someone who did not breathe frost, did not have skin the color of dirty snow. My breathing hitched; the first hot tears brought stinging and the taste of salt.

Shedding the cloak, I stumbled to the light switch, flipped the toggle, and the room faded to a windowless black. I curled into a ball beneath the covers and whimpered myself to sleep. Tears of loneliness soaked my pillow—this round was definitely a victory for the old, old man who reclined somewhere in the inky halls, who collected those tears in a tulip-stemmed glass and sipped, savored, analyzed the vintage.

I was left to myself for a long while, with ample time to reflect upon the various kinds of darkness produced there—for in the "morning" with my breakfast, Samuel Hain sent me a written report of the previous night's output of treated canal water. The meals were brought in by the same butler who had waited on me at Fifty-two Pink Eye Street, he of the oiled hair and swollen dough cheeks. Leaning against the sugar dish that first time, when I awoke to the unbolting of my door, was a card of grey paper written in large letters:

My Dear Dragonfly,

Good evening! Did you sleep well? I greatly enjoyed our little talk in the lounge last night. I hope you have a better understanding of me and my people now.

Some figures for last night that might interest you:

Guests admitted at Reception—4 boys, 2 girls
Graduating Pupils—7 boys, 6 girls
Tenebrous Liquid Output:
Premium Nightmare—75,000 gallons
Regular Instilled Water—400,000 gallons

These figures are for the Tenebrificium itself, not including random Instilled Water production at the pump houses.

Tonight I will be instructing your elderly friend on the performance of her duties. Until we meet again, do make yourself at home!

Most Sincerely,
Samuel Hain

The breakfast was better fare than I'd had in several days, but my appetite was tempered by the awareness that Willie was eating sparsely, that the cats might have nothing to eat at all. And Clara—was he feeding her, or was she being cruelly punished for killing the Frost Man?

Or had the Frost Man really died? I lay back against the headboard and rubbed my temples. Clara had said Hain's folk threw dead bodies into the canals—the two I had seen at the pump house appeared to be doing just that; but Hain had claimed last night to be immortal—Snicker was beside him in the medieval woodcut, representing a scene that had occurred six hundred years ago. Was Hain lying?

That first endless night-day I explored the three rooms of my prison: bedroom, bathroom, and commode. With a shock I discovered in the corner bookcase my own books from Uncle Henry's! Here they were, all the treasured collections of fairy tales, adventures, Dr. Seuss, Silverstein, Sendak; Marguerite DeAngeli's *The Door in the Wall;* Ruth Gannett's *My Father's Dragon;* and my tattered copies of the Bertram books by Paul T. Gilbert. They were all lined up neatly in alphabetical order by author or editor (*I* had never organized them in such a way—I pictured the pudgy hands of the butler laying them out as he did the spoons and forks, with precision). They were indeed my books, not merely copies of the same titles—but rather than comfort me, their presence here underscored Hain's threats concerning Henry; the funeral home was accessible—if my own books could be stolen from my room, Hain could make a target of my uncle whenever he desired.

I sat at the desk, inspected the drawers and pigeonholes. It was equipped with pencils, pens, markers, and crayons. On the side of a pink eraser I found the name "Susie" in childlike letters—so all of this was stolen from children's rooms. There were notebooks lined and unlined, sheaves of tracing and construction paper, tablets for sketching. An unopened package of red, yellow, and green modeling clay waited in a cubbyhole, and a plastic VIEW-MASTER with dozens of reels nestled in the drawers. Aiming the binocular device at the chandelier, I flipped absently through some of these, the three-dimensional figures strangely reassuring—they reminded me that there was still a world where children had toys, where the sun shone.

Expecting Hain to send for me or appear himself at any moment, I folded my hands on the desk top and stared at the door, then took a pencil and began to doodle on the sketch pad. When more than an hour had passed since breakfast, I found my jeans and flannel shirt and made my way into the bathroom.

The tub was covered by a metallic lid; although the gas flame underneath had been off for hours, the water was still warm enough to use. Soap and towels waited beside it. Putting the tip of my finger in, I waited for phantasms to dance in my mind—but none came. Leaning forward, gripping the side of the tub, I soaked my arm to the elbow, swished my hand around. Then I withdrew, studied the water dripping from my arm; it appeared normal, and my nerves remained steady. I suppose Hain wanted me clean—he had supplied me with a tub of untainted water.

I took my time, and when I was dressed again, I leafed through some of the books. Finding it impossible to concentrate on them, I rang the tarnished bell to call Mr. Angore. He arrived almost at once, sliding back the bolt, his square shoulders filling the doorway. The brass taper he had used to light my chandelier earlier that morning burned in his hands—he carried it diagonally across his chest like a weapon.

"How may I help you?" he demanded.

"Doesn't Mr. Hain want to talk to me today?"

His face was impassive. "If he does, he will send word."

I picked up my cape, tied it at the neck. "What's he doing? Will you take me to him?"

Mr. Angore did not budge from the doorway. "No. Mr. Hain calls for company when he wishes. You are to remain here."

I rolled my eyes, tossed my hair to show my impatience. "You don't know what he's up to?"

"That is his business."

"Well, then." I edged experimentally toward the door. "Just let me take a little walk around—"

"Absolutely not. You will stay in your room. There are guards at either end of the corridor and throughout the Tenebrificium. If you attempt to escape, you will be shackled hand and foot. If you require something that is not here, I will bring it."

"Did he tell you all that?"

"Those are Mr. Hain's orders." Backing into the hall, his eyes never leaving me, he prepared to lock the door.

"Mr. Angore—are there any other prisoners in the Tenebrificium?"

"You are a guest, not a prisoner."

"Any other guests, then?"

"The woman, Clara. There are no others." His muffled voice drifted through four inches of iron. "A meal will come soon."

TRAPPED!

I settled down with my chin in my hands, my stomach knotted with anger. This was Hain's game, and I didn't like it—another dungeon, but this one designed to keep me warm, fed, clean, and comfortable as I went mad with boredom. In a few hours I would be producing all the negative emotional energy he wanted; my frustration would whet his appetite, my fury provide a hot, flowing main course, and my howling despair would be the richest dessert he had ever tasted. When my mind was utterly gone, I might put on a gown of velvet, ride down in a carriage to the village, take up residence in some cobwebbed cupola, and buy my funereal bouquets from a dark-eyed gardener.

I felt a desolate longing for someone to tell me my fears were foolish. At the sight of my quivering fingers, the pain sharpened—the shape of my hands, the familiar proportions defined the emptiness: I wanted my mother. In my mother's pragmatic world, I thought a place such as Harvest Moon could never exist. If only she could be here, I was convinced, if she could hold me in her perfumed arms, then the High Horse itself would melt away to nothing, and I myself would wonder if it had ever been. Once I had been glad Uncle Henry, too, could hear the sounds from the basement—now I yearned for a Disbeliever, one whose very presence would banish this whole kingdom to Is Not.

But it was she who was Not—nor Was I, in the world where she lived. I had vanished into Henry's basement—gone without a trace. What *would* he tell people? Would my parents forgive him? Was he on trial, in prison, or where they kept crazy people, locked up and well fed, just like me? Or was he hiding, peeking out between stalks in the millet field while detectives tore up the floorboards of the funeral home, chopped holes in the basement walls?

I saw them in my mind's eye, my father taking some time off work at last, sitting with ruffled hair and beard stubble—my mother twisting a handkerchief through her fingers, her eyes ringed beneath with shadows. They wouldn't be talking to each other, not once they'd asked all the important questions; there'd be nothing to say. As they listened for the phone, the television's glow would bathe their faces, but they wouldn't be seeing or hearing the sitcoms, the news about war somewhere or the Chili Festival in Mt. Pleasant. They'd be lost inside themselves, thinking of birthdays missed, and deadlines that couldn't wait. Every film my mother had been in during the last ten years would be an abhorrence to her now, and my father would be trying to make sense out of his briefcase, wondering why it suddenly seemed so heavy.

I realized Hain's victory was complete: he'd gotten all of us. It didn't matter *where* someone was; Hain could devour agony bled from any continent, any house on any street. All the people I loved were hurting now, and I, with the intensity of a child's feeling, was hurting for them all. Once the lord of Harvest Moon introduced a little pain, it grew in cycles, propagated itself; there is no functional Tenebrificium like the human heart.

The butler arrived with lunch, taking no notice of me as he positioned the serving cart within easy reach of my chair, removed lids from dishes.

"Hello," I said, glad for even his company.

His eyes flicked over me, but he said nothing.

"Do you talk?"

He laid out silverware without a glance at me.

"You *must* understand words!"

He scooped noodles into a bowl.

"Is this food poisoned? Will I have nightmares if I eat it?"

Not responding, he arranged mushrooms, pudding, a salad of pure white leaves.

"Would you yell if you burned your finger?"

Duties finished, he padded away.

"Anyone who doesn't say anything now thinks Samuel Hain is an all-time loser!"

He looked once over his shoulder—then he closed the door.

I nodded. "I agree."

I contemplated the stew of chicken and herbs. *Was* it treated with witches' brew? I had eaten breakfast and been fine; when I thought about it, what choice did I have? I could send it back uneaten, and my supper, but eventually I would have to eat something. This meal was all right, but it was like Russian roulette; Hain could doctor it any time—he might let me get to trusting it first, then start with nightmare pudding on the fifth meal, or the tenth.

Mr. Angore had said there were no other "guests" in the Horse. If that was true, it meant that Mothkin and Singer, *if* they were alive, were at least not here in captivity. If, if. It also meant that Clara and I were truly alone. What would Mothkin do, I wondered, if he were trapped in this room? Assuming he had no mysterious tool that would allow him to open a secret panel in the wall and—*secret panel!*

Leaving my lunch in progress, I went over every inch of wall space, tapping, pressing, tugged at the legs of the furniture. I scrutinized the ceiling for any faint lines, thumped the floors for any hollow sound. The butler returned while I was doing the bathroom and looked blankly from the tray of food to me.

"Not finished yet!" I called brightly. "Come back in a while, please!"

Finding nothing, I returned to my lunch. Listening to the gas lamps, I supposed I could set the bedclothes on fire; that would cause some confusion—I might hide behind the door and try to hit the butler with the chair—but there would still be guards throughout the Horse. It appeared waiting was the only alternative.

When the dishes were cleared away, I busied myself with remembering all the good experiences of my life—the stories in the Numinous Wood, the Pea Mummies, summer picnics with Henry, outings with my grandfather and my parents long ago. Taking a black ink pen, I started a list. I wasn't sure what Hain planned, but I wanted to arm myself if possible with a solid reminder of who I was.

Rechecking the room for any crevice I had missed, I read *My Father's Dragon* all the way through. My signature at age three was scribbled inside the cover, across the map of Wild Island; it comforted me to think of myself at that age, a child who claimed books for her own.

Supper came and went; I gave up trying to talk to the butler. After supper I pulled out Richard Scarry's *Busy, Busy World,* the sanest and most cheery of the books on my shelf. Studying the colorful pictures of animals around the world, rehearsing their adventures, which I knew by heart, I was working—mostly by instinct, of course—to exercise my sense of well-being.

Mr. Angore appeared, asking if he should heat the water in my bath. No, I told him, I was ready for bed, and he locked me in. Changing back into my nightgown, I read over my list, said my prayers, and turned out the light. As I stepped over the folded pile of my clothes, I executed a Defiance Attack, standing in the darkness; I parted the curtains, gripped the comforter, and lifted the hem off the floor. Facing the bed, I was now exposing my bare feet and ankles to whatever waited in the deep space underneath. It wasn't easy to make myself do it, but I crammed my toes in farther, wiggled them. When I climbed into bed, I was pleased with myself.

Slowly the bed warmed. I lay on my back, faced the unseen canopy above. Wriggling, I found a comfortable position, tucked the covers under my chin. The multicolored patterns of the black night pulsed behind my eyelids—I always marveled at the resemblance of these patterns to cloth prints—Paisley, floral, plaid. The room was utterly still.

I yawned, drifted, tension seeping away. Just once I jolted awake as muscles relaxed, but then I slipped downhill. Sleep encumbered me like a robe whose arms were too long for my arms, its train doubled over my feet and piled on me in warm folds.

My next recollection, deep in the well of the dark, was of someone sitting on the bed. I was aware first of the weight, of the mattress's contour stretching. My eyes flew open. The night was impenetrable, but by the feel of the air on my face, I knew the bed curtains had been drawn open. Although I sensed no warmth, heard no breathing, I knew I was not alone.

No sound came from my opened mouth. My right hand squeezed my left wrist. Suddenly chilled from head to foot, I waited.

"Dragonfly," husked a whispery voice.

The pounding of my heart was the only reply.

"Dra-gon-fly."

The bed groaned as someone shifted weight. Air moved, pushed out of place. The hairs of my eyebrows tingled.

"Don't be afraid of me." The voice rose to a hoarse murmur, painfully familiar—like a well-known map with a few lines re-drawn. It belonged to someone I knew; I was sure of that. But something was wrong, something . . .

A match burst in the dark. I had to shut my eyes against the brilliance.

"Look at you, sweetheart. And look at me!"

When I tried, cautiously, I made out a big, leathery hand, its arthritic fingers knobbed around the match. That's when I figured it out, even before I saw the windburned face.

His cane was balanced between his knees. One of his roses rested in a buttonhole; its fragrance was different from that of Sylva's roses, and I understood the difference at once: this one brought with it a whiff of summer sunlight.

He lit the stub of a wax candle, fished from his jacket

pocket. There always were dozens of things, children's treasures, grown-ups' junk, in his pockets. My eyes were filling with tears. "Now you know me, honey, don't you? I can't stay long." Tilting his face, he pushed back his grey fedora hat, the white hair ruffled at his temples, just like chicken feathers. And there was his dear, crack-lipped grin, his perfect dentures that he even let me try once in my own mouth. He shook out the match a second before it would have burned him, dropped the spent stick into that marvelous junk-pocket.

I wanted to throw my arms around him, but was uncertain; what if my arms had passed right through him? *He's a ghost,* I thought.

"I know you're glad to see me. You got so big! But I got to tell you—got just this one chance—are you list'nin'?"

My head was swimming with roses, with crayon sketches. "I—" I squeaked, hardly aware of what my voice was saying, "I've got some crayons. Here, Grandpa."

He shook his head. "Later for that, honey, later. Listen to me now, girl. Okay?"

Dragging my sleeve across my eyes, I nodded.

"This Sam Hain." His face was close to mine. I could see the tobacco stains on his lips. "Maybe you don't like him, but you can't ever get away from him. When you go down into the ground like me, you *belong* to him, so you ought to make friends with him now. Do you understand me, Dragonfly?"

Tears turned to ice on my face—I *did* understand more than the ghost intended. "Nice try," I said evenly. "You know a lot about my grandfather, and you look and talk like him. But he's in Heaven now, not 'under the ground'—and he never called me Dragonfly. Uncle Henry didn't start calling me that until after Grandpa died."

His brow lowered. Steaming over, his eyes became twin pits of tar. The face contracted, as if a dozen rubber bands that had held the semblance of my grandfather's kindly expression had been released all at once. The mouth turned down its corners, pulled back from rotting teeth; now the fragile scent of the rose was obliterated by the stink of corruption.

I recoiled.

Spitting an ugly curse—further proof of its false identity—the apparition rose, its colors draining away. The hair dissolved, clothing shrunk inward as if it hung on a frame of pipe cleaners.

Now I screamed, twisting handfuls of the comforter against my mouth. Thrashing my feet I scooted to the far corner of the bed.

Shaping grey lips into a foul doughnut, the creature blew out the candle.

Fear crushed me, and I waited for the rake of fleshless claws. My heartbeat rebounded from the walls. Instead, there came a scratching of footsteps on the carpet—footsteps receding. They scuffled into the bathroom and then, abruptly, stopped. The thing, I guessed, was stepping into the mirror.

The terrible dry ghost of my grandfather did not return; I huddled for hours in the pitch dark, my face in my knees, my ears straining. For the remaining hours of that night, Hain's mastery was complete; despite the nearness of my precious books, my list, I shivered and wept. When at last Mr. Angore came in the "morning" and lit the lights, I was scarcely better off; my visitor had left behind his cane. Sliding free of the nest of bedclothes, their cedar scent tainted now with the bitterness of my perspiration and the essence of decay, I lifted the briar stick from the carpet, studied its dull brass head, its no-slip rubber tip. Every knot was in place, every detail exact—even a scratch I had made near the tip, when I used the cane as a lever to move a concrete block.

Turning the wooden shaft over and over in my hands, I sank into my chair, weary to the depths of my being. What had visited me in the night, speaking in my grandfather's voice? Conceivably a denizen of Harvest Moon could copy his appearance and mannerisms from my mind, probing deep after memories of the experiences we'd shared. But this briar cane was no facsimile. I stared at the scratch which even I had forgotten.

LAYING my head on my arms, I dozed. It was the opening of the door that awakened me, the arrival of breakfast. I had little appetite, but for the sake of the struggle I ate; I would need my strength.

In the bathroom I found no trace of the apparition. I had

noticed, however, when Mr. Angore had come to light the chandelier, that the bathroom door was standing wide open— I distinctly remembered closing it before I'd gone to bed. The mirror was hard, cold, innocent. My reflection gave me a start—it seemed my face had edged closer to adulthood during the long dark stretch.

Mr. Angore had heated the water, but before taking a bath I covered the mirror with Mothkin's cloak. Dressed again, I located my shoes and socks, sat in my chair to put them on. Would I truly be alone here forever? Listening to the ceaseless exhalation of the lights, I interlaced my fingers, squeezed my palms together. Waiting was unbearable; I had resolved to ring the bell and ask again to see Hain—but while I was contemplating my grandfather's cane for the twentieth time, the door scraped open.

Angore entered, stood to one side. Mr. Snicker stooped to bring his hat under the lintel.

I gripped the cane tighter.

Puffing cigar smoke he advanced, a twiggy mantis, his scissors jingling like spurs. He blew the smoke away, and I saw his face; glaring down from the shadow of his brim, he pointed his cigar hand at the ceiling, extended the thumb toward the door. "Let's go talk to the boss," he said. "Leave the cane."

Escorted by Snicker, Angore, and three sword-wielding guards, their faces etched with mold like shadowy soot, I delighted in walking so many steps in a straight line—I'd practically worn a path in my carpet. I made an effort to remember the route we took, reasoning that all I could learn of the layout would help me in an attempt to escape, but I was soon confounded by the turns and side passages, the preposterous number of stairways. Every passage looked exactly like the next, black and polished. In the absence of moonlight and windows, I could not even guess at our direction, which changed often.

On four different occasions, we stood in a section of hallway that rotated on pulleys or rollers to realign itself like a piece of railroad track. Twice the tube behind us came to rest against a blank wall, allowing us only forward movement; the other two times we swung around into a completely new corridor. The sections that moved were indistinguishable from the rest of the hallway, the seams perfectly invisible until we halted and the section began to turn. On one rotation, I saw two possible connecting corridors whisk by before we linked up with a third. How this rearrangement of the hallways was controlled remained a mystery. I never saw any of my escorts touch a switch; if they did so, the action was performed with deliberate subtlety, the switch concealed in the wall or floor. Possibly the movements were triggered by our weight, as in the kaleidoscope chamber; or maybe our progress was being monitored by watchers through pinholes who jerked levers to spin the floors at the appropriate times. At any rate, this system of rerouting corridors discouraged me further from ever attempting to flee; without the proper alignment of halls, there might not *be* a way to the exit.

At last we descended a stairway that wound in coil after coil around an enclosed shaft to our left. The right-hand wall was unbroken by any aperture, but the inside wall was marked every hundred feet or so by a window, a single pane of glass facing a black emptiness like an elevator shaft. The lamps here were turned low, so that I had to be careful of my footing.

Mr. Snicker paused before an iron door, mashed out the stub of his cigar in a silver cup with a lid that screwed on and off. It fit into his vest pocket and was shaped like two-thirds of an egg. The door was a black oval, devoid of knob, hinges, or markings. He rapped three times, laid his palm against it, and pushed. Without a sound it swung inward, rebounded slightly from the wall.

Inside, on a deck of iron, stood Samuel Hain. Imperious as always, he leaned on a guardrail, his feet set wide. Amusement was gone from his demeanor.

"Good evening, Mr. Hain." I marched toward him, my steps ringing on the giant plate. "What came into my room last night?"

He regarded me without passion. "Your grandfather."

"My grandfather is dead."

"Dead. A relative condition. You saw him, spoke with him. Do you doubt your senses?"

"It's Hallowe'en, Mr. Hain. I think it was someone in a costume."

"Then how do you explain the walking stick, which I understand he left? Who else but he would carry it?"

Who indeed? I looked at my feet and saw beneath them letters of red glass; an inscription had been melted into grooves, inlaid before the curving rail.

"Do you read Latin, Dragonfly?"

I shook my head; that was one thing Uncle Henry hadn't taught me. The letters spelled out "NEGOTIUM PERAMBULANS IN TENEBRIS."

His finger pointed out each word. " 'The Pestilence That Walks in Darkness.' " Lifting me by the scruff of the cloak, he dragged me to the rail, pulled back my hood. "It lives down *there.*"

Beyond the deck was a black well, a pit of inestimable depth. The ceiling above it was also a shaft, pierced by lamplight from the windows on the stair. From below drifted a preternatural chill, laced with the odor of a breath I can describe only as the evil reek of attics long closed, or of some huge and alien animal corpse, rotting away in a well of slime and dead air. I give thanks that no light shone down into the pit; at the smell alone my stomach roiled, and Hain dropped me back on the floor not a moment too soon.

I retched, crawled on hands and knees away from the rail, and lay gasping on the cold floor. Snicker and the guards stood in a semicircle, their faces all smiles.

Hain approached as through a mist, his movements slow, his steps like drumbeats. "We are in the left foreleg of the Horse, the home of the Thanatops. Also, I have found a job for you to do."

THE job was not in the left front leg of the High Horse; it wasn't in the Tenebrificium at all. He told me about it after we'd climbed the stairway and meandered again through the valves and channels.

"I will not go through mirrors for you," I said firmly, hurrying up behind his spreading cape.

"No. There are others far more inclined to that task than yourself."

His reply surprised me; I was sure he wanted me to help steal children. Considering possibilities, I tried again. "I don't think I could have any beautiful dreams now if I tried. You've shown me too many ugly things."

He was unmoved. "The time for dreaming is past. This is the hour of actualizing. It is time for Project Nowhere; the fields are golden unto harvest."

Snicker, Angore, and the others clattered behind us; their faces told me nothing. I had to run a few steps to keep up with Hain.

"What are you going to do?" I almost caught his arm, but thought better of it.

He turned into another hallway, smiled down at me. "Your world stands ready, anointed by the pipes and pumps."

"You're going up?"

"Nowhere but up!" He reached back to accept a cigar. "You see, there's no longer a need to hide down here in the dark. Things are always changing." Puffing smoke, he turned again, jogged down a flight of three stairs. "In the dim old nights, when we used to leave changelings in cribs and carry the babes off in our arms, we had to fight. You don't know what a changeling is, do you? It was a—a service we used to provide. Anyway, people believed then the forest was the place of devils; whole crowds of villagers would come after us with torches and weapons, right down the stairs of crypts, into the hollow hills—they could *see*. That's why the time of the Druids wasn't the time for Nowhere. So we waited. Sure enough, given time, the human race banished monsters and fey folk to legend; today no one can find our doors. We've grown stronger as your people have grown weaker—they no longer believe in anything."

"What will happen to the people on Earth?"

He blew smoke, swung his arms grandly. The others trooped with bared teeth, their footfalls in step. "Humankind will suffer. You're an intelligent child; you can work out the details for yourself. Every shadowy corner will harbor terror for them—there will be no reason or law. I will reign for thirty years and one, the number of days in October. By that time, I suspect, the Earth will be depleted, and we will move on to another world. There are always new kingdoms to be shaped."

Stopping at an intersection, he waited until the crossroads turned one-eighth, lining up with four new passages.

Hands on his hips, he watched me. "You really thought your A.P.K. friends would save you."

I fanned away smoke. The hallway, spinning like a giant starfish, clicked to a stop. "Where are they?"

He looked me straight in the eye. "They're dead. One was torn apart by werewolves—I guess your little boyfriend never told you that. He wanted you to be happy. *Happy—here!*"

Snicker and the guards roared with laughter.

My knees wanted to give way, but Hain hauled me forward, chuckled around his cigar. "The other one climbed all the way up here looking for you. You know what I figured out from that? I deduced that if *he* couldn't find you in all of Harvest Moon, the only place you might be was in the Numinous Wood, so we went to pick you up. See, if he'd known your whereabouts, he'd never have scaled the mountain and fought his way through so many guards. I let Mr. Anselm drink his blood as restitution for the Glassworks—Adrian, you see, was Mr. Anselm's uncle."

"You're lying!" I stumbled along in a blindness of tears.

"Afraid not." He stopped again at a branch in the corridors. "Mr. Snicker, you know what to do."

Nodding, Snicker headed off down the right-hand hall.

"Really," said Hain, handing me a silk handkerchief. "Cross my heart and hope to die. Your old friends are dead, and it's time to go forward. Do you want to hear what your part is going to be?"

17

THE THANATOPS

M Y last memory of the inside of the Tenebrificium is a stairway without a bottom. There *was* an end to it, of course, in the Horse's right front hoof; but the descent of that leg, round and round and round, seemed a journey of *weeks*. Repeatedly my shoes slid, and only Mr. Angore's hand saved me from a headlong pitch down a thousand stairs. There were no landings, although dozens of oval doors opened directly off the steps into the central core; what the rooms in this tower contained is forever a mystery. As in coming down a mountain slope, the muscles in my legs cramped and began to quiver, making the journey even more precarious.

At last we reached the massive outer hatchway, the iron skin two feet thick. The two front legs, pillars holding up the sky, rested in a wide rocky basin of the mountainside. Behind the Horse soared the black ridges; straight ahead, the lurid *Jolly Jack* rolled at anchor over the steep slope. Blocking our view of the village, the balloon leered at us like a lawless god of wine and flame. Occasional bursts of red light within kept it airborne—as it twisted on its moorings, it resembled a molten planet in the throes of birth.

The exposed stone and packed earth between the Horse's

hooves was devoid of any plant growth. A pool of oil-dark water at the low center of the concavity glowed lavalike with the moonlight. A hot gust from the snorting craft rushed past us, circled the basin.

Three conveyances waited: two ebony coaches, their teams ready to charge, and a wagon like a boxcar, plated with armor, drawn by ten horses—a troop carrier. From within came the clink of weapons, the glitter of wintry eyes at the window-slits. Mr. Snicker was the driver of the far coach; catching sight of me he winked, stooped over to ignite his cigar at the flame-pot beside him. The door of the nearer carriage stood open, waiting for me. A dozen guards flanked the exit, men with barely enough flesh to cover the protuberant angles of their skulls.

Whatever operation was getting underway, its proportions were epic: at the far hoof, another line of cloaked figures waited at attention, and on the cliffs behind us, hundreds of torches and lanterns dotted the jagged skyline—a multitude of the people of Harvest Moon had assembled to watch. Angore helped me climb into the coach, then ascended the driver's seat. Hain leaned on the door, pushed his face close to mine. The balloon's dragon-light, the swirling drafts, his slicked hair gave his features the aspect of a hawk diving toward its prey.

"Escape is impossible," he observed gently. "An armed guard will be riding with Mr. Angore, two more with you in the coach, and three more on the rear fender. I will be on the *Jolly Jack*, so I'll give you your instructions now.

"Doubtless you are wondering about the other coach. Its passenger is your friend Clara. She and Mr. Snicker will monitor the progress of your mission. If you fail us—if you deviate from your task in any way, even for a moment, the old woman will be put to death—*snip!*—just like that." He paused. "You understand me—good. The coach will stop first over there, at Left Front. The door will be opened, and the Thanatops will come out."

I squinted at the distant leg of the Horse, noted the difference in its construction. The entire hoof was a gate, hinged at the top; even from here I could make out chains looped through pulleys, chains the line of servants would use to hoist the huge door, to open the way for the entity within. At the corners of the gate, wisps, hardly visible, curled upward—these were not smoke, but something closer, I think, to the swallowing of light.

"The Thanatops is Pestilence Itself, Dragonfly, the last living child of the horrors that were Typhaon and Echidna. My father's present of six centuries ago—you will lead it now to the Gypsies. They alone stand in our way."

I sank against the velvet cushions. My head was empty; Hain exerted the force of his will, and my hand was so weak I could not make a fist. "I don't know where they are."

"I do. They inhabit the Numinous Wood. When Pestilence walks in the forest, nothing among those trunks will live."

"Why do you need me?"

His eyes blazed. "Gypsy magic. They have woven new spells of protection into the wood. My people cannot enter uninvited. But *you* may enter—and you may *invite*."

So it *was* to be the Trojan Horse, and I was to play the part of Sinon, the deceiver, the gate-opener. Had I been left any strength or courage, I would have begun searching for some means of escape, but the news of the deaths of Singer and Mothkin had stolen my hope. In a sense, by coming into Harvest Moon, I had thwarted their mission; had they not been protecting me, I told myself, they might not have died. I had doomed all my friends and quite possibly the whole world above.

"The Thanatops will follow the carriages down to the edge of the wood. Leave the coach when you are told. Walk alone, then, with Pestilence at your heels, to the edge of the forest. Enter between the trunks. A silk curtain will appear, like spiders' thread, from the branches high overhead to the ground at your feet. The Thanatops cannot break this web, but you will remember Clara and Mr. Snicker, who will be watching you; you will stretch out your hand and part the web. For you, it will be easy." He smiled ingenuously. "Clara's is the last life you can save. The Gypsies you do not know; what are they to you? They will die anyway, even if I must bomb them to oblivion from the *Jolly Jack*. This way will only be faster, Dragonfly. The Pestilence kills quickly, with little suffering."

I didn't fall for his lies; he would never choose a method of destruction that caused anyone *less* suffering—but under his mind-control, these particulars no longer seemed to matter. Maybe there *had* been something in my food that allowed him such influence.

"Finally, my girl, I will show you my appreciation. Do this, and I give you your freedom. If you want to live, step aside, let the Pestilence pass you by, and come back to us. Then you may go or stay, as you like."

"Go?" I blinked, focusing on his eyes. They convinced me of the inevitability of what Hain planned, of how useless it was to oppose him.

"Yes," he laughed, "go. Out. Up There. Why not? Soon, the Kingdom comes, the Epiphany of Darkness; what will it matter where anyone lives?"

I closed my eyes. The smell of the moon hung acrid in the air.

"Farewell, Dragonfly! I know you will perform well. I have *faith* in you."

Why should he not have faith in me? Of all his cunning and unscrupulous servants, I was the greatest, proven time and again. My brokenhearted gaze was for him the perfect parting note.

"Dragonfly?" His voice was almost a whisper.

I waited, without strength.

"You were the first child ever to come to my kingdom freely. And you were the best of the dreamers."

He left the burning, loathsome touch of his fingers on my cheek. Then he smiled, let two guards in, and shut the door.

WITH a jolt, the coach began to roll. The two expressionless guards sat across from me, wearing the shining black of high rank. Stiff-backed, they did not converse, did not glance aside from my face. I turned and watched through a glass window no bigger than a slit as Hain strode toward the lowered stairway of the balloon.

I could tell by the jerkiness of the ride, by the stream of harsh commands from Mr. Angore, that the horses were not eager to approach the left front leg of the Tenebrificium; more than once I heard whips crack. The carriage bearing Clara and the troop carrier rattled past us, the latter's ironclad wheels churning through the margin of the stagnant pool. I could not see forward, but the hoof and its expansive gate slid into view beside us as we ran the length of the row of guardsmen, who stooped to heft the chain lying at their feet. Like a team preparing for a tug-of-war they tested the links for grip, planted their feet.

Slowing, we banked again, pointing toward the slope and the Numinous Wood. The horses screamed and reared, straining at the harness. Someone was barking orders, now ahead of us, now behind. We were barely creeping, poised like a pebble before the hoof of the colossus.

Grating, the gate rose. I felt a corresponding chill in my spine, beginning in the small of my back, crawling up toward my shoulder blades as I envisioned the increase of blackness behind the coach. A sensation of *exposure* swept over me, of eyes that looked through the rear of the carriage as if it were glass. Creaking the suspension, the guards from the back platform crept forward, clinging to the sides of the coach, their bodies blocking the windows as they perched on the running boards. There was a dread hush. The horses stopped their protest; the carriage came to a full stop. In the near total darkness of the cab, I saw only the whiteness of the guards' eyes.

From above and behind came a sliding, a whispery tearing—as if a velvety shadow were ripping itself loose from a wall.

And then—*poch . . . poch . . . poch . . .*

Footsteps descended after us, the rustling perambulation of something huge, but almost without weight.

The coach bucked, continued its journey at a walk. Breathing in labored gasps, tossed and jounced, I lay back, tried to think, tried not to think.

Poch . . . poch . . . poch . . .

In nightmares I will never stop hearing the scratch of its feet; a television science program not long ago featured an amplified recording of a cat's footsteps, and my breath grew short indeed—not an exact match, but *awfully* close. The only other sounds were the tocking of the horses' hooves and the

steady shrieking of the brakes as the drivers of the three rigs
strove to keep their vehicles from plunging downhill.

After perhaps a half-hour's steady descent, the carriage
stopped; I felt the jostle of guardsmen leaping to the ground.
Moonlight flooded in again at the windows. My guards made
no move until the door was opened. Seizing my wrist, Mr. Angore steadied me as I stepped down. I noticed at once a deeper
than usual freezing edge to the air; judging by the touches of
their hands, I reasoned that the body temperatures of Harvest
Moon's folk were lower than mine—yet in the icy swath
which ran before the Thanatops, even their breath showed in
clouds.

I stood still in the light of a moon which had advanced
quite close again; the *Jolly Jack* drifted to my left, fifty feet
above a spur of limestone which thrust itself up from a skirt of
tightly-spaced trees. This grove lay like an island off the leafy
continent of the Numinous Wood; the road ducked into the
heart of shadows, then crossed a shallow, open ravine and entered between the gnarled stems of the forest. A cobbled path
veered off from the road to run along the bottom of the ravine
toward the nearest arm of the town, a row of dark roofs and
hedges perhaps a quarter-mile to my right. The troop carrier
rolled ahead through the outlying copse, patrolling the road,
and turned right at the crossroads; gaining speed, the armored
wagon vanished into the town.

The moon rotated, its toothed grin sliding into view. Three
mooring ropes were down, and I watched guards working
their way up the bare rock surface to catch them and secure
the craft. I could see the crimson splash of Hain's figure on
the extended corkscrew of stairs. Almost directly beneath
him, near the summit of the rise, was a low building, its walls
of piled limestone blocks.

Trying to ignore the presence behind me, the prickling of
my scalp, I studied the building. It looked like a guardhouse,
an observation post of some sort, its roof of planks sloping
low over a row of slit-windows. Weeds sprouting flowers of
midnight and violet grew in a tangled mass over the founda-
tion, leafy vines probing tendrils in and out of cracks in the
walls. I guessed the edifice was a relic of another time, when
guards might have gazed out the slits in three directions: to the

wood, the town, and the mountain. Now it sagged against the overhanging summit ridge, which was its rear wall.

The other coach was stopped just ahead, although Mr. Snicker and Clara were nowhere to be seen. Guards shuffled from foot to foot somewhat nervously, I thought—and none of them looked up toward the face of Pestilence. Rather, they kept their heads concealed in the shadows of their cowls.

If I turned toward the monstrous entity behind me, I wondered, would I be changed to stone like those who met the gaze of Medusa? Would I go mad?—fall lifeless where I stood? Yet I had not been warned against looking. Nor was my will to live, at the moment, very strong. All the same, I had never been so aware of the host of tiny movements involved in rotating the body to face behind. My heel slid backward, my opposite toe crept into a turn . . .

When I was a child, I was haunted by a question that no adult ever answered to my satisfaction. "What do pictures see?" I asked my uncle. "Nothing," he said, "because they don't have eyes." "But they *do* have eyes!" I'd protest, pointing to George Washington's portrait. "Not *real* eyes," he'd say. "Those are only painted there—they're strokes of paint." I always felt, however, that the fact that the paint was arranged to make them look like eyes indeed *made* them eyes in one sense; after all, if you pointed at them and asked what they were, anyone would tell you, "*Eyes.* George Washington's eyes." So, "Darkness?" I'd ask. "You mean they see just darkness all the time?" "No, Dragonfly. Darkness is *something,* and you'd need a brain to perceive even that. Pictures don't have brains, or optic nerves. They don't see." But all the time, there they were—there George was—looking out through his eyes.

Why do I tell you this story now? Because I think it helps make the point that I couldn't begin to see the Thanatops. My eyes were no more equipped to *see* the totality of it than canvas George's eyes were built to look into mine. No mere physical shape could contain it. I saw all that the impulses of my brain could decipher for me; but certain sounds and colors are beyond the range of human perception. The beast appeared as a rippling, an immense black smudge. Within two days, I was to have a clearer view.

"Go," said Mr. Angore, pushing me toward the forest. "Walk slowly and straight." A guard drove the coach away.

As my gaze passed over the abandoned building once more, I saw two figures framed in a brick archway at the corner nearest the road—Mr. Snicker and Clara. They stood just outside the building, on the verge of weed-choked lawn atop the slope. At their feet, the rock wall fell sharply, thirty feet down to the road, which in the thicket of trees ran along its base. This was the perfect vantage, from which Snicker could observe every step of my journey. He was within earshot of Hain, and Clara, her hands tied behind her, was visible to me as incentive.

The ground crew had tied one rope to some point on the far side of the building, and the *Jolly Jack* descended over the copse, the pilot keeping the tethering line stretched tight. Hain, I guessed, was scanning the trees for enemies.

Woodenly I started forward. I knew Snicker loved to use his scissors. Pulling a cigar from his coat pocket, he wiggled it between his finger and thumb in my direction. As I neared, I saw that Clara had been blindfolded.

"Say nothing," ordered Angore, "or the old woman will die. Here I turn aside—you go on." He hurried up the slope to the coaches parked well back from the road, out of the way of advancing Pestilence.

Now I was past them, the trees drooping to meet me ahead. Still playing with his cigar, Snicker peered at the nightmare behind me, the thing that came on with slow, even steps. It walked but did not breathe. In the dust of the road, its steps were the sliding of snow from branches, *floof, floof* . . .

Clara's face jerked left and right as she sensed its approach. Her features looked older than when I had last seen them, her dress spattered with brownish stains like dried mud; I wondered what torments she had undergone in the High Horse. At this distance, in the absence of wind, I could hear her words easily: "What's that? Who's there?"

Part of me longed to call to her—not so much, I'll confess, to comfort her as to receive her comfort. But I trudged on in despair, burdened with my guilt, remembering Angore's threat that I must not even speak. I am Hain's servant, I told myself bitterly. Clara and I will never talk again.

Noting my silence, Snicker grinned and nodded his approval. He fumbled in his vest pocket for a match.

I plodded into the deep shadow of the grove. The moonlight fell in leaning shafts through the overgrown trees; now the balloon was masked from my sight by the dense autumnal leaves, frozen forever in shades of blood, gold, copper, and black. The sere carpet exhaled a wandering mist, and something scuttled, fast and close to the ground, across the road in front of me. With equal suddenness, a figure loomed out of the mist to my right—a man with a droopy hat, his odd, lanky frame reclining against the boards of a fence returning to nature. In the wan light, his face was a featureless patch of white. The light shifted, and with a shock, I realized he *had no face*—his malformed, dangling hands were—were . . .

Then I saw he was not a man at all, but a scarecrow. It seems so strange to me now—the incarnation of dark disease skulked forty paces behind me, and I was frightened by a scarecrow!

I had reached the depth of the thicket, where the branches groped across to weave a roof over the road. Snicker and Clara were high above me, the moon still invisible, although I saw its straining tether angled across the road overhead. Here in the frosty cellar, a sea of red apples covered the road and the ditch—apples which would have been beautiful under different circumstances. A deep gully plunged down beside the path at my right; I could hear the gurgle of a stream at its bottom. Mist flowed out of the ferny crevice like steam from a bath, but its breath was frigid on my skin. The copse scrabbled and whispered.

As the Thanatops glided into the wood, I imagined the underlying roots groaning beneath a weight that would not register on a scale—and wondered what would become of the apples in its path. Would they blacken and shrivel, swell and burst with worms? Or would they glow with a jewelled beauty, becoming as deadly as the poisoned apple in "Snow White"?

The road opened out not far ahead, crossed the ravine toward the Numinous Wood. Soon I would be there; soon I would accomplish my mission. Out on the moon-glazed crossroads, a werewolf was bringing down his prey, a man of Harvest Moon who tried in vain to escape on horseback. The man's hat was gone, his hair streaming, his eyes as white and rolling as those of his horse. Enjoying the sport, the werewolf loped easily abreast, launched itself through the air, caught the rider in a flying tackle. They toppled from the saddle, fell among the bushes, and were gone.

I stopped to watch, my eyes following the riderless horse as it bounded over the tangles, its ears back. The bushes thrashed; all this was far from me, so I heard no sound. Then they were still. A prolonged howl echoed from the far trees, and I thought of Sylva. Watching the kill, I remembered his forays and the lesson Harvest Moon had taught me again and again: *Everything that lives must eat.* This was the cycle, the reality. I had lived in Sylva's house of my own will, had held his hand and danced, had turned the soil of his gardens. Just as he was a slayer, so was I; corruption and self-service and the celebration of doom—these were as much my melodies as his—or as Hain's. Ultimately, it mattered nothing that my eyes lacked the cold fire, the undead light of theirs. Long ago, with a heart I believed pure, I had resolved to help a band of captive children. Now, at the end of things, I knew what a fool I had been—for my will to help was a lie, my power to do good an illusion. I had not only failed, but actively *added* to the misery of everyone I had encountered. Would it not be better, I asked myself, to run with all my speed into the arms of death? It waited behind me for my journey to continue.

I turned, looked up at Mr. Snicker. The rope that held the balloon was rising, tilting the moonbeams.

Snicker had the cigar halfway to his mouth, his other hand still buried in his pocket. He stared hard at me. There was a frown on his face as if he smelled something bad. He stiffened suddenly, his gaze fixed on something just behind me—

—A hand clamped over my mouth.

Too stunned to struggle, I felt powerful arms lifting me, dragging me to the brush-choked ditch. A strange, knifing odor pervaded my head, some chemical that soaked a cloth pressed to my nose. My vision remained clear, but my thinking was swept over as by a layer of gauze.

"Don't be afraid," said a low, reedy voice in my ear. "Just watch!"

Lying back in a cushion of weeds against my new captor, I

was amazed to see a small, slender figure rise out of the mist to my right and step nonchalantly into the road. Dressed in a hooded cloak identical to mine, this person strode forward, headed toward the Numinous Wood. The Thanatops seemed to hesitate a moment, then padded on, its bulk a filmy darkening of the trees across from me.

Mr. Snicker gestured wildly into the air, his face livid. Spitting the still unlit cigar like a dart, he seized his scissors, whirled on Clara.

She tottered at the edge of the dropoff, her face beneath the blindfold a rictus of dread. Turning this way and that, she heaved her shoulders, tried furiously to free her hands.

Snicker opened the scissors, raised them to the height of his chest. That is the portrait of him I will always remember most vividly: coat like a crow's tail, twiggy striped legs, black hat shadowing his eyes—and those horrible, gleaming blades, reaching for the throat of an old woman in a blindfold. Nothing, I think, could be a truer picture of Harvest Moon.

The *Jolly Jack* reared up out of the trees, crossed above me, and hung straight over the building. On the stairway, Hain screamed orders into the body of the balloon, then dashed one round lower to yell something to Snicker—but Conflagron roared, the brass dragon in the gassy core, and Hain's words were obliterated. Gesticulating, he leaned over the rail. Black-garbed soldiers poured from the balloon's hatchway, spiraled down the steps. The moon settled lower.

Tails swirling in the downdraft, Snicker closed the distance to his victim. I sucked air for a warning cry, but the hand covered my mouth again, and someone whispered, "Ssssshh-hhh!"

A voice hollered from somewhere on the craggy ridge—a familiar voice, but one I was unable to place; the curious odor had numbed my mind.

"STONE BREAKS SCISSORS!"

On the height of the rise, just beneath the twirling stairway, someone sprang from concealment, and with all his strength, hurled a rock at Mr. Snicker.

Thud! It was a miss, aimed too hurriedly. Landing directly behind Snicker, it rolled between his feet. Gaping down at it, he spun like an ice skater, the scissors coming around in an arc. Anyone standing behind him would have been decapitated; since there was no one, the point of one blade scythed along the stone-block wall, dragging a tail of sparks.

In the next instant, the abandoned building exploded in a tower of meteors and flame. Unable to comprehend what I was seeing, I watched the slats of the roof soar upward like boomerangs, saw the whole face of the cliff flare with a prismatic color spray. The ridge was shaken to its bones, the ledge cracking. Clara pitched forward and would have fallen—but a figure in a black hood slid down the rock face beside the disintegrating building. I knew who it was even before a spark illuminated his face: Mothkin, alive! He dashed to Clara's side and caught her, pulled her back toward a cleft in the limestone.

Snicker, however, took a fateful step backward when the edifice erupted—and tumbled, a bundle of belly and sticks, toward the road. Still high in the air, his plummeting shape slowed, passed into what seemed a gelatinous haze—the corona of the Thanatops. Kicking, thrashing, his arms and legs left silvery trails as he bounced over the monstrous shoulders, hit the ground. If the Pestilence took any notice, it never faltered in its stride.

It was from within that the building had ignited; the flimsy roof had allowed an easy escape for the blast, the block walls sheltering Snicker and Clara from the brunt of the explosion.

The *Jolly Jack* seemed to be drinking a river of fire. Incinerated guards flew from the stairway, which glowed and lost its shape, white-hot in places. The jack-o'-lantern face yawned, its mouth a black hole that widened and widened as flames raged through the bowels of the ship. Almost at once the blistering updraft batted the moon skyward, away from the inferno, but already gas canisters within it were going off, blowing holes in its skin, lashing out like solar prominences across the dark.

I remember my grandfather burning colonies of bag worms from the limbs of his birch tree. As their silky webs shriveled in the flames from a gasoline-soaked rag, the worms, dozens and dozens of them, spilled out writhing, trailing smoke through the air; you could even hear their bodies sizzling. *I don't like to kill,* he used to say, *but you gotta draw the line somewhere.* I thought of the bag worms as I watched the crew of the *Jolly Jack* die. Those not hurled out by detonations or consumed in the flames were scalded by the rupturing of the inner hot bag.

The column of fire that had burst from the building waned, shrank to a smoldering glow. With walls still mostly intact, if somewhat blackened, the ruin resembled a lantern set into the side of the ridge.

Mothkin—alive! As if the purging flames had rolled into my heart as well, my weight of lethargy and self-punishment dissolved. He had not died in the fight with the werewolves— that had been, like so much of what Hain uttered, a lie.

Then a joy I thought could be no greater was multiplied in a breathless second: for the figure at the top of the ridge, the person who had hurled the stone and shouted "Stone breaks scissors!" climbed to his feet, waved both hands over his head.

It was Uncle Henry.

I laughed, wept, and coughed, tried to talk, tried to walk, tried to fly like a bird to the rocky summit. The person holding me thumped my back and said, "Take it easy, girl!"

Free of the arms, I turned to see a row of smiling faces among the fronds and weeds. Men and women, dark of hair and eye, knelt in the steep-sided ditch. The man who had restrained me was perhaps thirty, and he wore a broad-brimmed felt hat.

"We're Gypsies," he said.

"Thank you!" I threw my arms around his waist, squeezed, and thanked the people behind him until they gathered close around me, laid fingers over my lips.

"We're not out of danger yet," said a woman in a purple skirt that seemed woven of twilight.

I looked up to see Henry, still on the pinnacle, his glasses flashing in the light of the fire beneath him. Mothkin had joined him, pointing toward a descending path; but for one more moment he stood at the summit of Hallowe'en night, a Hallowe'en with some of the glory of the Fourth of July.

Now the sky was darkening; I could not see the balloon. And although the building's fire still cast a gloaming into the forest, I could not see the Thanatops.

18

LURKWICK

THREE women stood up in the ditch, crept to the verge of the road. She that wore the skirt of twilight led them, a lantern in her hand. The other two were younger, but of the same lithe build and cascading hair. They all wore loose-fitting blouses, richly-hued silk skirts, and shoes of supple leather. Black hooded cloaks draped their shoulders.

"Pestilence has passed along this road," murmured the man nearest me. "It must be cleaned before we can cross it."

The two younger girls dipped their hands into baskets and flung handfuls of what looked like fine sand in arcs; the grains were pale purple, bursting into gaseous tongues of flame when they hit the road's packed earth. The tallest woman held the light for them as they worked their way to the far side, the knee-high flames streaming and leaping before them. Burning green, pink, and blue, the swaths of fire extinguished themselves quickly.

We were just rising to hurry after them when a sound like the growling cough of a great beast rang through the grove, echoed from the cliff. The color of the sky began to lighten again; tree shadows lengthened, spun in half-circles. The coughing grew louder, became a rumble.

"Stay low!" ordered the man, pulling me down among the ferns. On the other side, the three women melted into the brush, their faces—dark-browed, beautiful faces—scanning the air above the trees.

To my amazement, from behind a horn of the mountain, the ragged moon arose. It was no longer completely round, nor was its skin as taut as before—now it resembled a tomato which had been hurled against a wall. Parts of the wooden skeleton were crushed, patches of the outer skin flapping in the hot, escaping breeze. It bobbed unsteadily, wheezed clouds of oily smoke. The engine in its punctured bay roared constantly to keep the craft in flight. It was obviously difficult to maintain a straight course, but the pilot headed in our direction.

"Let's go," said the man, "before he can see us."

Smoke was still rising from the cleared section of road. We scurried across, and there, framed by dark mistletoe, were the faces of Mothkin and Uncle Henry. I sprang into them with such force that they both fell backward from kneeling to sitting in the soft bracken. Their arms were around me, their scents of charcoal and warmth mingling in my nose as I pressed my face against the roughness of Henry's lapel and wept with him. Mothkin's voice whispered close beside my ear, "My cloak! I'm so happy to see my cloak again!" Laughing at my wide-eyed glance, he squeezed my shoulder, ruffled my hair. Clara crawled toward us, and although she'd never met Henry and hardly knew Mothkin, she kissed us all!

"Is everyone all right?" Catching my breath, I surveyed the three for injuries. Mothkin's swarthy face bore several new, healed scars; Henry and Clara looked haggard but intact.

Henry nodded, rocking back to look me over.

"Clara," I said, "this is my Uncle Henry; Uncle Henry, this is Clara—she and her grandson rescued me from the canal and have taken care of me since I left Languor House."

"Madam, I'm in your debt." Henry shook the hand she offered. "I can't believe you're a grandmother! But—your grandson? Is he here?"

A troubled look filled Clara's eyes—but Mothkin spoke up just then. "He *is*. The Gypsies have rescued the children from Meagerly's cavern. They are waiting for us not far away."

And Clara kissed him again.

Could it be true? Was Willie, too, soon to join us?

However, Samuel Hain's part of the drama was still un-folding. "Look out!" said the Gypsy in the brimmed hat, pointing toward the ridge. The *Jolly Jack* reeled over the sum-mit, yawed like a tilt-a-whirl car, its crumpled stairway still glowing red at its lower end. Hain clung to the top spiral, just below the hatchway; he was smudged, and his clothing had lost some of its luster, but he was unquestionably alive. Al-though I lay in the gloom of the trees far beneath him, his eyes were fixed on mine. Raising his arm, he pointed a long finger directly at me. The gantry rolled like a top losing its speed, but he moved his arm, keeping the finger trained. I hid behind Mothkin as we watched the wobbling phantom in the sky. So Hain *was* immortal, I told myself; he'd come through fire to find us again, and he would not ever stop.

The balloon hovered above the cliff. As it spun, we caught sight of the wheelhouse through a gash in the outer covering. The pilot was Eagerly Meagerly.

I believe those two were the last aboard the ship, the only two capable of surviving the heat of the leaking bag, the gales searing the bushes which clung to the rocky height. Mea-gerly's coat and hat were blackened, smoke rising from him. Conflagron shot incandescent flame with such intensity that the dragon's lower jaw sagged, beginning to melt.

"At that rate," breathed Mothkin, "his fuel can't last long."

Two of the mooring ropes still hung like dead tentacles be-low the craft. One dragged over the summit, the other brush-ing along the face of the cliff.

"Look!" said Clara.

We followed her gaze to where the bare slope emerged from the treetops. Something was stirring there, a shadow that doubled, hitched itself upward like an inchworm. Looking closer, I saw arms, legs, and the glint of something like an ici-cle . . .

It was Mr. Snicker; he moved as if no longer in full control of his limbs, shoving his elbows and knees into the cracks, his face turned away, mashed against the stone. He was covered in a veneer like glue, his spindling legs brushing a trail of the sil-very mess across the rocks. I put a hand over my mouth; what

I had thought looked like an icicle was a blade of his scissors. When he fell, it had pierced his bloated body and now protruded from his back.

"Horrible!" gasped Clara, hiding her face.

Snicker stretched a hand toward the moon, strings of pollution oozing from his arm.

Hain saw him, scowled over the rail.

Lunging, Snicker caught the dragging rope. Wrapping the line around his arms, he struggled to lift himself. No matter how foul a being I knew him to be, there was no pleasure in watching him grope upward, his breaths more and more spasmic. Hand over hand he went, a dying spider ascending its web for the last time.

The balloon tipped just enough to allow Hain to catch the top of the rope, near where it was anchored. Physically as strong as a vampire, he hauled on the line, coiling it at his feet, and Snicker rose like a bucket from a well.

I should have known Hain by now, but still his cruelty took me by surprise; he wasn't helping Snicker, had no intention of saving him. Face set in adamant lines, he pulled in rope, faster and faster.

In the last seconds, Snicker knew where his long ages of loyalty had gotten him. But who can say? Perhaps in his thoughts, this was only the just punishment for his mistake in abducting Willie without permission and keeping his presence in Harvest Moon a secret. I cannot begin to guess what goes through the mind of a being who, having thrived on children's pain for untold hundreds of years, comes, at last, to die. He emitted one awful, gurgling scream.

Then he was yanked into the twisted, glowing wreckage of the stairway, impaled and cauterized, branded inside and out. Hain jerked, shaking his body, letting him sag and then forcing him upward again. The metal hissed, scorched the velvet vest, the waistcoat. I'm sure Snicker let go of the rope, but it was snug around both his wrists.

Henry caught me in his arms, turned my face against his chest—but not before I saw the rope burn mercifully through, and Snicker drop like a smoldering rag beyond the trees.

"The compassion of Samuel Hain," said Mothkin.

I tried to steady my hands, looked soberly into Henry's face.

"My poor little Dragonfly," he whispered. "What terrible things have you seen here?" Stroking my hair, he held me close.

The fire was shrinking in the core of the *Jolly Jack*. The rift in the balloon had turned so that we could not see Meagerly, but he must have spun the wheel. As the moon lurched away over the darkening landscape toward the Tenebrificium, the figure of Hain stood facing us on the stairway. Unlike a balloon of the world above, the *Jack* left not a shadow but a *shine* slipping over the hills. The heat was withering; Hain's clothes curled like paper. He grew smaller and smaller, until the balloon vanished over the ridge.

"He's gone to get his soldiers," said the Gypsy, pulling a cloak about himself. "We'd better move."

I studied his lean face, rugged as with many fights, his hair long and so darkly brown that I had mistaken it for black, gathered in a ponytail that fell to his shoulders.

"Are you Lurkwick?" I asked.

He laughed, not unkindly. "Only in my dreams! I'm called Tefan. It's a great honor to meet Dragonfly at last!"

"Lurkwick!" said Mothkin, handing a lighted lantern to Henry. "With your uncle's permission, Dragonfly, I'll show you Lurkwick. Climb this hillside with me—the show is about to begin!"

"Take care of her," grinned Henry, offering Clara an arm as the Gypsy girls beckoned us deeper into the woods.

"We'll join you shortly." Mothkin parted the bushes, led me up a series of ledges toward the high cliff. He steered by the light of the ruined building, where something on the inside burned with an orange glow.

The trees climbed with us; we were still in their shelter when Mothkin turned, pointed away across the road to the town. The moonlight from the region of the High Horse was quite faint, but the torches, bonfires, and smudge-pots of Harvest Moon were going strong; by their flickering I saw the quiet road, the somber hedges.

"Do you understand what happened down there, Dragonfly, at the ditch?"

I shook my head, remembering the black-garbed figure that had stepped out in my place, a figure shorter than I was—a Gypsy child?

"When Tefan seized you, he covered your nose and mouth with a cloth soaked in a Gypsy formula."

I thought of the biting smell, the sudden emptiness of my mind. "It—it took away my thoughts."

"Yes. For a few minutes, you were conscious, but your fears, your pain, your imagination—all of those were effectively disengaged. You became invisible to the Thanatops."

"It was following my mind, not my shape. Another girl with an imagination could step out, and it would follow her as if nothing had happened."

He nodded. "The girl who took your place and led the creature away was Alycia. She says she knows you."

Alycia! What a brave little girl!—There was so much I did not yet understand.

"Now this is the good part." He grinned impishly. "Guess where she led the Thanatops?" His eyes strayed down the road to the ravine, along the edge of the Numinous Wood, and into—

"The town!" I cried.

As if on cue, a rising chorus of shrieks drifted our way over the treetops. Voices shouted, cursed, and wagon wheels began to rumble, flames licking suddenly up the side of a wooden gable.

"Good place for a Pestilence, don't you think?" He stroked his chin. "The Thanatops was sent to follow a girl and destroy the place of her leading. Oh, they're a tough breed—most will get out of town before they're *destroyed*. But this will keep them busy, and it will take Hain longer to muster his troops; that should give us the time we need. Also, they'll have to burn down about a third of the town before they can move back in."

The wailing increased, sunken-faced people appearing on the rooftops as if trying to escape a flood. Some leaped from high windows, ran limping across the plains; others charged out by side gates, on horseback or piled in wagons. I peered over my shoulder at the glowing building. "You set this up—you knew Hain's plan."

"The Gypsies knew. Their greatest seer told us where to put our fireworks—the Gypsies make them with chemicals from plants and minerals. That building was piled full of them, floor to ceiling. We intended it, though, as a diversion while we switched you and Alycia—we didn't know Hain would park the moon over the roof."

"That was luck?"

"That was the hand of God. There is no luck."

"What made it blow up?"

"The same thing that flies that balloon and lights up this whole place—gas, collected from the insides of the mountain. We put two open canisters of gas in there and let them leak. Henry and I were going to drop a torch from the summit at the right moment."

I was staggered by the thought of all that might have gone wrong. "Mr. Snicker did it for you, hitting his scissors against the wall."

Mothkin straightened, squinted into the distance. "I said I would show you Lurkwick. Here he comes."

A carriage sped around the corner of a hedge. Pulled by frenetic Untowards, it rocked, rose up on two wheels, slammed jouncing down again. Dust flew in clouds behind it, its swinging lanterns casting sparks. As it neared the copse—but avoided the Pestilence-tainted road—I saw two brass lions on either side of the driver's seat. A hooded driver held the reins, and beside him was a six-year-old girl.

I broke into a smile, then a laugh. "It's Alley Singer, isn't it? *He's* Lurkwick."

Mothkin leaned back against the fractured trunk of a tree. The caverns of Hain deepened with dusk around us—after many sunless days, divine grace had brought us together again. This time I, too, was a veteran of Harvest Moon.

"Mothkin—I'm sorry. I have so much to tell you—I'm sorry I left you at the cliff. I—"

He shook his head, the fading glow of the building flashing on his grin. "You're doing fine, warrior. You've survived, and now our troops are together."

I felt the suggestion in his words. Now the real fight would begin; Hain had been stung too deeply to allow a quiet end. He was no longer out to feed, to extract pain—now, with millennia of accumulated cunning and strength, he would seek to destroy us. And since his doors opened wherever he chose to put them, there would be no hiding on Earth.

Far below, Singer's coach vanished among the pillars of the wood. As we rejoined the others, he would work his way up by one of the mysterious Gypsy roads, so secret and narrow that they seemed to open just for the Gypsy wagons and close in living gates behind.

19

UNTOWARDS

IN the new darkness, the forest was quickly losing its
friendly face. Shadows pooled, flowed together; there was a
stirring overhead and along the living quilts of the floor—a
whispering of time grown short. Hidden tangles snatched often at my feet as Mothkin led me down the slope. Sliding between stark deadfalls, brittle as the carapaces of things
gigantic that slithered by night, we overtook the others, hurried on as quickly as the groping branches would allow. The
faint lights of flowers pulsed in the arches of roots; hollow,
mulchy drippings filtered through the brush. Lanterns in the
Gypsies' hands wore halos of mist. The air was cold.

I squeezed Henry's hand in both of mine, drank with my
eyes the outlines of his face. How he had come to find me was
a mystery I was dying to resolve; but for the moment, I was
content to cling to him, to assure myself that his hand, with all
its sharpness of angle and bone, was real. He had found me—
he had entered this place and survived. Tears of gratitude
flowing freely, I felt a resurgence of the strength that had left
me on the road. My curiosity had gotten Uncle Henry into
Harvest Moon; now I had to help him get safely out. Hain's
lies and the discouragement they inflicted dropped away like a

tattered garment—I shrugged them from me, focused on the devotion that had brought me back my loved ones. We must fight, I told myself. We must stand against our enemy.

Fragile though Henry had been, there was a new toughness in his expression. His stride asserted vigor, as if this silver-haired gentleman supporting Clara with his free arm was unburdened by years. Clad in his black undertaker's suit, he had come to reckon with the people in his basement.

Not far beyond the hill we reached a clearing, its floor a griddle of the interlocking roots of straight trees, their lowest branches three stories up. Water dripped and caught the light of luminescent vines; frigid pools lay in beds of thick, black ooze. Four wagons stood half-concealed in a fern brake of prehistoric proportions. The Untowards that drew them were sitting on their haunches, their heads cocked in attitudes of listening. More Gypsies waited in the shadows, long bows ready in their hands, swords at their belts.

The Gypsies and Mothkin greeted each other, but kept their voices to a whisper. Even as we scrambled toward the wagons, the men and women prepared for departure, each taking a position in the driver's seat of a wagon or vanishing inside. As they studied me, most of the faces were impassive, but the woman in the twilight dress reassured me with a kind smile.

Tefan opened a door on the far side of a wagon. Willie emerged, peering first around the edge of a wheel, then dashing into Clara's arms. His clothes were dirty and his hair unkempt, but he looked unhurt. I let out my breath, thanking God. Now we were all together—almost.

"As soon as Singer arrives," instructed Mothkin, "you should get into his wagon."

"What about you?" I asked.

"I'll be at the rear, with Avim—there will be pursuit. All the captured children are here, in the wagons."

Huddling in my cloak, I tried to penetrate the darkness between the stems of the trees. "I thought no evil power could come into the Numinous Wood unless it was invited."

Mothkin accepted a bow and quiver of arrows from one of the men. Bending it deftly, he looped the string into place, tested its tension. "Some evils are already within."

Remembering Hain's words about the Gypsies' magical protection of the forest, I looked back the way we had come, where the town was the feeblest of glimmers among the leaves. At first I saw only trunks on trunks marching away toward the plain; but then, in the spaces between the boughs, a rippling, filmy mesh appeared, stretching up from the forest floor to disappear among the high limbs—a curtain so nearly invisible that all I could actually see was the accumulation of dust on its surface, like smoke in a beam of light. Although we must have passed directly through it on the way in, I had seen or felt nothing.

A rumbling began, at first no more than a vibration in the springy turf. Following the Gypsies' gazes, I could not make out any entrance to the clearing, not so much as a path; yet a flicker of orange flame danced beyond the leaves, the brass head of a lion gleamed suddenly through the trees, and with a thundering of hooves, Singer's wagon crashed into the glade. Maybe it was only that the Gypsy roads were so narrow and winding that they were invisible unless viewed from precisely the proper angle; but it seemed that the forest itself parted to disgorge the coach. Singer's wagon was smaller than the Gypsy conveyances, more slender of line, elegant despite its battered condition.

Alley Singer's owlish face grinned down from between swinging lanterns. He was garbed now as a Gypsy, with a hat and vest of midnight blue, a loose-sleeved shirt the color of cream. "Good evening," he called softly in that voice like no other on Earth.

I ran forward, waved my fingers. There was so much I wanted to say, but words tangled in my mouth. I could only lean against the sideboard and gawk up at him, like some shining exalted being on the high seat.

"Dragonfly, you look well," he said. "That is good!"

I nodded stupidly.

There beside him was Alycia, blinking her violet eyes, waving one cherubic hand as with the other she clutched the voluminous cloak at her throat. The cape trailed down well past her feet, so that she resembled a doll. I will confess that I envied her the crucial role she had played in leading away the

Thanatops—and her getting to sit in the driver's seat with Singer as the rest of us were admitted to the passenger compartment. I was not the only youthful warrior—it was ironic how my pride flared within me; I, who had been ready to die on the road—I, who had so recently counted my shortcomings, I who had nearly brought disaster to us all—*I* was offended! I didn't want my place usurped. Such is the human heart.

Without ceremony, we were underway. Leaping and bucking, those fiery beasts pulled us deep into the woods, and the four wagons came after in a line. Putting my head out the window I watched Tefan's team yaw into place behind us, his carriage lanterns glowing with a pink flame—the two young Gypsies on the seat beside him were just lighting them as we rattled uphill along another secret road, the boles and branches actually *curving* around the trail like the walls of a tunnel. Behind Tefan's, the other wagons were blocked from view. Glancing at the impenetrable shadows, I was flung by a sharp turn back against my seat.

Untowards, you see, do not so much *pull* a wagon as *thrash* it. The Harvest Moon teams, even these employed by the Gypsies, appeared to view every run as a wrestling match with each other, with the harness, and with the road. We could hear the frequent slamming together of heavy bodies, the grunts and growls as the beasts crowded each other, forced each other into the bushes, sent each other glancing off tree trunks. They snorted, strained, each attempting to scramble over the top of the other's back. This behavior was their nature; it indicated no displeasure or ill will. At times the team behind us crouched down in a moment of rare concerted action, put their horned heads nearly to the ground, and leapt up, dragging the front wheels of the carriage three feet into the air.

"Daughters of black goats and nightmares!" I heard Tefan bark at them. "Mind the stones to port, now!"

Henry chuckled as our team pulled in two different directions, causing the carriage to fishtail like a car with a blowout. "Do you know why they're called 'Untowards'?" He held one knee between interlaced fingers and tried to bounce in cooperation with the seat. "Mr. Alley Singer explained this to me. It's for three reasons. One, they are highly unusual, like an *unto-ward* notion. Two, they seem at times *not* to be taking you *to-ward* where you want to go at all: hence, *un-toward*. Three: they ultimately get you there; they *ward* you well *unto* your destination. So they're called *Unto-wards*."

"Amazing!" said Willie. He ricocheted like a pinball be-tween Henry and Clara.

The woman in the twilight dress had climbed in with us, and was sitting beside me. "What is more," she lilted, her voice low-pitched and smooth, like a long, dark ribbon, "the Untowards are always born as twins." Her liquid eyes passed from face to face, her olive complexion dimly lit from the windows. "They are always together—one will not be teamed with any other partner to pull a load. They live a hundred and thirteen years, or so it is said, and then they die together. Each dies within a few hours of its partner."

"Happy creatures," said Clara with a sigh.

Uncle Henry was silent, but his brow wrinkled briefly.

"My people hold them in the highest respect. A Gypsy would give his life to save an Untoward, as an Untoward would do for a Gypsy."

"What are their names?" I asked.

The woman smiled, dimpling her cheeks. "These drawing us are called Few and Far Between."

We all laughed at that. "The ones behind us?" I asked.

"Tefan's team is Hither and Yon."

I watched her brush a strand of hair from her eyes. Her fin-gers were surprisingly long.

"And your name?"

"Muriel."

I had to find out how Henry had gotten here. "Oh, Uncle Henry! You must have been so worried—I'm sorry—" I didn't want tears, but they were coming. When a bounce of the wagon flung me across into Henry's arms, I stayed there, clung to him, and bawled.

He told me it was all right, stroked my hair. "Your story is more interesting than mine, I'd guess, Dragonfly. You sur-prised me on Hallowe'en night."

I tried to apologize again, and we were both laughing and crying, rocking with the carriage.

"Didn't anyone ever tell you curiosity killed the cat, little one? Didn't anyone?" His voice was hoarse. I'd never heard him cry before, not at all the hundreds of funerals that went on in his house.

"What—what did you *do?*" I asked.

"First, I wanted to go right down that chute after you. Then I thought, 'No, Henry, you've got to trust Mothkin.' He said not to go down under any circumstances. I knew you were with him, and thought he'd bring you right back up—"

"Oh, Uncle Henry, he *couldn't!* They were guarding the stairs—we could only go down!"

"I know it, Dragonfly. And I knew he'd take care of you. I sat right down and asked God to help you both, to get you out of there. Then I waited, but you didn't come out all night. All that next day I prayed you'd show up; that evening, I *had* to go down after you. Even if the basement people tore me limb from limb, it was better than leaving you down there."

Clara patted his face. "You're a brave man, Henry."

"I thought my best chance," he continued, "was to try to go down someplace where they might not be expecting me. The basement door and the laundry chute were out, so I took some rope, a knife, and a flashlight, and went around to the basement windows at the back of the house. Trying to get one open, I ended up breaking it—so I just slid on in.

"Well, I couldn't believe it! The basement had completely changed, all right. I was in a gravelly cave of some kind, and there were no signs of any people; just this cave with a low, lumpy ceiling, like frozen oatmeal, and the shattered basement window behind me. I probed around in the dark for awhile, shining the light into cracks in the floor, trying to figure out where to go—and it wasn't long before they found me."

"Hain's men?"

"Yes. A group with swords and dogs. Clapped me in chains, loaded me into a cart, and hauled me off to the marvelous Tenebrificium. Looking out the windows of Hain's glorious Hallowe'en Lounge, I had my first real view of Harvest Moon. Hain said in my ear, 'She's down there, your little niece. My boys have just gone to collect her. Too Quiet

Street,' he said, pointing; 'that's where she and your friend Mothkin are. They've been disturbing the peace in our city. Now they think they're hiding from me.' "

Too Quiet Street: I remembered the end of my first exhausting night in Harvest Moon. So Uncle Henry had been captured even before I had been, before I'd ever guessed he had come after me. He'd gazed down from the head of the High Horse at perhaps the very hour I had looked up through the windows of the shed; that was when I had slept in this very coach.

"What did he do to you?" I searched Henry's eyes for echoes of pain. "Were you in a dungeon?"

"No dungeon. You were in a dungeon, weren't you, my poor girl? No, he only threatened me. 'I have a job for you, Henry. You are free to refuse—unless, of course, you hope to see Dragonfly again.' "

"He has a job for everyone," muttered Clara.

"What was it?" I asked.

"I got to go with Mr. Snicker and the boys on various graveyard raids both inside and outside Harvest Moon."

"Graveyard raids?"

Henry braced himself against the wall as we rounded a particularly sharp curve—the carriage rose up on two wheels and skimmed along for a dozen yards before coming down with a jolt.

"It's all part of how he maintains his kingdom," Henry went on. "Hain calls these raids 'the Harvest of the Earth.' It seems fairly complicated. Among his people, I gather there are ranks, gradations of position and ability."

"That's right," interjected Muriel. "Greater spirits and lesser."

Henry rubbed his elbow. "They don't have bodies as we do—not initially, anyway."

"So they steal children," I said, the image of the children flooding my mind, the horrid, *changed* children in the kaleidoscope chamber: the *graduates*.

"Yes. When they've finished torturing the poor little ones, they steal their bodies."

"Hain's favored servants are allowed to inhabit these fresh, new vessels," said Muriel. "Outside blood rejuvenates

their weary stock. They mix with the populace of Harvest
Moon—in time, they produce children of their own. Wearing
the bodies of humans, Hain's people bear offspring." There
were children native to Harvest Moon—the colorless waifs
who chased each other about the arbors and played the
Game.

"There are never enough children from the outside," continued the Gypsy. "Once stolen, you see, once the living spirit
is cast out and the foul spirit of Harvest Moon comes in, the
body—however young—begins to decay. Fresh youth decays
less swiftly, but all too soon the vigor fades. Hain's people
must constantly seek renewal—new bodies to occupy."

"But until he's ready to reveal himself to mankind," said
Henry, "Hain feels he has to move discreetly. He's afraid
someone will guess at his existence, so he doesn't steal
enough children to satisfy the needs of his people. Five, six,
seven a night, snatched from different countries, different
continents."

"His people lose their bodies at a faster rate, though," I
said, recalling things I had seen.

Henry nodded. "The oldest ones just crumble into dust. So
they need 'the Harvest of the Earth.' For Hain, the Earth is a
big warehouse. From graveyards, he gathers in the dead;
they're not as good as the stolen bodies of the living, but better than nothing."

"You had to help them steal bodies?" asked Clara.

"I am a funeral director. Who would know better than I
where to find the recently buried?"

I shuddered, envisioning Henry guarded by ghouls, skulking in cemeteries, his trembling finger pointing the way for
their shovels. "They led you *outside?*"

"Oh, yes—they had the run of the funeral home. We
marched up and down the main stairs every night. I was kept
handcuffed, of course. Then I'd drive them all, a hearse full of
hijackers, out to Woodbine Cemetery, or over to Stockton, or
Langley—all the towns around. On about the fourth night, we
discovered that the police had my house staked out—by this
time, Dragonfly, you and I were missing persons. So from
then on we went at it from *inside* Harvest Moon. They'd mea-

sure, calculate, and dig a tunnel—we'd come up *under* a cemetery, and load down coffins like boxes from an attic. They can filch a casket without disturbing a blade of grass!"

"Wow," breathed Willie.

"Awful," said Muriel.

"Well, the dead are the dead," said Henry. "No one's using what's planted in Woodbine. I'd help them steal all the bones they wanted if I thought it would spare one living child."

"I understand," said Clara shakily.

"I slept in a guest room on Pink Eye Street," finished Henry. "Whenever I raised a question or made a demand, Mr. Snicker—or whatever boss he left in charge when he was away—would remind me that only my cooperation would ensure your safety."

"What lies." I sighed, watching the gloom speeding by outside our window. "They didn't even *have* me as a prisoner most of the time."

"I couldn't be sure. I did try to escape; Snicker came close to snipping off my thumbs."

Another piece of the puzzle slid into place—a piece I didn't care for at all. Hain's men robbed graves; they had access to the contents of any coffin in the world. *There* was the explanation for why that ghost in the bedroom had carried my grandfather's cane. The briar stick had been beside him on the day they laid him to rest—and these monsters had not allowed him to rest.

My mind raced; ghosts, sightings of dead friends, loved ones, or enemies that walked the Earth by night: throughout history these might have been phantoms of Harvest Moon, wearing the faces of the dead to torment the living, all for the furthering of the Kingdom, for the maximization of pain. It chilled me to think that perhaps my grandfather's body, too, had been stolen from its casket—obviously they had opened his grave to get his cane. What if that which sat on my bed had been his commandeered form, the same I had sat beside in the gazebo years ago?

I pushed the thought from my mind; disturbing what he had cast off could never disturb the soul that was my grandfather.

"How did you get away from them?" I asked.

"Finally, as we were coming down the central stairs after a gruelling night, we were ambushed by Gypsies. Mothkin and Lurkwick were with them. The Harvest Moon group was slaughtered. Snicker was off somewhere that night. That was—oh, I can't keep track of time here; maybe a week ago. Since then, we've all been looking for you, Dragonfly."

Muriel giggled, tipping back her head. "It never occurred to us to look under our noses." She patted Clara's arm. "We searched everywhere but at your house!"

"But when the balloon came and burned you out, it was obvious." Henry shook his head, reflecting. "From across the canals, some Gypsies saw you taken aboard."

"Then Mother Iva began to plan your rescue," explained Muriel. "She is a seer. For a long time she has studied Samuel Hain and his movements."

"No wonder he hates the Gypsies," I said.

"We must give him something more to hate," she replied. "There is now no going back. He will turn the Thanatops and find a way of forcing entry—the wood will give us no more protection."

Willie frowned. "The people here age, and the bodies they're using die. Why doesn't Hain himself die—or Meagerly?"

"His spirit is very great, full of unbelievable force. He and a few of his chief servants have the power to preserve their bodies by strength of will, to shed years like water, crush centuries beneath their heels."

"Then there's hope!" I exclaimed. "Snicker *was* one of the strongest. His face hadn't changed since the Middle Ages—I saw his picture. They can be defeated—even the worst of them."

"Right!" agreed Clara.

Henry's eyes glowed. "What a mess we're all in!" But his tone was not entirely one of dread, or of regret. Of course he wanted to know all about my adventures. I filled him in as best I could, but I was interrupted while I was still on Languor House.

* * *

THERE *was* pursuit.

A yell from Singer told us to keep our heads inside the coach. The Untowards bellowed, and a chilling, feral howl echoed among the trees.

I knew a pang of bittersweet memory with the fear of that sound: it was the cry of a werewolf. This utterance was more prolonged, more savage than any I had heard over the gardens when Sylva was hunting; but once one has heard the voice of a lycanthrope, it is easy to distinguish such from even the most unnerving howl of an ordinary wolf.

The drivers urged the Untowards to greater speed, and our coach sprang like a grasshopper, the suspension wailing in protest. From all around us came throaty barking, howls, the indescribable thick utterances of tongues half-shifted from man's to beast's. Shapes on two legs or four pelted through the brush; we glimpsed them as they flashed past the square of the window. Willie pressed himself back into the hollow between Henry and Clara.

Muriel's eyes searched my face, then peered into the forest. "There must be a hundred of them out there, by the sound. Too many to fight. They're inseparable from the Numinous Wood—Gypsy spells do not hold them out." Again, she studied my face. I knew she was thinking of the story I had just told, of my closeness with Sylva, of the horror of his murder and burial. These were his brethren—doubtless Hain had issued them an incontestable command: *"Overtake the Gypsy wagons. Destroy all who occupy them."*

With a suddenness that hurled Clara, Willie, and Henry on top of Muriel and me, Singer threw the brake, and the carriage plowed the road on locked wheels. I could hear the stiff-legged sliding of the Untowards, their agitated cries, and the squealing of brakes behind us.

Disentangling ourselves, we all tried at once to push our faces to the window. The carriage had spun partly around before it came to rest, and we had a view of the road ahead: three dead trees blocked the track. Determined Untowards at full speed might have bounded over a single log, or even two, yanking the wagons behind them; but three, spaced as they were, would have broken legs and splintered the rigs to kindling. This was no accidental deadfall.

Three werewolves crouched on the farthest treetrunk, their teeth glistening in the light of our lanterns. A terrible silence settled with the dust as their ember-eyes scanned over us, their tongues trailing, tails beating the air. Two had gone completely feral; the tallest had let something of humanity remain in the structure of his head and throat, so that he could address us. He approached with ears twitching forward, his silver-grey fur magnificent. A wolf attempting to stand on hind legs is awkward at best; yet the werewolves of Harvest Moon were all lethal power and grace, masters of the worlds of wolf and man. He that drew near was regal, ready to pounce, to leave nothing behind but his shadow and the mangled dead.

"No closer," growled Singer's voice softly; I surmised he must be holding his crossbow.

The werewolf stopped, spread his wiry limbs, his muzzle peeling back in a grin. His attitude said, *"I see your silver arrow, and I am not afraid."*

The two on the log stopped wagging, opened and closed their mouths expectantly. Dozens of pairs of eyes winked in the thickets to right and left.

"Have you come to do what your master could not?" asked Singer.

The werewolf bunched his brows. "I am a werewolf." His voice was refined, gentle, the words slurred by his labial length. "I have no master."

Singer chuckled. "I see you've left your collar at home on the dresser to prove it. Convincing!"

The werewolf cocked his head, rested his clawed hands on his hips. Suddenly, his smoldering blue eyes were locked on mine.

I wanted to look away, to huddle back in the depths of the coach, but I was unable.

"Now, *this* must be our little troublemaker, our fussraiser." He poked an index finger at Alycia. *"You're* too sweet-faced to be the infamous Dragonfly."

"Is that your business?" asked Singer. "To find Dragonfly? No closer, I said!"

"Ooooo!" The werewolf waggled his claws. "You scare me spitless, Mr. Lurkwick!"

"I don't believe we've met," said Singer.

"I am Cawdor," said the werewolf, "for what it's worth to you. You are all about to die."

"Going to have a fur-flying bang-up, are we? Going to pull hair and bite ears and make each other rue this day?"

"Why not?" grinned the werewolf. "It's Hallowe'en!"

20

THE ABANDON

CLARA put an arm around Willie, who looked weary far beyond his years. The werewolf Cawdor took a few padding steps to the side, his eyes on Singer. His two companions sauntered closer like languid gunfighters. The forest seethed with the shifting of weight, with panting, and a sound I will never forget erupted from all sides at once: the fierce growling of a hundred inhuman throats. The werewolves' noise as they tightened their circle set the frame of Singer's carriage to vibrating, the many-pitched chord rising in volume first on one side, then on the other.

The Untowards were uncannily silent. Horses or mules would have fought to free themselves of the harnesses, kicked the wagons to pieces in their terror. But the Untowards stood with planted hooves and lowered horns—bound as they were to the wagons, they seemed to understand that the Gypsy archers afforded their best chance for survival.

Was our adventure to end this way? Henry's hands lay palm up in his lap, his expression serene; having meditated so often upon death in his work, he could stare unmoved into its narrowed eyes. Clara and Willie gripped each other, faces toward the window. Only Muriel stared not at the werewolves but at me—she knew what I would do before I knew myself.

I couldn't just *sit* there and wait for the end. Time had slowed down for me, exactly as it's supposed to in moments of extreme crisis. I observed every motion in minute detail—the rising and falling of Cawdor's feet, the tiny clouds of dust they raised; the sparkling of lantern light in a sea of amber eyes; the slow twirling to earth of a red autumn leaf.

I followed its downward spiral. On these eternal autumn trees, I reflected, there were just so many leaves—a finite number. Spring never came with its buds, its showers, its tender green. One by one, one by one to decay: that was the way of this kingdom. There was no returning. The dark, given time, devoured all.

What did I have to lose? Once more, I looked at Henry's kind old face.

And then I was pushing open the door, leaping to the rutted surface of the road, staggering to keep my balance. Henry called my name, but again I left him gaping down a laundry chute.

Straightening, I felt a universal scrutiny. Cawdor took me in at a glance but ducked behind the head of an Untoward—he was too wise to let Singer use me as a diversion.

I squared my shoulders, turned in a circle, watched the bristling shadows between the trees. Behind Singer's coach stood the other four wagons, Gypsies armed on each driver's seat to defend their cargo. It was clear that I had stepped out in the second before the first pounce, the first whistling arrow's flight; no one had any idea what I was up to. I brushed hair from my face, clipped it behind my ear. Taking a step, two, I might have been any girl stretching my legs after a carriage-trip.

"Yes," muttered Cawdor, one galaxy-blue eye framed by an Untoward's horns, "this *must* be Dragonfly."

Muriel's voice whispered urgently behind me as she leaned out the door. "I will tell you a charm against werewolves, Dragonfly. Repeat the words aloud." Her voice was so low that only I could hear it. "I don't know if it will work, but let's try!"

I nodded once and faced Cawdor. In the boldest tone I could muster, I said each line as she gave it to me.

> *"By the Holy Rood and the sacred rune*
> *And the bloody light of this aye moon;*
> *By the skin beneath the lurkwick tree*
> *I charge you, set not your teeth to me!"*

My heart caught in my throat. *The skin beneath* . . . She had woven Sylva into her charm. When I had finished, there was utter silence.

Saliva dripped from Cawdor's muzzle. "Mighty words, little one. Mention of that holy—*object*—may turn as many as thirteen werewolves, but not, alas, a hundred." He stalked to the far side of the Untoward team, shadows playing over his shining fur. "The moon you invoke no longer rides the sky." Rearing his head, he faced me across the backs of Few and Far Between. "But what, pray tell, do you know of the *skin?*"

I looked to Muriel for help.

Speak freely, said her eyes.

"It was the skin of Sylva." I swallowed hard. "I buried it under the lurkwick tree."

Cawdor's snout was wrinkled back, so that I saw every one of his gleaming teeth. "Why?" he asked.

"Because I loved him."

The long face twisted, the ears lay back, and Cawdor howled—a sound of rage and heartbreaking melancholy. Hackles rose on the backs of the Untowards. A grand chorus joined him, a hundred snouts pointed at the sky.

A whisper in the dark, Cawdor dropped and rolled beneath the team, arose directly in front of me. The crossbow pivoted, covering him. He thrust up a finger, its claw two inches long. "I found his skin under the tree—I found them both." His chest heaved. *"I was his father."*

I should have known—the eyes—those ice-blue eyes. I had no words to say; Cawdor's grief tore through me. Pain was the eternal product of Harvest Moon—no one was untouched.

"It seems, then," said Muriel from the doorstep, "that both of you have suffered at the hand of Samuel Hain. For it was he that took Sylva's skin."

Cawdor's breath hissed through his nose, his ears pointing straight back down his spine. "My son . . . and my father." He flexed one vicious claw, opening and closing his palm. "You . . . you loved him?"

I nodded soberly, wiping at my tears. "He was my friend. He spoke to me when I was lost—rescued me from Noyes's house on Pink Eye Street. He brought me home, and I lived with him. We worked and played together."

The werewolf turned away, dragged his feet in the dirt. On the high seat, Singer held his crossbow steady on his knee. Alycia sat with a pale hand covering her mouth. Muriel hung on the door, her lips set.

Burying my face in my cloak, I thought of Sylva, of all that I knew about werewolves through him, remembered the story of his grandfather, who had raised his hand against Eagerly Meagerly. Of all Hain's subjects, werewolves were the hardest for him to control. The undead vampires were purely evil, as predictable as a moonless night. Witches were united in the work of pollution, and the general populace were Hain's own people; he understood their hunger for pain. Only the were-wolves were truly *wild*, which is the nature of lycanthropy: the werewolf's supernatural disease confers on him or her incred-ible strength, longevity, and immunity to ordinary instruments of death—it forces regular changes upon the body, and the un-controllable passion for slaughter. But it is essentially an *ill-ness*, an outside force at work on a human being; at the core remains a living, beating heart. Sylva had loved me—had longed to have with me a life of all the normalcy he could manage. He had been a boy at war within himself, a boy of dreams and laughter, striving to cast out the savage.

His father, who stood before me on the road, was also a man of war within and without. He turned back now, folded his arms. "Assuming we don't rumble . . ." He eyed Singer. "Where will you go?"

Singer fingered his dagger. "That's hardly something it would be wise to discuss with you."

"Never mind. I can guess anyway; I've lived a long time beside the Gypsies of the wood. And I'm tired, I can tell you—bone-weary of it all. It's fine to play axe-man and re-ceive commendation after commendation: what nice teeth you have, Mr. Cawdor, what lovely claws! Then one day a were-wolf moves into a marvelous retirement home—as the rug."

He paced nearer, stood glaring up at Singer. "I have not forgotten, bolt-slinger, how you and the Grey Man left many of my brothers dead in Too Quiet Street. Had I been there, things might be different now."

"I'm sure they would be," said Singer. "We would have been kinder in Too Quiet Street if your brothers had been. That is a law you understand. We do not hunt werewolves."

Cawdor's baleful eyes probed. "You sprang the children; you knocked down the moon. You're going to finish it this time, aren't you?"

Singer nodded. "Soon."

For a long time Cawdor watched him.

The eyes blazed steadily all around, amber and crimson and green. They belonged to men and women trapped in a terrible predatorial cycle. Mist stole over the roots. Alycia shivered. Two more falling leaves crisscrossed slowly to the ground.

The forest was a world without wind, a frosty autumn world where no crickets sang. From its depths no sign was visible of the town, no glare on the sky, no creeping smoke. Except for a distant lurkwick grove, a few scattered fey glimmers, the only light was from our lanterns.

Cawdor bent his muzzle so near I could feel his breath on my face. "Infamous Dragonfly," he whispered gruffly, "remember my son."

Quickly, I caught his matted silver claw between both my hands and squeezed it. "I'll never forget him," I whispered back.

He extracted it, glancing at his comrades. "Don't press your luck." Winking as only a father could, he surveyed the row of wagons, linked his hands behind his back, and with the unhurried gait of a werewolf on two legs, he made his way back to his companions. Each of the three lifted a treetrunk in his arms and dragged the barrier into the woods.

Singer picked up the reins. Snorting, Few and Far Between shook their heads as if waking from a nap. Alycia and the Gypsies appraised me with shining eyes. When I hopped up into the carriage, Muriel wrapped me in her arms.

As the battered coach rolled forward, everyone was hugging me and thumping me on the back. Beyond the window, the eyes were vanishing; the rattling of the wagons covered the sounds of padded claws.

AS the wagons plunged deeper and deeper into the forest, the road meandered in curves so prolonged it almost seemed we were going in circles. There were countless branches, alternate tracks shooting away to right or left; I wondered whether Singer directed the Untowards, or whether they were choosing the course themselves. Our firelight flared along the groined arches of trees so thick and ancient that entire houses might be hollowed from their insides—my fancy set the houses there, windows tinted rosy with inner light, living shutters of moss. Odd sets of eyes flashed now and again in the gloomy thickets, and once, in a vaulted avenue of purplish leaves, I glimpsed the shaggy back of something like a monstrous bear.

"Is the Numinous Wood a dangerous place?" I asked Muriel.

"It can be, especially in the deeper places—it is so old, you see, much older than the rest of Harvest Moon. Hain did not make the wood." She watched the tangles sweeping by. "There are places in there, creatures the like of which no one has seen. Some of the old ones have many a tale that would keep you awake at night, staring at the ceiling of your wagon, your ears straining for every little snap of a twig . . ." She smiled at her memories. "Tefan's father, Avim—he tells of seeing what his grandfather called the Ouolaughag—something like a man, but with arms so long they touch the ground."

Willie's eyes grew round in the dimness.

"Others are Muaudhen, the Ghost-Witches, who come into camps sometimes when they need something."

"What things do they need?" asked Willie.

"There is Rokurokubi, the Long-Necked One. My mother was awakened one night by something scratching—*scritch, scratch, scritch*—it was like the sound of a cat lapping milk from a saucer with its rough tongue, only louder. When she opened her eyes, there was Rokurokubi, her neck as long as her body. With her ghastly tongue, she was drinking the oil from a hanging lamp. My mother buried her head under the covers, and when the others were awake, Rokurokubi was gone—and so was the oil from all their lamps!"

Gooseflesh tingled on my arms. Willie sat back, his gaze shifting uneasily around the compartment.

"Are we sleeping in the forest tonight?" grinned Henry. "If so, it might be wise to abandon this topic."

Everyone chuckled pleasantly, but I was thinking again of that shape I had seen—or thought I had seen—back by the canal near the cottage. From what Willie had said then, it had been a result of touching the tainted canal water. But now we were far from the canals—and the phantoms of the Numinous Wood were apparently all too real.

"We build our wagons sturdily," said Muriel, undeterred, "for good reason, and we always sleep inside them; there are wild animals—bears, pigs, great cats . . ."

"Splendid, splendid," said Henry. "Remind me to ask for a bow and arrows."

We rode in silence for a while, and then Willie told us all about his captivity, of how he and the forty other children traveling with us had been shut up in dank cells in a wall of crumbling bricks. There were a few feeble candles only part of the time, with long periods of total darkness. The cells were wet, very cold, and smelled of rot. Guards passed through at times with trays of steaming food and hot chocolate, none of which was given to the prisoners. They were not allowed to speak to one another, and the whole group came together only to eat sparsely, when Meagerly strode up and down among the tables. Every "morning" the children were made to gather the sparsely, which grew on the rubble-strewn floor of a cave somewhere deep inside the wall beyond the dining room. Green tubers on the walls shone softly there with their own light, and somehow this dubious illumination sufficed to nurture the sickly, colorless fronds that probed up through the jagged rocks. Climbing among the boulders, the children twisted ankles, bruised knees, scraped elbows raw. Sometimes the guards drank the aforementioned hot chocolate as they watched the children work, and if any prisoner sat down on the job, a fat man with a whip delivered a lash—usually his approach was incentive enough.

"I tried to start up our story-telling," explained Willie. "You know, to try and cheer us up. But one of the guards heard me. He picked up a live coal in a pair of tongs and told me *that* would be my next meal if I didn't shut up."

We all shook our heads sympathetically.

"Poor Sweet Pea," sighed Clara, hugging his shoulders.

The track dipped abruptly, and the carriage began a curving descent. Huge boulders crouched between the trees. Few and Far Between slowed to (more or less) a walk.

"We're here," announced Muriel.

Roots crept over and under each other like nets covering the rocks. The silver trails of slugs spread in sticky fans, and old humus, heavy with damp, sagged over the lip of a hole in the ground.

As the Untowards pulled us straight down into this crater, I studied the crumbling walls of granite, bearded with black fern and softly luminous creepers. At some time in the past, it appeared, the floor had dropped out of a forest glade. Several hoary trunks, having been sucked half into the collapse, had locked whitened knuckles on the rim, dug themselves in, and grew now horizontally, thrusting ghostly crowns out over the pit. The rank of trees immediately behind them leaned at a less precarious angle, their cross-beam limbs intertwined, dropping an occasional leaf as if in endless vain attempts to fathom the depth.

The roaring of a river overwhelmed the sounds of the wagons, and with a mixture of thrill and uneasiness, I recognized the powerful call of the River Abandon. It arose with curtains of icy mist from the gulf beneath us. Steepening, the road darkened as the lights of plants were left behind. The four swinging lanterns on Singer's carriage threw crazy shadows down a stark slope of shattered debris which plunged away just beside the track. Listening to the river, to the steady shrieking of our brakes, I felt as if we were driving over the edge of the world. Once again, perhaps with self-preservation in mind, the Untowards went quietly, sliding cautiously down a cleared lane barely wide enough for them to pass abreast, between the scree slope and a wall of rock.

I peeped into the frigid abyss, my senses attuned to the thundering entity in the caverns below, the living, roaring Thing that wound back and forth through Harvest Moon. Stretching, I searched for the reflected glimmer of our lights, but the river was much farther down than I had guessed; its voice was borne up by the stone throat, amplified.

"Better lean to the inside, Sweet Pea," advised Clara.

"Feel us slowing down?" asked Muriel. "We're coming up on Cullen's Shortcut."

The carriage was creeping along, negotiating a sharp curve throughout which the road slanted, the outside edge much lower than the inside.

"What's Cullen's Shortcut?" asked Willie.

Muriel nodded toward the window. "Look, but don't lean."

We sighted down our noses. There was a bottomless gulf, where droplets of water fell from the cracked ceiling, flashed through the lantern light, and vanished from the Earth. "I don't see anything," said Willie.

"Look lower."

Pushing our faces a few inches closer to the opening, we dropped our gazes to the glistening mountain-side of detritus, where tons and tons of a former ceiling had amassed. Far, far down among boulders the size of Clara's cottage lay a shape of a different color from the rest.

"It's—it's a wagon!" exclaimed Willie.

The splintered boards had warped and swollen, and the tongue stood up like the mast of a shipwreck. What Willie had recognized, though, was a spoked wheel a few yards from the hulk.

"I'd guess it belonged to Cullen," said Henry.

"That's near where we're going," explained Muriel. "But we generally try to take the long road."

LOOPING around, doubling back, the road brought us eventually to the floor of a dripping cavern, perhaps a quarter-mile beneath the forest. To this day I puzzle with the question of whether the Abandon in that deep channel flowed through a part of Harvest Moon, or whether we had passed beneath Hain's kingdom to journey through the margin of another—for there are countless such worlds.

Anyway, here at last was the river, wide and surging. Its majesty, the awe of its might again swept over me, but my admiration was more controlled than before, less perilous—perhaps the presence of the Gypsies had a stabilizing influence—or perhaps the difference was in encountering the river here, away from the sights and sounds of Hain's dominion. Eager to expand my view beyond the rectangle of the window, I hopped down when Muriel did, let the spray wash over me, let the clean blast of its breeze lift my hair. The lanterns of the five wagons whipped and guttered, and the breath of the Untowards wreathed their heads in clouds. We were at the bottom of a well, a valley of the deep; walls climbed behind us and before, across the river. But that was as far as the light extended—the cavern's ceiling, the road down which we had come were lost in impenetrable gloom.

The Gypsies, Singer, and Mothkin busied themselves with something beyond a pile of rubble, their torchlight and shadows dancing on a stone shoulder above them. I wandered to the edge of the current, skipped a flat stone across the tumbling surface—my tiny projectile was folded under on the first bounce.

The others from the coach joined me; we stood together, watching the foam explode over boulders and against the bank. Where we stood had once been underwater, I guessed, for it was a bed of stones as smooth and flat as faceless doubloons, their dates and the pictures of the kings who minted them long ago washed away and forgotten. Kings came and went—rivers and stones, I mused, would outlast them all.

Clara hunkered down and sat on a rock, her hair fluttering around her ears. Head erect, taking in the view, she was a grandmother at the beach, and Willie hopped around her, stretching his legs. Finding a driftwood stick, he dragged and poked it into the muck. He stooped, picked up a stone he liked for reasons such as only little boys know, and put it in his pocket to keep. Henry shuffled along the water's edge, his hands behind his back. I will always cherish that strange, sacred moment we all spent together there, smiling and breathing and watching on that sunless shore. Perhaps our situation was not so unique, after all—perhaps it only seemed that way to me as a child. Certainly in that dark place I was charged with wonder, and a light shone around us far beyond the power of the lanterns to deliver.

We looked up as the Gypsies drew from its hidden cove a broad wooden barge. One man steered with its tiller as others hauled on ropes, wrestled it into the shallows. Boots sliding in the gravel, they brought it aground, dropped a section of the square bow on hinges to become a ramp.

"Come aboard!" called Tefan, waving to us as he leaped onto his wagon. One by one the wagons were driven up the plank, the teams unhitched, and blocks placed under the wheels to keep them from rolling. Muriel and the others moved around the railing with torches, until a hundred lanterns cast a warm and wavering glow across the deck.

"A ferryboat!" cried Clara happily.

"On the River Styx!" said Henry, spreading his arms.

"The Abandon!" I corrected. "We're going to ride the River Abandon!"

21

THE GYPSIES

CHILDREN streamed from the wagons.

They sprang down the short wooden stairways, elbowing, chattering, dashing along the deck. However dirty and etched with privation their faces were, the sight of them brought a sense of relief; Meagerly's treatment seemed to have done no lasting damage. The scratches would heal, the thinness and pallor would be remedied by food and sunlight. With all the vitality of children anywhere they set about exploring the barge, marveling at the scenery. All had shoes and practical clothing—jeans, sweatshirts, skirts, and cotton blouses. As Willie explained, the guards kept a stock of clothing pilfered from drawers and closets, so that even children kidnapped in their pajamas could be outfitted. There was no laundry, however, in Meagerly's hole in the wall; day and night, the children had to wear the same set of clothes until they fell to grimy rags. By the time his clothes wore out, the typical child, dejected and sick, was dragged off to "graduation." I did not yet understand what happened to the children when their time as prisoners concluded—but I was soon to learn.

Most of the old group, the group I had vowed to help, was

gone. Of the faces I still carried in my memory from that first awful glimpse, only a few remained. In that sense, I had failed: help had come too late to save some.

Tefan and Mothkin pushed off with poles, and once we had swung into the current, the pilot was able to guide us easily with the tiller. The channel was deep toward its center. Flat and heavy, the barge handled the river well. "Be glad we're going downstream," said Tefan, stashing his pole against a gunwale. "The other direction, all the Untowards and some of us would have to get out and pull!" Following the line of his finger, I saw two dry ledges on which men and beasts could walk along the river.

A wide square of deck remained in the bow after all the wagons were parked, three across the stern and two before them. The men built driftwood fires in two iron pots at the center of the open deck, and I helped to organize the children, to get them to sit close around the fires. Heating kettles of water, the Gypsies assisted everyone in washing hands and faces with the first soap any of the children had seen in many days. Again and again, dirty water was emptied over the side, fresh water heated; and old Mother Iva, her shawl like the midnight welkin, tended the worst of the rock-cuts. Sitting cross-legged, she washed the wounds, applied ointment from a blue bottle—smelling of something on fire, the stuff made each patient grit his teeth or cry, until Mother Iva bandaged the cut and gave the child a piece of hard candy; these resembled frozen raindrops.

Next the Gypsies made tea. A broad-shouldered man in a green silk shirt appeared, his arms full of cups. Of course there were not nearly enough of these to go around, so everyone drank in shifts, beginning with the smallest children. The oldest man, his face a study in long, steely lines, poured scalding water over tea leaves, then handed the cups to me to pass around.

As we finished the first distribution, he nodded cordially. "I am Avim," he said. "Welcome aboard the *Quo Vadis*." His accent was strange, though I could not have begun to guess at the country of his origin—his vowels were held slightly longer than mine or Henry's, his consonants more carefully pronounced.

"Dragonfly," I said, shaking his hand. "Thank you, Sir, for everything."

Avim was Mother Iva's son. Together, they led this particular group of Gypsies. Avim knew Clara and Willie; these were among the same Gypsies who had built the cottage in the wood. He rose and bowed to the gathered children. Since their rescue, there had been little time for introductions. Mother Iva, he announced, was a seer, wisest of the family. His wife Rocy was a roundish, warm-faced woman with salt-and-pepper hair.

Avim introduced Tefan, Irah, and Hewin as his sons. Irah was a tall, muscular man, younger than Tefan; the two of them were seeing to the Untowards, but they paused to wave. Hewin was the pilot, dark and lean, like a shadowy pillar on the stern.

As Avim sat, the green-shirted giant leaped to his feet. "Alon!" he boomed. A beard rioted from his nose to his collar. "Amarah is my wife." He indicated a small woman whose face was dominated by enormous, gentle eyes. "The girls are our contribution—Muriel, Ganymede, and Io."

I studied the two younger sisters, who were helping to brush and water the wagon teams. Ganymede, second in age, was a whirl of tangled hair and a pearly smile—her mouth, it seemed, was always open to laugh. Io was a teenager, as brooding as Ganymede was summery.

Once again my foolish envy flared up; I was always so painfully anxious when I felt I was on the outside! I wished I had known the Gypsies first, even for a day or two. No, of course it mattered nothing, but envious I was, and I countered by trying to get to know all the children in a hurry, to make them "mine."

Not much time passed, however, before I realized I couldn't communicate with those who spoke different languages. A brown-eyed girl spoke urgently in French—a dark-skinned boy answered me only with a blank look, and two girls in matching hats blinked long lashes and kept repeating "Japan" and "Hello."

But the Gypsies, I noticed, *could* speak freely with all the children. "Oh, I guess you are," said Rocy soothingly to the French girl. "I'm sorry; all we have now is tea. But when we land, we'll all eat a-plenty."

The girl nodded and sat quietly, watching the dancing river-foam.

I blinked. Rocy hadn't spoken French; her words were the English I understood. Why, then—?

Rocy giggled. "Are you so sure I'm speaking English, Dragonfly? Are you so sure?"

It *sounded* like English; her lips moved in English. Yet across the fire, ruddy-faced Alon was telling a story to a group of children about five years old. Clearly from various countries, his audience hung on his every word.

"How is it possible?"

Rocy's hands flew as she washed out teacups. "We are an ancient people. Can't say 'old as the hills,' 'cause we're older than most hills. Do you know, Dragonfly, why the world is full of languages?"

Once again, my education at Henry's knee came through. "Because of the Tower of Babel."

"Bull's-eye!" Her round cheeks grew rounder. "Back when that monstrosity was being built, there were some among men as said the Gypsies just didn't want to *work*. But the truth was, a Gypsy can always smell trouble comin'—and that proud tower smelled of trouble from the start. So the Gypsies loaded up their wagons, steered hard by the Great Bear in the sky, and had no part of it. They went down the back slopes of that world and in and out of others—and when God mixed up the languages, the Gypsies just *weren't there.* As a reward for their good sense, they've always kept that gift of language, providin' they use it wisely. It's not English I'm speakin' to you, girl—you just *hear* it like it is."

"And isn't it fitting," said Henry, who had also heard Rocy's story, "that those same good-sensed people now are at war with Samuel Hain? After all, he's building a tower of his own."

Rocy snapped her fingers. "Hey, there's nothin' new under the sun."

Mothkin and Singer had the same gift, although they were not Gypsies—and this original tongue of mankind was also, I gathered, what the ancient ones of Harvest Moon spoke. The younger Gypsies sounded different from their parents because they had grown up here, with the voices of the present age in their ears.

THE river swept us along, through magnificent caverns and narrow cracks, in deep, slow stretches and over frenzied rapids. The *Quo Vadis* took an occasional grinding impact, dragged itself over a submerged shelf, but the hull was quite worthy of the Abandon, and Hewin knew his business.

There were children whose language I *did* speak. Willie introduced me to his friend Chris, who had worked with him in the sparsely gardens. Chris was a year younger than Willie, but was tall for his age. A vampire had brought him into Harvest Moon. Playing hide-and-seek, Chris had come face-to-face with the vampire hanging by his heels among the coats in a closet. "Who are you?" Chris had asked. "I'll tell you the truth," said the vampire. "I'm a vampire, come to snatch you away to a place where you're going to be perfectly miserable. Do you want to come with me?" And before Chris could answer, they'd carried him off through a door he'd never seen before at the back of the closet. He wondered how long his cousins had looked for him.

Alycia had finally been abducted through the mirror in her *parents'* bedroom, where they were letting her sleep on a cot. If Hain really wanted you, you weren't safe anywhere.

Avim stood with one foot on a keg, a violin in his hand. He began to play a wandering melody that enchanted and calmed us, and seemed even to assuage the hunger pangs many of the children felt. The music rose into the unseen heights, defying the dark. In the shadowy space between two wagons, Ganymede began to dance. It wasn't a performance—maybe no one saw her but me. She was dancing for herself, responding to the music, celebrating life. Lantern light etched her hair with fiery gold. Her shoes lay cast aside, her feet soundless on the deck.

HOURS slipped by. The Numinous Wood was left far behind as we rode the river deep beneath the mountains. As most of the children watched Alon juggle, I strolled among the Untowards, patted their formidable heads. They snorted and studied me carefully but were unalarmed. I worked my way to the starboard rail, behind a wagon, where the lanterns flickered and the river's whisper was as calming as Avim's music. I was not far from where Hewin stood at the tiller. Dark of complexion, long and angular, he closely resembled his father. He raised a hand in answer to my wave, then continued scouting the channel ahead.

The Abandon forked often in this region, its force diminished. Rocking, the barge entered a wide, echoing tranquility that was almost a lake. I leaned on the rail and breathed the pure, chilly air, let my thoughts float unfocused. Lantern highlights on the waves made it look as if the barge wallowed through nets of gemstones, strings of pearls and diamonds. A ray of gold shot suddenly across the surface, and I saw a light far away.

"What's that?" I asked.

"Another barge," said Hewin quietly. "A Gypsy barge."

I stood for perhaps half an hour, and the other barge drew steadily nearer, cutting toward us as if making for the same point. The single flame became a line, wavering, sometimes vanishing as it passed behind an island; and finally it resolved into the separate winking lamps such as burned along our deck. Then the dark outline of the vessel itself was visible as it veered and glided parallel to us through a cyclopean archway and into another cavern of oceanic proportions. The volume of water led me to suppose the Abandon must be joined here by hundreds of other rivers.

The last several hours of our voyage were spent drifting. Avim replaced Hewin at the helm, the barge hanging nearly motionless. He steered an erratic course, riding a complicated system of invisible currents. Islands loomed out of the darkness, the river lapping at their rocky sides. I could not tell just how far the cavern ran, but it was immense; a third barge appeared a half-mile away.

Children dozed, their heads on their knees, or talked quietly, clustered into language groups. Bearded Alon, ever the entertainer, performed magic tricks with silk handkerchiefs and colorful glass eggs. A tiny Asian girl draped contentedly across his knees like a cat. Irah and Ganymede sat together on a wagon's roof, intent on a conversation that made her laugh and toss her hair. Willie and Chris pumped Tefan for information. He answered good-naturedly, drawing diagrams for them with his finger on the deck. Muriel knelt with them and warmed her hands on a cup of tea. Perched on a hawser and a barrel, Henry and Clara had found a lot in common. Clapping her hands, Clara was not at all the ashen-faced grandmother that had pulled me from the water.

Mothkin and Singer occupied the starboard prow, their cloaked backs like the outlines of two owls. Their conversation was punctuated now and then by a nod, though as always, they wasted no words. When Singer climbed down to talk with Mother Iva, I scrambled up to join Mothkin.

He smiled. Dangling his feet over the gunwale, he faced the murky channel like a strange figurehead. Again I noticed that the left side of his face was lined with new, silvery scars.

"You did well on the forest road, Dragonfly."

I let my feet dangle, too, but clung to the stanchion of a lantern. With a shrug, I said, "I didn't know what else to do."

"It was the best thing you could have done, appealing to the father in Cawdor. Nothing else would have worked. You saved us all."

"But I—I *left* you—at the cliff." I fought to control my voice. "I didn't know if you were alive or dead, but I went off with Sylva."

Mothkin nodded. "If you hadn't, Cawdor would have had no reason to spare us. He certainly has no love for any of *us*. But you chose to love a werewolf boy—and here we are."

Images from my adventures flooded my mind. We sat in silence. Ripples flashed with firelight and disappeared.

"Are those scars from the fight on the cliff?"

"Yes. From the werewolves."

"You're not going to turn into a werewolf, are you?"

"No." He chuckled softly. "I am immune."

"Tell me what happened after the fight."

He'd been seriously wounded. Singer had saved his life by getting Hain's people to follow him, leading them away. It took some clever dodging, but he returned and carried Mothkin on the back of an Untoward to the Numinous Wood, where the Gypsies treated his injuries. Singer had searched for me up and down the sewer ditch, and had figured I must have been captured. The Gypsies watched, but I didn't turn up at Meagerly's. Singer knew Hain was working on something at Number Fifty-two Pink Eye Street. Before Mothkin had even regained consciousness, Singer and the Gypsies sneaked in and hit the enemy hard there, hoping to find me. (Henry and his captors had been away on a raid.) They turned the place inside out, from the attic to the dungeons, and found evidence that someone had been kept there recently.

I sighed, leaning my head against the torch-pole. "I was already in Languor House, with Sylva."

Mothkin swung his legs, the heels of his shoes drumming slowly on the wood. "We would never have guessed that. No one we questioned knew anything. Friends in various disguises infiltrated the town, looking for any sign of you. But you weren't downtown."

"No. The garden district."

"We feared you'd been taken to the High Horse. A surprise attack on Noyes's old house was one thing; an attack on the Tenebrificium would be something else entirely."

"No way in," I agreed, "and no way *through*."

So Mothkin and his friends bided their time, kept their ears open, and studied every move Hain made. Unfortunately, he was *always* moving, sending people and wagons here and there. With Mother Iva's help, Singer planned the rescue of the children, and at about that time someone spotted Henry. No sooner had the Gypsies gotten him away from Hain than others in the wood, watching the moon balloon when the cottage was burned, caught a glimpse of me at last. All was ready then, so they broke into Meagerly's prison and brought out the children. Mother Iva was sure that would force Hain's hand, make him so angry he'd parade me and Clara out as hostages to threaten the Gypsies with. Her auguries told her of the coming appearance of the Thanatops, of Hain's plan to destroy her people.

"Hain *despises* the Gypsies," Mothkin added. "They foil him time and again, only to vanish into the forest. He's sent werewolves before, but their numbers were much smaller in the past. The Gypsies are well-armed with fire and silver;

werewolf attacks never met with much success. Back on the road, though, we saw more than a hundred. Hain's been breeding them, spreading the disease among his townsmen to create an army."

"An army of werewolves!"

"It's all part of Project Nowhere. He's planning to turn them loose outside of Harvest Moon. But their first task, I'm sure, was to be the annihilation of the Gypsies—so you see what a serious thing it was for Cawdor to decide to let us go."

Far ahead, a light was growing, stronger than the barges' lanterns. The third barge, which had slipped in front, drew ashore against a craggy cliff. The light became a flaming beacon, and beyond it rose the wall of the cavern's end.

"That's where we're going, isn't it?"

"Yes." Mothkin lifted his head. "The City of Echoes. The end of all this, for better or worse, is just ahead now."

22

THE CITY OF ECHOES

A murmur of excitement stirred along the deck, children
waking up, shaking each other, pointing at the lights
ahead. The Untowards rolled their heads; Gypsies darted in
and out of the wagons to stow gear. Mothkin and Singer
climbed onto the bow with ropes. Steering in close to where
the Abandon gurgled against peaked rocks, Avim held us
straight. The cathedral rocks, sheer-sided islands on which no
boat could land, towered to right and left; as we squeezed between them, the men on the gunwales pushed against the rock
with poles. If an unexpected current were to throw us sideways, the blades of the rock, honed by centuries of swirling
water, would shear the barge in two.

I watched at the port rail with Henry and Clara. The ceiling
angled down into the scope of the light; curtains of flowstone,
glittering with flecks of bright mineral, hung between
columns whose fluted surfaces resembled thousands of windows. Fires danced below us, and we saw marvelous fish, their
sides aglow with red light. These circled in great, flashing
schools through the submerged pillars of another world.

"Dream-fish," said Muriel.

The wall of the city before us must have taken ages to construct, each stone—the lower ones a dozen feet across—carefully placed on two others, the whole a forty-foot barrier that held together without mortar. Bonfires blazed at the top; these were the lights we had seen from afar. Two wooden ladders climbed to narrow twin doors near the parapet. I could see no other entrance to the valley beyond the wall.

Avim shouted greetings toward the barge threading among the towers behind us. On the boulder-strewn shore, the crew of the first barge waited to help us dock.

"Mind the ladders, children!" Rocy held up a finger. "Poultices can't put you back together if you fall."

Mothkin and Singer tossed their ropes. Hands on the ground caught them, drew us in.

"Hail to the Liberators!" cried a scar-faced man from a high rock. He flung his arms wide, and the chest that emerged from his loose white shirt was as hairy as an Untoward's, crossed by the pale lines of old wounds. Spying Avim he called, "Moses! Well done! Let's drink!"

"Let us indeed!" bellowed Alon, pulling a bolt to drop the prow.

Two rows of men and women from the barge to our left climbed the ladders, the rainbow hues of their clothing, their dark skin aglow in the firelight. From his vantage the scarred man watched the third barge's landing on the other side.

Shouldering packs and boxes, the Gypsies from the *Quo Vadis* led us up the shore, Irah and Alon carrying two sick boys on their backs. The footing was treacherous with shifting fragments, slick with moisture. Henry and I lent Clara our arms to lean on; when we reached the foot of a ladder, she rested on a stone.

Mother Iva shoved her shoes into her belt and scuttled up the rungs barefoot. The children ascended, some timidly, some so eagerly I held my breath as they shrank in the distance.

"Can you climb up there, Grandma?" asked Willie.

"'There was an old woman went up in a basket,'" she quoted.

Henry recognized the poem and joined in: "'Fifteen times as high as the moon.'"

Hewin, Tefan, and Ganymede brought the Untowards, hooves clattering on the ramp. Fascinated, I watched as the animals trotted without hesitation to the ladders and started up. Moving one hoof at a time, the teams kept pace in pairs, one partner on each ladder.

"That's the trick," Henry observed. "Slow and steady."

" 'Shall I go with you?' " asked Clara, finishing the rhyme: " 'Aye, bye and bye.' " Gripping the heavy rails, she inhaled and climbed, muttering verses to herself all the way.

Mothkin was the last one, following me, his cape spreading like a dark wave. The river, too, seemed to utter rhymes under its breath as it lapped around a bend and onward, lost from our sight.

It didn't take me long to figure out that this was not a city of the Gypsies. The hollow valley was a fortress built long ago, said Muriel, by a people called the Vin Avarem. For the Gypsies, the ruins were a camp, a hideaway where the widely-scattered families could meet. No one lived here permanently; the Gypsies were happier in the vaults of the woods.

A stairway led down behind the barrier to a well in the canyon floor. Surrounding the central space rose three levels of ancient buildings, each structure set against the slope so that it required only three walls. Slabs leaned together tent-like to form the roof, the open fronts sealed by piled and interlocking stones. There were no doors in the doorways, no panes in the arched windows. The houses, large enough to seat from ten to a hundred people (the largest was a common hall), contained only stacked-stone furnishings and fire pits. Smoke escaped through cracks where the slabs met, the bare walls blackened with soot.

Not all the buildings, however, had fire pits; I ran from house to house with the other children, exploring. "The fire places are new," explained Muriel, "made by my people. The Vin Avarem burned no wood, and made no smoke." Tables were fashioned of flat, often irregularly shaped stones placed across three legs of stacked, smaller debris. Simple stone cubes served as chairs. In alcoves were rectangular depressions I assumed to be beds.

"How did they cook?" asked Alycia.

Muriel pointed to an alcove. "Food and warmth came from the Madar, a fungus that shared each home in a place of honor."

Alycia wrinkled her nose. "They *ate fungus?*"

"The Madar fed them on itself, yes." Muriel passed a hand over the rough concavity in the wall. "And taught them many things. It had a mind, you see—it *was* a mind—it sang to them when they slept on it."

"What happened to the people and the Madar?" I asked.

"Both finished their work here, it is said. Madar and Vin Avarem are gone into the Hurlim lands, the darkness under the Earth."

The crack in which the city lay narrowed and closed a few hundred yards behind the front wall. The steep sides rose to a shelf on either side, where columns grown between floor and ceiling marched away like stone forests. Having extinguished the beacon fires, sentries lined the wall's ledge, their eyes on the river.

The Gypsies called us to gather in the courtyard. A fire crackled beside the well, and beyond it was a low table on twenty legs—a stage, perhaps—where they laid out a feast. Here were all the staples we had eaten at Clara's and more, from pickles to potatoes, from stewed mushrooms to roast rabbit. There were seed cakes and hot rolls, apples and blackberry pie. "We sent out the call," said Rocy, seating children on semi-transparent cylinders of stone. "Said we were comin' with a boatload of hungry little ones. We can all thank our good Lord for Bailley, Abbie, and Levim!"

"Yes," said Avim, standing across the table. "Let's thank our good Lord."

The children fell silent, and the Gypsies uncovered their heads.

Avim offered a prayer of thanksgiving, mentioning the deliverance from werewolves, the Creator's abundant gifts. "Be with us in what lies ahead," he finished. "If some of us are to leave this Earth, then take us quickly Home. Deliver us from the evil one. Keep us till Shiloh comes."

The children ate ravenously. The scarred man, Basalom, brought out a keg of beer, and Ganymede danced in the shadows when Avim played his violin. Others danced and sang; some told stories so original and amusing that I forgot the passage of time, though I remembered the stories ever afterward. When the children began to nod off, and the tales turned to the ribald misadventures of one or another member of the families, my thoughts wandered back to Avim's solemn prayer.

How could the Gypsies laugh and dance, knowing what must lie ahead? Yet their peace was contagious. Lulled by the warmth and the food, I slumped against Henry and was drowsing when a flash of golden light jolted me awake. I saw that the dishes were being cleared away, and many of the children were asleep. Mother Iva held a globe of crystal in her wrinkled hands. Muttering to herself, she shuffled back and forth, staring into its depths.

Firelight pooled in the sphere, shone from its perfect roundness so powerfully that the globe seemed to generate the light itself. The glow bathed her walnut face, her fingers turning the crystal slowly round and round. "Coming," she murmured, her feathery hair lifted by a draft. "Black horse, black goat, blood moon risen anew—coming!"

"Hain!" whispered someone.

"How soon?" Avim asked.

"Now the bones of the cliff rattle—passing—"

"Bones of the cliff?" said Rocy. "Hangin' roots? They're even with the Five Pools?"

"Aye," croaked the seer, "bye and bye."

"Along the Great Valley, behind the Horse," said Avim. "They'll be here in twelve hours."

"Weave in the haste of hate," Mother Iva said, "and make it ten."

Henry shivered, drawing the lapels of his coat tighter. So Hain knew exactly where we were: I suspected his witches had crystal balls as well, or the equivalent—sticks and bones, magic cauldrons or mirrors. His forces were descending on us, their bloodless hands clutching swords, their iron wheels crushing gravel. The stone wall wouldn't hold them when they arrived. We'd be trapped, as if at the bottom of a well.

Avim waited, his hands on his hips, the fire casting shadows on his sharp-angled face.

Mother Iva hunched over the sphere, turned it from palm

to palm, her lips moving without words. The only sound was the soft singing of the fire. Her eyes widened, darting left and right as she probed a tableau visible only to her.

"You see an answer?" prodded Avim. "You know what must be done?"

The old Gypsy held the ball still, locked knobby fingers around it. "The fire that swims . . ."

"The dream-fish," said Tefan.

"Fire that swims—falling from darkness. Falling from the darkness of dreams."

"Falling fish?" Rocy asked. "What does it mean?"

"No human foot may walk—shadows ascend . . ." Her knuckles whitened. The glow faded from the crystal ball— although maybe that was a trick of the fire; a log settled, sending up sparks. Rubbing her brow, the seer sank to her knees beside the embers.

Rocy leaned over, placed a hand on Mother Iva's shoulder, her face a pale question.

Avim let his breath out slowly. On a rugged boulder at the edge of the light, Basalom folded his arms. His golden earring caught the glow, flashed like a star. Mother Iva polished the sphere on her shawl.

"Well?" said Irah. "What's to be done? What do the visions mean?"

"The High Dark Shelf."

It was Avim who spoke. "The source of the dream-fish, high above us, where the black stream springs from the rock. Are we to go up to the Shelf, Mother? No one I know has ever been there."

"Hain's power," said the old one, "burns with the blood of his moon. Find the Upper Darkness. There—there is the fight."

"The Shelf . . ." Tefan stared into the fire, but his gaze seemed focused on some distant place. "If you say it exists, I believe you. But the stories tell of unscalable cliffs . . ."

" 'No human foot may walk.' " Singer appeared so suddenly behind them that Ganymede and Io jumped. "The Black Goats can reach it."

I had no idea what kind of place they were talking about, but there was no chance to ask. I did my best to keep up as they discussed logistics: since there were not enough Unto-wards, of course not everyone could go. Most would remain here, the children hidden in the cellars, under Mother Iva's spells of protection. The seer decreed that Basalom, Avim, and Alon must see to the defense of the wall. "Here, strength," she said. "There, speed."

"Right." Singer stepped forward. "Mothkin and I will go."

"Go alone, and the moon-master lets you go." The wizened seer turned slowly in my direction. At once, I understood: Henry, Clara, Willie and I were all a part of the design now, in the front ranks of Hain's enemies. He might ignore the two A.P.K.s, plan to deal with them later; but if we went with them, all of us together, he was sure to pursue.

Henry grinned, twiddling his thumbs. "Wild cards, Mr. Lurkwick; that's what you need. That's us."

I expected Avim to object, but he was almost imperceptibly nodding.

"Dream-eater comes for the bright circle," said Mother Iva. "Is it complete?" Her gaze shifted to Clara.

"We're going, aren't we, Grandma?" Willie tugged at her sleeve. "We have to lead Hain away from here."

"That's right," said Clara, buttoning her sweater. "We're going."

Mothkin reminded us of the extreme danger. No one knew what awaited above. There would be no shame in choosing to stay. I gripped his hand. Curiosity had led me after him down the laundry chute; I had much better reasons now to follow him upward.

"A Gypsy should be with you," said Tefan, gesturing with his hat. "Let me go, too."

"Good!" said Mother Iva.

Irah swaggered up beside Tefan, his thumbs in his scarlet sash. "Where my little big brother goes, I will go." He clapped his hand on Tefan's shoulder with a force that nearly buckled the elder's knees. "Someone's got to keep reminding him which end of the goat is which."

"Two is best," confirmed their grandmother.

Avim nodded once; Rocy's mouth twitched, and as she stirred the fire, sparks leapt. Muriel's gaze clouded. Leaning carelessly against a roof-slab, Ganymede stretched and yawned.

The Untowards needed sound sleep: before their fitful doze on the barge, they had run twice the length of the Numinous Wood—to Meagerly's and back, and then to the river. Singer said we would start in seven hours, and we should try to sleep. Even as he spoke, the Gypsies began carrying supplies and leading the weary children to the cellars.

Clara and Willie went ahead with Singer to the guardhouse at the wall's base. Mothkin conversed with the Gypsies, then rejoined Henry and me. In the dying light of the fire, we stood for a moment together—the three of us, like on the Hallowe'en night when it all began.

Then Mothkin steered us toward the wall, the sweet strains of Avim's violin rising from where he sat on a rock in the empty court. As we moved away, I understood the city's name. Avim's music swelled in the caverns of the slope, hummed among the columns of the high shelves. We stopped walking to listen. The city was a gigantic, resonating instrument, as if the single musician had awakened from the dust a grand chorus of ghosts.

Now Ganymede did not dance, but stood face-to-face with Irah. They were two statues, lovely and somehow apart from time: I would always remember them that way.

None of the others were about as we crossed the floor of the ravine and approached the guardhouse. Basalom walked a gantry high above, his arms loaded with quivers of arrows. The violin faded away, and an eerie silence settled over the long-empty city. I thought of the Vin Avarem, who had piled up these stones. What had they looked like, and why had they chosen to live in a world of everlasting darkness? Now they were gone, and a handful of the living nestled in the cold, ancient Madar-beds.

Singer, Clara, and Willie arranged the bedding on the floor of fitted stones. The Gypsies had lent us warm feather pallets, small pillows packed with aromatic beans, and colorful blankets of a material I did not recognize. Two lanterns burned in corners; the chamber was otherwise bare.

I don't imagine sleep came to any of us during those hours. At least the Untowards were sleeping, I kept telling myself. I lay as quietly as possible, trying to *will* myself to rest. My head overflowed with memories, faces and voices as clear as on the days they'd gone in.

Mothkin and Singer sat for quite a while before they blew out the lanterns. I supposed they were praying; when I tried, my thoughts were too erratic to sort words from. Then I began to pray in pictures—children returning home, parents weeping for joy. The mothers were all my mother, the fathers my father. My tears came, warm and silent.

Listening to the others turn themselves over and over, I tried to block out visions of the wagons and hooves racing toward us down the canyons. I crept to the dank restroom, a malodorous shaft at the back of the chamber, closed in by leaning walls. Clara found me sobbing there, led me to my bed, and rocked me long into the night.

23

NO HUMAN FOOT

EXHAUSTED by hours of pushing myself from my right side to my left, I had at last sunk into a warm, somnolent comfort, my body heavy and limp. I was drifting in a murky, echoing state just below consciousness when a change in the light brought me fully awake. A lantern in his hand, Tefan waited in the doorway; I doubted he'd even tried to sleep.

Singer and Mothkin sat up instantly, as if they'd been awake and listening for a signal. Seeing our movement, Tefan nodded soberly and left without a word. Mothkin struck a flame; in the flare I saw Clara curled on her side, a wisp of hair rising and falling across her nose at each breath. Willie was a ball beneath his covers. I shook the ball, and it moaned.

His back popping, Henry sat up, fumbled for his glasses. Clara pulled her false teeth from the pocket of her sweater, slid them into her mouth, and clacked them experimentally. Willie crawled out of his burrow, his hair standing straight on end. I wonder what the two A.P.K.s thought as they surveyed us in the dawnless dawn of that stone room.

Irah, too, stood in the courtyard by the table—during the night, I had not heard either of the brothers enter the guard-house, where their bedrolls awaited. Hewin served a breakfast of hot cakes, toast, and a thick stew. Avim, Rocy, Mother Iva, Bailley, and quiet Amarah clustered around, drinking tea and speaking little. Weariness showed in their faces. Tefan and Muriel led four teams of Untowards, two by two, from a large edifice near the common hall. Stamping, swishing their tails, the beasts looked ready for action.

"The children are sleeping soundly," said Avim as we ate.

Lanterns crossed back and forth atop the wall, where Basalom and Alon had been busy: I glimpsed archers, stacks of rocks, and even two catapults which Basalom's crew had carried in pieces from their barge. The barges, Irah explained, were in a hidden harbor upstream.

The catapults commanded the river, but Hain was not coming by boat. They could also be turned to cover the shelves above the city. Singer pointed to where flowstone formations grinned like opening jaws. "That's where he'll come from."

Mother Iva had laid spells across every approach, but one seer's devices would do little more than slow the enemy down. Archers would harry the attackers until they broke through the forest of columns, and then fall back into the city. Advancing, Hain's soldiers would face a hail of stones from the catapults.

Singer and Avim agreed, however, that the attack would come from both sides and quickly overwhelm anyone on the wall or the ravine's floor. Barricaded in the cellars, the Gypsies would be a difficult and dangerous prey. Still, Hain had the numbers and the witches to ferret them out. The best hope was that he would demand to be present for the victory, that he would order his warriors to encircle the defenders and await his return from the Shelf.

Singer smiled, gripping Avim's shoulder. "You've done what can be done."

"God go with you, my friends," said Avim, taking our hands.

"And may He stay with you," answered Mothkin.

Between two Untowards, Tefan held Muriel in his arms, tenderly brushed away her tears.

Clara missed Ganymede and Io; Amarah explained they were with the children, neither being adept at good-byes. With misty eyes, we thanked and took leave of our friends, praying that we would meet again.

The Untowards had leather collars fastened over their fore-quarters. Two curved wooden pommels on the top of the collar gave the rider a secure grip, but there were no saddles, stirrups, or bridles. Although the animals stood no more than five feet at the shoulders, I was acutely aware of the distance from their backs to the ground.

Mothkin cupped his hands to make a step for me. Clinging to his arm, I let him hoist me onto Few's matted back, where I grabbed the pommels, one over each of the animal's shoulder blades. Few sidestepped as I landed, his hide, which smelled powerfully of goat, twitching violently. Mothkin patted the shaggy neck, and he calmed down. His broad back—impossibly broad, it seemed to my stretching legs—rolled with every shuffle of his hooves. I held on, hoping the collar wasn't going to slip.

"He likes you," said Singer, twisting his hat to tighten it on his head.

Willie's mount was a lanky, even taller Untoward called Steeple, whose head bobbed as if it were on a spring. Receiving Willie, the creature whipped around in bounding circles, rodeo-style.

Watching Steeple's antics, Clara's expression was completely blank, like those of students during the second week of a physics class, face-to-face with the incomprehensible.

"Don't worry," reassured Tefan; "he's just happy to have a light load. Chase, here, is steady and runs straighter than any of the others." Before she could protest, Tefan and Irah boosted her onto Chase's back. Rocy had outfitted Clara with an over-sized skirt, which she had pulled on over her faded dress; sidesaddle, Bailley had said, Clara would never stay on an Un-toward's back—the skirt was large enough that Clara could hike her dress up to her hips and ride in modesty. Half-buried in a cascade of purple cloth, she and Chase made me think of one of the magi arriving by camel from the mystic Orient.

Lighter in color than the others, Chase cast one glance at her rider, snorted, and kicked her hind legs, heaving upward at the back end. She slammed back down, let the shock wave snap her front end into the air. Somehow Clara held on, leaned close to the animal's ear, and said, "Now that's enough of *that*." And it *was;* after three lashes of her tail and a tentative circular prance, Chase seemed to give her approval, and bleated demurely. Clara straightened her sweater, a smile creeping over her face as Chase plodded into line.

As Singer helped Henry onto a particularly long-haired beast, I noted that Henry and Clara had wisely tied strings to their glasses; one line went around behind their heads, and another ran from an earpiece to their top buttonholes. Henry swayed fluidly with his mount like a pro. Tefan swung onto the Untoward to Henry's left; their team's names were Hither and Yon.

Singer climbed aboard Far Between, who reared and actually took four steps on his back legs before he came down. Irah and Mothkin mounted the jet-black, flame-eyed team at the rear of the column, Fire and Flood.

"Don't concern yourselves with steering," instructed Singer. "The Untowards will follow their leaders, and they'll do better at choosing their path than we would. Give all your attention to holding on. Where we're going, there'll be an awfully long way to fall."

The Gypsies crowded around us one last time, clutching our hands, wishing us well. Then Few's back was undulating, the rock-strewn floor of the canyon sliding away beneath us. At first, my legs and tailbone whacked painfully against Few's back at every stride. I had seen Henry buy paint at a hardware store once; I recalled the machine that had clamped the sealed bucket and shaken it into a whizzing blur. Rocks and buildings vibrated before me, each visible in multiple images stacked one atop another.

"Relax!" called Singer into my right ear. "The only muscles you need are the ones in your hands!"

I tried to become a mass of jelly, and it helped. The landscape bounced as it streaked past, but I wasn't being ground to powder.

"Oh-my!" Clara's voice drifted over the clopping of hooves. "Oh-my-oh-my-oh-my-oh-my!"

"Roll with her, Grandma," piped Willie. "Like this!"

"I-*am*-rolling-tell-*her*-to-roll!"

Singer led us through the tiers of the city and up the slope to the right. The Untowards leapt expertly over patches of glistening flowstone, keeping to the solid boulders, cracks chinked with the dust of centuries. Free of the wagon harnesses, the beasts were clearly at home now, their lungs filling with the chill air. Avoiding the loose cairns, they surged up a forty-five-degree incline, sometimes moving in single file, sometimes two by two. Hazarding a glance behind, I saw Avim, Rocy, and Hewin, already mere flashes of color around the fire, and beside them Amarah and Muriel. Mother Iva hunched beyond the flames, her arms upraised.

The City of Echoes itself diminished, its dark outlines fading to invisibility. Torches gleamed like fireflies along the great wall. In a matter of seconds, the well behind us looked utterly black, no different from any of the other cracks and gulfs of the deep Earth. I wondered at how frail a thing man is, at how the mere absence of a torch in such a place casts the greatest of his works into obscurity. Where was the wall piled up by the Vin Avarem; where were the houses they had built? What did the stones care that a few beings in a barren valley would stir the dust in battle? After that climb among silence and eternal apathy, I am always awed by the passage in Luke 19—when Shiloh passed among them, stones such as these were ready to cry out in praise.

Singer, Tefan, and Irah all had lanterns glowing, which locked on metal rings at the tops of short poles. The poles, in turn, were inserted snugly into sheaths on the collars of their mounts. Shadows pressed around our wavering circle of light—it was unnerving not to have any idea what lay a few feet beyond. Hain's entire army could have crouched a hundred yards away and watched us go by. As we topped the slope and entered the field of columns, I began to imagine with increasing conviction that they *were.*

The silence was maddening. It amplified the footfalls of the Untowards, made their breathing harsh. To my consternation, my palms broke out in a clammy sweat, the pommels growing slippery. Frantically I rubbed them with my cloak.

Singer seemed vigilant but at his ease, his crossbow ready. I had seen him wind it, but he had not laid a bolt in the track; probably he didn't want to risk firing accidentally from his jouncing perch. The lantern swung above his head, sending the shadow of his brim up and down across his face.

Behind me, Tefan held his long bow, his purple vest resplendent; the scrollwork of its embroidery flashed and changed as the twirling light picked out different stitches—his chest was a midnight sky of scudding clouds. Henry rotated his head to admire the cavern columns, wide around as the trunks of oaks, but older by millennia. The ceiling was draped with curtains of stone so thin I could see the light of Irah's lamp behind them. Soda-straw stalactites filled the gaps between their larger cousins, and dazzling mineral flowers spread petals delicate as crystal—some of their filament strands actually fluttered in the updrafts of the lanterns.

Willie and Clara, too, had adjusted somewhat to the quirks of the Untowards. The old watch glinted on its chain around Willie's neck—he had hidden it in his pocket, and the guards at Meagerly's had not taken it away. The sight of that watch brought back the memory of our stories in the cottage; I reflected happily that Willie was experiencing now a journey as fantastic as any his imagination had conceived. But time was limited for this foray, as surely as we had imposed limits on our story times then—I didn't want to think of the consequences of failure.

Mothkin and Irah both carried bows across their knees. The darkness closed behind them, sweeping up all traces of our passage—of our existence.

WE traveled for perhaps an hour through the weird, dripping forest, where the "petrified trees" had grown from both ends to meet in the middle. We could see Mother Iva's enchantments hanging in the air like helicoids of blue mist. There were other avenues, much wider than this one, said Singer, through which the enemy might approach; it was difficult for the Gypsies to know exactly where to concentrate their spells of defense. The surface we traversed was fractured like earth that bakes in the sun. The stalactites bunched along cracks in the ceiling. Again and again the Untowards stepped up or down a foot or more where the floor had buckled; sometimes the rock had separated, leaving a crevasse dozens of feet deep. I gripped the handles and held my breath when Few edged gingerly along the slick edges and hopped across to the far side.

The gardens of ice-like mineral blossoms would have been a speleologist's paradise; crusting the surfaces above and below us, they glimmered foam-white, emerald green, ruby and sapphire. The regular falling of droplets *plok, plokked* in the stillness, swept away at times by the subdued roar of the Abandon, now separated from us by tons of limestone, now so near we turned in hopes of seeing it.

THE ground began to slope downward, the columns diminishing in number, just as if we were coming to the edge of a forest. Ahead, an eerie red glow shone through the last pillars. It was a flickering, shifting light—the umbrages of the stone formations swung around like the shadows of sundials. The Untowards came to a dead halt, their noses testing the suddenly smoky air. Listening to the increased volume of the river, I swallowed hard—I knew the color of that light. Only one source burned with the fire of an obscene jack-o'-lantern. Glancing at Singer, I read confirmation in his face.

Hain had raised his moon again. It was not far away.

"Lights, gentlemen," said Singer, sliding his lantern pole from its sheath. Blackness crept in behind us as two of the lanterns went dark. Singer kept his burning, but held it lowered almost to the ground, so that its light was reduced to a circle at his mount's feet.

We sat in the gloom. Hain's light grew, and with it came the sounds of his people—although the river masked the falling of hooves, we could pick out the grinding of wheels, the metallic clash of the wagons, the unmistakable snort of the *Jolly Jack.*

"They're in the channel," murmured Tefan.

"Where are we, exactly?" asked Mothkin.

"Across from the Dead Sea," said Singer. Far Between stamped his foreleg, gave a small, uneasy bleat.

"This is your territory," said Mothkin, walking his mount up beside Singer. "What do you say?"

Singer did not answer at once, but moved his arm, playing his light in a wide circle over the floor. "The stone is wet here. Easy to slide right off into the river." He glanced back at us. "Hain won't have them *all* in the channel. Some will be up here; most will go through Heavensdrop Hall or the Thousand Ghosts. If he hasn't smelled us already, he will. I don't see any point in hiding out."

As if to punctuate his statement, the dry whisper of foot-steps sounded somewhere to our right, frighteningly close by. A loud baying echoed among the columns, answered from a half-dozen directions.

"Werewolves!" hissed Tefan.

A bluish light floated in the darkness from which we had come.

"They're already back there," growled Irah, "breaking an opening in the guard spells."

Few jerked back and forth, so that words seemed to leave my mouth sideways. "I thought the werewolves were on *our* side!"

"Not hardly," said Tefan. "Cawdor did us all the favor he could do on the road, but Hain's with them now."

"We'd better move," advised Irah. "Do you know the way to the Bridge of Despair?"

"If I explore a little," said Singer. "Do you know it better?"

"By heart, from my Dead Sea camping days."

"Good." Singer handed him the lantern. "We haven't got time to explore."

Now Fire and Hither took the lead, carrying the Gypsies, who steered by the formations as a mariner would use stars. Glistening shelves, rainbow pillars whistled past as the Unto-wards followed the bobbing lantern.

"Heads down! *Keep* 'em down!" warned Tefan just in time—a jagged curtain materialized and whisked off my hood as I ducked. We lay against our mounts' necks as the low ceil-ing brandished an array of stone spears and lances. I shud-dered, *feeling* the unseen blades scything over my back.

I didn't even see the attackers until it was over.

"Aa-HA!" shrieked an inhuman voice. Something growled, and Few screamed, skidding.

None of my companions said a word; I'm not even sure whose arrows flew—but as the Untowards sprinted forward again, three huge black werewolves lay among the rocks. One's leg was still kicking spasmodically as Few bounded over her.

The horror of war spilled through me like an icy liquid. We had killed—without question, without hesitation; there could be *no* hesitation. No one was asking questions any more. When Steeple drew even with me I saw that Willie's face was colorless. Still unable to straighten, we held on and wondered when furious claws might strike. Once I stared into a were-wolf's eyes—fire-blue eyes that flashed nearer, nearer—then suddenly sprang away, dodging a barricade of stalagmites that swept between us.

"The Bridge!" called Irah, tossing the lantern to Singer. There was no further need of lamps.

We emerged on a shelf some fifty feet above the river, which had regained its frenzy in a high-walled ravine. Foam burst around pinnacles of rock, jutting up like the fingers of a twisted claw.

And there, hanging ripe and poisonous under the mammoth arch of the ceiling, was Hain's balloon. The jack-o'-lantern face was a ruined mask of horror, the skin sooted dark, the nose and mouth engulfed by a ragged hole; only the eyes remained—the scarred and floating head was frozen in a scream of rage. If the craft's purpose had once been primarily observation and the lighting of Harvest Moon, now it was clearly a grotesque battleship. Wire netting had been rigged to stand out from the entire lower hemisphere, an apron for the screening of missiles fired up from below. Though we could not see the pilot, enough of the interior was exposed to display the ranks of canisters and explosives lining the platforms within; the crippled giant was a flying arsenal, stripped of everything but bombs and fuel. Even with the inefficient loss of huge quantities of heat, the balloon carried enough of the mountain's gas to power Conflagron while Hain dropped burning death on his enemies.

"Old Jack's not so jolly any more," muttered Tefan.

In the river canyon marched the forces of Harvest Moon, troop haulers plated with iron, black carriages, warriors on horses and Untowards. Werewolves ran in circles along the slopes, their noses to the ground; rows of the skeletal death-guard clacked in formation with raised spears. Fires blazed in pots all along the host, blanketing them with a fog that dis-torted shapes, made the army look like a single living, creeping mass. They were heading upriver in a file so long its vanguard was already out of sight around a bend a half-mile distant. With a sinking of my heart, I saw that the Gypsies were outnumbered at least fifty to one.

Ahead and to the left, downstream, rose the bridge. Unable to believe my eyes, I looked at Singer; he seemed unperturbed. The bridge was in ruins. Once an apparently natural arch of stone spanning the river gorge at our level from cliff to cliff, it had lost its middle; a twenty-foot section had fallen into the roiling water, leaving the slender tongues on either end, ramps to nowhere. Surveying its interrupted length, I understood its name; *despair* was a logical feeling for anyone who had counted on crossing.

Even worse, we had been spotted. The werewolves commenced a frenzied barking and howling. The far wall of the cavern lit up in a series of flashes as someone aboard the *Jack* signaled with a bull's-eye lantern. Seething, the column of the enemy slowed, heads turning in our direction.

"Here we go!" said Singer, clapping Far Between with his knees.

Few followed his twin's lead, lurching ahead, hooves splaying on the wet flowstone. My breath caught in my throat as we slid toward the lip of the canyon. Dislodged, stone pieces rained down—Henry's face tilted away from me as Few's hindquarters spun around. But Few had a level head; ceasing to struggle, he redistributed his weight, stood still, and let his momentum burn itself out. When we skidded to rest against a dry outcropping not ten feet from the rim, he chose his route carefully and climbed out of danger.

The forest of columns erupted with loping grey shapes. Fangs bared, the werewolves charged in from the flank to cut us off.

Arrows flew. Once the lycanthropes closed with us, there would be no contest; a claw's swipe could remove an Untoward's throat—the only chance was to reach the bridge at a dead run. Had I been alone, I would never have tried it; I didn't believe even these agile goats could clear that distance.

Swwitchh! Singer's silver-tipped bolt caught a werewolf in the chest, spun him around. Letting fly simultaneously, Avim's sons dropped two more. I couldn't help but hear Sylva in their strangled yelps; I saw his anguish in their glowing eyes. There'd been no remorse at the destruction of the vampires, but even fleeing for my life, I wept for the werewolves—they were victims, as surely as the children were, caught between two worlds.

Pelting ahead, Mothkin drew up with Singer, shot a shape-changer in midair. Handing him the still-burning lantern, Singer nodded and galloped forward. Mothkin pulled back, working with something under his cloak. Leaving the ground, Flood careened over an astonished werewolf, who looked around just in time to meet Hither's shoulder. Tackled, the werewolf cartwheeled through the boulders.

At the approach to the bridge, two lycanthropes danced from paw to paw, claws raised. Far Between never slowed his pace, stones crunching, flying away beneath his hooves. With calm efficiency, Singer wound the key of his crossbow, *scritch, scritch, scritch.*

The balloon turned itself like a weary hippo, smoke pouring from its ears. The ribbons of its torn skin flapped in the breeze.

"Come ON come ON!" yelled Willie to his mount. His yellow hair lay straight back from his face as he hugged Steeple's neck, patted his shoulder.

Irah lay on his belly and fired backwards, using the sweep of his bow arm to draw the string. His shot only grazed his attacker, but it cost the werewolf a few strides.

Clara's voice was muffled, her face buried in Chase's back. "Run, Sweet Pea! Run!" So now Chase, too, was a Sweet Pea.

Henry's expression made me look forward again. Fifteen feet from the bridge, Singer slid a bolt onto his deck. Ten feet out, Far Between went airborne.

Their pouncing strategy confounded, the werewolves had no time for a second plan. The Untoward swiveled as he flew, his back legs coming forward, hooves like spiked maces. Rotating his arm, Singer fired point-blank. A couple thousand pounds behind the blow, Far Between plowed into the second guard, touched down, and got his balance, flip-flopping in three doughnuts. Both werewolves soared into space, their dark forms like those of cliff-divers against the whitewater far below.

I had no time to watch them fall; I was in line behind Singer. Few and Far Between barreled up the bridge, gaining speed. As the gulf drew nearer like the end of all space and time, I think I screamed into the wind.

I'll never forget that leap. There was *nothing* beneath us— only hanging vapors, blue-grey and frozen, far, far below. I remember the bunching of muscles in Few, and then silence—the pounding of hoofbeats suddenly gone, the emptiness whistling in my ears. We hung there forever. Over my head passed the ceiling of curtains and canyons, the lower edge of another world, and my insides were nothing but laughter. Few hit the farther span at a run, skimming down after Far Between. I looked back under my arm, saw Tefan and Henry landing, Clara and Willie crossing the gap.

A werewolf sprang at Mothkin, would have landed on his back, but Irah's arrow found its mark. As the beast fell from the cliff, Irah pulled ahead, vaulted with Fire over the river.

Last up the span, Mothkin ripped apart a flask with his knife, swung it behind him. The bag's contents gushed out, viscous and heavy, to cover the bridge. It was oil, the fuel of Gypsy lamps. Just as he prepared to flip the lantern over his shoulder and ignite the oil, leaving our pursuers a flaming barricade, an enemy pounced from concealment, lunged for Flood's neck.

The werewolf had wriggled in under the hail of arrows, worked his way up to the edge of the bridge. His bow over his shoulder, his knife in its sheath, Mothkin held only the lantern.

Without pausing to think, he shattered it over the snapping head. Grunting, the lycanthrope missed his target, glancing off Flood's chest. Mothkin caught the pommels as Flood stretched out, sailed across the bridge, and galloped down the other side to join us.

If the fire had failed, the oil had served well enough; slipping, wheeling their arms, the beasts could not approach the dropoff at a run—with the springing power of the lycanthrope, they might have been able to follow us—but not from a standing start.

"Perfect!" cried Singer. "Now after me—there's no time to lose!"

"The Bridge of Despair," chuckled Tefan. "If it weren't a broken bridge, we would all be dead." He leaned across and gripped Irah's shoulder. "Good work, big little brother!"

The look on Willie's face was almost rueful as we sped away; I'm sure he wouldn't have minded trying a second leap. Clara gasped for breath, sagged over Chase's head. Few and Far Between were in the lead again, with Hither and Yon so close behind that a sudden stop would have resulted in a pile-up. "Not so close, girls," laughed Tefan, pulling on Hither's horn.

The trail down from the bridge narrowed, plunging to the water's edge where the Abandon ran into a smaller cavern. About a third the size of the one behind, this channel wound slightly, walls glistening with the river's spray. There was something ominous in the darkness, in the confined thunder. We all hung on tightly as the Untowards tripped along three feet from the hurtling foam. Although I couldn't see what was happening at the bridge, I knew we wouldn't be safe for long. Crossing the river would slow Hain's people down, but I was sure they had ways. The balloon could be negotiated into this corridor; for the sake of those in the City of Echoes, I hoped the *Jack* would follow us.

We hadn't gone more than a quarter-mile when the ceiling shot away, the cavern became once more colossal, and five passages radiated from the chamber before us.

Whole mountains of rubble climbed the sides of the bowl-shaped floor, tons and tons of debris, I supposed the oldest solid objects on Earth. A lake became visible as we mounted a slope, still, black water, separated by a scree-slope from the river.

But what immediately captured our attention was a water-fall of liquid fire. Descending like a continuous sheet of thunder from darkness above, folding, folding on the stones below, it lit up the entire cavern. The fire was not constant, but flared and leapt in spirals *within* the water, glowing deep in the pool at the base, and sparking in glory as it spilled over into the Abandon. Spray rose in clouds, bathing our faces, dampening our hair as the Untowards climbed to the edge of the pool.

Singer had to yell to be heard: "Each streak of fire is a huge school of dream-fish!"

Was it possible? There were millions of flares, an aurora of red flames, and millions of tons falling every second. How many years had this gone on, minute by minute? For how long would it continue? Never had I been so aware of the imminence of God.

"The Gypsies call this Immemorial Hall," said Mothkin, "or the Fire Falls. But the Vin Avarem had a better name. The word they used means 'The Hall of Creation.'"

Yes, I had to agree; that was the best—Light plunging out of a Void; water; a roaring as of the formation of stars and worlds—and washing over us from the fathomless darkness above, the exhaled breath of an omnipotent Spirit.

"Life," said Tefan, "and Death. Over there is the Dead Sea, a body of water thirty feet deep, with no inlet or outlet that anyone knows about. The seers say it's here to remind us what water looks like when it stops moving." That *sounded* like the seers, I've often thought: Keep Moving was the philosophy by which the Gypsies lived and died. The Dead Sea was cut off from the source of the dream-fish; it had no access to what fell from above. To Gypsy thinking, understanding sources was all-important.

The Abandon charged on into a cavern where the shores were wider, and a convergence of currents threw the flood up in curtains of mist. A faceless darkness gathered under the arched entrance, hung over the flats of mud and grey sand along the walls. The blackened hulk of a ruined boat lay half in the water, half on the shore. Loneliness and *lost*ness were etched in the vanishing lines of the cavern's depth.

"We call it Charon's Porch," said Tefan. "You're looking at the very end of the Abandon, where it flows into a darker river."

"What river?" I asked; I could not really see the other river—only the mist, the tumult of its passing.

"I know only the name legend gives it," answered Tefan. "The Styx."

Zig-zagging, the Untowards carried us up beside the falls from rock to rock, in and out of the mist veils. "Hold on!" called Singer. "From now on, we're wall-climbing!"

There was no way I could see to continue upward, only the sheer face of the rock, illuminated by the Fire Falls; but the

Black Goats of the Rocks skipped from chimney to chimney, over the shadowy rooftops of a world unseen by human kind, up the eaves of castles of darkness. People say you should never look down in such a situation, but who can resist? When I saw how far below us the water pooled, I prayed hard I wouldn't faint. If Henry, Clara, or Willie had any observations on the ascent, they were saving their breath.

24

EVENT HORIZON

IT was a world of darkness in vertical lines, shades of grey and black, broken only by the falling fire—a world without compromise, where a wrong step had only one result. The cliff, with its buttresses and promontories, was a grand sculpture that shared its echoing sanctum only with air. After hours of leapfrogging from pinnacle to pinnacle, straddling crevasses, and wriggling upward through cracks in ledge after ledge, we trotted onto an expanse of smooth rock a hundred feet long, sheltered by an overhang. Singer rode in a wide circle to investigate the shallow cave.

"Is this it?" I asked. "The High Dark Shelf?"

"Not yet," he answered. "But the Untowards need a rest."

Clara hobbled with assistance to a boulder, her joints creaking. "I shouldn't have gotten down," she said, "if I have to turn around and get right back up." Willie made the rounds of all the Untowards, patting and thanking them. The animals lay down to catch their breath.

"They don't usually have to climb so far so fast," explained Tefan, stroking Hither's muzzle.

Several hundred feet overhead, the cavern closed in a cathedral dome; the burning river fell through a rough hole, crashed on the stairsteps of ledges. The fire-fish, I thought, must be a tough breed to survive their journey.

The A.P.K.s and the Gypsies spread out along the edge, watched below, but there was nothing to see. Our ascent had doubled back and forth so often I could not have traced our course, even with a searchlight. Tefan altered his position by a few paces, scanned the well of shadows. "Nothing. Not a torch, not a movement . . ." His voice trailed off. *We* didn't carry torches, either. Beautiful as it was, the water masked sound; we might not be able to hear any pursuit—and there was no guarantee that we'd be able to see it.

The men checked their weapons. Irah passed us a water-skin; the Untowards, too, drank from a basin in the rocks.

Squinting upward, Tefan stood with fists on hips. "This is as far as anyone I know has ever come. Through this hole, it may be a long way, or it may not be far at all."

I stood on tiptoe beside him, craned my neck. "How do you know it's there at all?"

He laughed easily. "The seers see, and we believe. But getting there may not be easy."

Clara said, "Getting *here* wasn't easy!"

A tortuous trail led up through the enormous hole in the dome, following cracked defiles so narrow that in one place, we had to dismount and squeeze in single file. Once above, the Untowards were faced with a slope of debris, little more solid than sand, steep and wide; there was no place to jump to, nothing for it but to inch upward on their bellies to firmer ground. Using ropes, we were able to belay one another, anchoring, untying, passing the ropes back. It took more than an hour, and when we were all safely past, enough of the loose material had been dislodged that a nyone following would have a much easier go; we'd cleared the way for the pursuit.

The steeples resumed, and we bounded higher and higher, sometimes passing between the falls and the cliff. Exhilarated by the mist, the fiery fish tumbling past my head, I was thrilled to think that no one had ever seen these grottoes, unchanged since before the pyramids were raised. Only air had occupied this space before us—or so I thought.

The wall tipped back, became a steep slope, and we angled away from the falling water. I didn't notice until Singer told me, but we had broken out of the caverns; we were again in that vast airspace where Harvest Moon lay.

"We're much higher than the High Horse," he said. "It's back there." He pointed toward a maze of ridges. "We may be able to see some lights when we're even higher."

The rock opened at our feet, and the Untowards leapt across the first of thousands of apparently bottomless cracks winding throughout this region. Some were a yard across, some so wide that the Untowards had to get a running start. Hills of slag loomed to right and left, their shadows shifting eerily.

Once again it became necessary to rest. There was no relief to the uphill grade, the footing was hazardous, and our mounts were burdened with our weight. They lay down in a level hollow, but this time they found no water.

The Gypsies climbed a hillock to search the slopes. It was dimmer here; the Fire Falls was a half-mile distant. Gazing up into darkness, I thought I could just see the point, a long way off yet, where the water bent over a lip of rock.

"Yes," said Singer over my shoulder. "I think that's the top."

Henry propped up his feet. "I wonder why Hain hasn't caught up with us in the balloon?"

"He's being careful with his toy this time," Mothkin said. "We could shower it with rocks and arrows from above; the netting only protects its underside. His ground crew will try to overtake us first, and he'll be just behind—with the balloon."

ANOTHER hour's foray brought us the knowledge that we were not the first to scale these heights; piled-stone structures of the Vin Avarem, empty and silent as those in the City of Echoes, began to appear on ledges.

"Why would anyone build a house here?" asked Henry, when the Untowards crept in a line up the spine of a ridge.

"It's not a city," Tefan answered, studying the dark windows. "These were mystics, I'd guess. Holy seers. Perhaps their vision was clearer the closer they got to the Shelf."

Topping the ridge, we reached a section of broken layers and yawning cracks. The gargantuan slabs lay at irregular angles as they had fallen eons ago, their surfaces heaped with debris; though our path lay almost horizontal in a series of wavelike shelves, the stones rolled and slid beneath the animals' hooves. Choosing each step, the Untowards skirted the chasms, leaping only at need.

On a difficult stretch, our line expanded. The ridges steepened, sharp peaks separating the lead riders from those behind. Tefan and Irah rekindled their lanterns after a brief debate; whereas we didn't want to spotlight ourselves, the footing was simply too hazardous in the murk. Better illumination gave the Untowards confidence, and we made for the relative safety of higher, more solid ground.

"What is it?"

Mothkin's sudden question brought our heads around.

Irah sat unmoving on Fire, whose nostrils flared. The Gypsy's face was toward the jagged wilderness behind us. Pulling an arrow from his quiver, he turned Fire back in our direction. "They're coming. We should get off this washboard."

Glancing often over our shoulders, we pressed on. It was like those nightmares in which you try to run from some horror, but your feet are bound by quicksand. On the grinding pebbles, among the ditches, the Untowards could not sprint. A crack whispered open to my left as Few crossed a slab that bridged it; I saw a shower of rocks vanish over the edge.

The next events unfolded with a rapidity that left me gasping.

First, with a terrible crash, the stone slab gave way. Half-covered by loose silt, it had looked as solid as the other Earthbones, but it must have been precariously in balance on the rim of the crevasse. Though the weight of an Untoward was nothing compared with the slab's tonnage, the tip-tap of hooves was just enough to unsettle it. For centuries, nothing had touched the rock; no wind had pushed, and no rain had hollowed it a secure bed. When Few and Far Between danced across, the center of its gravity altered by the slightest fraction. Rotating on gravel ball-bearings, it dropped away under the feet of Hither and Yon, who barely scrabbled to safety behind their leaders.

Wheeling sideways, Steeple and Chase teetered on the brink. Willie and Clara held on, the collars saving them from a pitch over their mounts' heads into the crevice, now unbridged.

Mothkin started to say something, but his words were swallowed up; the rocks were not done moving yet. Loosened by the vibrations, a second stone wobbled forward above Clara. Chase backpedaled, flailing her hooves.

The lanky Untoward just got clear as the megalith hurtled into the pit, wedging itself a dozen feet below the edge. Dust spiraled in the light; we covered our heads against a shower of grit.

A deep groan rose from the crack, supplanted the screams of the Untowards. The floor beneath Hither and Yon tilted; it was actually the top of a rectangular monument, resting on end in a trench. Now the block was tipping, forced over by the second falling stone. The crack between us widened, and the jammed block disappeared into the depths.

Before their riders could react, Fire and Flood jumped instinctively over the gap to escape the rain of stones. Flying from the moving platform, they carried Mothkin and Irah back to our side. A baseball-sized rock bounced down, and *bang*—Irah's lantern was gone in a flurry of glass and sparks.

Steeple and Chase whirled and bucked, half-screened from our view by falling rubble. With horror I saw both Clara and Willie lose their grips, slide from their seats as the block struck the trench's far wall. The titanic *boom* shook the mountains.

Panicked, Steeple and Chase bunched low and sprang across the trench, now so wide they nearly fell. Grabbing their collars and forelegs, Irah and Mothkin helped them scramble up beside us.

The twin Untowards had come without their riders.

As the repercussions faded, we searched the dust clouds.

"CLARA!" I shrieked, fearing the worst. "WILLIE!" Pebbles sifted over the lips of the pit. Nothing looked the same; cracks had appeared everywhere. Perhaps the whole field of mazes had become unstable, and was about to slide off the cliffs. So many tons of stone—could anyone be alive across the gulf?

"There!" Irah pointed.

A flash of yellow stirred beneath the detritus. In a split-second of silence I could hear the ticking of Willie's watch—and there, shaking pebbles from her hair, was Clara. Heart leaping, I called their names again.

"Are you pinned?" asked Singer. "Can you move?"

I saw what concerned him: Willie and Clara lay just at the juncture of the capsized platform and the wall behind it. If an arm or a leg had gotten between the surfaces . . .

"We're okay!" shouted Willie, digging Clara free. She looked stunned, unable to stand yet.

Irah handed a coil of rope to Mothkin. "Tie this around something solid." He nudged Fire away from the edge, but the shattered ground left no room for a running start.

Tefan led Hither after them. "We're with you," he said to Irah.

The crack continued indefinitely on one side, and it ended in the sheer blade of a wall on the other; the only way to reach Clara and Willie was to jump across, but the wide gap made for a dangerous leap. When the Gypsies had mounted, the two Untowards backed into the boulders and then unfolded, flying over the gorge. Hooves skidding, they landed and thrashed to safety.

Gently, the brothers helped Willie and Clara onto the animals' backs, but stayed on the ground themselves. Clara recovered quickly, clutching the pommels. Even her glasses had survived intact, dangling on their strings.

Irah smiled. "Hold tight."

"The Untowards can only carry a single rider," explained Mothkin to Henry and me as he secured the rope around a chimney of rock. "And that jump is too hazardous to risk any more than necessary."

We held our breath as the Untowards vaulted back to our side, where Mothkin and Singer caught and pulled them to solid ground. I hugged Clara and Willie, and Mothkin lobbed Irah the rope.

"You first," said Irah, hitching the rope around Tefan's waist.

Singer crouched on the first ridge with the remaining lantern. "Take care," he advised, "but come quickly."

Hearing the urgency in his tone, Irah fastened the cord's end beneath his own arms, too. Lashed together, the brothers moved to the edge of the crevice. Taking up the slack, Mothkin tied it off, double-checked his knots. Singer slid down to help him.

"Ready?" asked Tefan.

"When you are." Irah stood behind him and reached around his brother's body to grip the line.

Together they leaped. Irah's hat was swept from his head and remained there, rolling in a circle on the ledge.

Sleeves fluttering, they glided down, arcing toward us as the rope broke their fall, their legs extended to absorb shock. They swung below my line of sight, down into the darkness.

A blaze of fire on the far slope snapped my gaze upward. Lanterns glared among the rocks; hoofbeats pounded nearer. My heart forgot to beat.

"It's *them!*" cried Henry. "Look out!"

Mothkin spun, dragged Willie and me up the embankment.

"We can walk ourselves!" I said. "Help Clara—I'll get Henry!"

He dropped me without argument. "Get behind the ridge fast—they'll come shooting."

"The boys!" Henry tried to help Singer pull up the dangling Gypsies.

"Go, Henry!" Mothkin deposited Clara and Willie behind the protective balustrade. Sliding down to us, he elbowed in, seized the rope. There wasn't room for three to stand; falling back, Henry staggered with me up the loose rock of the ridge.

At Irah's command from below, the Untowards, too, took shelter. His voice echoed, sounding far away.

Kneeling behind a rock at the summit, I saw three Untowards poised opposite, their black-cloaked riders leering beneath silk top hats. Lantern light filled all the hollow behind them. They were not alone.

A fourth rider appeared, wearing a long, tan coat like Meagerly's. Unkempt blond hair flowed to his shoulders, and his mouth *bulged* with an abundance of teeth. Braying laughter, he lifted his bow. "You haven't time, Grey Man!" he shouted. "That rope is too long!"

Singer and Mothkin saved their breath, struggled to reel in the Gypsies. Irah and Tefan, too, must have been fighting upward, hand over hand.

A rider walked his mount to the precipice, hung sideways from the saddle, and snagged Irah's fallen hat with his bow. Twirling it round and round, he flung it to the man in the trench coat.

Five more riders, ten, scaled the ridge. Men and women of Harvest Moon lined up, casually fitted arrows to their strings. Glittering eyes surveyed the laboring men. A woman stared at me and waved fingers rife with blue veins.

"*Go,* Lurkwick!" cried one of the Gypsies. The voice was strained; I couldn't tell which of the brothers was speaking. "Stay with the others."

The leader drew his bowstring, the barb pointed at Singer. "Ashes, ashes!" he cackled. "We all fall down!"

Singer looked straight into his eyes, and the arrow struck.

Mothkin caught Singer as he jerked and fell, the coil of rope at their feet snaking over the edge. Below, the Gypsies grunted in pain as they dropped a dozen feet and were yanked to a halt.

Again the blond man rocked with laughter, throwing skinny arms wide.

"Jehu!" growled Irah's voice. "Is that you?"

"It is I." The man pulled Irah's hat over his greasy hair. "Come to send you to Charon!"

"Have you?" asked the Gypsy. "Then let's go. You and me, with knives."

"I think not." Jehu smiled. His teeth jutted almost straight out from his sunken cheeks. "We have no time to waste on honor." He nodded to his archers.

I leapt to my feet. Henry pulled me down by the cape, cutting off my cry. Arrows whistled through the space where I had been. The shafts clattered against the walls, vanished into the shadows.

Irah's voice rang out again:

"Save them! See it through!"

Then bowstrings were twanging, Jehu was laughing, and beside me, Willie had begun to sob.

In the protected basin, our Untowards bucked and bleated. Watching the arrow shafts that rolled down between their feet, I noticed something else: the ground was shaking. Puffs of dust rose, new cracks crawled everywhere, and the rock beneath me trembled. Still unstable, the masses were shifting again.

In the enemy ranks, Untowards bellowed, voices shrieked; and the cliffs groaned as with birth pains.

Despite Henry's restraining arms, I peeked out a window of rock. Tilting backward, the dividing block on which Jehu stood came to rest against a farther wall. The row of Untowards had been heavy enough to overbalance the stone, knocked askew in the earlier slide. The chain reaction we had started probably continued throughout the day, blocks on gravel bearings readjusting themselves to angles of repose. This latest upheaval had not destroyed the enemy, but it had further widened the chasm—now, as Jehu and his shooters realized, it was just a little too far for an Untoward to jump.

They shook themselves, let fly another volley of arrows. But Mothkin had utilized the seconds of confusion to drag Singer out from behind the pillar where the rope was tied, to half-carry him over the ridge. When they landed beside us, Mothkin rolled over, nocked an arrow, and shot it through an aperture.

"Can you see them?" gasped Singer, slumped against the rock and fumbling with his crossbow.

"No." Mothkin ducked as an arrow snagged in his hood, nicking his ear.

There was no cover for the Gypsies on the rock face, but we could do nothing to reach them; arrows filled the air, rattled over the stones. I could feel Mothkin's frustration as he wriggled for a better vantage. Even seeking for a way to circle back would mean climbing the exposed ridge above us—we were trapped.

Jehu's shot had pierced Singer's left shoulder. Blood soaked his shirt, and his face was drawn as he lifted a knife, gripped the arrow in his left hand. Gritting his teeth, he sawed off the shaft's feathered end. We clustered around him, Henry supporting his weight.

"Can we help?" I asked.

Shaking his head, Singer picked up a flat stone, held it against the end of the arrow, and pushed the barbed point out through the back of his shoulder. His breath was slow and deep. My eyes flooded with tears; I could not begin to imagine his pain.

When the point emerged, Henry took the knife, cut away part of Singer's shirt, and helped to pull the arrow on through. "I think it missed anything important," he said. "It's bleeding, but not bad."

Wincing, Singer bent the arm. "It will take more than that."

As we worked, Mothkin slid from crack to niche, emerging to loose a shot and then dodging the response. "They can't cross the gorge," he reported, pausing to examine Singer's wound. "But it won't take them long to find another way around."

"Tefan and Irah?" asked Singer.

Mothkin shook his head. Somewhere below, they had been under the direct hail of the arrows. Willie wept soundlessly against Clara's arm.

Edging to the left, Mothkin glanced out toward the rope, which hung taut, I supposed, with the dead weight of our friends' bodies.

His eyes widened.

Jehu snarled a curse. "It's impossible!"

There was the sound of arrows whistling, *thunking* horribly into a target.

Jehu repeated: "Impossible!"

"Keep watching," came Irah's voice, strangled and suddenly much nearer. "You'll see greater things than these." The voice lowered. "Walk, brother. Three more steps."

As Mothkin fell back, as both Gypsies lurched over the ridge, I understood. They were still roped together, the line dragging at their feet. Irah held his brother in a bear hug, shielding him with his broader body. Tefan dropped to a sitting position. Irah sagged to his knees, and before anyone could catch him, he slid on his face down the scree slope, coming to rest between the hooves of Fire and Flood. More than twenty arrows protruded from his back.

Tefan dove after him, sharp stones gouging his chest. Fighting for breath, he lifted his brother, turned him over.

We hurried to his side.

"Brother," Tefan rasped, touching Irah's face, stroking his hair.

"Never could out-wrestle me, could you?" Irah grinned. His complexion had gone grey, like a Harvest Moon face. "Tell—the others—"

"We'll tell everyone," said Mothkin quietly. "You saved your brother's life. And without you, we—"

"Not *that*." Irah shook his head. A cough spasmed through him, his breath growing shallower. "Tell them—see them—again."

"Yes, Irah," said Singer, leaning close. "We'll see you again."

Tefan's tears fell on Irah's neck.

I had never watched a person die, at least not up close. In Henry's parlor I had looked upon many a corpse, but they were, as he always reminded me, empty shells, waxen and only vaguely reminiscent of the human beings that had used them in life—so it had been with Sylva's skin and my grandfather. This was the first time I'd seen someone at *the moment*. Like so much else I witnessed in Harvest Moon, I'll never forget the translation in Irah's features.

His breath caught; his glassy eyes became remarkably clear, focused at a spot just over Tefan's shoulder, and his lips parted in a laugh. "Look, brother!" And then, although no one had said anything, he added, "*Here* I am."

Finally, his eyes faded like powerful lamps switched off. His head fell into the crook of Tefan's arm.

I will *certainly* never forget this part: Mothkin and Singer raised their heads and *smiled*, a reaction which I could hardly have understood then. Irah left the world with a grin of childlike delight; and whatever he was celebrating, Mothkin and Singer were truly happy for him.

25

THE SHELF

THERE was not much time to act. The men removed what arrows they could easily, but were forced to break off the heads of most; if there were the leisure of a funeral later, the steel points could be taken out then. Wrapping Irah in his cloak, we bound him carefully with rope to the back of Fire, who stood with lowered head.

While Mothkin kept an eye on the enemy, Singer tore a strip from his own cloak, and Henry bandaged his shoulder as best he could. Blood seeped out, staining the cloth, but it appeared Singer was in no immediate danger.

"They're gone from the ravine," reported Mothkin. "They'll try to cut us off." Jehu's warriors had not seen, from their position, that we were trapped. Supposing we had already found a way upward, they left no archers behind.

"Then we move now," said Singer. He gripped Tefan's arms, looked into his face. His growling voice was soft. "Let's ride."

Tefan nodded. "That's what he died for." He slung Irah's fallen quiver over his shoulder.

Chase stooped to allow Clara onto her back. Without his previous enthusiasm, Willie pulled himself up onto Steeple.

Sliding the lantern pole into Far Between's collar, Singer led us at a trot up a pebble-strewn basin. I don't remember much of that last climb, the walls and fractures shimmering through the veil of my tears.

Irah was gone: I struggled with that concept as the light of the waterfall drew nearer. His rugged, laughing face would not leave my mind. I thought of Avim, of Rocy, of Hewin, waiting for our return—and of dark-eyed, dancing Ganymede. I think what frightened me the most was the realization that Mothkin and Singer, for all their competence and rightness of purpose, could not stave off the hand of death.

NOW the end of the story is near.

From the ravine, it was not as far to the Shelf as I had guessed.

Mothkin saw lanterns behind the rocks to our right. Veering away from them, the Untowards sprang across an abyss to a rock platform standing out from the cliff, its base invisible far below. We pounded across its top and leapt to a second, higher pinnacle—then to a third, higher still—and there it was above us.

Far Between reared, striking the air with his hooves. Ragged cloak billowing, Singer shielded his eyes from the light of his lantern. The Fire Falls gushed from a cliff thirty feet above us, a quarter-mile to our left, dropped frothy and glowing to burst over a slab far beneath; from there the river wandered among the mazes like the molten discharge of a blast furnace. Yet the air was chill and pure.

We had risen to a height just under the roof of the Harvest Moon cavern—the cracked ceiling, dozens of miles long, of Hain's kingdom. It sloped down from here, so that we were tucked away in the highest corner. An uneven stairway of stacked stone led up from the last monolith to the corner of the Shelf.

Slowly mounting the steps, we studied this final shadowy realm. The stairway had been constructed by hands. Obviously someone—many someones—had come here often in the past. Was it a hundred years ago, I wondered, or ten thousand? A Shelf it certainly was; from its front edge, the cliff fell sheer to a fathomless gulf. The Falls angled away several hundred feet down, winding over other ledges, but the pit beneath the cliff was swallowed by darkness.

At every step, we could see more and more of the Shelf's cavern, a mammoth ellipse, wider than it was deep. On a hill of rubble near its back wall was a single building of the Vin Avarem, small and windowless, but with an open doorway—where light glowed, as from a torch. The implication was not lost on us; torchlight suggested a presence.

My cheeks stung with drying tears. Straightening my back, I peered over a field of boulders. This place had a vigilant stillness, as if the rocks themselves kept watch.

Despite the fiery river, the darkness resisted penetration. I have never seen the same phenomenon, though I've encountered strange enough things in the years since. Light could come *in,* flowing in the water, wavering around our tiny lantern, but the darkness *lived* here. The Shelf was not a part of Harvest Moon; every sense told me this lofty, remote cavern was far more ancient. Nor was it a part of the Earth, for it was beyond the sway of many natural laws. Maybe that was why Mother Iva had sent us here, to a no-man's land where Hain was as much a stranger as we were.

WE gathered on the Shelf, on a level floor of limestone, worn smooth by the tread of countless feet. The Untowards took a few tentative steps, tested the air. Stones clustered in weird cairns, some a foot high, some towering twenty feet over our heads. Light spilled steadily from the doorway of the solitary building, the rays bending curiously around the stones. Their shadows seemed to waver as my eyes passed, to glide when I no longer watched directly.

Suddenly Few and Far Between bristled, squared themselves against the shadows ahead. Singer's crossbow was up.

Something darted among the rock piles. Then another motion pulled my gaze in a different direction. To right, to left—the shadows rustled, coming forward.

Clara sucked in breath. Lifting his glasses, Henry squinted. Willie's mouth was an O. Something in the jerky movements around us bore a chilling familiarity.

Reeling on legs of mismatched length, the clay children emerged from their hiding places. Lips working, fingers groping, the children of the pump houses staggered toward us, firelight glinting on the black buttons of their eyes.

Pressing her hands to her mouth, Clara wailed and would have fallen, but as the Untowards edged backward, Henry drew even with her on the right. He caught her fainting form and held her across his knees.

I wanted to cry out, to tell the others of my encounter in the pump house. But my throat twisted shut.

Hairless, with clothing merely molded from the clay of their bodies, they dropped a fine rain of particles at each step. Some had lost appendages in the long climb to this place; some, undoubtedly, had never made it at all, had crumbled to powder or melted in the mists. Their mouths opened and closed, mouths with no depth, no tongues or throats. None of their hands were fingered alike.

Singer raised his weapon, then lowered it, shaking his head. Although they ringed us round and still swarmed from the darkness, it was impossible to shoot anything so pitiable. None of the lumpish heads was higher than the Untowards' flanks; they swelled in a tide of misery without voice, incapable of tears.

Hain's sense of completeness, I thought: he would finish us not with arrow or sword, but with the misshapen zombies of his creation, the symbols of generated suffering. The sheer weight of their bodies would press us off the cliff. There would be no satisfaction for our warriors in piling up enemy bodies in a last stand; we would not strike a single blow.

Tefan sat woodenly, seeing but not seeing. His bow was limp in his left hand, his right resting on Irah's back.

So we have failed, I told myself. Few snorted, backed up step by step. Some of the children were close enough to run their hands over his side, and his skin twitched. He lashed out with a foreleg, and one of the figures' arms exploded in a shower of clods. The child ignored the loss, and stood gazing up at me. Only their eyes had depth, like wells of midnight.

It was Clara who understood. "Let me down." She clutched Henry's arm, slipped to the ground, and took the nearest fig-

ure in an embrace. The clay child hid his face against her,
awkwardly encircled her with his arms.

Standing beside Flood, Mothkin gently held the out-
stretched hands. A dozen figures jostled around him. His
scarred face softened as he worked his way through their
ranks.

Tears spilled down my cheeks, hot with shame. I had been
wrong, completely wrong. Whatever the grotesque children
had come for, it was not to kill us. But because of their
hideous shapes, I had believed the worst of them. Sliding from
Few's back, I squeezed a reaching hand, felt the fingers
crack—but as I wept my apologies, as I touched the grainy
face of a girl with three eyes and an upside-down nose, I saw
her forgiveness and relief.

They crowded on all sides, hugging me with nerveless
arms. Some had trumpet-like ears, some had only smoothness
where mouths should have been; but all had the hearts of children, fearful and wretched, starved for the closeness of a human being. My tears left tracks over their faces as I pressed
them against me, one by one, the taste of clay dust in my
mouth.

The crowd parted before us, urged us away from the ledge.
It was only when they formed a protective wall between us
and the stairs that I stood straight, looked over the bobbing
heads. Turning, they faced a growing pool of firelight.

Jehu had returned.

Lips drawn back in a ghastly grimace, hair streaming, he
charged. Still he wore Irah's hat, and his coat flapped behind.
Clenching his Untoward with his knees, he held his bowstring
taut. His people came in a leaping file across the towers,
lanterns swinging. Though Mothkin's arrows had thinned
their numbers, I counted thirteen riders and several unencum-
bered mounts. Polished bows glistened as they bent.

"Down!" ordered Singer, pulling collars, making the Untowards kneel. Henry crouched with Clara behind Yon's shaggy
bulk. Willie and I tumbled in beside them. Tefan laid an arrow
against his string.

The backs of the children blocked my view, but my ears
told me what was taking place. Arrows hissed, fragments rat-

tled as clay figures were struck. Jehu's people were shooting at the children.

Mothkin, Singer, and Tefan sprang up with bows raised, but the children surged forward, a dun-colored wave. Now I had a clear view of Jehu, who shrieked as they descended the stairs. I recognized his mount as Louder, one of the team that pulled the Welcome Wagon. Behind them, the other twin, Louder, tossed his head in terror.

Jehu whirled and fled, glancing off his archers along the lower stairs. The children threw themselves upon enemy and Untowards alike, wrapped their arms around necks, scrambled onto shoulders. The goats struck back in a frenzy of horns and hooves, and the dust of shattered clay bodies filled the air.

Still they poured down from the Shelf, grasping, crawling over the fragments of others, crushing forward. A howling woman on the second Louder swung her sword, sliced the legs from under a clay boy; the upper body clung to her waist as two more children broke like crockery against Louder's horns. Three more gripped her hands, a fourth rode her back, a fifth hugged her neck. Her screams echoed as they all plunged together off the steps.

So it was with every one of Jehu's warriors. Sometimes the Untowards were spared, the riders dragged from their backs; sometimes mount and master plummeted in the embrace of a dozen children. It took nearly all the clay bodies to do it, but in seconds, only Jehu remained.

Louder had spun around on the highest of the stone towers below the stairs. Attuned to the voice of his twin, he had gone no further from the instant the other Louder had fallen. He stood with legs apart, head hanging over the lightless pit.

Tefan approached them now, his bow at his side. He stepped over the mounds of fractured clay, boots crunching in the powder, eyes never leaving Jehu's face.

Jehu kicked and slapped at Louder, cursed in a voice grown shrill. Yanking at the reins, he fought to turn the goat, to follow the escaping Untowards down the trail.

Slowly, Louder raised his head. His black eyes were liquid, mournful.

Tefan stood an arm's length from Jehu. He fixed the man of Harvest Moon with his unflinching gaze.

Frantically Jehu grabbed his bow, dropped three arrows before he got one against the string. But Tefan's stare held him, pierced him.

The Untoward expelled breath in a long sigh. From beneath his huge, age-chipped horns, he studied Tefan, then turned toward the abyss, where his twin had gone down.

In the last second, Jehu understood, tried to hurl himself from the saddle; but the stirrups held his feet. He wrenched around, hands jerking like white spiders.

Louder launched himself high over the pit.

I almost believed he had taken flight, that he would soar away with his screaming rider. But he leveled out and dove. He and Jehu shrank in the dim light, smaller and smaller, and were gone. If the pit had a floor, it was so far below that we never heard them hit bottom.

Tefan looked after them, then trudged back through settling dust.

"Who were those children?" asked Henry weakly.

I looked from Mothkin to Singer, but their faces told me nothing. "I saw some of them in a pump house."

Tears shone on Clara's face. When she was in Hain's dungeon, she explained, she'd had to help make them, big dolls of clay that Hain said he'd bring to life and use to work his plumbing.

But the distorted features, the malformed limbs . . . "You *made* them like *that?*" I asked.

"No, not like that. I rolled and rolled the clay, worked on each little face until it was perfect." Hain had told her that, by helping with the dolls, she was saving the real children from hard labor. She had not believed him, but Mr. Snicker had threatened to cut off Willie's thumbs if she didn't meet her assigned quota. Hain twisted and bent them before they went into the kiln. Singing, cackling, he mashed them into walls, rearranged faces, resculpted arms and fingers.

Just before being taken out to the woods, Clara had been forced to watch a "Graduation." Meagerly had marched some real children into the room—sick, tired children, bled for all the pain they could feel. Some other people entered by another door. Clara trembled remembering these others; she had been unable to look at them, but she glimpsed—and *heard*—them as they pounced on the captives and *folded over* them like rippling, hideous blankets.

These were the people of Harvest Moon undisguised, who sucked the souls from their prisoners, spit them into the clay dolls, and inhabited the living bodies themselves. Left in their malnourished bodies, the children would die and escape Hain; but by putting them into tormented jars of clay, he could continue to extract the hurt of their souls forever. Meanwhile, the vacated bodies would suit his people well, being much fresher than stolen corpses from the ground. New genetic material was injected into Harvest Moon, and pain, as always, was maximized. That was the terrible secret of Fifty-two Pink Eye Street; the operation must have gone on there before the High Horse was built.

None of us knew, though, why the real children, the ones in clay bodies, had climbed to the Shelf. They had saved us from Jehu, and their bodies were smashed, scores of them, on the stairs and far, far below. I pictured them in their journey, abandoning the pump houses, the brown line of their shapes filing across the midnight fields. Some would have broken themselves simply opening the doors; if they had been pursued, hundreds of them might have been pulverized to buy the others an escape. Then there was the climb. Since they could not jump from spire to spire, each gulf meant descent to a distant floor or else miles of backtracking, and climbing on ungainly limbs would leave casualties littering the gorges. If I'd known by what secret route they had come, I was sure I would see a continuous trail of clay dust among the peaks. Mothkin said their souls were no longer trapped, that Hain could hold them no more. All of them, snatched from bedrooms throughout the ages, were free at last.

All except one.

We were gazing over the mountains behind the High Horse; from our vantage above the highest, we could see the fires of the outlying districts, glittering like a bed of banked embers. The Horse faced away from us, overlooking the central sweep of the Abandon, where the whole smoky show still

frolicked full swing. I was impressed again with just how far
Harvest Moon sprawled. The perhaps fifteen hundred warriors somewhere in the caverns below us were a mere pittance
of the population.

Just then Clara gasped, and I turned to see a small figure in
the shadows. It was the last of the clay children, a boy with an
egg-shaped head. Both his eyes were on the left side of his
face, like a Picasso painting, his hands upside down. Dragging
his stubby legs, he stopped in the middle of us and turned his
head to look at us one by one.

I knelt before him, took the hand he offered. It had three
fingers and a thumb that pointed at the ground. "Thank you," I
whispered. "Thank you all."

The boy wiped dust trails from my cheeks with his other
thumb.

"My name is Dragonfly—or Bridget Anne, if you like that
better. What—" I faltered, knowing he had no tongue to tell
me his name. He could hear me, though: Hain had given his
captives ears for hearing orders.

Bending, he traced with his thumb on the stone. I watched
his hand move in steady arcs: letters. He was writing his
name.

"John." I slid my arms around him, held him as gently and
tenderly as I could. "Thank you, John. You saved our lives."

He clamped his hands behind me for a long time. At last he
pulled away and pointed to the stone building.

I peered at the open doorway. "We should go in there?"

John nodded, pulling me forward.

Our footsteps called up echoes as we followed, winding
among the rocks. I touched some of the rough surfaces, feeling their cold permanence. Distance was hard to reckon here;
the building seemed to retreat before us. I clutched John's
hand as his cracked feet moved unsteadily. His warped
anatomy kept him constantly off-balance, one ankle's twist
away from a destroying fall. The others watched in all directions, Henry once again supporting Clara. Her voluminous
skirt was a hindrance now, threatening to trip her. Willie
turned in circles like a soldier on patrol.

Tefan waited with the Untowards as we climbed the broken
slope. He had not spoken since our arrival on the Shelf. Only

his left hand moved at his side, the fingers clenching and unclenching.

At last we reached a sharper incline, which I saw was a set of steps buried in debris. Searching for solid footholds, we approached the simple, flat-roofed structure. We all could have entered side by side through the yawning doorway. The bare chamber was long and scarcely wider than the entrance, the floor of natural, unpaved stone. Not a pebble littered the hall. Walls of mortarless blocks shone with a red glow, a suffusion of the air, appearing to emanate from everywhere at once. I had mistaken this for torchlight, but it was steadier and left no shadows.

There was also a damp, ferny odor. Our footsteps rang in the hush. Advancing the length of the building, we found at the back a place where the walls formed a T, extending in alcoves to the right and left. The stone floor gave way in these recesses to beds of earth, where a profusion of wild flowers grew, bathed in the red light. Water trickled down the Shelf's rear wall and reached the flowers through vents in the building's roof.

"Pea Mummies!" cried Willie, dropping to his knees. They crowded the beds with delicate copper leaves. Clara, too, pressed her face close to drink their aroma.

The blossoms of gold and silver, green and crystal brought me memories of our cottage. "Here, of all places! Who could have planted them?"

"I think," said Mothkin, "that we'll find answers here." He was studying the curved walls and ceilings of the twin alcoves, which seemed covered in plush red velvet; when I looked more closely, I saw strings of roots. The light originated there.

Singer scanned the plants with his luminous eyes. "Yes. It is Madar, the fiery fungus of the elder times." He and Mothkin seized each other's arms, laughed aloud, and turned back to the Madar.

"What does it mean?" I asked. "What should we do?"

Singer crouched near me, rubbing his chin. "If Madar is growing here, then this is a place of great power. The Vin Avarem must have planted these beds long ago."

"Long, *long* ago." Mothkin knelt beside John, whose

mouth stretched in a broad smile. "It called you, didn't it, John? You and the others, when the time was right. 'Leave the pump houses,' it said. 'Climb to the Shelf!' "

John nodded vigorously.

Mothkin pumped the clay hand. "The Madar knew we would need your help. It has been waiting for us all these years—for us to come here and stand against Samuel Hain. The seers of the Vin Avarem knew, just as Mother Iva knew."

Singer nodded. "This is the battleground."

The A.P.K.s rose, glancing toward the entrance.

"This building has a purpose," Singer said. "We'll have to learn what it is. But Hain is very near. First, the animals—"

Mothkin agreed. "There are high ledges on the Shelf's back wall."

"Tefan and I will take the Untowards there and try to see the enemy's position. If it's clear, I'll come right back." Singer grasped Mothkin's arm. "Learn what you can, quickly."

I caught his hand, peered into his owlish face. "How's your arm?"

"It hurts." He winked. "Now let's get to work."

"Be careful!" called Clara.

Singer waved and was gone.

We touched the Madar's downy contours. Mothkin paced, brow furrowed. "Do you know what we should do, John?"

John shook his head, his arms hanging limp.

Hands shoved into his pockets, Henry examined the walls. Mothkin prodded the floor between the alcoves, listening for hollow spaces. Willie buried his face among the Pea Mummies, probing in the soil.

Just as I stooped beside him, the blossoms began to tremble.

I whirled to face the doorway, and an ominous exhalation thundered over the Shelf.

Mothkin sprang to his feet. Henry jumped with such a start that his glasses flew to the length of the strings. The cavern we could see framed in the archway flooded with incarnadine light. As Mothkin sprinted toward the door, the *Jolly Jack* swelled over the ledge like a pocked bubble of molten steel, completely filling our view. It slid forever past us—ripped seams, gaping wounds, and the net of wires.

Finally, swinging beneath it on cables rose the derelict

barge from Charon's Porch. Hain's men had lashed it on as a makeshift gondola; a small army of them crowded the warped deck, reminding me of bloated crows on a wire.

In the building's entrance, Mothkin nocked an arrow. Already the balloon was too high for a shot at the unprotected upper side. He dodged back as something fell from the barge, and the Shelf's edge erupted in flames. Gravel rained over the building.

Through a cloud of black smoke, I saw the gondola twirl slowly as Hain steered toward us, saw a torch's flare as another explosive barrel was lighted.

"Lie flat!" ordered Mothkin, gesturing wildly. "Cover your heads, and open your mouths!" Hurling himself from the archway, he shot his arrow straight up and dove behind a rock outside. By the light, I could tell the balloon was directly over us.

When the bomb hit the roof, there was a sound like the Earth splitting in two. The explosion itself wasn't as loud as I would have expected, just a pressurized WHUMMPPP! that threw me on my face. Henry covered me with his body, dragging me against the back wall. The biggest noise was a catastrophic groaning as the Madar's house caved in.

I remember chunks landing beside us, acrid smoke, and the sifting of sand long after the crashing stopped. Then Henry stirred and looked anxiously into my face. His lips moved, but it was several minutes before I could hear any voices. Clara and Willie had survived another burial.

John had not even gone for cover, but sat in the middle of the floor. Huge stones lay all around him, but he had received only a sprinkling of dust. Dazedly he got up and put his hands to the roofslabs, which had fallen, leaning upright between us and the building's other end. Mothkin was somewhere outside; I hoped he was alive.

We were in a perfect igloo of rubble, completely walled in. The only light was that of the Madar. I pushed on the blocks to John's left, felt no give to their weight; nor had the back wall or the ceiling above us suffered any weakening. Muffled rose the cheers of Hain's people, the swinish snorting of the balloon.

Willie found a crack and peeped out onto the Shelf. "They're landing!"

I shoved against the rocks, but it was hopeless; we were entombed.

26

A Swelling
of the Ground

I gave place to panic. Dashing from side to side I pushed on walls, set my back against stones a draft horse could not have budged. *Trapped!* Mothkin, Singer, and Tefan were alone out on the Shelf, and we could do nothing to help them, just as it had been with Irah. The masonry bounced my rasping breath back at me.

Spinning, I nearly bowled over John, who had come to pluck at my sleeve. He pointed, pulled me toward the Madar.

Willie knelt there, his head hidden among the flowers. Coming up with leaves in his hair, he motioned excitedly. "What do you think this is?" He pushed the coppery fronds away to uncover a metal wheel, dark with damp, in the right-hand alcove. Purple-blossoming vines had threaded through it, masking its shape.

Bending over Willie's shoulder, Henry raised his glasses. "Some kind of machine?" It looked like the wheel for shutting a pipe on and off—spoked, like something on the door of a bank vault. Whatever its axle was attached to was under the soil. "I don't see what it would control."

Heavy footsteps pounded outside, and a garble of voices

filtered in. Quite soon, Hain's people would start digging us out.

A breeze riffled my hair, and I glanced up at the Madar. Its millions of threadlike tufts fluttered; its edges shimmered. I whispered, "Look!"

With a loud hiss, the fungus was changing. Its light crept toward its center, leaving a greyish blanket of dead growth on the walls. Where the light passed, a red mist seeped from the velvety cushions, swirled in the air—the Madar's spores. Some of these were drawn to the chill of the trickling water, flowed into the soil and beyond; but most of the spores rode a draft, touched the back wall in long, filmy fingers, and were sucked through the cracks between blocks. As the last of the light faded, the cloud disappeared.

"Where is it going?" Willie murmured, as if to himself.

The only light in the cramped space came from the crack behind us, where Willie had looked out onto the Shelf. Although the glimmer wasn't nearly enough to see by, Willie and I stood and slid our hands over the opposite wall, through which the Madar had gone. There was a feeling of space, a hollowness behind the stones.

My palms pressed to the rough, wet surface, I let the faint draft flow over my face. Sweat plastered the hair to my brow; the air cooled my head, helped me think. Willie pushed his nose toward a crack, called my attention to the air's scent.

The current wafting through our prison was not the dusty breath of the Shelf. I caught the salty, life-laden odor of a sea—and when we shoved our ears closer, we could hear waves breaking over rocks.

Willie shook my arm. "This is a door! That's what the Vin Avarem wanted us to find. It's a way out of Harvest Moon!"

A doorway! Of course: Hain's people were not the only ones who traveled from world to world. The Madar could not speak to us directly, as it once had to those who built this edifice; but it had shown us the building's function.

"If we could open this," I said, "we might surprise Hain. He thinks we're cornered." I groped along the blocks, searching for a button, a trigger. There must be a concealed portal, and we needed a larger exit than the Madar did.

"The wheel is the only control we've seen," said Henry. "But we have to be careful; we might end up somewhere worse than Harvest Moon."

"The Vin Avarem must have thought of that," said Clara.

I had not considered the possibility that the door would lead anywhere but to our own world. "Maybe it only goes to one place," I said.

The flowers rustled, and Willie announced that he had the wheel.

"Turn it quick!" Clara blocked the light, peeking out. "Here they come. I can't see Mothkin."

"Urrnnh!" Willie strained against the long-unused fixture. "Somebody'll have to help me."

Henry and I felt down his arms until our fingers touched cold metal. "All together now," said Henry.

Clara's tone rose in pitch. She saw Mothkin, a prisoner, surrounded by enemies.

Stones clattered as someone outside climbed the wall to our left. Iron crashed against the fallen roof slabs, and something else made a scratching to the right.

"Get them out of there!" snarled a voice we all knew much too well.

Clara gasped, falling away from the crack. "Hain is walking straight toward us!"

We threw our weight into it, the cold biting our skin. At last the wheel ground loose, spun haltingly clockwise. As we turned it hand over hand, we heard the shrieking of some massive hinge or pulley under the rock. There was a sliding behind the wall, a subtle alteration of the pressure on our ears.

Suddenly an ear-splitting roar shook the walls.

Deafened, terrified, we all screamed together.

Blue light knifed through the cracks before our faces as the wall rippled, struck from behind. The growling shriek was some huge animal's voice, savage and throaty. A shape moved across the beams of blue radiance, and something slammed the blocks again.

"Keep turning!" cried Henry. "This is the wrong world!"

A limestone block shot over our heads, smashed against the slabs. What I thought was a sickle thrust through the rectangular hole it left; a foot-long crescent shape hooked into our chamber, glinting, curving to a needle point: a gigantic *claw*.

We wrenched the wheel. A slithering passed behind the wall, and something splintered. The claw, severed, dropped beside Henry. The light and the bestial utterances faded together, as if we were on an elevator moving to a different floor.

When the wheel clicked, we sagged over it, catching our breath. Behind us, the people of Harvest Moon dug and tore at the stones. I could not decide if we were in a protective fortress or a tomb.

Next, silvery light glazed the walls.

Through the window left by the claw, we squinted into the brilliance of another world that was not our own. Despite our hurry, we gaped at its astounding beauty. The light came from the crescent edge of a sun, blazing from the starry void of space; there was no blue sky here, but only a titanic black circle that filled three quarters of the heavens and screened most of the sun.

Stretching down toward us was a dim bridge of stone without moorings or rails, miles wide, whose far end seemed to connect with the dark, cratered disc. All around the bridge's base at our end were sharp, leaning mountains, and the transparent air was scented with mint. Shrubs and arbors tangled the ground, pale lavender flowers bobbing in a warm wind.

Green eyes shone in the foliage, and a sleek black cat glided like a shadow up a branch, arched its back, and blinked languidly in our direction.

"It's the Kingdom of Cats!" cried Willie, pulling loose another block to widen the hole. The breeze drifted over us, musky and alluring. I began to wonder about Willie's imagination; the murky land before us was exactly as he had described his "Kingdom of Cats" on the island behind the moon.

Moreover, I was positive, seeing a white star pattern on its forehead, that the cat on the branch had been the leader of that shadowy parade which had passed me in the forest of Harvest Moon, before I reached the canal; though how it had gotten here or there, and what its errand was, are still mysteries.

"Well, then," said Clara, "we must be only one away from Earth. Turn the wheel, and hurry!"

Had a stream of gravel not reminded me Hain was digging, I would have been reluctant to turn away. Gripping the ring, we sent it around several more rotations.

I wished I could have lifted my head to the window while twisting the spinner; I wondered what the worlds' edges looked like as they tilted away. When the device set itself into another notch and the wheel jerked in our grasp, we heard the agitated barking of a dog.

"That's it!" Clara clapped her hands. "We're home!"

Our four faces vied for position in the gap, Willie hoisting himself by our shoulders.

No other world's air was so delightful as that streaming from the night sky beyond the window. We were certain at once; until I'd been away, I'd never known that my own world's air even *had* a distinct smell. Full of the coolness of grass, the damp, clean aroma of spring, a breeze lifted our hair. *Spring!* It seemed impossible we had been in Harvest Moon for half a year, but the snows had long since become water for the lilacs. A dazzling array of stars filled the sky, and a new crop rippled in Uncle Henry's millet field: that was where we emerged, with the funeral home towering dark in the background. We really were home.

This strange dimensional gatehouse had opened by overlapping with a ruined shed at a corner of the field, a remnant of some long-ago farm, gloomy even in the daytime. I had always suspected it of being haunted. Now we were inside it at night: that prospect would have terrified me once, but no longer.

Floodlights whitewashed the grain. At the field's edge, someone had fixed halogen lamps to a row of tripods.

My mouth fell open as I saw people, more than a dozen of them, standing here and there in the millet. Cars, a van, and a jeep were parked along the road. More people had gathered under a tent canopy, where they worked at a console. A woman with a hand-held machine seemed to vacuum the crop. Straight ahead, a man in a blue windbreaker crouched and twirled a plant between his fingers. Staring at us, he jumped to his feet. "Someone's in there!"

A bearded face bounced up right outside the window, giving us a start. Its owner trained a flashlight at us. "Who are you?"

"Henry Logan," answered my uncle. "We need out of here fast!"

His name caused quite a stir. Suddenly people crowded the window.

At the same moment, a hole opened behind us, dust showering the Pea Mummies. A ghoulish face glowered there. Through a second aperture, a decaying arm slashed at us with blackened nails. Shouting a war cry, Willie bashed it with a rock. Hain's people were trying to dislodge one of the leaning roof slabs. As they jimmied it backward, lines of firelight danced around its edges.

"The door's jammed!" yelled someone from the field, from our world. "Looks like half the roof is caved in!" Out there, of course, they were tugging at the shed's door, believing it led only into this crumbling relic.

The woman glanced in through our window and yelped when she saw the cadaverous arm. "They're in trouble! Pull down the wall!"

Warning us to stand back, the man in the blue jacket swung a pickaxe, widening the hole.

The grey hand grappled Willie, tearing his shirt. Clara picked up the severed claw, fallen from the roaring beast that had first broken the wall. She wielded it like a dagger and sank its point into the bony wrist. The arm's owner howled and withdrew.

Now the roof-slab groaned backward, a dozen clawed hands around its edges. "Quickly!" hissed the voice of Hain. I could feel his nearness, his hate. Stooping, I found a rock that fit my palm.

But even as I prepared to fling it at the first ghoul through the gap, artificial light inundated the room from behind us, dissolving the shadows. What saved us, I suppose, was that the Madar's house was built far sturdier than the slipshod shed, whose wall yielded to a few stout blows. A large block landed squarely on the control wheel, snapping it from its shaft. The floor lurched, but the doorway remained open to our world. Stones rolled through the Pea Mummies, crushing the blossoms, their brilliant juices streaking the blocks with liquid fire.

We flung ourselves into the crowd. Hands caught us, dragged us from the jagged hole as we pushed with our feet.

"Mr. Logan!" People pressed around us. "Bridget! Are you all right? Are you hurt?" Light flashed from eyeglasses and cameras.

Blinking into the camera lens, I pointed back to the hole. "They're coming!"

Clara waved people away from the shed. "They're coming out!"

"*Who* is?" asked the man with the pickaxe.

"You might need that," said Henry. "Get ready."

The cameraman came forward. All eyes turned to the hole. For an instant, firelight glared within, and our rescuers gasped. Then there was a resounding *boom*, the rattling of gravel—and silence. Flashlight beams played over the inner wall. The broken roof-slabs still leaned in place; there was nothing to see but the inside of the collapsed shed.

"Samuel Hain, you coward!" Henry shouted into the hole. "Afraid to show your face now?"

"Mr. Logan—" The blue-jacketed man shook his head, offered his hand. "This is incredible. I—my name is Russell—"

We didn't hear his last name, since the young man with the beard screamed and fell over his legs in his haste to get away from the shed. A bristling dog colored like a wolf rounded the shed's corner, bared its teeth at the gloomy interior.

I remembered John.

Shuffling into the glare, he shielded his eyes with an inverted hand.

There was another collective inrush of breath. Russell raised his pick, but Henry told him this was John, a friend.

The people had no idea how to react; some backed away, some stood dumbfounded, and one made the sign of the cross. At Henry's reassurance, some edged forward.

Now we were behind the people, and Henry whispered into my ear. "Mothkin needs us in there."

I nodded emphatically.

"Keep them busy, Dragonfly. I'll be back in a wink." With that, he was off at a crouching run, making for the funeral home. No one noticed until he was halfway there. When Russell shouted after him, I told him Henry would be right back.

The people were trying to talk to John, but the dog barked and snarled so that they couldn't hear *themselves,* let alone realize no sounds were coming from John's lips. He smiled up at them as they shouted questions, clicked his picture, scanned him with a Geiger counter.

He wore the patient, serene face of a grandparent. I wondered if he was still a child. Had he been a prisoner in the clay body for five years? Fifteen? Fifty? Without him, we would never have found the doorway in time. I have often thought of that face with two left eyes and a mouth on the lower right; sometimes it floats before me when I am worked up over something insignificant, and then I see things more in perspective.

John turned from the gawking crowd, trudged a few paces away through the trampled millet. He walked among a stand of fresh plants, letting the stalks sweep around him, swishing his thumbs through them.

The people followed, shining their lights.

He stopped, smiled at me, and raised a hand.

I felt tears again as I waved back.

Then he burst apart. It was as if he simply relaxed, spreading his arms to the wind; he had finished his task. Cracks shot up from his belly, raced to the top of his head. Still smiling, he fell in four directions, and a puff of dust swirled over the grain.

"Good-bye, John," I whispered, pulling my sleeve across my eyes.

Glancing toward the house, I couldn't see Henry.

The people came surging back, a few stopping to examine John's remains. Russell tried again to introduce himself. His team was mostly from the university, and they were studying the bizarre subterranean rumblings that this area had become famous for. All his instruments said the ground for miles around was solid. This was not a fault zone, and the noises didn't sound like anything in his experience. The phenomenon had reached an alarming peak this afternoon—and now we, the disappearance victims, had emerged from a shed at the epicenter. He hoped we could give him some answers. Clara asked how much time he had.

A car's headlights flared across the field. The driver pulled in beside the van and cut the engine. Turning, I felt a sentence vanish on my lips. I knew the car, had ridden in it every now and then, when the situation had been "workable." For me, the whole world vanished and I saw only the car, its opening doors.

Two figures stepped out, scanning the crowd—and finding me. As one, the three of us broke into a run. My cloak streamed behind me as I bounded over the millet.

My mother sprinted in tiny red sneakers, her high heels abandoned beside a dresser somewhere; her coat flapped open to reveal bluejeans. With her simple hairstyle, she looked like a taller version of me. I couldn't remember my father's hand without a briefcase in it, but both his hands were gentle when he spun me in the air. My parents called my name over and over, touching my hair and face with the wonder of blind people who have suddenly received sight. Weeping, laughing, the three of us squeezed together, cameras flashing around us.

Hearing a car's horn, we saw the hearse approaching straight across the field, bottoming out and bouncing like an Untoward.

"What's he doing?" cried Russell. "Watch out for the power cables!"

The hearse roared over a spaghetti-like bundle of cords, and a satellite dish teetered in a circle. Henry braked beside us, showering us with sod.

Willie and Clara were already sliding into the front passenger door.

I beckoned my parents, dashing toward the hearse. "Come on! Come on, all of you! There's something we have to do!"

My parents weren't going to lose me now. The three of us dove into the back seat, and Henry leaned over to embrace my mother, to thump my father's back. Then he aimed the long rear of the hearse at the hole in the shed wall. The university people were flabbergasted. Hefting his axe, Russell signaled the others to follow him after us.

His foot on the brake, Henry gunned the engine, peered over his shoulder to gauge the strength of the stone blocks. I sat crossways on my parents' laps. They looked from the shed to me to Henry, their lips parted. Willie and Clara knelt on the front seat, clutched its back; reaching up, I caught their hands. I read my question mirrored in their eyes: could we re-enter the door? Was Harvest Moon just beyond those heavy slabs, or was it now infinitely remote, no more accessible than a fading nightmare?

Letting out his breath, Henry studied the silver moon, clean as polished chrome. The cloudless sky itself was breathtaking—not a shadowed ceiling, but limitless air, ablaze with stars.

"Hang on, and keep your heads down," advised Henry. "The windows will probably break."

"What are we doing?" my mother asked.

"You'll understand in a second—I hope." Then he glanced at me. "Did John get clear of the shed?"

"He broke apart in the field."

Henry nodded slowly, holding my gaze. I could see the doubts roiling inside him: where was the wisdom in driving a carload of his loved ones to meet Samuel Hain?

Of wisdom, there was none. But Mothkin had come to help us when we needed him.

I touched Henry's hand.

The broken wall lurched toward the hearse's rear window, our tires whirling in the soft earth. Russell rapped on the fender and yelled something. Before we hit, Willie and Clara ducked, and my father shielded my mother and me.

A shuddering crash forced us deep into the padded seat, my mother's throat vibrating against my neck as she screamed. Then we were moving again, stones crunching under the wheels as the car ground on its springs. Walls tipped, shattered; the hearse was tilting, the front end rising as we fishtailed backward.

Before I even lifted my head, red light flooded the car's interior. Sounds changed to echoes, and I smelled smoke. I knew we were back inside. Hain's people had pulled off most of the rocks; knocking over the roof-slabs, we careened down the slope. Henry put all his weight on the brake. Lying on the horn, he jerked the emergency brake, but still we were rock-surfing, the scree coming down with us. Black-garbed figures leapt out of our way.

Hitting the bottom of the rise, Henry spun the wheel,

backed us around. The headlight beams swept across the High Dark Shelf, flaring in a hundred pairs of eyes. Our rear window had fallen to junk in the space designed to carry a casket, and several of the side windows were spider-webbed with cracks, but we were unhurt.

Rock dust mixed with the balloon's smoke over the slope. Pouring in from our world, floodlights illuminated the ruins of the Madar's house; a jagged circle of the night sky was visible, and Russell stepped through. Silhouetted by the powerful halogen beams, his team clambered among the stones behind him. They pointed, waved for their comrades to follow. Steadying himself on one knee, the photographer shot pictures in all directions, pausing only to thumb the advance lever.

"They see it!" said Henry with relief. "They see it all, and they're in!"

"You showed it to them!" laughed Clara, hugging him. I'd been worried, too, whether they'd see the Shelf or not. But my mother went white, her hands to her mouth; my father opened his door and stepped out. Sliding down the stone heap, Russell had almost reached us when he saw the people of Harvest Moon.

Taken aback by our dramatic reappearance, squinting into the headlights, they held their swords and bows ready. Though my mother had been in a few horror films, I was sure she'd never seen a set like this. Taking her hand, I tried to reassure her.

"There's Mothkin!" cried Willie.

Two silk-hatted ghouls gripped Mothkin's arms, a dozen more surrounded him, and Samuel Hain looked to have been in the act of interrogating his prisoner. Mothkin's shirt was torn open; Hain had made several scratches across his chest with a dagger.

Turning toward us, Hain spread his arms in welcome. There was power in his eyes, grandness in his every move. Restored, his crimson clothing flashed. Immense and glowing, the *Jolly Jack* waited over the pit, tethered to the barge, which had landed at the Shelf's front edge.

I had the presence of mind not to look toward the ledges, but I saw no sign of Singer, Tefan, or the animals.

Gazing over an army of archers, Russell eyed his pickaxe and stopped where he was. A string of the university team occupied the slope above him at varying heights.

"My dear Dragonfly," crooned Hain. "You couldn't stay away."

27

NEW MOONS FOR OLD

"WHO are you?" demanded my father.

Hain approached, his spangles throwing glimmers along the sleek hood of the hearse.

"Who are you?" my father repeated. He was tall, but Hain towered half a head above him.

"I am the ring-master," said Hain. "Welcome to my circus."

At last I knew why God had made my father a business-man, had let him square off against corporate cutthroats when he could have been watching my school plays; he had been in training for this moment. An ordinary man would have wilted under that inhuman stare, but my father slammed the car door, leaving no barrier; hands on his hips, he was every inch my hero. "A circus?" He raised his eyebrows. "Well, then, let's have a show!"

"Yes!" I wriggled out of the car, thrust my own chin at Hain. "Project Nowhere is over!" I pointed toward the slope, the glowing hole into spring. Flashlights danced in the hands of technicians. "Those are grownups, Mr. Hain, not scared kids. It's the mob, just like in the old days. They're here with torches to burn you out!"

"No more nightmares!" shouted Willie, climbing out on the far side of the car. Clara stood with him; Henry exited on the driver's side and crossed his arms.

Hain's soldiers waited, their sunken eyes darting, the death-skeletons clenching their teeth. My mother was the last one out of the car. Reopening my father's door, she slammed it even louder, put her hands on my shoulders.

"Your passion is impressive." Hain's predaceous gaze flicked from face to face; then he turned his back on us, paced among the rocks. "I'm a family man myself, you know, a provider." His gesture took in his army. "My family is big and diverse, and I take care of them. Do you really have a quarrel with me?"

My father watched him levelly. "I think I do."

Hain stood on a rock, glowered down at us. "Let me put it this way. What if I ordered my archers to shoot you all where you stand?"

His people raised their weapons, fear and hatred in their eyes. We were as repulsive and terrifying to them as walking corpses in the land of the living.

My father placed himself between us and the enemy. A muscle twitched at the side of Hain's jaw. His troops shuffled forward, putting on a display. Gaunt scarecrow men and women readied arrows; nearby, a werewolf licked his lips; lank hair masking their faces, two teenagers flipped out switchblades. A vampire waggled fingers beside his mouth as if eating corn off the cob. Old, old stern women, their features made reptilian by the grave's ravages, showed us dentures of black metal; experienced and vicious soldiers, they clutched implements of hooks and barbed wire.

As Hain met my gaze he looked genuinely regretful. "You should have been kinder to me when you had the chance." Then he shrugged, as if to say *but that's life: live and learn.* "I won't let Project Nowhere be stopped; I owe it to my children, as my father left an inheritance to me. So this is farewell." He raised a hand to signal the archers.

My father pushed us down behind the hearse.

"WAIT!"

Hain looked around. The commanding tone had been

Mothkin's, who hung in the grip of his captors. "You have something to add, Grey Man?"

"There's a better way," said Mothkin quietly.

Spectral faces watched him; someone on the slope shined a beam on him like a spotlight.

"And what," asked Hain, "might *that* be?"

"We have a conflict of interests," Mothkin said. "Those of your children, and those of the children of Earth. I suggest we settle our dispute with honor."

Hain eyed him carefully. "What do you propose?"

"A shadow-duel."

Hain grinned. "A shadow-duel is to the death."

"To the death."

Hain considered, then glided in a long circle before his warriors. "Tonight we will remove the last obstacle." He gestured dramatically toward the world outside. "Tomorrow evening you will feast in the land of your inheritance!" They cheered, waving swords and claws, the werewolves chasing their tails. Flinging his arms wide, Hain delighted in the applause. "What could be more auspicious than to usher in the Epiphany of Darkness with the defeat of our old adversary, the man who burned us out nearly ten years ago and came back to do it again?"

Vampires clapped, the teenagers raised fists into the air, and the old ones murmured approval. The scientists' flashlights played over the crowd. "Let it be a shadow-duel!" shouted Hain, swooping toward Mothkin again. "I only regret that Jehu dispatched your Gypsy friends and the brave Lurkwick so soon."

"Have no fear," said Mothkin; "their combined animosity lives in me."

"Splendid." Hain drew Mothkin's captured silver dagger from his own belt, offered it back by the ornate hilts. "Daggers?"

"Daggers." Shrugging free of his guards, Mothkin took it as Hain unsheathed his own. The crowd parted in a wide circle.

"Back, back!" said Hain. "A shadow-duel needs more room than that!" His people withdrew toward the Shelf's center, leaving a block-square space on the near side of the barge. He ordered a lantern to be brought.

As the balloon descended slightly into the pit, throwing the arena into its former shade, I prayed that Mothkin knew what he was doing, that God would help him. Obeying instructions, Henry switched off the car lights and engine, and Russell's team extinguished their flashlights. Once again the Shelf thrived with furtive shapes and incomprehensible angles. Caped vampires blew kisses to Hain; werewolves bayed with upturned snouts, and the German shepherd from outside bared his fangs, standing with his master near the exit.

I stole a glance at the stony heights, but the gloom was too deep now even to see the ledges. If Singer and Tefan were there, I told myself, maybe the dimness would give them a chance to come down unnoticed—though an honorable duel, I supposed, must be between two duelists.

Mothkin walked toward us.

He clasped our hands, his battered face tranquil.

"Mothkin has been Uncle Henry's friend for years," I explained, "and he's mine, too."

"You can be very proud of your daughter." He shook my father's hand. "She's an extraordinary person."

"Mothkin?" I hugged him quickly around the waist. His face was still as enigmatic as it had been on Hallowe'en night, half a year ago—it seemed half a lifetime. "You've got to win."

He said, "I will guarantee you this: no matter what happens on the High Dark Shelf, Shiloh's kingdom will come." Then he crouched and laid a hand on my shoulder. "It was a foolish thing you did in following me down the chute."

I nodded: there was no argument on that point.

Mothkin smiled. "But I am glad you did. And I thank you for coming back just now. You've done very well, Dragonfly."

Hain waited, the lantern at his feet.

The braver scientists worked their way down to the car for a better view, speaking in whispers, trying to comprehend their entrance into a cavern that couldn't exist. "Some kind of religious cult?" I heard Russell ask. A woman beside him said, "That *makeup* they're wearing—!"

Mothkin crossed the uneven floor to Hain, and they linked hands, the two knives jutting upward from fists locked each in the opponent's palm. Shadows of their pronounced features pulsed on their foreheads, the lantern on a flat rock between them.

A young woman in black served as arbiter, her chestnut hair matted with mold. "Find your targets where you may," she instructed in a voice so breathily unclean it would have stained a filter. "In flesh or in shade." Lifting her shrunken hands, she blinked red eyes at them, smirking. "No rules, gentlemen. Are you ready?"

Each combatant studied the other's face, trying to anticipate the first move. A hush fell over the ranks of basement people. When Hain and Mothkin nodded, the arbiter backed away, her task finished but for a final word: *"Begin!"*

Instinctively my mother slid an arm around me, just as she'd done when I was a baby. I held her arm tightly with both hands.

Hain and Mothkin separated, circled, a lynx and an alley cat. As they stalked, their knives caught the light, their steps padded on the foot-polished stone. Strangely expanding, their shadows slipped over the rocks. Watching them I thought of my own shadow-dueling on the sidewalks, the old tap-dance game of trying to beat my shadow's feet to the pavement. My shadow had scared me with its lagging, when its carelessness of imitation suggested I hadn't begun to fathom the darkness of October; now I understood the owl season, and those umbrages still made me tremble. Swinging at the duelists' heels, the shadows mimicked, but did not mirror perfectly: their inscrutable wills were awake.

Hain sprang over the lantern, putting its light behind him. His shadow blackened, spreading to twice the size of Mothkin's. Using one hand as a fulcrum, Mothkin dodged and retaliated with a quick upward slash. Although his knife was nowhere near Hain, the knife's shadow plunged into the shadow of Hain's cloak—and by whatever dark laws governed the duel, the *real* cloak opened with a *rrrip!*

Hain brandished his knife, pressing Mothkin backward. When the A.P.K.'s shadow hit a rough patch of ceiling, the outline wavered; taking the advantage, both Hain and his shadow aimed daggers. Ducking Hain's arm, Mothkin parried the *shadow's* knife on his own.

Such a duel, you see, was really two against two: Mothkin

and his shadow circling the lantern, trying to outmaneuver Hain and his.

Two blades whistled past Mothkin's ear, one silver, one black. As Hain leapt over a boulder, he avoided Mothkin's knife, but the shadow-blade tore a shallow wound from Hain's shoulder to elbow. Howling, he feinted with a kick at Mothkin's face. Hain's shadow caught the other's wrist, and the two shadows fell into the lantern, which burst in a flurry of slicing arms. The darkness deepened, the shadows gaining strength, swiveling away from the Fire Falls. Hain lunged, his dagger's tip scratching Mothkin's forehead.

Hain's shadow sidled up onto the barge's deck, stretched a sinuous arm; maybe the distance and poor lighting played tricks, but I was certain Hain took his own shadow's hand and pulled himself aboard. Mothkin followed, scrambling up a rope net, his shadow slinking behind him like a dark bridal train. They clashed in the stern, blades ringing. The shadows flashed on swirling smoke.

Mothkin thrust quicker than the eye could follow, and his knife caught the enemy's side. With a groan, Hain lurched into the rotting tiller, slumped to the deck, his shadow pinned beneath him. Mothkin was facing us, his shade capering on the smokescreen above; he advanced, intent on the eater of pain.

It was too soon to feel relieved. I expected treachery from the Harvest Moon warriors.

Sure enough, a corpulent old man pulled an arrow from his quiver. Squatting like a toad on a boulder, he drew the string back to his ear, sighted on Mothkin.

Willie and I screamed together, but we knew in an awful, endless moment that Mothkin would have no time to react.

There was a *twang* and the *th-wock* of an arrow striking home—but who toppled was the assassin from the rock, his arrow coursing into the air. Before the skewered body had even hit the ground, we saw Tefan on Hither's back, slipping from the darkness behind us, a second arrow already on his string.

"Hooray!" Willie jumped up and down.

"Let the duel be fair," said Tefan from atop a high outcropping, half-visible in the dimensionless darkness.

Hain climbed to his feet, blood on his fingers. "You told

me your friends were dead. I thought your deity did not approve of lies."

"He doesn't," Mothkin agreed. "Come closer, and learn how poorly I measure against His list of virtues."

Moving to the far side of the barge, Hain leaned on the rail with his back to the distant village bonfires. His arm clamped to his side, he chuckled. "Nothing is what it seems; death is a mask life wears, and life is the mask of death."

He raised his arms, the knife twirling in his hand. His voice grew louder, more alien as he laughed not from his humanoid throat, but from the belly of what he *was,* that green-eyed thing I had glimpsed in the hold of the *Jack.* "Masks, MASKS!" he roared. "TRICK-OR-TREAT!" As I watched his spread-eagled form, lighted from below by the balloon, I noticed a rippling at his ankles, a distortion of the orange light that crept up his legs, encircled his waist. Drifting in the smoky air was the odor of something horribly corrupt.

"The reek of decay!" shrieked Hain, his arms coated with a sticky, slithering plasm. "The final smell of all flesh!" He waved a dripping hand at us. There was a sickening suction noise, and a huge, mucous shape slid up from the pit, onto the barge.

Seeing it more clearly now than I had on the forest road, I recognized the Thanatops. It crawled, a hideous giant, after its master. Still it was mostly transparent, visible only at certain angles of the light—and then, mercifully, in none but the haziest outlines. Pulling itself over the gunwale, the foulness resembled a tremendous human embryo. It penetrated Hain's shadow, dragging it on like a garment. Part of the monster remained in or on Hain, swelling his skin, rejuvenating him; but the bulk of it inflated his shadow, giving it substance. Heedless of the direction of the light, the blackened shadow stretched its limbs, its reach half as long as the Shelf.

The people of Harvest Moon cheered: "NOWHERE, NOWHERE, NOWHERE." Slowly, the chant refocused, the words separating—"NOW *HERE* NOW *HERE!*" When Hain took a step, the pulsating darkness behind him followed, anchored to his heels. He controlled it like a gigantic marionette. Dwarfed, Mothkin's shadow hung back opposite the flicker-

ing light as he edged along the barge's rail, head tipped back
to see all of the Thanatops.

Willie looked as if he were trying to climb into Clara's
pockets; Henry shook his head, staring at Pestilence. Tefan
held his position as most of the scientists raced up the slope
past him. Not far from the hearse, Russell trained his flashlight at the giant, tried to comprehend what he was seeing.

Mothkin jumped down from the barge an instant ahead of
the monster's fist, which was corporeal enough to smash the
railing, to hurl the tiller after him like a spear. Dodging among
the boulders, Mothkin buried his shadow in darkness.

He could not hide for long; the Thanatops could span the
Shelf in three strides, its disproportionate head brushing the
roof. Pressing its palms against the ceiling, Hain made the
shadow bunch its shoulders, stand with feet apart. "WHO AM
I?" shrieked the puppet master.

"The mighty Atlas!" answered the vampire Anselm, and
the people of Harvest Moon were in stitches.

In the Hallowe'en Lounge of the Tenebrificium, I had
vowed to remember the lesson of the Celts; their fear had allowed Hain to dominate them. If I were to be of any help to
Mothkin now, I must not let terror paralyze me. Russell's
flashlight had given me an idea—a strange one, but normalcy
was no standard here. Slipping from my mother's arm, I
dashed around the car, grabbed the light, and followed its
beam across the rubble field, the bizarre distances of the Shelf
telescoping around me. I ran six steps, and already the hearse
seemed a block away, my parents calling me, holding out their
hands. Praying I wouldn't twist an ankle, I hopped over the
rocks to where a limestone slab the size of a dance floor lay on
end. Pausing at the top of a rise, I looked in vain for Mothkin.
The grim barbed-wire ladies pointed me out to skeleton
guards.

Sliding down the bank, I shielded the flashlight from the
rocks. The dust made me cough. I had reached the slab, its
face like the open lid of a grand piano angling high above me.
Clamping my hair behind my ear, I wedged the light between
stones so that its beam shone up onto the slab. The surface
glinted with veins of onyx and quartz, giving it the appear-

ance of a frozen, snow-covered lake: a perfect stage. I took a deep breath. Leaning into the beam, I raised one hand in the shape of a twisted claw.

On the stairway below the laundry chute, Mothkin had "woken up" Quillum, the Great Shadow Lord, to help me against the mocking shadows. Now I was trying to return the favor. Yes, I knew it was only a trick that had boosted my courage at the journey's beginning. Mothkin needed more than courage now, but I couldn't just stand and watch the unfair fight. Spreading my cape to heighten the effect, I pantomimed an enormous creature waking up. I tossed my head, yawned, unfolded great shadow wings and arms. My theatrics, projected in crisp contrast on the sweep of stone above, were impressive, at least from the angle I saw them. Still, I felt a little foolish. Swirling my cape, I bounded right over the flashlight—

—And that's when it happened.

I landed, looked up, and my shadow was lagging like never before. It *hadn't jumped,* but was leaning against a corner of the slab, and as I stared, it snapped its fingers, acting completely on its own.

"What are you *doing?*" I gasped.

The enormous shadow folded its arms, cocked its head as if waiting. As its face turned, I saw that it wasn't even *my* shadow—it had a long, curving beak, like an eagle's.

"Quillum?"

Spreading its wings, the shadow bowed.

I pointed toward the barge, my voice a quavering whisper. "Would you help Mothkin, please?"

A wind gusted out of nowhere, smelling of dust and feathers, the forgotten odor of attics. Peeling himself from the wall, Quillum rustled over my head, rode the wind like a sheet free from the clothesline. The clacking of skeletal feet brought me to my senses; grabbing the flashlight, I climbed on hands and knees out of the concavity, then doubled back to the hearse.

By the time I arrived, the Great Shadow Lord was flashing in and out of the vapors around the Thanatops, which swung its slimy fists, beating the air, fanning the smoke. His sword a black icicle, Quillum struck and whirled like a helix of leaves on the autumn wind, vanishing again, yet omnipresent as the smell of burning. Now he billowed on the ceiling's arch; now he rivered under the feet of the Harvest Moon warriors themselves; now he waxed on the gas-clouds, taunting the enemy. Perforated in half a dozen places, the Thanatops rained its unclean ichor over the barge as it tore loose timbers, fought to disperse the smoke and keep Quillum at bay.

Hain was outraged, but he could hardly complain. If Quillum was not Mothkin's shadow, neither was the Thanatops Hain's. You must remember that, if you're ever challenged to a shadow-duel: there really are no rules. As one might expect, Hain had a final nasty trick in store. Pulling a canister from his coat pocket, he flipped the top open, lobbed it over the pit. The powder within mixed with the air and burst into a nebula of green flame.

Below the lip of the drop, Conflagron exhaled in response. A displaced desert sun, the *Jolly Jack* rose, driving back darkness. I glimpsed Meagerly through a rent in the fabric, his heat-blackened form hunched in the captain's chair as he pushed the engine to five times its intended output of heat. The balloon's skin had ripped back even more since I'd seen it at the river, displaying the network of timbers, the bomb-laden decks. Fire from the dragon's jaws showed between the craft's exposed ribs like the flaming sword at Eden's gate; the vapors parted, and Quillum paled. Dependent on the dark, he had no place to stand. His form broke apart, seeped into the hollows and corners. The Thanatops raked its claws among the boulders, sifting the debris for Mothkin.

Posing on the barge's transom, Hain swung his leg, made the Thanatops kick a hillside, and rubble showered the cavern's rear wall. The crowd raised weapons in salute, tossed silk hats into the air as Meagerly glided in low, flooding the Shelf with garish light.

The Thanatops crumbled massive stones to sand, dug through the hills and cairns in our direction. Coated with dust, the horror became more distinct, the bald, bulbous head pulsing like that of an octopus. Russell didn't wait for me to return his flashlight; he seized two of his colleagues, helped them climb.

"COME OUT," shouted Hain, "WHEREVER YOU ARE!"

"We can't leave them," I started to say—but then I saw Alley Singer. He was kneeling with Mothkin in the hollow behind a rock, a little to the left of the earth-moving claws. Backs to us, the men conferred, then sprinted in opposite directions, staying out of sight. Mothkin headed right, toward the Shelf's center; Singer skirted the pit's near edge, close by the head of the stairs.

Fresh blood had seeped from Singer's shoulder. His crossbow was up, but he knew it would not help him; keeping an eye on the balloon, he moved in.

The *Jolly Jack* was the problem: as long as it bathed the Shelf in noonday brilliance, Quillum could not appear, and Mothkin had none but the slightest shadow. On an Untoward, Singer could have leapt across to the balloon, still hovering over the pit; but the mount would have fallen, even if Singer managed to grip onto something. He had chosen not to endanger the faithful goats. I lost sight of him when he had almost reached the barge.

Hain's people joined the hunt for Mothkin, sniffing in the cracks, listening for what they alone could hear, grasping for his anxiety. Anselm led them, skipping from ridge to ridge, his crowish shape flitting across the red moonbeams.

I looked at Henry, at Clara and Willie, my companions on many dark roads. What could we do? At the end, we were out of ideas. "Lord, help him," said Clara.

Suddenly Mothkin stood on a ledge, probably not far from where the Untowards were hidden. In the deepest recesses of the Shelf, he faced Hain over the warriors' heads. At the edge of the light, he had a shadow again, long and low at his heels. Hain's arms fell to his sides, and the Thanatops stopped digging. Imbued with Pestilence, the monarch of Harvest Moon had nearly shrugged off his human guise, his face little more than rabid green eyes. Silence reigned in the cavern.

"Here I am," said Mothkin. "Surely our duel isn't *over?*"

It *could* be in only seconds: all Hain had to do was move the *Jack* in, disperse Mothkin's shadow, and end the fight with one stroke; Mothkin had left himself nowhere to hide. But such a conclusion was too simple. Hain's eyes narrowed to emerald slits as the balloon raced its burners.

"STAY WHERE YOU ARE!" Hain ordered Meagerly, and the Thanatops's arm held the craft over the pit. I followed his logic: if Tefan was alive, then Singer might be, too, and the Shelf was a maze of cracks and hillocks where he could hide. Keeping his light source out of danger, Hain would finish Mothkin shadow and all.

He descended the gangplank, his enhanced shadow sliding its feet under his. Mothkin stood his ground, and the *Jack* hung over bottomless darkness. As Hain moved among his people, he acknowledged their applause; meeting Anselm, Hain shook his hand, and the vampire bowed, sweeping his fingers toward Mothkin. Rows of skeletons stood in rigid salute.

Thunderous cheers carried him up a pile of rocks, closer and closer to his enemy. "OPEN THE KINGDOM!" yelled the crowd, and "NOW *HERE* NOW *HERE* NOW *HERE!*"

Unnoticed at the back of the assembly, someone darted toward the Shelf's edge—someone from the ranks of Harvest Moon, who knocked a skeleton guard out of his way, the bones smashing apart in a ravine. No one but me saw the runner until he broke onto the open rock of the front ledge.

I crawled onto the hearse's hood for a better view.

Willie hopped up beside me. "It's Cawdor!"

On four legs, the werewolf flashed over the mounds like a low-flying bat, his ears flat; his magnificent silver shape bounded across the barge.

"What's he doing?" asked Willie, gripping my arm.

"He *is* on our side. He *is!*"

Hain glanced behind, warned by the cunning that had served him for centuries. He saw the werewolf fly from the barge, soar through surging heat to the iron grill under the balloon. For a werewolf, the jump was easy.

Catching the grates, Cawdor dangled below the craft, his thick tail swinging, legs splaying as he handwalked to the aperture on the bottom, where the remains of the ladder were fused into junk. Confused, Hain's people looked around.

"A traitor!" wailed Anselm. "Archers! Arrows!"

Cawdor was inside long before anyone could shoot, his tongue out as he climbed a ladder. We could see him through the open bag, but the very screens that protected the *Jack* now prevented Hain's warriors from eliminating this new threat. The balloon tilted slightly, Meagerly letting go of the wheel to glower at the werewolf. Cawdor's fur began to smoke, but he gained a platform, leapt through a hatch to a higher deck.

"Werewolves *hate* fire," said Willie. "Tefan says fire and silver are the only two things that can kill them."

I recalled the werewolf at Fifty-two Pink Eye Street, leery of a blaze contained in a fireplace. The balloon was an airborne furnace.

Gauging the distance to Meagerly, still high above him, Cawdor must have realized he'd never make it; already runners of fire licked his singed fur, his tail a smoking ember—I could not imagine his agony. He wriggled between braces, attained the central hot bag. With a howl that rang in the cavern heights, that would echo forever in the hearts of all his kind, he plunged his claws into the membrane, ripped it asunder.

Only his grip on an engine strut kept him from being hurled through the outer wall as a withering blast consumed his fur. He was a flying candle, diving into the core, where Conflagron hung nose-down. The dragon was melting, raging so far beyond capacity that its surface streamed, details running together. Instinct guided Cawdor at the end; he had fixed on the engine's position, and when he fell sizzling against it, he wrenched the head up and around, held it fast. His last act was to wrestle Hain's flagship to the ground.

Meagerly put all his weight on the controls, but he could not steer. Losing stability, the balloon banked left, nosed down as the core became a ball of black smoke. He hauled on the elevation lever—I recalled the copper knob above the pilot's knee—but it did not respond; Conflagron was shooting fire backward. *Jack* didn't clear the ledge. There was a fracturing of wooden ribs as he rammed the cliff, squashed himself oblong.

Cawdor was gone now; the engine jarred, and Meagerly regained control. Reversing thrust, he sent a jet of fire against the Shelf. Nodding with satisfaction, Hain started to turn, but another movement snared his attention.

The moment of nearness was all Singer had needed. He stepped through a tattered hole not six feet from the pilot's chair, that exquisite throne of faces and claws. Meagerly rose to meet him, hissing, swinging long-nailed fists, his charred coat flying.

Singer's bolt struck Meagerly full in the chest, but had no effect; the creature had nothing resembling a heart. His backhand sent the crossbow spinning overboard; I watched it clatter onto the edge of the Shelf. Singer ducked under a strut, and the slave-master's claws gouged slivers from the wood.

Droplets of liquid metal from the engine fell among the barrels of explosives. As detonations rocked the ship, the decks buckled, one by one. The floor of the wheelhouse scattered into boards. Willie's scream was a soprano thread.

The pilot's chair reclined, falling through a bulkhead that no longer existed. Singer threw his arms around a crossbeam.

Cruel mouth twisted in annoyance, Meagerly found himself standing on air. The hat sloughed from his hairless head; his coat peeled upward like a leathery seed pod. Plummeting, he grasped at struts on the way down, each one breaking more of his bones. At last, with a sudden, brilliant blaze of the molten core, his ancient flesh was incinerated.

Singer lowered himself to the wheel, balanced his feet on the remaining supports. Smiling wearily, face covered with soot, he groped for the elevation control and lay on it. The singed tetherline snapped. Still backing, the balloon rolled up and headed for the ceiling, gathering speed. Fuel exhausted, Conflagron coughed like a firing cannon. Higher and higher the *Jack* climbed, raining explosives from its hold, the triangular painted eyes at last shriveling away. It illuminated the stalactites and fantastic draperies of the cavern's roof.

Singer!

At full speed, the warship struck the millet field from below.

It was like looking into the sun. All the incendiary kegs went off, shattering the windshields of every car along the ditch. Russell's van was tipped on its side, and we had to replace seven windows in the funeral home. People two counties away saw a fireball that rose "half a mile" into the sky. Chunks of the cavern roof came down along with halogen lights. There wasn't a lot of the *Jolly Jack* left to fall—a loop of cable, a shred of burning cloth, a fine rain of splinters.

My father had pulled us down behind the car again, but I watched over the fender as a cooling silver light streamed in through the ceiling's gaping hole: the pure, soft radiance of the real moon. Somewhere outside, as dogs have done from time immemorial, the German shepherd greeted the orb in long syllables.

Hain reeled as the light swept the Shelf. Warm spring darkness poured down into volatile October; and by whatever laws governed this place between worlds, as clean moonbeams struck its putrid flesh, the Thanatops took fire, its globular head snapping backward. Hain's warriors shrieked, covered their faces, tried to hide among the rocks. Fire devoured the monstrous shadow from the inside out, spewing, sizzling from its vile skin. Its hands painted the walls as the enormous body, a vortex of silver flames, crumpled to its knees.

Mothkin and Hain glowed in the wild firelight, alone in a crackling circle where no shadows had substance.

With a growl of hatred, Hain sprang, his dagger aimed for Mothkin's heart. He was as quick as a striking serpent, but Shiloh's warrior was the merest fraction faster. Somehow, Mothkin got his wrist against Hain's forearm, knocked the thrust wide.

The evil one's momentum carried him forward, unstoppable. Mothkin's dagger received him, driving deep. They stood together unmoving, framed in the dying light like old friends embracing. Then slowly, Hain lifted a hand, patted the side of Mothkin's neck, and pulled himself loose.

Quillum and Mothkin's shadow regained their shapes, flanked Mothkin on either side: but the duel was over.

The Lord of Harvest Moon sank onto a boulder, blood soaking his crimson coat. Unhurriedly, he surveyed his people. Finally his gaze found mine, and again I saw in his eyes a tired grandfather, older than anyone should have to get.

" 'Then fall, Caesar.' " His voice was a whisper, but it echoed from every direction.

Gradually, the smoldering Thanatops overbalanced. Shapeless, cloaked in the stench of its burning, it toppled into the abyss.

On the moon-washed pavements of my childhood, I had danced with my shadow, trying to shake my feet free of their silk-slipper counterparts. Mine are still inseparable, and Hain's were then; his falling shadow pulled him by the heels, his limp arms dragging, his face in the dust.

At the very edge of the Shelf, he thrust his dagger and his

fingers deep into the stone, anchoring the whole titanic weight of his shadow. Slowly he raised his head, green eyes aglow, for one long, feral snarl.

Then he slipped backward into darkness.

The ground trembled, ledges splitting. Orphaned, the pain-eaters knew in themselves the terror and anguish on which they had so long thrived; gibbering, tearing at their hair and clothes, they ran in circles. White bones flew as landslides swept skeletons away. Vampires sprouted ribbed wings and glided screeching, mindless and purposeless.

Quillum vanished into a ceiling crack. He started by putting in a foot, then flowing upward like black thread from a spool. Last to go, his trailing hand waved good-bye.

Untowards leapt from between the sliding cairns, kicked hooves in the air. Riding to meet them, Tefan led them toward the base of the slope. Mothkin ran a slalom course between avalanches to the hearse. Clara, Henry, Willie, and I intercepted him, spinning him around.

Mothkin pointed to the far-off fires of Harvest Moon under their pall of smoke. People there must have looked up and seen the column of moonlight; they must have stood in stirrups, stopped in mid-brawl, dropped kettles, pushed back thorn-boughs to stare.

I saw the orange lights waver. Dust swirled from the gambrel roofs. At the town's center, a row of fires vanished. Air rushed in that direction, stripping autumn leaves from the trees, sucking light from firepots and beacons. They winked out in a widening circle, leaving the stern Horse alone in blackness. In response to the outside light—reflected from the moon, but born in the fiery sun—Hain's night kingdom collapsed.

Too Quiet Street split open from end to end, and into the yawning crack the light poured. Side fissures followed the winding streets, swallowing carts and fence-posts.

I watched the last bonfires go out, siphoned away. I imagined the arbors, the yards where the children's Game had finally come to a stop, the players cowering under hedges and in the branches of bittermite trees. And somewhere down there, I knew, was a harp on a table, surrounded by the most perfect roses, locked behind a secret door.

"They have been hiding here," Mothkin said. "But the crack in the Earth is open, which they thought to keep forever closed."

Then I understood that Hain's people had come from that crack, had crept up to escape a place of infinite chill and darkness. They had preyed upon our world for a time, plundering our pain. Now the Dark Place drew them back, gathering its own as a glob of mercury overtakes wayward droplets. The incontestable vacuum stripped them at once of all that was mortal, all that they had worn to mask themselves.

They tumbled from the Shelf as on hurricane winds, and in their last seconds, I saw the people as they truly were. Their claws groped, desperately trying to check their flight. Thin, furry limbs scrabbled, cat-like eyes flashed from faces wasted with eternal hunger. Their trunks were empty and flattened, blankets caught in a midnight wind, flapping and twirling away. It was one of these people, I was sure, that had nearly folded over Henry at the laundry chute.

But not all of them were taken; a few vampires, a handful of werewolves remained in the shadows, fleeing toward the spring night of our world. "Those are the real ones," explained Mothkin. "Outside ones, not Hain's—immigrants, lured by this land of opportunity."

Watching them go, I felt a weight lifting from my chest. "Was Sylva an outside one?"

Mothkin smiled. "Only you can answer that."

"Sylva?" asked my mother, seeing the flush of my cheeks.

"It's—" I began, ready to tell her it was nothing. But it was something, a part of me. I felt a trembling excitement. "It's a long story."

"I can't wait to hear it." Drawing me close, she kissed my forehead.

The cataclysm continued. Every ward of the city disgorged its people, even those tall houses in corners, bordered by arms of the mountain. High in the distance Hain's pipes ruptured, spewing nightmare water in falls of purple darkness. Flooding the lowlands, the far-looping canals extinguished peat fires, swept up glowing apples, scarecrows, and the old grey blankets of the leaves. Last to go was the Tenebrificium, plowing a swath through the trees.

On the High Dark Shelf, far above the tumult, floated a sea of lovely air.

28

AN EVENING IN JUNE

THE people in the basement were gone. No one heard their scratchings in the small hours; the mysterious rumbling beneath the field stopped, and I'm sure mothers in every country, lying undisturbed till dawn, wiped away a few tears and thought, "No more nightmares. My child is growing up."

Russell had some remarkable photos: Untowards, John, the balloon, and leering faces of Harvest Moon. We repeated what we knew for this professor or that, but Russell never achieved the acknowledgment of his colleagues; although his team backed him up, they were unable to persuade anyone who had not been there. The problem was that the hole in the field had a *floor* the next morning, making it nothing more than a sinkhole some thirty feet deep; police and fire fighters who had shined flashlights onto the vast Shelf that first night were as baffled as he was. What was anyone to say or think? The cavern had disappeared, and all instruments and subsequent digging *still* indicated no hollow spaces under that part of the state. The Madar's door resealed itself, as such doors do automatically within a few hours. If they weren't built that way, we could scarcely walk down the street without pitching headlong into other worlds—it happens often enough anyway, Mothkin explained.

Of course we didn't say much about Harvest Moon to anyone else. Our neighbor Mr. Wiggins went to his grave believing a gas line had exploded. I learned that spring to question what I read in the news, because every one of three different papers I saw ran its own version of what had happened. We could take our pick of the broken gas main, ignited natural gas, or our favorite: "a most unprecedented and spectacular display of earth-bound atmospheric discharge." Yes, all the fuss had been over a ball of heat lightning.

Since my mother was in movies, the tabloids carried the photos of my parents and me reunited in the field, along with the sketchy suggestion that I had been kidnapped by a cult. We turned down offers to tell our story on national television, and it wasn't long before the whole event was forgotten.

We all stayed at the funeral home that night, including Mothkin, Tefan, and a garage full of Untowards; mostly Henry, my father and I handled the questions from police in the kitchen, and they never knew about Irah's body, still strapped to Fire's back. When reporters began arriving, we locked the door. Before dawn, Mothkin and Tefan had slipped away with the animals, but they left a note saying they'd be back. Making use of a Gypsy door, they rejoined the others below.

The next morning I climbed out a window onto the porch roof to watch a helicopter buzz the field, where cars and trucks ground this year's millet to juice. I sat for a long time with my eyes closed, letting the sun warm a half-year of autumn chill from my bones. Mixed with the grit of pulverized stone, fine wood splinters dusted the roof: I swept a handful into an envelope, knowing they had come from the framework of the *Jolly Jack*.

What happened to us after that? Well, my mother got a job on a new weekly television show that ran regularly through twenty-three seasons. Best of all, it was filmed in a city only an hour away from Henry's. Mrs. Cain retired, and Dad and I moved in with Mom. My father announced there was no business that couldn't be conducted by computer and fax from a small town.

Henry was a widower; Clara was a widow. It wasn't long before they were married, spending Sunday afternoons picnicking on the green cemetery grass and their evenings watching my mom's show and hosting visitations.

We saw Mothkin and the Gypsies again; there never have been any lasting good-byes. We even joined them on other adventures, each of which is another story. What I will tell you about is the first time they came back. It was in June, about twilight on a Sunday evening, when new green on every tree was gaining confidence. School was out, and Willie and I were coming to grips with the fact that we'd have to repeat our interrupted grades. I'd missed a year, and Willie had missed two—but to his relief, his teachers decided to waive one. "After what we've been through," he said, "they ought to let us each skip three." We'd been having a picnic on the elm-shaded knoll at Woodbine Cemetery, Clara reciting a poem from memory, Willie reflecting on how a lot of the graves beneath our feet were empty now, though the families that brought flowers would never know it. "What difference does it make?" asked Uncle Henry, ex-grave robber's accomplice. "They'll *all* be empty on the Last Day."

That's when I saw Mothkin strolling toward us through the trees. He wasn't wearing a hooded cloak; for once, his hands stuck in the pockets of a new pair of durable grey trousers, he looked almost like an ordinary person. Tefan and Muriel were a few steps behind him, Tefan carrying a large cardboard box.

"*Pax sit vobiscum,*" greeted Mothkin, staggering under Willie's and my flying hugs.

"A *pax* on you, too," said Clara. "What's in the box?"

Tefan set it on the grass. Muriel swung me in her arms.

The lid flaps pushed open, and a furry tiger face looked at us. Out hopped Stover, Wonder, and the kitten, Snowball (now a young cat). Willie shrieked with delight, trying to hold all three at once.

"These three found us," explained Tefan, "looking for you, I guess. The others are here and there on the errands of cats."

Muriel knelt beside Willie, stroked Stover's back. "In her visions, Mother Iva saw Egor. His throne was waiting for him."

"In the Kingdom of Cats?"

She nodded. "Behind the moon." Her brass circle earrings shone in the evening light.

"Tell us about everyone," said Clara.

Muriel spread the twilight folds of her skirt. "Irah is buried. We made a monument for him in the Numinous Wood—for him, for Lurkwick, and for the werewolf Cawdor."

"My father sends his thanks to all of you," Tefan added. "He hopes to thank you someday in person. There was a battle at the City of Echoes, but the enemy was waiting for its leader. The defense held."

"Our families are well," continued Muriel. "Thanks to you." Her liquid eyes took in all of us, including Tefan. They rested on his, in fact, for quite a while.

"The children," Tefan finished, "have been taken safely back to their homes. When the Gypsies scattered from the city, each family took a child. Delivering them all in secret has kept us busy for the last month." I imagined the happiness of parents around the world when their sons and daughters came skipping up front walks in the gloaming, perhaps with the rattle of a wooden wagon fading in the street.

"Thank you," I whispered.

"And Hain?" Henry peered over his glasses. "Is he dead? *Can* he die?"

His power was broken forever, Mothkin told us.

"Then his spirit is alive?"

"In one sense, yes. In another, it never was." Mothkin's words were often as cryptic as his facial expressions.

Willie and I wanted to know when we could visit the Numinous Wood again.

"Learn and grow," Mothkin said, leaning against a tree. "You have a lot in your own world yet to discover. But if you're offering, I could use your gifts again someday. Shiloh could use them."

"I'd like that," I said.

Willie agreed, showing us his watch. "I'll keep this handy."

The trees burgeoned with leaves that would learn the art of making deep, cool shade through the hot months and be ready for the glory of next October. Scented of the mock orange that clustered along the fence, a warm breeze set the hedges to whispering. I ran my fingers through the clover around my knees, watched fireflies coming out, each tiny lamp adding color to the night.

I wondered aloud. "Why are fireflies always going *up*, never down?" If you watch them in the summer dusk, you'll see that it's true.

"There are some things," laughed Muriel, "that not even a Gypsy can tell you."

FREDERIC S. DURBIN spent his childhood in the deep oak shade and sun-baked dust near Taylorville, Illinois, climbing trees and avoiding shoes. His parents opened the town's first bookstore. While still in elementary school, he discovered the works of H.P. Lovecraft and J.R.R. Tolkien, his earliest literary influences.

He spent most of his spare time throughout high school and college writing draft after draft of an epic fantasy novel, best described, he says, as "a learning experience." He majored in classical languages at Concordia College, River Forest, Illinois, where he edited the fine arts section of the college newspaper.

After graduating summa cum laude in 1988, he traveled to Japan as a Lutheran volunteer missionary teacher. In 1995, he became a full-time instructor of creative writing and English at Niigata University. It was here, among the pine groves and pounding surf of Japan's northwestern coast, that Durbin began to see the faces and hear the voices that became *Dragonfly*.

Coming November 2005 from Ace

Polaris
by Jack McDevitt
0-441-01253-1
New in paperback from "perhaps the best pure storyteller working in the field today...an exemplary merger of mystery and science fiction" (*Washington Post Book World*).

Age of Conan: Heretic of Set
by J. Steven York
0-441-01345-7
The next installment in the *Age of Conan, Anok, Heretic of Stygia* trilogy.

Also new in paperback this month:

Kris Longknife: Defiant
by Mike Shepherd
0-441-01349-X

The Winter Oak
by James A. Hetley
0-441-01255-8

Gilfeather
by Glenda Larke
0-441-01348-1